YOU'RE GOING TO *MARS!*

ROB DIRCKS

GOLDFINCH  PUBLISHING

Published by Goldfinch Publishing
An Imprint of SARK Industries, Inc.
www.goldfinchpublishing.com

Library of Congress Cataloging-in-Publication Data
Rob Dircks, 1967-
You're Going to Mars!
by Rob Dircks
p. cm.
ISBN 9781733017909

For Mom

1

FROM THE BEGINNING

"Tell me everything, Paper. From the beginning."

"It's a lot. You sure you want to me to go all the way back?"

"Yes."

"Okay, well, the day I was born– wait, hold on."

I look over to the display across the two-tank chamber I'm trapped in. In ninety-two minutes, it'll either light up green, indicating I'm going to live, or it'll light up red, indicating this ship – and me – will explode into teeny pieces no bigger than 50 microns in diameter. So no, I don't think I have time to go all the way back to the day I was born. (Although that story *is* pretty darn cute, if I do say so myself, and it's relevant to this whole mess, so I'll try to sneak it in somewhere.) I'll have to start somewhere closer to the present so I don't run out of time, so that they can hear the truth about Mars, the incredible truth – they have no idea. But where to start?

Wait, I know: I'll start with the subway poster we found. The ad for *You're Going to Mars!* It was that exact moment that

I gave up my childhood dream. The day I knew for sure I'd never be going to Mars.

It's funny, thinking about it now. How my dream laughed back at me and said, "Oh, not going to Mars, are we? We'll see about that."

START THE COUNTDOWN

It's the perfect day out, cloudless blue skies, very light winds from the northeast (the Everpresent Stink isn't even that bad), so we're good to go with launch. This cardboard subway poster we found is the perfect size and thickness, so we're using it as the launch platform.

"Duggie, okay, you ready? Start the countdown."

Duggie claps. Counting is his thing. "Tee minus five... four... three...

"Ignition."

"...two... one..."

"Lift off!"

We jump back to avoid the blast, and peer up in wonder as my two-foot-tall homemade rocket, Mark 76, shoots up into the sky, becoming a little dot in just a few seconds. For the seventy-sixth time, my eyes well up and I have that magical feeling: that's me in there, a little me escaping the Earth's clutches, shooting up where I really belong, into the unknown, free, with a little know-how, a little imagination, and a lot of luck.

"Talk about luck. Duggie, do you remember how many failure points there were in the last Mars rover mission?"

"Um... not sure, Paper..."

"Thirty thousand four hundred eighty-nine. If you really think about all the ways a mission can fail, it's a miracle it ever works."

"Um, did it work?"

"Don't you remember?" Sometimes memories just slip through the cracks in Duggie's brain, including every single Mars story I've told him. "*Mars Inquisitor*, July 2065. Perfect launch. Perfect landing. Not only did it work, it's still sending back data twelve years longer than it was supposed to."

"So... what happens to Mark 76?"

"Come on, Duggie, try. I know you can do it. Remember."

"It... it comes back?"

"See? Who said you weren't smart?"

He grins and scratches his beard, flipping his trucker hat backward and pointing his binoculars up into the blue. I slowly pull him back with me another hundred feet or so, just in case. He doesn't remember what happened the last time we tried this.

"Paper? I don't see anythi-"

"Duggie!"

I lunge at him, throwing us both just out of the way as the harmless-rocket-turned-supersonic-death-missile crashes into the landfill three feet from where we were standing. The impact crushes the fuselage, releasing the methane composite fuel. And *BOOM!* it explodes into a fireball, singeing our shoelaces.

Duggie immediately shoots to his feet and resumes clapping. "Let's do that again!"

"No. It wasn't supposed to do that. It was supposed to

perform a soft landing, right back there." I point to the subway poster. I can still make out, under the methane scorch marks, the words on the poster screaming up at me in purple letters: *You're Going to Mars!* It's cruel, the way the picture of silver-haired Zach Larson, world's first trillionaire, points a finger at my face and taunts me. Like he knows I want nothing more than to run away screaming from Fill City One, to break out of this suffocating hellhole, suck some fresh air into my lungs for once in my life. Wait. That's not true. I have, on rare occasions, on a cool spring day here and there, caught a fresh whiff of "clean" on a breeze. Just enough to remind me that the Everpresent Stink is not all there is. I've inhaled clean air just enough to learn that things smelling bad is not normal or shouldn't be taken for granted and forgotten, like a train that passes by so often that you don't hear its thunderous rattle any longer.

In any case, I look down at the poster, and the remains of Mark 76, and realize: it's over. Time to grow up. Give up my rocket hobby. It's been all failure points and no miracles, and that's all it'll ever be. I'll never get where I'm supposed to be. I look deep into Zach Larson's paper eyes, with his *still-running-triathlons-at-sixty-years-old* confidence, and whisper, "Your little sweepstakes is over in a week. You got any miracles left up that sleeve?" Larson just keeps smiling, smug, so I give him the finger. "I didn't think so."

"You talking to me, Paper?"

"No, Duggie." I walk over to a discarded French armoire wedged into the mud. "Okay. Show's over. Back to work. This piece looks like a re-new. Pick up the other end and let's get it on the lift."

As Duggie dutifully ambles over and bends down to help me heft the monster furniture, I dart back and snatch the poster, roll it up and slip it into my satchel. Obsessions die hard.

"You know, Paper. I saw what you did there, just now." Duggie shoots me his goofy three-teeth-missing smile, picking up two clawed oak feet and grunting with effort.

"Oh, you saw, did you? What exactly did you see?"

"*You're Going to Mars*, it says. The poster you picked up there. From that TV show. Printed four-color process, nice heavy cardboard for a rocket platform, probably two-hundred point stock. Too contaminated to recycle, though." He thinks about it for a second, looks back up into the sky. "*I'd* like to go to Mars."

Poor Duggie. He's like the trash savant of Fill City One, smarter than any ten Hunters combined when it comes to sifting the piles, but certain memories, and basic facts, like every space story I've ever told him, or that it's virtually impossible to find a winning scarab medallion to land a spot on *You're Going to Mars!*, or the fact that there's only a week left in the sweepstakes anyway, or the fact that you can never leave Fill City One even if you want to, escape him. I think it was a bowling ball that did him in, bonked him in the noggin. Stupid mainlanders throwing out perfectly good bowling balls.

"I'm pretty sure neither one of us is going to Mars, Duggie."

"Why not?"

Ugh. I don't want to get into it. But he's tracking the scent. I need to distract him. I pat the armoire. "Hey. Give me the specs on this thing."

"Oooh. I like this game. Lessee..." he looks the massive piece of furniture over, scratching his beard. "...it's definitely

Ethan Allen. French Country collection, yes. I think they call the color 'brie.' Isn't brie cheese?"

"Yes. They painted this the color of cheese."

"And it's solid oak frame, drawers are poplar with oak veneers. And the SKU is..."

"You don't remember the failure points on *Mars Inquisitor*, but you remember the SKU on this armoire?"

"...135321603. I think."

I still don't know how he does that. "You're amazing, Duggie. And to think, you're just a wee lad. Twenty-one years young."

He tucks his chin into his chest, like he always does when paid a compliment. "Thanks, Paper." Then he looks up. "I'm twenty-one?"

"Yes, Duggie. We're the same age. Come on, you have to remember that. We were born on the same day."

His eyes widen. "Oooh. Yes! Tell me the story! The story of the three sisters!"

"No. Not again. Please."

But it's too late. I guess I knew it was too late the moment the words left my mouth. He loves hearing the story about my two sisters and me, mostly because he's not-so-secretly in love with Scissors, the youngest of us by five minutes. Although it might also be that he likes to hear a woman's voice, not having a woman in his own life, a mother or a sister or a lover. And thinking that thought always triggers my weakness for him, that mixture of pity and simpatico that I can never shake, so of course I tell him the story again.

"Okay, Duggie. But this is the *last* time." I wink at him, like it's ever the last time. "Once upon a time..."

THE STORY OF THE THREE SISTERS

So I tell Duggie the story I was told again:

My father brought us home, in shock, still not believing that he had three girls instead of one, and that his soon-to-be ex-wife wouldn't be coming along for the ride. "Good luck, Harlon" were the last words she said before climbing into the transport cab in her hospital gown and disappearing forever.

My Nana, on the other hand, was giddy with delight as she swung open the screen door. "Oooh!! Look at them! They're just like three buttons on a shirt! What are their names?"

"Names?"

"Names, Harlon, names!" She plucked the nearest one, I like to think it was me, from Dad's armpit and raised me up and looked me in the eyes. "Well?"

"I, uh, listen, it's been a long…"

"These children will not cross my threshold without names, Harlon James Maxwell Farris."

The always-ready twinkle sparked in Dad's eyes and he

grinned. "Okay. How about we do Rock-Paper-Scissors?"

Nana didn't understand, had somehow never heard of the game Rock-Paper-Scissors in her entire seventy-six-year-old life, or more likely had forgotten decades ago. So she didn't understand that he meant to play the old game with her to determine who would pick each girl's name. (Dad's got an idiotic sense of humor. Actually, they both do. They're quite a pair.) Bouncing me around a bit, turning me this way and that, looking me over, Nana, instead of asking for a little clarity, just said, "Paper. This one looks like a Paper."

"No, Mom. That's not what I meant. What I meant was-"

"Rock. That one under your left arm is Rock. Looks solid. Solid as a three-week-old loaf of bread." She squinted at my last sister and let out a laugh. "And Scissors. Oh, yes, this one's going to be sharp. You'll see, Harlon."

"Mom. No. That isn't how this works. You can't just-"

But Nana was already shooing Dad away, and making a nest for the three of us right there in the middle of her double-wide trailer, flapping her bingo wings, making a fuss over every little peep and squeak and fart and, I imagine, already planning the designs for the three custom-knit sweaters with our ridiculous new names emblazoned across the front.

Dad technically won the argument, making sure that our actual, real-life names – Becca, Robin, and Nance – were recorded on whatever semi-official birth documents they kept stuffed in an old drawer somewhere here in Fill City One. But practically it would make no difference, because from those first moments forward, Nana ruled the roost, and took to calling us Rock, Paper, and Scissors, and well, when Nana gets an opinion in her head, it ceases being an opinion and becomes cold, hard fact.

THE CITY OF GOLD

See? I told you I would sneak that story in here somewhere.

Anyway, Duggie has fallen asleep listening, as always, with a sloppy grin on his face and a beer in his hand. I shake his shoulder. "Come on. Up. You can nap later. Close up your cooler and let's get this over to the Body Shop."

We finish strapping the armoire to the lift's forks, climb into the cab, and buckle in. Wrenching the ancient vehicle into gear, I tap the dashboard. "Autodrive. Destination Body Shop." Static fills the cabin, as usual, and I hear *affzzmtth*, which I translate as "Affirmative."

As we head, for the zillionth time in my life, out to the Body Shop, I ponder once again how miserable and boring and smelly my existence is here, but how genius the Gitano family was in creating Fill City One. Take this one junk armoire: it'll require a single hour to repair, it's only missing one leg, and some of the veneers are lifting, and within a second hour it'll be back on a flatbed, ready to deliver to an

Ethan Allen in New Hampshire, for sale as new. Cash from trash.

And that's just the teeniest tip of the iceberg. Those crafty Gitanos aren't lying when they call Fill City One the "City of Gold."

Although let me be perfectly clear: Fill City One is *not* the city of gold in any positive, feel-good way, and no one living here will ever call it that. It is, rather, the largest, stinking trash heap in the world. That is not an exaggeration, or a figure of speech, either. It is literally the world's largest garbage dump. By a mile.

Ah, my wonderful home.

Fill City One was once called "Staten Island," one of the five boroughs of New York City, until the fifty-eight square miles of premium "waste-ready" land was auctioned off by the State of New York in 2025 to become the country's very first privately owned city. Well, less of a city and more of a landfill. Actually, it's nothing at all like a city and one hundred percent like a landfill.

WasteWay Corporation won the bid, not because it made the most sense, but because generation upon generation of the Staten Island Gitano mob family – founders of the privately-held corporation – had perfected the arts of intimidation, graft, bribery and, of course, making people disappear. So they made some people disappear, stuffed the appropriate pockets with the appropriate amounts of cash, won the bid, and planted their flag on the highest hill in the land – which, of course, was already the borough's massive garbage pile. Then they moved everyone out, built a thirty-foot wall around the whole island, knocked down all the bridges, and constructed a single drawbridge across the Arthur Kill into New Jersey.

One way in, one way out.

They say if you see it from the New Jersey Turnpike, it looks like a medieval castle, with a drawbridge and a moat, and gun turrets that resemble ancient battlements every quarter mile or so. How quaint. It must be nice to see it from the outside, passing by and then forgetting about it forever.

Oh, yes. I said gun turrets. It would be fair to wonder why the Gitanos feel the need to be so protective. It's just garbage, right?

Wrong.

While the new owners might have been mobsters, they weren't the mook types from the old twentieth century movies. The Gitanos are shrewd bastards, hoarding trash and making coin off it over and over and over again. Hence "The City of Gold."

First, of course, they get paid for hauling the trash for the entire East Coast into the most gargantuan landfill on the planet. *Cha-ching.* Then they recycle just about everything – including this mint-condition French armoire with one leg missing, an unopened gallon of Benjamin Moore eggshell white, prescription drugs, cars, and more laptops than could ever be counted. The Hunters – a subset of the Fillers, the group to which my family belongs – sift and sort and prioritize. The armoire will go to the Fill City One Body Shop, then back to that Ethan Allen store in New Hampshire. *Cha-ching.* The paint will go back on the shelf in a hardware store in Virginia. *Cha-ching.* The same with the drugs, the car and computer parts. *Cha-ching. Cha-ching. Cha-ching.*

Next are the plastics, papers, glass, and batteries. And after that, the compost. WasteWay Corporation is now the number one provider of fertilizer to the entire country. Every bit of organic matter and waste from Maine to Florida is corralled into The Pit – a godforsaken Circle of Hell I try to stay as far away from as humanly possible – and mixed with who-knows-what to stew for a while. The end result? According to WasteWay, "FertiFood: the finest growth medium on Earth." According to me? The most putrid and lethal substance in the solar system, possibly the universe, able to maim – no, kill – with a single sniff. If you look up "foul" in the dictionary, you'll see a picture of The Pit.

Finally – and this is the real secret sauce of Fill City One, and all the other Fill Cities – is *energy*. The real reason for the walls and the gun turrets. The real "gold" that makes all the other work done here seem petty and irrelevant. During the decomposition process, evaporation, chemical reactions, and microbial action create gas, mostly methane and carbon dioxide. The chemists here supercharged the process and refined the end product, creating a top secret, patented, prized fuel called Fill City Turbo. And they created it just in time, too – just as the Great Gas Crisis of 2030 gripped the world, with global oil reserves drying up almost overnight. Pretty insanely perfect timing, I'll give them credit. And yes, in case it wasn't already obvious: the federal government is Turbo's number one buyer. So the Feds pay for the trash to be taken away... and pay for it again when it comes back as desperately-needed fuel.

Yes, the Gitanos are smart, extremely smart, but they can't resist the lure of the less-elegant aspects of organized crime; it's in their blood. So they continue to loan, pimp, deal, gamble and make people disappear. Of course, they need a place to put all the bodies... hmm... how about a hundred-foot-deep pile of trash everyone on Earth wants to avoid? *Good idea, Sal!* Not only does it turn out to be a convenient dumping spot, but it sends the right message to sellers and buyers and potential energy competitors that they all – very literally – should treat the Gitanos and WasteWay Corporation as if their lives depended on it. And how big is this dark side of the business? Well, officially, Fill City One has no cemetery – three hospitals, ten elementary schools, one orphanage, fifty-five streets, nine thousand dwellings, twenty-five thousand permanent residents who work the refinery and the fill, and a mortuary for the locals, but *no cemetery.* Unofficially? It probably has the biggest cemetery in the tri-state area.

Let me put it another way: be careful where you dig.

So sure, Fill City One is the model of waste management and energy production, operating the world's largest landfill and the most massive network of refineries and pipelines the world has ever seen.

But it's hell.

It's dangerous.

It's corrupt.

It smells.

And us Fillers are never allowed to leave.

My Nana signed a contract for a bare bones salary and a free home, like all the other original Fillers, back in 2028 or so. She absently scanned the fine print that declared she was no longer a citizen of the United States, but a "citizen," in air

quotes, of privately-held Fill City One, with no rights whatso-
ever, and no visa to leave. Even temporarily. The fine print
also noted that the contract was to stay in effect for eight
generations. Not years. *Generations.* Her children couldn't
leave. Her children's children couldn't leave. Her children's
children's children. And when the eighth generation comes,
it's likely they'll have no leverage, nothing to show for their
indentured servitude, so they'll have to renew the contract. Et
cetera. The outside world forgot all this after just one generation. The mainlanders are mostly ignorant, retaining just a
wisp of a memory about some strange and dirty beings
named Fillers who make their trash disappear and magically
supply their fuel. To hear the word "Filler" on TV is like
hearing a curse. It makes me mad.

But I don't blame Nana. Life was hard already, and she
thought this was a way to make it better.

It just didn't work out that way.

"Paper! Paper!"

I snap back to reality just in time to watch three Body
Shop workers diving out of the way of our lift, and Duggie
frantically reaching for the dashboard controls.

"Exit autodrive! Exit autodrive!" Jamming the override
levers hard right, I narrowly miss one of the giant stanchions
holding the whole place up, and brake hard, sending us into a
spin, missing another stanchion by millimeters. We jerk to a
stop.

"*Whew.* That was close. System glitched again."

But the momentum of our spin has already jettisoned the
armoire like a bullet from beneath its straps. We watch help-

lessly as it skids down the drive, right into a concrete wall, smashing into splinters.

Duggie asks, in all seriousness, "You think they can still repair it?"

"I don't know. Ask him."

The foreman, Tom Bradline, moves his toothpick to the other side of his mouth, scowls at us, and pulls out his tablet. "Well, well. That's another one, idiots."

"Hey! Don't call Paper an idiot!"

"Duggie, it's okay. Mister Bradline, listen." I point to the staticky speaker in the lift cabin, a zombie autodrive system that's been resurrected too many times. It's wheezing, pleading with us to let it die for good this time. "She's dead. It wasn't our fault."

"You know what I hear, idiots? Opportunity. You've got three hours to make up for that loss and hit our numbers, or you're docked for the day. Now get the hell out of here."

Tom Bradline is a dick.

5

PORK DUMPLINGS

Three hours later, we finish up, after processing a few more loads, nowhere near breaking even on the damn armoire. I fix the system and the autodrive on the lift again – against its hoarse pleas to finally euthanize it – and we call it quits.

"G'night Duggie. Sorry about getting docked again."

"No worries. Worth it to see another one of your rockets. G'night Paper. Say hello to Scissors, will you?"

"You bet."

I walk the gravel path I've walked virtually every day of my life, the one I've trampled grooves into with my footsteps, in the dark, under the methane lamps, back to Nana's. She has dinner on the stove: Nana's Famous – Infamous, rather – Pork Dumplings, that I would testify in a court of law actually do stick to your ribs, but not in a good way. I guess they're better than Prepper Pots, those freeze-dried food bags for the apocalypse I see on TV with the tagline, "Let's Hope You Never

Have To Eat It." In any case, we're lucky to even have food on the table, so I say a silent *thanks*.

I sneak into the tiny corner of our bedroom, behind the New York Jets blanket, my little two-foot-by-three-foot sanctuary, the only space in the world I can truly call my own. I pull out the *You're Going to Mars!* poster and tack it to the wall, next to the other three, above my pile of ratty old astronomy textbooks, laptop, and my telescope. Four Zach Larsons now point out at me. "Oh well. It was a good fantasy." I sigh dramatically, it feels good to do that sometimes, and take out my box cutter, hesitating, reaching up to cut them all to pieces.

"Paper! Dinner's on! Get it before it gets cold!"

I rush back to the dining room table, because the only thing worse than Nana's Infamous Pork Dumplings are Nana's Infamous Cold Pork Dumplings, and immediately notice the mistake.

"Nana. You set a place for Rock again."

Nana gives me her sly look that only my ninety-seven year old grandmother can, and Rock peeks her head out from behind the refrigerator. "Surprise!"

"Oh Rock! Rock! Rock! You're home!" I run up and squeeze the life out of her.

"Whoa! Whoa!" She pulls away and points to her growing belly. "Don't crush the merchandise. Don't you want to be an aunt?"

"Sorry. I can't help it. It's just so good to see you." It's been six months since I've seen Rock, the oldest of the three Farris sisters by seven minutes. She found a mate, Dill, applied for the proper permits, and the WasteWay Corporation allowed their union, on the condition that Dill would continue to work the Refinery. The Refinery is on the very opposite end of the city, underground, and intra-city transport cabs are only approved at the stingy whim of the dispatchers. "Rock, how did you...?"

"I told them Nana was on her deathbed."

The springs on the screen door squeak at that moment, announcing Dad's arrival. "I heard that. Mom? These kids trying to kill you off again?" He waltzes over and hugs Rock. "Nice to see you, love. You know Nana's immortal, right?" Tosses a half stick of butter to Nana. "It's a special occasion." Then he grins at Rock and points his chin at me. "Have you told Paper the real reason you're here?"

Rock shakes her head and a corner of her lip curls.

Something's up.

I don't like when something's up.

I give her my best penetrating stare, but she looks away and scratches her cheek. That's her tell. Yes, something's up. Then Scissors barges into the trailer behind Dad. "Hey Dad. Thanks for waiting for me. Oh, hey Rock! Wow, you got fat!"

"It's not fat, you idiot." But Scissors is already putting her dirty hands all over Rock's belly, whispering sweet nothings to the baby inside. Then she takes a whiff of the kitchen air. "Do I smell pork dumplings? Or is somebody burning a tire out back?"

Dad's not the firmest dad, actually the polar opposite, a pushover for his girls, but he states with all the authority he can muster, "Yes, it's pork dumplings. And they smell as delicious as always, don't they girls? *Don't they?*"

"Yes, Father." Nana smiles at our singsong chorus, not because she believes us, I think she just likes to know we're not spoiled, not that anyone in Fill City can afford to be spoiled, and that we'll eat what's put in front of us. Period. Except egg salad. But that's a story for another time.

We wash our hands and eat.

"Dad, we were processing this armoire today, and it kind of broke, splintered into quite a few pieces actually..."

"I'm shocked."

I smack his arm. "...and Bradline docked me for a full day. How unfair is that?"

Dad raises an eyebrow. "You're lucky. Back in my day, we'd get docked for a *week* if we broke something like that."

Nana harrumphs. "A *week?* That's a luxury. Back in my day, we'd get docked a month, and the lifts only worked two days a week."

Rock grins and nods. The game is on. "You had *lifts?* We had to hump armoires uphill with our bare hands. In the snow."

My turn. "You had *snow?* I wish. Back in my day we had to walk across shards of glass barefoot, and we prayed for snow to heal our bloody feet."

Scissors squeals, "You had *feet?*"

It goes on and on like this, my favorite Farris family game, "Back in My Day," until eventually, every time, it gets to something like, "You had *water?* Back in my day, we had to suck the moisture out of each other's bad breath for a droplet of water. Still we considered ourselves lucky." And the game always ends when we're all howling with laughter, bent over from the pain in our guts, unable to think of anything worse.

When we finally settle down, and Nana moseys back into the kitchen to get dessert, I notice she looks a little more frail.

At ninety-seven, degrees of frailness become very fine, but still, something's different. "*Psst.* Dad. Is Nana okay?"

Those eyes twinkle for a second, Dad's got a tell too, but he shuts them tight before I can confirm. "Work."

"Work? Nana doesn't work anymore. She stopped when she turned eighty. That was like a million years ago."

"She had one last hunt. It was a doozy, too."

"What are you talking about?"

"Let her tell you."

Nana shuffles back to the dinner table, with a candle and a little box. She lights the candle – and strangely on cue Dad dims the rest of the lights – and we sit, hushed. Other than the sea shell wind chime in the yard, absolute silence.

"Nana. Are we having a seance or something? Are we trying to talk to PopPop again?"

She pretends not to hear me, looks around at the three other people at the table, nods to them, and begins.

"Paper Farris."

I decide to go along with this, for the moment, for Nana's sake, I don't want to disrespect her if she's finally succumbing to dementia. But my senses are telling me this is another in a long history of jokes, and if so, the whole bunch of them will be woefully sorry. "Yes. That is my name."

"And you have studied astronomy and physics since you were a wee little girl."

"Yes. I have. Is there a portable black hole in the box?"

"I don't know what that means. And when you were that little girl, did you not pretend to be from Mars, and even wear a homemade shirt that said, 'My Real Home is Mars'?"

I roll my eyes. "God. You remember everything."

"I'm only ninety-seven, of course I remember everything. And is it true that you are the first Filler ever to build a rocket from computer parts, develop your own methane-based propellant, and launch and land said rocket successfully?"

"The first two parts are true. The landings..."

"No matter. And have you said, Paper, on many an occasion, that space exploration is the only dream worth pursuing?"

Scissors snickers. "Objection. Nana, you're leading the witness."

Dad raps his glass of bourbon twice on the table as a gavel. "Overruled. Answer the question, Paper Farris. The jury is waiting."

"Yes. It is my dream. Just a dream. To leave Fill City One in my dust, and reach for the stars. Or it *was* a dream anyway. Until today. Are we done?"

But Nana's just getting started. With a flourish, she wiggles her flabby arms across the little box, as if performing a spectacular illusion, though her glasses fall off in the middle of the maneuver, sending Rock and Scissors into a fit of giggles. Then she pushes the box towards me. "Open."

All eyes are on me and the little box. I have no idea what's inside, but it must be important because my fingers begin trembling as I slowly lifted the lid.

And there it is.

The Red Scarab.

6

THE RED SCARAB

As I lift the large beetle-shaped oval out of the box, I admire the craftsmanship. Not that it's handmade, of course. The producers made fifty million of these buggers, the official lottery devices for Zach Larson's *You're Going to Mars! Sweepstakes*, so no, they're by necessity cheap molded plastic knickknacks, barely worth more than the air they're displacing. But still, whoever carved the original mold took great care to make it look like an ancient Egyptian artifact, with fine grooves for the wing covers, and perfectly fitting hinges. The paint job is excellent too, for such a mass produced item: a metallic reddish gold, almost iridescent, darker inside the grooves and shiny on the smooth parts. It hangs from a budget-friendly leatherette necklace.

Nana straightens her back proudly and announces, "And now, like the mythical scarab beetle of millennia past, you are about to be reborn, into a new life, and usher in a rebirth for all mankind."

Dad applauds. "Wow, Mom. Very eloquent."

"I printed it off the website."

I hang the trinket around my neck. "Awww. The Red Scarab. Thank you Nana. That was sweet."

She harrumphs. "You don't seem too impressed."

"No, it's sweet. Really. I'll keep it with my others."

Yes. I'm embarrassed to admit I already have twelve Red Scarabs hanging in my secret corner, part of my pathetic shrine to the impossible dream of *You're Going to Mars!*, so one more isn't about to send me to my fainting couch. The scarabs are nice looking baubles, something to decorate the disappointment, I guess, like other Fillers who keep laptop backgrounds of beaches they'll never visit. I could easily go out to any of the nearby fills and find more, because when you produce fifty million cheap scarab medallions, and every single one gets thrown out – except thirty lucky winners – a majority of them are going to wind up here in Fill City One. Like the dream, they're discarded everywhere, no longer worth the plastic they were molded from.

Nana flicks her bony finger at the scarab. "Press the head."

Now even the sea shell wind chime stops.

Dad, Rock, and Scissors hold their breath as they stare at my index finger, hovering over the head of the Red Scarab.

It can't be.

Can it?

The odds are – sorry for the pun – astronomical. If this is one of the thirty winners, when you press the head the beetle's wing covers will spring open, its wings will unfold, a red glow will emanate from the inside, and it will announce in Zach Larson's annoying voice, "You're Going to Mars!"

Everyone – and I mean every single TV-watching human alive – knows this, because we've seen the commercials so many times it's seared like a radiation burn into our collective consciousness. We know that thirty lucky winners will compete in a ridiculous reality show/astronaut training/popularity contest starting next week, in lavish accommodations, until only one contestant remains, and earns the single coveted spot on the crew of humanity's very first manned mission to Mars, aboard Larson's privately-built ship, *High Heaven.*

If this is one of the winning scarabs, my life will change forever. All our lives will change forever.

Against every rational thought, every calculation of every betting odd, every past disappointment, against every fiber of my being telling me it's impossible, my heart begins to race, and I close my eyes, and I press the head.

Click.

And nothing happens.

"Nana!"

Dad, Rock, and Scissors look equally shocked and angry, and a chorus of "Nana!"s fills the little dining area. "Boo"s and "Tsk"s follow in great numbers.

Rock shoots to her feet in a huff. "I blew a travel allowance for *this?*"

Dad tries to stop Rock from storming out the door, calling back, "Mom? *Really?* I have a number of things to say about this."

And I can't tell whether Scissors is crying or laughing, so I flick her earlobe for good measure. She hates that, and shouts, "Hey! I'm not the one who screwed you out of a trip to Jupiter."

"Mars, you idiot!"

"Whatever, it wasn't me, it was-"

"STOP!"

Nana has both her arms raised, like I imagine Moses did to tame the Red Sea. We all freeze, having never heard such a stern command leave her mouth in our entire lives. And again, while we stare, wondering once more if her brain is reaching its expiration date, she does the wiggling thing with her arms, producing from behind her, from some previously unseen pocket on her housecoat, a *second* little box.

She winks at me, chuckling. "Sorry about the first box, Paper. I couldn't help myself."

But I won't put up with more of her shenanigans. I grab the box from her hand and rip open the lid. "Ha ha. What a surprise. Another scarab. You're hilarious, Nana. How many more of these boxes are you hiding in that housecoat?" And with a dramatic, angry jab of my finger, just to show her how mean she's being, preying on the impossible dreams of her granddaughter, all for some cheap joke, I press the head.

And the wing covers spring open.

Dad, Rock, and Scissors' jaws drop in unison. Nana smiles so wide her dentures threaten to pop out.

Slowly, the beetle's wings unfurl, and tears stream down my face as I watch the red glow burn inside.

Scissors squeals, "Now say it! Say it, TV guy, say it!"

And as we all lean in to hear, in the cheapest-quality sound possible – though it sounds like a high-fidelity choir of angels to me – an eight-bit recording of Zach Larson's voice croaks, "You're Going to Mar-"

Rock snorts. "You're going to Mar? What's a Mar?"

Panicking, as if the absence of the final letter of Zach's catchphrase might nullify my winning scarab and doom me to permanent exile here in Fill City One, I flick the beetle.

And this time, as clear as day, we hear the words that will change our lives forever:

"You're Going to Mars!"

LIGHT A FIRE IN THE SKY

I can't stop staring at the red glow.

It's impossible. But true.

"Nana... How...?"

Dad collects me and Nana in his arms. "Remember her last job I told you about? It was to find *that*."

"But... the odds. Literally thirty in fifty million. Point zero zero zero zero zero six percent chance."

"Yes. Terrific odds. But here's how she narrowed those odds..."

Dad proceeds to tell us how Nana uncovered one of the most intricate scams in history, one with fake websites, diverted shipments of cardboard boxes full of scarabs, and lots of dirty money changing hands, all in a bid to win a spot on the show, because it meant guaranteed fame and fortune even if you never got to Mars. Nana followed the leads of these grifters, connected the dots, patiently waiting and toiling.

I'm too entranced by the glow of the scarab in front of me to listen.

"...and once Nana triangulated the spots in the fill where the discarded scarabs were being dumped..."

"Wait. Nana, how many scarabs did you sort? There must've been millions."

Nana shrugs, as if millions of scarabs aren't a bother. "We stopped when we hit the winner."

It turns out Nana had harangued a group of old-timers to spend five weeks, day in and day out, searching through the unopened cardboard boxes of scarabs that had been discarded. The grifters behind the scam didn't even have to open the scarabs or the boxes they were in to determine if they were winners – they had stolen some kind of infrared scanner that could tell if the winning chip was inside. Except that, unbeknownst to them, the scanner they stole didn't work, and they weren't actually scanning – or more important finding – anything. Whoops! Karma had won.

Nana's fist shoots into the air in triumph. "Mainlanders overestimate themselves, and underestimate us Fillers. I knew they'd miss it, there's no such thing as a cut corner. But I'm a *Filler*. I don't cut corners. I don't miss nothin'!" She leans over and gives me a kiss on the forehead, opens her fist and points to the heavens. "And now, my sweet Paper, you're going to light a fire in the sky."

I smush her cheek with a big, wet kiss of my own, and look around at Rock and Scissors. We all laugh, and start jumping up and down, hugging and screaming and waving our arms in the air. "I'm going to Mars!" I shout again and again and again. Until my hand accidentally knocks the candle over.

"Oh, shit."

The tip of the candle lands a little too perfectly against Nana's fake plastic flower centerpiece, setting it ablaze. In a panic, I reach for the nearest liquid – Dad's glass of bourbon – and throw it on the fire. Unfortunately, alcohol doesn't put out fires as much as it feeds them, and within seconds the vinyl tablecloth is also engulfed in flames. Frozen like four deer in headlights, we watch as Dad lunges for the fire extinguisher, pulls the pin, squeezes the handle, and aims the impotent little spittle of expired foam at the growing conflagration. He looks up, and I almost laugh.

"Run!"

I've seen fires before, many, but never one that grew so fast. I imagine that the older trailers like Nana's must've been built from sapwood soaked in kerosene, that's how fast this fire tears through our little home.

Luckily – if you can call it luck – Fill City One takes fires *very* seriously. With all the landfill's methane, and an entire underground refinery with pipelines branching out in every direction, a house fire here could blow a crater in the Earth the size of Texas. So firemen are on the scene in forty-five seconds, and the blaze completely out in under two minutes.

In the charred remains of the place where I grew up, I can just make out the corner of my New York Jets blanket, somehow the only thing not black, hanging from a nail like a flag of surrender. I want to cry, but it's not the time. Right now is about Nana. I turn to her, expecting to see her weeping, or gearing up to spank me for the first time in my life, because I really deserve it this time, of all the infinite times I've tested her infinite patience. But she puts her arm around me instead. "You know, Paper, when I said light a fire in the sky, I didn't mean it literally."

I laugh, and start bawling in her arms. And I don't stop. Dad, then Rock, then Scissors envelop us, and we all cry through the night.

8

I'M GOING FOR A WALK.

The next morning, as rain soaks our clothes, the only clothes we now own, our neighbors come out to the leaky overhang they let us sleep under and offer hot coffee. Nana continues, as always, to see silver linings. "You know. The rain is good. Makes sure all the embers are out. Keeps Fill City safe."

Dad holds out his mug under one of the leaks to let a little rainwater cool off his coffee. Another silver lining, I guess.

I can't see silver linings right now. Yes, I have a winning scarab around my neck, the ultimate silver lining, one in fifty million, a chance to live my childhood dream. But Nana has lost everything. Because of me. I have the sudden urge to fling the scarab out to sea.

"I'm going for a walk."

I make it maybe a quarter mile before I'm confronted by Tom Bradline. "Well. I heard. You really did it this time, didn't you, Paper Farris."

"I know. I'm an idiot."

"Yes. You are. Grade A idiot." He takes the toothpick out of his mouth and traces a little "A" with it in the air.

"Listen, Mister Bradline. I lost a day's pay, our home burned down, and now we're standing here in the rain. Can I go on my way?"

"No. You're coming with me."

And so Tom Bradline escorts me in the direction of the Body Shop, I suppose to find one more way to make my day even more terrible. Or worse.

"So, Paper, while we walk... tell me about Mars."

I stop. "What?"

He pulls me along. "While we walk. Tell me. Mars."

Does he know? About the scarab? Is he going to steal it? It's worth taking my life for, easily. It can probably fetch a million credits or more. Maybe even secretly buy a family's way out of this filthy shantytown they dare to call a city. Tom Bradline always seemed like one of the good ones, despite his sour attitude, and that stupid ever-present toothpick, but you never know. People have disappeared for much less. I shiver in my wet coveralls, and pull up my collar. Maybe he hasn't seen it.

"Well, Mister Bradline... Mars is the fourth planet from the Sun. It was named after the Roman god of war. They also call it the Red Planet, because of the reddish iron oxide on the surface. It has seasonal cycles like Earth, and a thin atmosphere, and it's the next planet from us, so it makes an excellent candidate for terraform testing, and potential off-world colonization. The first manned mission is finally taking place, in December."

"You're going to Mars."

I jerk my hand back to my collar, closing it around my neck. "Excuse me?"

"The show. *You're Going to Mars!*"

"Oh. Yes. The show." I look around for a place to run, just in case. Not that there is one, Bradline knows every nook and cranny of this route at least as well as me. "Um, as you know, every fifteen years or so there's been a global economic crash. So every time NASA thought they had enough funding for a manned mission, boom – the money would disappear again. Finally, Groupie-"

"I hate Groupie."

"You're supposed to hate it. It's for the six billion people on the planet under the age of thirty-four who can't get enough virtual social media entertainment. It's not for fifty-five-year-old Fillers." He looks at me sideways. "No offense. So finally, Zach Larson, the world's first trillionaire and owner of Groupie and AceSpace, said 'enough,' and told NASA to hold his beer while he funded the whole thing himself. To help with the funding, he came up with a sponsored TV show that would auction off a spot on the crew to a random Groupie subscriber. The winners are picked by-"

"Okay. I've heard enough." He steps in front of me, blocking my path. Looks down at me.

Oh my God.

"Now close your eyes."

I try to run, but he grabs my upper arm hard. Instinctively, I turn opposite, flexing his hand backward, and, using a self-defense move Dad showed me a decade ago and made me practice endlessly – because, you know, we live in Fill City One, after all – I grab his palm, twisting his wrist sharply and sending him to the ground.

"Jesus Christ, Farris! Keep your eyes open, I don't give a rat's ass! I just thought it would be more fun!"

"More *fun?!* What kind of a sick–?!"

Just then, the members of Bradline's team, the Body Shop crew, turn the corner and approach us.

They're leading a caravan of lifts, carrying repaired appliances and reclaimed lumber.

A tow truck bringing up the rear hauls something big.

A trailer. A double wide.

Bradline wheezes through his pain and the broken toothpick threatening to pierce his cheek. "It's for your family. You ingrate. Now will you let me go, goddammit?!"

"Oh my God! Mister Bradline! I'm sorry!" I release his palm and lift him up and give him the biggest hug I can remember. "Thank you! Thank you!"

He brushes some of the mud off his coveralls. "Thank your Nana. She's one of the originals. She's watched over many of my men, and myself for that matter. Decades of warm soup on cold days breeds a fierce loyalty. And she's saved more than one life down here. So even one night in the rain is too much for her. She won't have any more. You can thank her."

I lean up and kiss him on the cheek. Strange. Not like me.

"And the other thing. The Mars thing. Your Nana told us." By now, the crew had circled me, smiling, expectant. They want to see, I can tell. I loosen my collar, take off the scarab necklace, and press its head. Again the wing covers spring open, revealing wings and a red glow, and Larson's silly voice. Some ooh, some laugh, and one says, "It's really true. You're going to Mars."

"No. I'm going on a show. And if I survive three months against thirty competitors, *then* I'm going to Mars."

Another one, Vera, turns to Bradline. "But... boss... the show starts in like a week. And she can't even leave Fill City One. Can she?"

. . .

Shit.

In all the frenzy of last night's fire, and my brooding guilt this morning, I haven't given any thought to this actually becoming a reality, the Mars dream, so I've never seriously asked myself the question: *how the hell do I get out of here? And how the hell do I get to Los Angeles in five days?*

My hands start to tremble, I feel tears welling up in my eyes. *No, Paper. Not in front of the damn Body Shop crew.* My head's spinning. Bradline sees my collapse coming, and takes my hands in his own.

"Miss Paper Farris. We – all of us – need you to hear something: You are your Nana's grandchild. I don't like to admit it, but you have her pluck, and then some, and you're smart as a whip with your little gadgets and such, a little scary even, considering you're about as graceful as a drunk raccoon and you make my life miserable. You, young Farris... you're getting out of here. And you are going to get on that show thing. And you are going to win. And then you are going to Mars. Do you understand me?"

I look at him blankly.

"Come on, Farris. Wake up. This isn't just about you." He points around to the fills. "This is no life, not really. It's servitude. A life without choices. We're 'free' only inside thirty-foot walls." Then he points to his companions. "Look at us. You're doing this thing for us. You're leading the way so that we can-"

"Whoa. Stop right there, Mister Bradline."

"Excuse me? I was in the middle of my speech."

"This is about me. It's my dream."

"No it's not. It's ours."

"Mine."

"Ours."

"Mine."

"How old are you?"

"How old are you, Mister Bradline? You're older than me!"

He puts his fingers to his lips, to readjust his new toothpick, but stops, and settles into a burning glare for a few seconds.

It works.

"Okay, yes. I understand. But I'm not some kind of beacon of hope. I'm just a twenty-one-year-old Filler with a dream. Anyway, it doesn't matter. Vera's right. I can't make it out."

He laughs, and the others follow his lead.

"What?"

Bradline flicks his toothpick aside, to join the million or so others he's littered the path with over the years. "We'll get you out. You just leave that to the experts. We have ways. We're working on it with your dad, and, um..."

"And, *um?*"

"...and your mother."

9

MY WHAT?!

"My *what?!*"

"Your mother. Listen, Paper, things are moving pretty fast..."

Dad tries to calm me down, to keep me from hitting my head again on the countertop. Lying on the linoleum floor squeezed into a corner of the kitchen with him, installing this reclaimed oven in Nana's newish trailer, playing with a methane gas line, is not my happy place at the moment. Normally I love this kind of time with Dad, because I'm the only one of us three that can install the more complicated gear, fix machinery, and improvise. He always looks at me when we work together, with this mysterious smile, like he's looking into his own past.

But not today. Neither one of us is smiling today.

Nana's busy with what she's considering for the moment the "important" stuff – hanging donated knickknackery on the walls – but really, I think she's just avoiding the "Mom" issue, and me, and Rock, and Scissors, and Dad, like we're the 2044 Thailand virus outbreak.

I slap the ratchet wrench into his palm. "I don't have a mother."

"Yes you do."

"No I don't."

He looks up, pleading. "Rock. Scissors. Help me out here."

Scissors, who's installing cabinet doors above us with Rock, kicks him in the heel. "Help you out? You betrayed us, Dad. And I'm not being melodramatic. What the hell?"

"I didn't betray anyone. Listen..."

But Rock stands firm. "I am not listening to this." Then she rubs her belly, which is probably not the right thing to do at that moment. "Do you realize...?" and tears burst from her eyes. The stress of the past twenty-four hours – from the potential departure of her sister Paper to Los Angeles, to the loss of our childhood home, to the discovery that Dad was secretly corresponding with our absent mother, to having a six-month-old baby inside her – it all finally gets to her. She wails like the infant she'll be delivering in a few months.

Dad, always a softie for waterworks – which, admittedly, all three of us have taken advantage of since we discovered its power many years ago – jumps to his feet, hitting his head on the countertop, screaming "Fuck!" and then, "Oh, sorry. Excuse my French. No, Rock, listen. All of you, come here."

So we stand around the new counter, glaring at Dad, stewing. Nana quietly slips out to the living room to attend to some crucial towel folding she's forgotten.

Duggie, who's gluing the curled-up corners of the linoleum back down in the far corner of the little dining area, gets up off his knees and joins us, giddy, ready for whatever game he thinks we're about to start playing. "Can I go first?"

"Duggie..." Dad politely motions for him to leave.

"Yes, Mister Farris?"

Dad motions again, and points to the door for emphasis.

"Yes, Mister Farris. Nice day out. Rain's finally stopped."

"Duggie. Go outside."

"Now?"

"Now."

Duggie's brain finally clicks, and he bounds out the new screen door, but not before casting one last backward glance at Scissors and giving her a shy little two-finger wave.

Rock is still whimpering, but manages a laugh. "Forget little old Mars. That one's over the *Moon* for you, Siz."

I add what I think is the necessary clarity. "The Moon is smaller than Mars. By a lot. Not something to forget."

"Yeah, okay Paper. Whatever. Blah blah science nerd stuff. Scissors knows what I mean. Don't you, Siz?"

Scissors' cheeks are red, though I can't tell whether it's from blushing or being angry. "Hey! You two. We're supposed to be super pissed at Dad right now. Focus."

So we refocus our rage on Dad. But before more shouts or tears can start, he clears his throat. "Your mother, her name is Jane, she is alive and well. Well-ish. She had a difficult childhood of her own, very bad, like a lot of childhoods here, much worse than yours I'd add. She couldn't handle being a mother, I guess. Did what she thought was best for you. So she snuck out of Fill City One. I don't know why or how, I've never known anyone else to do it. Please don't hate her."

"Don't hate her? How do *you* not hate her? How can you not be more angry at her? She abandoned us! All of us!"

"Actually, she did me a favor. She got her freedom, or whatever she was looking for. And I got the better part of the deal." He looks around at us intently. "I got you three." And for the first time today we see his way-too-calm smile, which can be either totally reassuring or totally annoying.

"Silver lining." I try to say it with anger, but we can't really argue his point. We are the apples of his eye, after all. Who *wouldn't* want to raise three girls like us on his own?

"I still hate her."

"Me too."

"Me three."

Dad has lost this round. "Well, okay, how about this: You can hate *her*. Fine. But don't hate *me* for trying to help her."

"*Help* her?"

"Oh, did I say help?"

"Yes, you said help, Dad."

"Well, she, uh, needed a few credits and some parenting advice last year, so she snuck me a letter and an untraceable phone."

"*Parenting* advice?"

"Well, it seems... no, I don't want to tell you. You'll gang up on me. I'll tell you some other time. A calmer time."

Rock stamps her foot and crosses her arms. Menacing. "Don't you think it's a little late for that, Dad?"

"Okay, okay. It seems... you've all got a brother."

"*A BROTHER?!*"

Rock nearly faints. Scissors face palms. I try to wrap my head around it. "We have a brother. Did you really just say that?"

"A half-brother."

"So this Jane person married again, and had a kid, after running away from her trial run with good ol' Harlon and his three daughters?"

"Come on, Paper. It's not like that. I didn't say she got married again. She didn't. And I didn't say she could handle it either. She can't. She's a terrible mother. The poor kid. Only six years old and he doesn't know which way is up."

Scissors picks up her screwdriver and walks away. "Good story, bro. I've already erased it from my memory banks. Just let me know when any of this has something to do with me."

"Actually, Scissors…"

"Oh, come on, Dad. Enough surprises for today. And I'm sorry, with all due respect, that smile of yours is getting annoying."

"No. I'm serious. Scissors, I'll need you and Rock to do me a favor. We'll be smuggling Paper out of here tonight, we don't have any more time, to get on the road with your mother – please don't hit me for mentioning her – she has a way to get Paper out to Los Angeles. But Paper can't look like herself. Just in case. No one can make the connection. She needs to look different. Much different. I need you to give her a haircut. And do something about the color."

Rock and Scissors lock eyes on each other and smile, the smile of an evil supervillain duo. Then they turn to me, and Rock picks up a knife from the counter. "Hey Paper. Hear that?"

And I run out of the house screaming.

10

GOODBYES

I'm not attached to my hair, it's not like that.

But the three of us all have had long, thick, dark braids going all the way down our backs, for as long as I can remember. It's just never been any other way. When we were little and bickered – which was pretty frequent to be honest, and we still fight like feral dogs over a bone sometimes – we would threaten to cut off each other's braids in the middle of the night. I can remember mornings waking up in a panic to feel if mine was still there.

But it was always still there. Of course it was. The three of us would sit in "braid circles" weaving intricate patterns for each other, taking time to make sure they were perfect, because everything else we had was either dirty or damaged, or simply smelled bad. Some of my favorite memories were of those braid circles.

Huh. Maybe I am attached to my hair.

Scissors isn't looking quite so sentimental. "Ah, revenge! For all those earlobe flicks. Finally!"

She and Rock have me pinned against a light pole. "Siz. Please don't. I'll bring you back a Mars rock."

Rock snorts. "What the hell does she want with a Mars rock? Look around."

I look around, and yes, we're in a section of the nearest fill reserved for concrete. Rocks twenty-five feet high. "Point taken. But you don't really want to do this. Do you guys?"

"Of course not. Well, maybe just a little. It would be cool to see what we would look like with something different for once. Wouldn't it? Like a blonde crew cut."

"Ha! You're kidding."

Scissors reveals the scissors from her satchel.

Oh my God. She's not kidding.

I close my eyes.

Suddenly a new feeling washes over me. The feeling that maybe I need to change. To take the first step. It's just like Nana said. I'm being reborn. Like the scarab.

I open my eyes. "Okay. Let's do this."

So Scissors cuts my braid, and we all gasp, unsure whether to laugh, or cry, or drop everything and walk away. She looks at me, searching, a little sadness in her eyes. I nod, and she gently lays the braid into her satchel.

"It's okay, Siz. That was the hard part. Keep cutting. And Rock, get the bleach."

To Dad's credit, he doesn't laugh when I return to help him with the new refrigerator, and he pretends not to notice. "Paper, good. I need a third hand with this freon injector."

I give him my hand, and he places it on the valve. "Great. Hold it just like that."

"You're not going to say anything?"

"I just did."

"Come on, Dad."

He studies me for a moment. Smiles. "It suits you. You look like a pixie."

I have no idea what a pixie is, but I don't like the sound of it.

Nana comes up from behind me and tousles my bleached little mop. "You're my hero."

Ahh. *Hero*. Now *that* I like the sound of.

After dark, a lift quietly arrives outside, and Tom Bradline and Duggie and a couple of others hop off.

"Okay, Harlon. We've arranged our end. Last-minute addition to Load 85332b, scheduled to go out on a trailer at exactly eleven-thirty p.m. We've lined the inside here with a special foil; it'll fool any scanners on the way out. She can remove it later and it'll look good as new, and it'll get delivered, so there won't be any inventory anomalies. Also, false bottom with four screws. She'll have a screwdriver and a flashlight, a pouch for urine just in case, and of course, air holes. Now, let's get her inside so we can package the whole thing up for shipping."

I step forward to see what kind of coffin they've invented for me.

It's an Ethan Allen French armoire, the color of cheese.

Of course.

Bradline sees me approach it and eyes me suspiciously. "Hey. Who's this?" But as the words leave his mouth, recognition sweeps across his face and he begins to howl with laughter.

He laughs so hard he starts coughing, God, it looks like he's going to choke on his toothpick, or have a stroke. "Paper Farris?" are the only words he can get out before resuming his death-rattle-slash-laughing-fit.

The others stifle their snickers, prep the false bottom, and motion for me to climb inside.

"Made you some snacks for the ride. Cashews, too. Your favorite." Duggie takes my hand and drops a bag into my palm.

I run back to my sisters, and hold them tight. Rock puts my free hand on her belly. "By the time you get back, he'll be running around and eating his own boogers."

Scissors gulps. "You are coming back, right?"

I kiss her on the cheek. "That's the plan." And I flick her earlobe. And for the first time ever, instead of swatting my hand away, she grabs it, and kisses it, and a tear runs down to her chin.

Dad fumbles in his pocket. "Wait! A picture. Stay right there." He pulls out his ancient instant camera– he can't use a phone for this highly incriminating photo, as every single packet of data is monitored by Fill City One Command – and hands it to one of the Body Shop crew.

"Okay, everybody. Make the face you want Paper to remember."

The flash blinds us. Then Dad kisses the top of my head, hugs me, and pushes me away. "I'm letting you go. Because I know this isn't goodbye." He's trying to hide it, but I can see him sniffing and wiping his eyes with his shirt sleeves. "Oh, hey, listen, whenever you fall down, just remember to get back in the saddle. And if you hear anyone talking down about Fillers, it's just ignorance. Now, go show them who you are."

I look up into his eyes. "Who am I?"

He smiles at me and shrugs. "I guess you'll have to find out."

"Hey, where's Nana?" I look around, but she's gone. I imagine this is all too much for her, this goodbye. She's probably in her bedroom, wailing, mourning the loss of her granddaughter. Poor Nana.

But the screen door creaks, and there she is. "Forgetting something?"

She raises the Red Scarab into the air.

"Yikes! I almost forgot the Scarab!"

Nana shuffles over and places it around my neck. "Now, look at me Paper. Take a good look at me. I may not be here when you get back."

"Nana!"

"Oh, don't be so sensitive. I'm ninety-seven, for Pete's sake. I say that to myself every night in the mirror. You just go and have a good time. Live your dream. I'll be fine. Now vamoose!"

"I'll see you when I get back. Count on it."

She nods, and waves her arms, and shoos me into the awaiting casket.

I climb in, and they secure the false bottom, and the lift starts moving.

And I instantly start sobbing and banging on the armoire. "Let me out! Let me out! This was a bad idea!"

I can hear Bradline, muffled, screaming back at me. "Shut the hell up Farris! What, do you want to get us all locked up? Or worse? It's too late for that crap!"

"Sorry!"

I don't know what's happening to me. For twenty-one years, I couldn't wait to shake off the dust and smell of Fill City One and escape. Couldn't wait to break out of that teeny trailer stuffed with four people (and trust me, with Rock as five it was even worse), finally get away and get some time and space to myself. On my own. And now I am alone, truly alone for the first time. Totally by myself.

And it sucks.

I can't cry again, Bradline will murder me, so I just whimper quietly. It's a new feeling, this alone thing. I hate it.

Then my foot touches something. My satchel! How'd they sneak that in here? I fumble for my flashlight and examine the contents:

Yet another poster of Zach Larson, this one with a mustache and goatee and horns added in marker. Next to the words "You're Going To Mars!" they've scribbled "(Maybe.)"

A little braid of my own hair.

A poem we wrote when we were probably around ten. It reads: "Our number is three, and in time you'll see, what each one will be, but on this you'll agree – there's nothing like we!"

And *this... how?* My little baby sweater, with "PAPER" embroidered in big letters across the front. Somehow Nana saved it from the fire. I pull it close, feeling it against my face, and though it smells like charred wood now, it still feels soft, just like always. I know it's only been three minutes, but wish I could see her face again.

Aha! I can! They snuck me the photo we just took.

I lift it into the light, and there she is, Nana, poking her tongue out at me, and sticking her finger in Dad's ear. I laugh. Dad, of course, is crossing his eyes and grinning like an idiot. Rock smiles and points to her dimples – she was the only one of us to have those cute dimples – as if to say, "you better get your ass back here soon so you can see these beauties again." And Scissors puckers her lips into a kiss and gives me the finger with both hands. Duggie's there, too, looking off to the right, blankly, as always unprepared for a picture. Even Tom Bradline is there, on one knee, barely breathing from laughing, red as a beet, pointing up to my hair. Across the bottom, Dad has scrawled *Greetings from Fill City One! Wish you were here!*

And right in the middle is me.

Hair butchered and blonde. Looking more sad and less excited than I should be.

I turn out the flashlight, breathing deep, holding the image of my family in my mind. In the darkness, behind my eyelids, the light still glows until it fades, and I'm alone in the dark, and I think:

So this is what it feels like to die.

I have the irresistible urge to beat on the doors of the armoire again.

But something stops me.

Little pinpricks of light.

The air holes Bradline drilled are letting in tiny points of moonlight, bouncing on the inside of the armoire inches above my face. I know it's a stretch of the imagination, but they look like a constellation, Capricorn maybe. I lift my finger and touch the door, where Mars would be at this time of year, and follow it as it crosses the night sky, from constellation to constellation, on its journey around the sun. My finger stops at the point where I know Mars will be when Zach Larson's ship intercepts its orbit, and I have the inexplicable feeling that I'm pointing to my own future.

A little jolt of anticipation surges through me, and I laugh.

Bradline bangs on the wood. "Shhhh! Shut up!"

I silence my laugh, but the feeling stays with me, like I'm shedding my skin and floating, up into the stars, surrendering to chance and fate, impatient to see where this ride takes me. I'm ready. And maybe, if this all actually works, I'll float back down someday and tell everyone what space is like, what the sand of another planet's surface feels like under your foot, and where we might all be headed together.

Feeling not so alone anymore in my custom-made coffin, I grin and say aloud, "So this is what it feels like to be reborn."

Bradline growls, "For the last time, shut the hell up, you idiot."

11

COME ON, CHUCK. HAVE A LOOK.

I can see nothing. I can hear almost nothing.

But I think we're at the gate.

My casket – *armoire* – is jostled and lifted, and I assume placed near the rear of one of the giant tractor trailers that constantly drive in and out of Fill City One, mine being a last-minute addition. I hear muffled voices, irritated, climbing in and activating the trailer's infrared scanners. They're designed specifically for this scenario – to detect the body warmth of a hostage – I mean, that's basically what we are, aren't we? – trying to escape Fill City One. But Tom Bradline knows his stuff. My little foil compartment will show nothing, no heat, and the tiny air holes are situated such that any heat escaping will register on the infrared as a mouse or some other small varmint.

"Hey. Bradline. What's this? An awful lot of metal showing in there."

"Armoire. With a steel safe on the lower half. Mainlanders are idiots. They keep their trinkets, and then throw the safe out! You want me to open, unpack, repack, so you can have a look?"

My heart stops.

"Come on, Chuck, have a look. It'll only take a half hour. You know what? If we hurry, twenty minutes." Yes, Bradline has a bad attitude, but he's no fool. He's delivered me five minutes before outbound time, knowing that no security guard in their right mind will hold up the queue for twenty minutes unless there's a clear and urgent problem. Plus they trust Bradline, maybe more than they trust the Gitanos – so I hear the guard *harrumph* and the trailer doors close. We move into the queue.

There's no driver, of course, but each tractor trailer has cameras, sensors, and weapons defenses that are in constant contact with Command, detecting external danger – thieves and other malcontents – and more mundane obstacles like road conditions and bad weather. They constantly monitor the interior as well, for humidity, varmints, and things like me – a stowaway. Their countermeasures are elaborate and fearsome. I might get beyond Fill City One for the first time in my life, but I will not be out of the woods.

Without fanfare, the truck stops idling and starts moving. I feel it bounce over the tire spike strips, one, two, three, four...

I'm OUTSIDE!

A little yelp of excitement escapes my mouth, and I nearly pee in terror thinking the sensors have heard me and I've been caught a whopping hundred yards from the walls of Fill City One.

But no sirens blare.

. . .

I'm on the road.

Mainland.

The trip was supposed to take an hour until my rendezvous, and Bradline had told me it would get a bit warm. But it's been over two hours now – my contact is late, very late, and *a bit warm* has become *blistering hot*. I'm boiling in my own body heat. In an effort to trick the infrared sensors, Bradline has sealed me in successfully, but in the process he's created an oven. Water isn't the issue, either. I have plenty. It's just the heat. It's getting dangerous. Extended temperatures like this will cook my internal organs. Sweat begins to pour off my body, and I feel my focus... getting blurry... desperately, I peel off my clothes and pour water onto myself.

It's no use. A few more minutes... I'm going to faint... then die. I turn my head and vomit.

I feel a shudder as the trailer grinds to a halt. I've been discovered... it's over... I'll probably be dead when they find my body.

The last thing I remember is a strange vibration, a cool rush of air, and a woman's voice.

"Well. Don't you look pathetic."

12

HOW I MET MY MOTHER

The sounds of clanking.

I open my eyes. I'm lying on the side of the road, looking up into the open trailer. The moon is full, so I can clearly make out a woman, reconstructing the armoire to its original specifications, according to instructions, and packing it back up. Perfect.

The woman turns and looks down, noticing my eyes open. "Well look at you. Naked and covered in your own waste. Just like the first time I met you."

"...Who... are you...?"

"I'm your mother."

Ah, my mother. Sweet as saccharin. Just like I imagined.

I pull myself up to a sitting position, though my head screams for me to lay back down. "...You're..."

"You look like your father."

"You... say that like it's not a compliment."

"It's not." She returns to the packaging, putting the last of the tape around it. Inspecting it.

"Hey! Dad is a handsome man." I pull my coveralls back on, and stand up, defiant. And fall to my knees.

She snickers. "Oh, okay. Sometimes. He had cute teeth when he smiled. I'll grant you that. And nice blue eyes. Listen, I'm in a little bit of a hurry here." She quickly looks at her watch. "Two minutes twenty. Time to wrap things up."

Leaping from the back, down to the pavement, she locks the trailer doors. Connects some wires. Walks around to the front, climbs into the cab, and does God-knows-what. When she returns, she grabs my arm and lifts me back to my feet. I almost pass out again.

"Whoa. You can faint in the ditch. Let's go." And she pushes me towards a berm on the side of the road, maybe fifty yards away, into some tall grass, shoving me down.

I swat her hand away. "Gee, you're a regular Florence Nightingale."

"How do you know who Florence Nightingale is?"

"I read. I had a lot of books around growing up. You know, instead of a mother."

"Oh for crying out lou- *stop!*" She looks down at her watch. Pushes my head down further into the grass "Get down! Not a peep!"

In that next moment, my eyes focus on her in the dark for the first time. This gray-haired, scrawny, leather-skinned woman has no connection to me, none at all, except... oh my. Her nose. We have the same nose. I've always wondered about that, where we got our good-looking noses. It's a really nice nose. Though I'm positive it's the only nice thing about her.

Suddenly the tractor trailer roars back to life. Its engines rev, floodlights swivel in all directions, sirens blare, and it ejects a cloud around itself, I'm guessing tear gas. *"Stand clear of the vehicle! Stand clear of the vehicle!"* it shouts over and over. After a minute or so of this, the sirens and the floodlights stop, and it silently moves on its way.

"How...?"

She smiles. "EMPs. It's the only thing that'll shut down all their systems at once without damaging them. After the electromagnetic pulse, which its sensors categorize as a weather event like a bolt of lightning, the trailer goes through a startup sequence, and it takes five minutes and forty-three seconds to get back online. Just enough time to drag you out, clean up your god-awful mess, get everything perfect and get the hell out of there. Then it goes through a one minute twelve-second inspection, for damage, inventory, stowaways, et cetera. Then back to the road."

"You generated an EMP?"

She lifts a box, about the size of a shoebox, and points to three red switches on the side. "Yup. EMP pulse generator. Made it myself."

"Who *are* you?"

"I'm your mother. Jane. You're into rockets, from what Harlon said, and I'm into... other stuff."

"Oh, look at us, we have so much in common. Is this where we hug?"

"No."

"Good. Now really – *you* made an EMP pulse generator?"

"Ahhh, I see. Not the vision of the abandoning mother you were expecting, am I? You were expecting some drug-addled drifter, or a prostitute, or some other lowlife, weren't you? Well, how do you think someone like *that* gets out of Fill City One?"

"I don't kn-"

"They DON'T. Damn, woman, you're only the fifth or

sixth one to ever leave, as far as I know, and you had a lot of help. I did it on my own."

"But... why?"

"No. I may have no right to call myself your mother, but you have no right to ask me that. I'll leave it at this: I'm very good at what I do. I don't always like what that means. But I am what I am. No regrets. Now I promised Harlon I'd get you to L.A. on time, and air travel's for zillionaires only, so let's get to the car."

We crawl out of the ditch, this Jane person and I, walking through a field of soybeans onto the far side, to another ditch. A red... thing... greets us.

"What's this?"

"A car."

I'm not sure about that. Any car this resembles has been crushed into a stack of at least fifty in Fill City One's junk yard and is rusting away to dust. This one looks like it belongs there too. It actually has a driver's seat. "You have to drive? Manually?"

"I like to drive. It's a 2038 Honda. One of the best engines ever developed. It's still legal to drive yourself out here in the mainland, in most places anyway. Get in."

I lean down to open the door, notice a movement, and jerk back. "There's someone in there!"

"Relax. It's Voomvoom."

There he is, in the back seat, sucking on a lollipop, content, rubbing his eyes.

My half-brother.

"You left him out here in a field? Alone? He's six! What kind of mother are you?"

She throws open the door and plops into the strange

cockpit. "He's *seven*. And I left the windows open. Jeez. See? That attitude? *That's* why I should never have had kids."

We both shout, "Hey!", Voomvoom and I, at precisely the same moment, and that makes him smile. He leans forward and offers me his lollipop. "Voom voom."

"No thank you. So, let me guess..."

"Yes. His name is Voomvoom because it's his favorite thing to say. He's perfectly normal otherwise. Aren't you, Voomvoom?"

"Voom voom."

I jerk my head around to him. "Wait! Give me that lollipop!"

Jane slams her hand on the steering device in front of her. "Lemme guess! You have a problem with me giving him lollipops, too!"

"No." Voomvoom offers it to me again, and I hold it close to my nose, and breathe in deep. "Strawberries!"

She shrugs. "Well, artificial imitation strawberry flavoring, but yes. So?"

"Just strawberries! Nothing else! No methane! No rotting! Nothing!"

I run from the car, to the edge of the soybean field, and fill my lungs with the first truly fresh air I have ever inhaled. "It's *CLEAN!*" I twirl around, hands in the air, breathing deeply in and out, in and out, and catch the scent of something else. A clump of purple weeds. "What is that?"

"Lavender. Go ahead. Stick your face in."

I kneel reverently and touch the purple stalks to my nose. Oh my God.

The aroma fills me completely. Sweet. Deep. Intoxicating. I begin to weep.

I've discovered a new world already! Just two hours

outside of Fill City One! The world of clean air, and sweet, unadulterated smells! And if I look up, I imagine even the sky is clearer, and that if I squint, up to the north and west a little, I can see Mars. Oh, the wonders of this world!

"Ahem."

Oh. Except for my mother. She's not so wonderful.

"Get back in, Pepper. Change those stinking clothes. We've got work to do."

"My name is Paper."

"Not for long."

Minutes later, a card pops out of Jane's homemade fake-identification-creating-machine.

"That's me?"

"That's the new you. Robin Smith. Photo, DNA code, address, interstate transport permissions, everything. And here's the kicker: our DNA matches. There's no way you can fake that. So when they check, take a swab, and believe me they do, you really are my daughter. It's legit. It's perfect."

"*Perfect.* You and me. Ha."

"You going to keep doing that? The passive aggressive thing? All the way to Los Angeles?"

"Yes. The entire way."

"Oh joy."

I look down at the name again. "Smith. Couldn't think of anything better?"

"Smith. It's the best name to use. Too many connections for them to check, too many false positives." She guns the engine and shoots out of the ditch, onto the highway, leaving a trail of dirt in our wake. It's strange to see her in control of the vehicle, this ancient car, without giving it audible instructions, turning the steering device and stepping on levers near her feet. It looks like a lot of unnecessary effort, and she can't move from her spot, or shift her focus from the road, or turn around to talk to me, or her son in the back seat. Why not let the car do the work? Manual driving is stupid.

"Pepper, lemme see the thing. The scarab."

"My name is *Paper*. Well, now it's Robin. And no."

"Suit yourself."

We drive in silence for a while, listening to the leaves rush out of our way as we hurtle down I-80, seeing nothing in the dark but the few yards of highway ahead of us. I still can hardly believe it: this is the start of a journey that might – no, *will* – take me 140 million miles. To *Mars*. I feel another involuntary jolt of excitement in my gut, a feeling of certainty, that fate has placed me in the middle of something big, and that I have a job to do, a place to be, and there's a reason it has to be me, and nothing is going to stop me. I look over at the woman driving the car, and have a pang of... something. "Thank you for doing this, Jane. But... you're still not..."

"Your mother? Sorry to rupture the fragile little denial you've got going there, but biologically, you're a hundred percent wrong. I'm your mother. Emotionally? Sure. Whatever helps you sleep at night. And you're welcome." Then she cackles and peers into the mirror above her head and shouts, "Who's your mother?"

From the seven-year-old boy in the back seat comes the answer: "Voom voom."

I look down at the ID card one last time before tossing it into my satchel, and think: *Well, Robin Smith – is there any possibility this plan actually works?* Fill City One keeps shoddy records, that just isn't their thing, they never even established a DNA database like the government on the mainland – they prefer simple walls and guns and constant monitoring – so WasteWay management will see me on TV around the clock for months and never know the truth. As long as the folks back home cover my work, and put my identical triplet Scissors in my place when needed, and fake the necessary documents with Bradline and the other willing Fillers, I should disappear for a while, be back in eighteen months, then slip back into Fill City One with no one the wiser. Hopefully.

It's not a fool-proof plan, not even marginally, I wouldn't bet on it, but it's our plan. It's the best we have.

I shift in my seat, getting comfortable, and reach back for the seat belt.

There is none.

13

BOLOGNA SANDWICHES

Morning.

I peel my crusty eyes open. "Can we stop?"

Jane laughs. "In forty more hours."

I peek over at her tablet, with its little antenna vibrating away, an ever-present indicator of just how *not* smooth this ride is. It's showing a live feed from the huge sweepstakes countdown clock mounted on the main Groupie Studios building – sixty hours. "We've got plenty of time to stop. Sixty hours to go two thousand miles. We'll need to stop. For fuel. For rest. For food. I'm not living on lollipops for the next two days."

"We're not stopping."

"I'm hungry."

"Good for you." She shifts in her seat, and harrumphs, like a younger version of Nana. Turns around, pointing to an old cooler in the back. "There are sandwiches in there. I hope you like bologna."

"Did you butter the bread at least?"

"What am I, Zach Larson?"

Oh, well. At least it's not egg salad. As she turns her head back to the road, I catch a glimpse of something reflective on her opposite cheek. Weird. "What's that?"

"Nothing." She's now actively NOT turning her head. I can't see the thing on her cheek.

"Show me and I'll show you the scarab."

I spy a little smile curl her lip, and Voomvoom claps. She turns her head to me. "Okay, here's your look. But you know what they say about curiosity." There is a bright blue tube making its way out of her sweatshirt, along her neck, over her ear, and up her nose.

"That's *disgusting!*"

"You wanted to see. Now show me the scarab."

"*Gross!* What the hell *is* that?"

"Listen. We can't stop. Yes, technically we have a little wiggle room, twenty extra hours or so, but you're not in Fill City anymore. Things happen out here on the mainland. Have you ever met a toll monitor?"

"No. What is that thing coming out of your nose?"

"Jeez. It's going *into* my nose. It's a Meal-in-a-Bag." She points to the pouch shape under her sweatshirt. "I made it myself."

"Of course you did. Gross."

"It's not gross. It's necessary. It's got every nutrient and stimulant I need to get to L.A., and then some, without stopping, thanks to a secret ingredient or two. I'm calling it my Mars Blend. Now back to the toll monitor. Tolls ideally take a few seconds, a quick ID/DNA check and you're on your merry way. But you hit a nasty monitor, for whatever reason, a bird shit in his coffee that morning, doesn't matter, and he'll take his sweet time with you. Hours. Overnight. We could easily miss our deadline. Easily."

"That's not fair."

"Fair? Oh honey, did you think you'd escape Fill City and there would be nothing but endless fields of lavender?" She taps the tube up her nose. "I've got an extra one of these if you don't like bologna."

"No thank you. Bologna's my new favorite." I motion to Voomvoom, and he passes me a sandwich from the cooler and points to the necklace hiding beneath my t-shirt. "Can I see?"

So I show them both the scarab, its dramatic little show, and Voomvoom yelps. "Voom voom!"

"Yes, very voom voom." His smile is adorable, he has such cute dimples. *Hmmm.* He looks a lot like Rock with those dimples. I tuck the scarab back under my t-shirt, and pull the family photo from my satchel, and show it to him. "See here? Wow. You look like her. Her name is Rock. She's my sister. We're triplets. But only Rock got the dimples."

Voomvoom grins even wider. "She's *my* sister too. Right?"

I want to correct him, to say half-sister, to explain the difference, and get in a not-so-subtle jab at this Jane person who claims to be my mother while I'm at it, but his smile disarms me, and instead I just smile back and say, "Voom voom."

We pass a gas station, the old kind that you see in vintage movies, and I'm surprised to see that it's still open. Most smaller vehicles are electric, of course, unlike the ancient jalopy I currently find myself in, so I thought I'd only see charging stations. The big rigs use fuel, but they mostly use some variant of Fill City Turbo, available exclusively at federal filling facilities. I suppose there are still enough of these vestigial cars rolling around the country, driven by old-timers and freaks like my mother who are on the run, or belong to some off-the-grid cult, or have something to hide.

"We should stop here." I point to the gauge that I assume shows the fuel level. "It's at the bottom."

She laughs and taps the gauge. "I don't know if that's ever worked. But it doesn't matter."

"Why? Is this car being powered by your limitless maternal love?"

"No. Nuclear."

"Excuse me?"

"Nuclear. There's an NRB back there. Under the back seat."

"You're running a *nuclear reactor* in here?! Right under Voomvoom?! Are you seriously trying to win some kind of *Worst Mother In The World* award or something?"

"An NRB isn't a reactor. Jeez, I thought you were supposed to be the smart one. Calm down. It's a nuclear radioisotope battery. Uses the energy from tritium decay to generate electricity."

"But the radiation! Voomvoom!"

"Okay, first, if I could have pawned the kid off on someone I would have..."

"You're terrible."

"...but me and Voomvoom are stuck with each other. And don't worry. There's a surplus of shielding. Way more than required. It's safe. Safer than an old gas tank. And it'll be running a lot longer than I will be."

"Silver lining."

"Oh, hey, here comes a toll. Open your window and shut your mouth."

We slow down as we approach the first toll. It's just like the toll booths I've seen, maybe from the same movie as the gas station. There are no people though. "Where's the toll monitor?"

"I said shut up." But she points with her chin over to the right, off to the side and above us. In a little elevated booth, an angry-looking woman raises her eyebrows at the sight of an old 2038 Honda, then goes right back to reading the news on her tablet, or playing Unicorn Battalion, or posting on Groupie, or whatever toll monitors do to kill the endless, mind-numbing hours alone supervising the road.

"Cards!" The dingy screen on Jane's side of the car shouts, and as she feeds it our ID cards, the machine sucks them in greedily.

"DNA!" The screen shouts again, and three rusty, spindly arms sprout from the bottom of the screen and explore the car's interior, until they find their prey. The arm nearest me grabs my hand and scrapes my index finger.

"Ouch!"

Jane shoots me a look that says, "If you make one more sound, we are going to die," so I shoot her a look that says, "You're insane *and* paranoid, did you know that?"

We continue to glare silently at each other while the machine does its work, and I notice out of the corner of my eye Voomvoom sitting perfectly still and quiet, eyes forward, expressionless. He has done this many times. He is much wiser than me, at just seven years old, I'm sure of it. I wonder how much he's seen that he shouldn't have, with a mother like Jane.

"Proceed!" The screen shouts one last time, and spits our cards into the car, where we have to pick them up off the floor. Its light turns green and Jane floors the accelerator like she's being chased.

"Jane. That's what you were worried about? It's a toll. Harmless."

"Oh, honey. You don't want me to go into one of my rants."

A quiet "Voom voom" of agreement comes from the back seat.

"But since you asked... you're correct. It's not a big deal. Not normally, not for regular folk anyway, who roll around in autodrive, around this glorious mainland of ours, the US of A. It really is still the land of the free you know, more free than most of the rest of the world anyway, considering we're all ten credits away from declaring bankruptcy and corporations like WasteWay are taking champagne baths. The people of this country still are compassionate and fun loving, even if they don't give a lick about all the Fillers slaving away to provide their fuel and keep their neighborhoods clean. And sometimes it takes my breath away still, how magnificent this land of ours is. It's worth fighting for, you know. For the mainlanders and the Fillers. All of 'em. Worth fighting for."

She expects some kind of acknowledgement, I think. I shrug.

"See, ironically, it's the fighters that don't breeze through this country, even though they're the ones fighting for it. The fighters have to sneak around, cover their tracks, lay low, move around, become invisible."

Oh dear lord. It hadn't hit me fully until this moment: my mother is an absolute nut job.

"Jane, do I want to know how you're fighting for it?"

"No. Still not ready. Still too pissed and foolish. We'll see, though. Thirty more hours is a long time."

"With you? Not at all."

Voomvoom laughs at this, and that makes me laugh, and Jane shoots us both a look that could kill.

14

CLANK, CLANK, CLANK

There's a weird clanking in the engine compartment. With no way for me to know if this is normal – there doesn't seem to be anything normal about this vehicle – I just try to block out the sound and focus on the infinite fields of wheat while Jane drives for never-ending hours and night turns to day. It is beautiful, as she says, the mainland. Amber waves of grain. Purple mountain majesties. All true.

Clank. Clank. Clank.

Even Fill City Three is impressive. We passed it on the western edge of Kansas, a castle in the middle of nowhere, a grand medieval fortress, with a continuous stream of rigs going in and coming out, like an army to battle, and several huge pipelines leading off into infinity. The Gitanos have thirteen private cities around the world, and there is always talk of expansion. How many gargantuan landfill refineries do we need?

Clank. Clank. Clank. *Clank!*

Uh oh. That last one sounded different. Something's not right. I look over to the driver's seat to see if Jane seems concerned. Her eyelids are closed and her head is bobbing. "Jane!"

She starts and swerves back into our lane. "What? What the hell is that clanking?"

"This is your car! You tell me! If it's not too much trouble interrupting your nap!"

She manages to control the car as it protests and threatens to explode, stopping on the shoulder, where, I assume, it dies permanently. She frowns. "See? You thought we had plenty of time. Stuff happens, Pepper!"

"It's *Paper*. No. It's Robin. What happened?"

"Sounds like a motor mount or a strut. Lesse." She hops out, humming, hiking up her sleeves like she's looking forward to the challenge of resurrecting this old heap for the umpteenth time. "Don't just sit there, Pepp- *Robin*, give me a hand."

I walk to the rear, expecting tritium to shoot out into our eyes, or at least seep out by our feet and kill us with lethal radiation.

"And don't worry about the NRB. It's safe. I told you it's safe. The whole thing would have to blow for any radiation to leak."

"Comforting."

She rolls out her tool bundle and dives in. "Hmm. Yup. Nope. Bugger. Really? Hmm." And finally, "Oh."

"Oh?"

"Oh. It's the left motor mount all right. Too rusted. Broke free from the engine block."

I look around at the entire car, which seems to be held together with rust. The whole car is trying to break free.

"And we've got another problem. When the mount

collapsed, it snapped two of the NRB cables. That's live power, so they've fused themselves to the engine block."

"Oh. Anything else?"

"Actually yes. The NRB's sprung a leak."

Radiation! I run to get Voomvoom.

"I'm KIDDING. Sorry. Kidding."

"You're terrible."

"Yes, you keep reminding me. No, so it's just the two problems. The mount and the cables."

"For the motor mount, I assume you have a spare."

She shakes her head.

"Then why don't you just *make it yourself*, like everything else?"

She smacks her wrench on the engine block and stands up, in my face. And I notice for the first time: I'm taller than her. I'm not sure why this would strike me as significant, being taller than my own mother. Maybe I assumed from her oversize personality that she'd tower over me. Or that I'm the child, meant to be smaller, but some strange change was happening, I was getting taller now that I was free. In any case, she doesn't seem to notice or care. She's just angry.

"'*Just make it yourself.*' Ha ha ha. Now you listen, Pepper. *Robin.* I know you're pissed at me. I can't blame you. But I'm trying to do something here for you. I know forty-eight hours doesn't make up for twenty-one years, but come on. Cut me the tiniest bit of slack. Work with me."

She puts her hand out. I'm taken back. I've been treating her with nothing but contempt and sarcasm, which was proving surprisingly unsatisfying, and through it all, this tormented woman with a blue tube sticking out – *into* – her nose is plugging along, doing something risky – according to her conspiracy theories – to help me, the only daughter she'll likely ever see. And she's not asking for anything in return. Just a little slack.

I shake her hand.

"Why are you shaking my hand? I was pointing to the trunk. Go get me the hand welder." She's scowling, but under the scowl I distinctly make out a little smile.

I scurry around to the front and pop the trunk. I'm not surprised by the absolute mess. It's like looking into the undigested contents of the car's stomach. Tools, circuit boards, housings, wires, an EMP pulse generator, a fake ID creating machine, chemicals, scanners, cardboard boxes. But no welder. "Is it in one of these boxes?"

She yells back. "Don't touch those boxes. That's none of your business!" She rushes around to me. "Damn. Forgot these were in here. You just nevermind them. Hmm." She rummages around, as if there was some mysterious organization to this clutter. "Nope. Damn."

I point to three green cylinders in a corner. "Are those full?"

"Spare conventional batteries. Yup. Why? Oooh, yes..."

"Yes... just what I was thinking." I pull out the three batteries, and some copper wiring, and begin connecting them together with some old clamps. "With three of these in series, and this rod, we should be able to get 300 amps output at least, enough to generate an arc, cut the steel and create a weld."

She nods and grins. "I knew all that. Now tell me how we don't kill ourselves."

"Disconnect the NRB and put it and Voomvoom and all these chemicals somewhere far away. Insulate ourselves. Remove the small rear windows and use them as shields."

"Good. Smart. And we can use this extra jack head as a new mount."

So we go to work. Our homemade arc welder makes quick work of the snapped power cables, throwing showers of sparks that threaten to burn holes through our primitive "shields" and blind us. But the mount is proving stubborn. It's spent its lifetime rusting into the rest of the chassis and doesn't want to surrender.

"Just can't get the right angle. I'll have to go underneath. Jack her up another ten inches."

"I've seen a blob of molten steel melt a hole in a Body Shop worker's arm. Be careful."

She scoffs. We cut the old mount free and weld the "new" one in place. It's actually just the right size, though we won't win any awards for beauty. And it'll probably last through this trip only. But this trip is the last one I'd have to make in this heap, and I say a silent prayer of thanks for that. One more weld point and we're done.

"Goddammit!"

A spark has found its way into Jane's ear, and she's writhing in pain. I immediately drag her out from beneath the car and disengage the welder. She's screaming, so I start screaming too.

Voomvoom runs over, hysterical. "Mommy! Mommy!"

And I don't know what comes over me, I shout, "Mo-!" and catch myself.

Immediately her screaming stops. She cups her ear and groans. "Did that thing just screw up my hearing? Or did you say Mom?"

"No." I ignore her and pour a little water into her ear, then take a good look. It only seared a little hole in the cartilage. Nothing in the inner ear. She'll be okay. Good.

She nurses her wound, and watches me closely as I finish the welding job. I turn when I'm done and see, before she can wipe it away with a rag, a single tear sliding down her nose. "Good job, kid."

"We're... a good team." It seems like a nice thing to say, but I immediately regret my moment of weakness.

"Team? Ten more hours and I'm rid of you. Then I just have to figure out what to do with *that* one."

Voomvoom lets out a little "Hey!"

"You're terrible."

"Get in the car. Let's see if this hatchet job of yours actually works."

I walk back to the passenger seat, but Jane puts her hand on the latch, and points me around to the driver's side. "I was nodding off back there. And my ear is killing me. Your turn to drive."

"But I don't..."

"Yes you do. It's just like the lifts back home."

"They have a dashboard with buttons. And autodrive."

"Right. Then I guess you'll have to learn."

She shows me the floor levers, the accelerator and the brake, and the steering device, or "wheel" as she calls it. Why the original designers placed levers at your feet, instead of your fingers, was beyond me, and it takes several minutes to coordinate. "Feet are for walking. Not driving. This is ridiculous. Vehicle... autodrive, destination Groupie Studios, Los Angeles, California."

"Ha! Yeah, keep talking to it if that makes you feel better. Now come on, time's a wasting."

I peek down at the tablet. The Groupie Studios countdown clock is at twelve hours. She's right. I better get driving.

So with a herk and a jerk, I pull us out onto the highway,

just as a big rig thunders by and nearly splatters us into tiny red spots on the pavement. "Whoops." Voomvoom ducks under a blanket in the back.

"Oh, forgot to tell you. Use your mirrors."

Soon enough, I actually am "driving." At first it's as awkward as slow dancing with Nana. It's awful.

But then... it's not.

Here I am, gliding across this great land, past farms and meadows, chasing puffy white clouds in an endless blue sky.

I feel powerful. The lifts at home are fast, but this is very fast. And I'm in total control.

It reminds me of those times, like with my rockets, where I felt like anything was possible, anything at all. I've fixed this rusty old 2038 Honda car-slash-rocket ship and I'm piloting it down the road, into whatever lies beyond, into the future. It feels wonderful.

I turn and smile at Jane. She has her arm out the window, lazily lifting and dropping her hand, playing in the wind. Her ear has stopped bleeding, and she's smiling too.

"I like manual driving."

She laughs. "I knew you would."

As my mind relaxes and wanders, I wonder aloud, "By the way, what's in those boxes in the trunk?"

Her face hardens. "Nothing."

15

AWFUL LONG WAY FROM NEW JERSEY

W e're approaching Los Angeles, and the last of fifteen tolls, at four a.m., with three hours left on the sweepstakes clock – plenty of time. The weather has cooperated, and the motor mount fix has held, and only three unhappy toll monitors have decided to delay us for no good reason. Jane warned me that they were all corrupt and sleazy and thought they were above the law, looking for drugs they could resell, or valuables they could force you to surrender that they'd fence secretly later. But I find them nasty at worst. She's just being paranoid.

On the drive I had tried to teach Voomvoom the Farris family's "Back in the Day" game, but he was too young to grasp it, so we settled on thumb wrestling and coming up with words that rhyme with "voom."

"Broom."

"Doom."

"Moon." He likes that one most, repeating it almost as much as "voom." I don't have the heart to tell him it's not a true rhyme. I wonder what kind of mother that will make me some day. Is it okay to let things like that slide? Or should I teach him the right way to do things even if it seems mean? And will I overthink every single little thing like this? Probably.

The toll goes exactly as I expected, "Cards!" "DNA!" spit our cards at us, and "Proceed!" The last toll. Los Angeles here we come.

But the toll monitor steps in front of the car just as the light turns green. "Looks like you're lost." He squats down and looks over Jane's license plate with his flashlight.

"No sir. We know exactly where we're headed."

"Awful long way from New Jersey. Sure you're not lost?"

"Disney. You know. Kids. Can't live with 'em, can't stop taking 'em to Disney."

He nods, smiling. "Sure. Sure. But Disney in Florida's closer to you."

"California one has more rocket rides." She nods over to me. "This one's into rockets."

"Pop the trunk."

Jane turns to me with a look that says it all: she wasn't being paranoid after all. You could make it through a hundred tolls, and all it took was one monitor like this. The one with the bird shit in his coffee. The one that could keep us here forever. He's not just angry, he's menacing. He wants something. Like he doesn't care what it is, but he wants it anyway. He's itching for it.

Jane shout-whispers to me. "You stay put." She gets out and strolls up to the trunk, like she doesn't have a care in the world, and opens it for him.

"What's with the thing coming out of your nose, lady?"

"It's going *into* my nose. Meal-in-a-bag. It's how I eat. I have an extra one if you want."

"No thanks."

I can't see, the lid of the trunk's blocking my view, but I hear the monitor's grumbles at not finding gold bars or plastic bags bulging with Allanol or Bliss-laced mushrooms – just the mess of an old crazy hoarder lady with a tube up her nose.

"What's in the boxes, lady?"

"Nothing."

A strange feeling arrests me. For hours and hours I desperately wanted to know what was in those stupid cardboard boxes, and just because she wouldn't tell me, I would've given what was left of my hair to find out. But now I'm paralyzed by fear, by the desperate desire for no one to *ever* find out what's in those stupid cardboard boxes, because it must be terrible, and I don't want to go to jail, or find out my mother is driving around with human heads in her trunk, or have to explain to the police why our perfect little family needs ten years' worth of prescription horse tranquilizers.

I hear the monitor tear open the first box, then the second, then the third, then grumble again with disappointment.

"See, sir? I told you it was nothing."

"Whatever. You're clean. But do you mind telling me why you have boxes full of those stupid scarabs from *You're Going to Mars?*"

16

CHEAT

Did he say *scarabs?*

I rush out to the front, and peer into the trunk, and there they are: three boxes filled to the brim with red scarab medallions. Thousands of them.

I don't even have to ask.

"It was YOU!"

Jane glares but says calmly, "Honey, this fine young gentleman has said we're okay to go. Let's get into the car and let him get back to work." She turns to the monitor and whispers, "Girl's got mental issues."

Ha! I am NOT getting back in that car. Not with *her.* "You grifter!" I reach down into my t-shirt and rip the winning red scarab from my neck, and thrust it in her face, pressing the head. "Is *this* what you were looking for?" The scarab once again goes through its little routine.

And I see the toll monitor's eyes light up.

Uh-oh.

I try to fold the beetle closed quickly and tuck it away, but it's too late. The monitor's greedy hand shoots out and snatches it. I stand frozen as he smirks and raises it high into the air, like a trophy, proclaiming his ultimate prize, the prize that would buy him a life of ease and privilege, or at least a better life than that of a highway toll monitor. "It's mine! Mine! Mine!" He looks down at us, eyes popping like a madman. "Do you have any idea how much I'll ge-"

Jane karate chops him in the throat, cutting off his little victory speech, and wrenches the scarab back from his fist as he falls to the ground. Then she hugs me – not in a good way – and shoves me into the passenger seat and slams the door. Before the stunned monitor or I can even react, she's already in the driver's seat, starting the engine.

But there's a hand in my window! The monitor's using my door to get to his feet, frantically grabbing for my neck. He's not going to give up his future life of ease and privilege without a fight.

"Jane! He's hanging on!"

"Not for long!"

She peels out of the toll lane, leaving a cloud of burned rubber behind us – but not the monitor. He's still firmly attached to the car. I smack his free hand, and some primal instinct kicks in, and... I bite him. He screams and lets go momentarily, and that's all it takes. He's gone, rolling on the highway in our rear view mirror.

Jane fumes. "Now why did you go and do that?"

"Bite him? He was hanging on to the car and trying to strangle me!"

"Not that! Why did you show him the scarab?"

"Why did you cheat a million people out of a shot at going to Mars?! That scam was you, wasn't it?" I smack her in the shoulder. "Stop this car! I'm getting out!"

She jerks her head around to me, to scream something at

me, and blue liquid starts running from her nose, and she starts gagging. "...the... meal-in-a-bag...help..."

Her hands are all over the place, trying to keep the car straight while it's shooting down the highway at eighty-five miles an hour, and simultaneously trying to pull the stupid tube out of her face. I force her hands back on the wheel... "You just drive!" ...and, wincing with disgust, I gently tug the tube until it's out of her throat, up her nose, and out. Blue food gel starts spattering everywhere. Voomvoom takes cover under his blanket. I look for a clamp or something to stanch the flow of gel, but then give up and just fling the whole mess out the window.

"Hey! That was mine!"

"Don't worry, you have an extra!" I take a deep breath. "How could you?! The scam! Who *are* you?!"

"What are you talking about?"

"The three boxes full of scarabs! It's kind of a giveaway!"

"I have no idea what you're talking about!"

"Dad told me. About some scam involving a million scarabs. In cardboard boxes. Just like those! It was you! I have eyes, I can *see,* you know!"

She glares over at me and points a shaking finger in my face. "You think I would CHEAT?"

"Yes!"

She jabs her hand over between my legs and turns a latch on a little compartment in the dashboard. "*Now* what can you see? You have eyes! Go ahead!"

I pull open the compartment, still unsure whether I might find a severed human head, but instantly the wind from the open windows sucks thousands of little pieces of paper out and swirls them into a tornado, blinding all of us. Jane cackles, somehow staying on the road through the paper blizzard, and shouts, "RECEIPTS!"

I pluck one of the pieces of paper out of the air. And another. And another. Each one is, in fact, a receipt from 7-Eleven, or Wawa, or Stein's. I thought only the oldest of old timers still used paper receipts, but, then again, this is my mother I'm riding with. The receipts are from states up and down the East coast, and each receipt is for the purchase of just one item: a *You're Going to Mars!* Entry Scarab, priced at an even one credit. I begin to think, *this poor crazed woman really thought she could go to Mars*, but a much more terrifying thought immediately replaces it: *I did the same thing. I am her. I am turning into my mother.*

I'm afraid to ask, but can't help myself. "What... could you possibly be looking for on Mars?"

"Crap."

"'Crap?' That's the last thing I'd be looking for on Mars."

She points to the rear view mirror. "No. Crap, that toll monitor's on our tail."

17

HOLD ON TO SOMETHING

L ights behind us. Gaining fast.

"He's going to arrest us! I can't go to jail!"

"Nobody's going to jail! Look, he doesn't have his flashers or siren on. He's solo, going rogue. Looking for his treasure. I told you they think they're above the law. What he's doing is illegal. Buckle up."

"There's no seat belt!"

"Oh, right. Just hold on to something."

She swerves the car to the left, brakes hard right, and spins us around, receipts flying everywhere, until we're facing the oncoming car, headlights ablaze, right in the middle of the highway. Voomvoom claps. "Voom voom!" I scream.

The effect is instantaneous. The monitor's truck auto-swerves to miss a head-on collision, but can't correct in time afterward, instead launching off the road, barreling so fast it takes flight over the roadside ditch, landing rough but upright.

Silence.

Jane reaches down into the space between our seats,

calmly, revealing a long steel rod. "Be back in a second. Taking my persuasion bar just in case."

"What in the hell is happening?" I seriously think about surrendering right then and there, and going back and kissing the ground of Fill City One, and begging forgiveness, and promising never to even think about leaving again, just to be rid of this demented woman.

She leaves her car there, the wrong way in the middle of the road, and walks the fifty or so yards over to the monitor's truck. He's inside, alive but still dazed.

She strikes the left headlight. It shatters. "No one..."

The right headlight shatters. "... is going to stop..."

The hood receives a significant dent. "....my daughter..."

She flips the steel rod in her hand, revealing an end sharpened to a point, and plunges it into the left front tire. "...from going to Mars!" She pulls out the rod to a loud hiss, and smashes the hood one more time for good measure. "You hear me, clown?"

In response, the monitor, now somewhat recovered, rolls down his window.

And points a gun at Jane.

She bolts back to the car, running serpentine to avoid his poorly-aimed shots. "Pepper! I mean Robin! Get 'er ready!"

Oh for crying out loud.

I climb across to the driver's seat, spin the car around – with a helpful "voom voom!" from the back seat – and throw open the passenger door. Jane lunges in and slams it shut. "Go!"

I pound my foot to the floor, and the car takes off like a rocket. In the rear view mirror I can see the truck return to the highway, swerving to stay in control with one flat tire.

"Steel bar versus gun? Really?"

"Hey! I didn't think he would *kill us* for that damn thing! And they're not even supposed to have guns! That's illegal!"

"Really? You think he's worried about illegal?"

She frantically fiddles with her tablet. "Get off here. Shortcut."

And so our grand entrance to the city streets of Los Angeles, instead of being all smiles and relaxed and wind in our hair, is a pre-dawn car chase, with first-time-manual-driver Paper Farris driving, and my lunatic mother shouting turn-by-turn directions through the worst parts of town, and a seven-year-old kid clapping his hands at all the excitement, and all of us running from a deranged toll monitor with a gun. Someday, if I live, I will remember this and laugh.

But first I have to live.

We hurtle down one-way streets the wrong way, into alleys not meant for cars, hiding, making our way in the general direction of Burbank, the home of Groupie Studios' *You're Going to Mars!* In addition to the giant clock – now showing just thirty minutes, where the hell did our time go? – the live feed shows the crowd, getting more and more energized. Hundreds of fans and scalpers have descended on the area, making it their temporary home, a little tent city, and for weeks lucky winners have come forward, submitting their winning scarab to a production manager in exchange for a real-enough-looking spacesuit and helmet, and a salute, and drunken cheers. The scalpers are willing to offer, right there at the entrance gate to the show, a million credits for a winner like me to just hand the scarab over and walk away. Four of the winners, that I've seen, have taken the scalpers up on their offer, walking away rich and opening up the gate to the scalpers' wealthy or celebrity clients. Zach Larson and his producers don't seem to mind, as unethical and even illegal as it seems, because the more controversy that gets stirred up, I guess, the better for ratings and ad revenue. They're Larson's rules. Or more accurately, his lack of rules.

Twenty-four of the winners have come forward. I'll be the twenty-fifth. And the remaining five winning scarabs will decompose forever in a landfill in one of the Fill Cities.

"Wait. Was that a... giraffe?"

"Yes. The L.A. Zoo. Turn right up here." The animals crane their necks and watch us zoom past. "And don't drive so fast!"

"We're in a car chase!" I bank into a side street.

"No we're not. I think we lost him."

We sneak back onto a main road, then onto a highway. "Ventura Freeway. Only half a mile to go. We're getting close, Robin! We're home free."

The monitor's truck appears, on cue, going in the opposite direction. It skids out, rumbling across the berm between lanes, and is on us in seconds.

"Shit! Faster!"

"You just told me not to drive so fast!"

"*Now we're in a car chase! Now you should go faster!*"

He's at our right moments later, desperately trying to manually override his autodrive with one tire out, and trying to aim his gun at us.

"Oh, enough of this shit already." Jane grabs the steering wheel and yanks it towards her, smashing us into the truck, and both cars into the guardrail, which is no match for the force being exerted on it. The truck snaps through it like it was made of popsicle sticks and roars off the freeway, plunging twenty or so feet right into the Los Angeles River.

Jane looks back. "Whoops. I hope he's okay." But we see splashing in the dark, and the monitor crawling to what I suppose you could call a concrete shore, shaking his fist in the air at us, totally defeated.

"Okay, no dead bodies. Good. Now let's get you to the gate, so I can ditch this car before the cops show up."

I'm still furious with her, for everything, for never being there, and for finally showing up in my life and making me want her to disappear all over again. But the car? "You're going to ditch your car? It's a 2038 Honda. It's your baby."

She smiles. "No. It's a car. *You're* my baby." Turns to Voomvoom. "And *you're* my baby."

18

I HAVE SOME QUESTIONS.

I pull into the parking lot of Groupie Studios, far away near some overgrown bushes, and the three of us shuffle, like weary warriors, toward our goal. I look up at the giant clock I've been watching for the past sixty hours. We made it with a whopping ten minutes to spare. Voomvoom kicks a can as we walk, and I step in front of him to give it a punt, and I don't know how, I lose my balance I guess, and both my legs swing out from under me. I crash hard on my butt and my left palm, scraping the skin off. I'm bleeding. After all this, the escape and the cross-country drive and the life-threatening car chase, I hurt myself walking the last hundred yards to the studio.

Jane looks down and laughs. "Harlon said you were a klutz. I didn't believe him."

"A little help here?"

They lift me to my feet, and Voomvoom swats the pebbles from my palm, spits on it, then tears the lower part of one his sleeves off and wraps it around my hand. Kisses it like a mom would do.

Jane drags us to keep moving. "No time to waste. I have some questions to ask you, Pepper."

"Paper. Robin. Me too."

"Me first. Do you know who controls virtually all fuel needs for most countries on this little dirtball we call Earth?"

"WasteWay. My turn. Why did you leave us?"

"Because I had a job to do. Why do you think we've never had a manned mission to Mars?"

"I don't know. What kind of job is so important you had to leave your husband and three daughters?"

"The answer to both questions is WasteWay."

I stop and turn to her. "All right. Can we stop with the riddles?"

She nods and takes a deep breath. Exhales. "I was a refinery engineer for WasteWay. One day – I happened to be pregnant with you three, by the way – I saw something I wasn't supposed to. A report about a compound, containing an element. An element that's not even on the periodic table. WasteWay is covering up something. I know it."

I shake my head. "Really. So you walked off in your hospital gown?"

"Listen, Paper. I had to be outside. Tried finding things out on the inside. Too risky. Not just for me. For Harlon and you girls."

Oh boy. I want to believe her. I do. Believe that WasteWay is up to something more than just garden-variety greed, that it has some nefarious larger goal like taking over the world, or Mars, or both. It would make a great excuse, something I could believe other than that my mother left us because she had a skull full of loose change. It would be nice to believe her conspiracy theory. But I don't.

"Jane. What would any of this have to do with Mars?"

"The element. It's not from Earth. Has to be from Mars, it's the only place we've sent missions in the past fifty years. When I saw your faces for the first time, you and your sisters, I knew. I couldn't sit by, live my miserable life in Fill City One, and give you the same miserable life, and give the same miserable life to untold numbers of people in the future, while WasteWay hid some terrible secret, for who-knows-what terrible reasons."

"And have you found anything in twenty-one years? Anything?"

I expect another excuse, another conspiracy theory, or maybe for her to cackle again and say "voom voom," but to my stunned surprise, she reaches into her pocket and pulls out a ratty old laminated sheet. "Here."

I look down at the numbers. It's a readout of something, chemicals I guess, too much math to make much sense. "I don't know. It looks like it could be a geological survey."

She smacks her knee. "Bingo! You *are* the smart one!" She points to one of the lines. "And what's missing?"

"It was a guess. I'm not a geologist."

"Look at the second report, down there. Now back up to the first one. What's missing?"

"The bottom one has a line that says 'anomalies: none'. The top one doesn't have that line."

She grins. "*All* reports have that line. Or at least they're all supposed to. This one doesn't."

"So?"

"So someone *deleted* the line. This is a *NASA geological survey*, Pepper. And someone there is deleting evidence of some kind of anomaly. On a *government* survey. This stinks. Stinks of WasteWay. They're hiding something that's up there. They don't want us to know. Why do you think there's never been a manned mission?"

Poor Jane. It's a simple error. A printout glitch. She's chasing an innocent rabbit down a bottomless hole.

"I had given up, Pepper, honestly. Ask Voomvoom here. I thought that trip to Mars was my last long shot at finding the truth, and I raced up and down the coast buying those damned scarabs, but I never found a winner." She peers up to the stars. "And then I got the message from Harlon. A miracle." She turns to me, and all the insanity in her eyes seems to disappear for a moment, and she puts her hands on my face and pulls it close to hers, and whispers, "I found the winner. You. You said you feel like you were meant to be out there. *You are.* And you said the folks back home are waiting for something. *They are.* It's all connected. You, me, them. I'm so terribly sorry I wasn't there for you, love. But we both have a job to do now."

"It's a piece of paper, Jane. Twenty-one years and one piece of paper. Come on. Please. I'm just trying to win a trip to Mars. Bradline thinks I'm leading the Fillers to some unseen destiny for crying out loud, and now you? With this?"

She sighs. "Sometimes life asks more of us than we planned on giving." Then she hugs me, like I imagine a real mother might do when her daughter doesn't believe her. "Forget I said that. You know what? It's all right. Believe in *yourself,* Pepper. Go have your adventure. Enjoy every second. Don't give my crazy theory any mind. But... if anything does happen, and you need me, I'll be right here." She reaches once more into her pocket, lifts out a small, thin rectangle, pulls open my satchel and tucks it deep inside.

"A stick of gum?"

"It's your Get-Out-Of-Jail-Free Card. It just looks inno-cent, like a stick of gum. I made it myself."

"Of course you did. But I have no idea what you mean."

"Just hold on to it and don't show anyone. You'll know if you ever need it."

By this time we're at the fringes of the crowd, pushing our way to the front. Only six minutes remain on the giant clock. Closer to the gate, revelers are drinking and singing, awaiting the final countdown and the launch of the show they've been waiting months for. A scalper notices our little threesome, maybe it was just that we were the only ones without red plastic cups in our hands, sloshing beer everywhere. "Hey, kid. Got something you want to sell?" He flashes me a card with two million credits displayed on its face. *Two million.* It would buy my mother all the help she needs, and Voomvoom a normal life, many times over. I look back to her. She shakes her head and pushes me forward, her expression saying *this is not for anyone else. This is yours.*

I turn back to the scalper. "I've got something. But not to sell."

The crowd stops their party like a freeze dance. Someone turns off the radio. All faces turn to me as I push to the iron bars of the studio gate. I slide my hand through, shaking, holding the red scarab out to the production manager on the other side. His name tag says "Ted." He bows, dramatically. "Please press the head."

I do, and the wing covers spring open one last time, and the wings unfurl, and Zach Larson speaks.

And the crowd does nothing.

They know, as I do from watching the feed, that counterfeiters have tried to fool the producers on at least a dozen occasions. Instead, they watch in silent, rapt attention as Ted drops my scarab into a mysterious looking box.

The next few seconds are endless.

Then a green light on the top of the box lights up.

"It's a winner!"

This time the crowd erupts in cheers, raising me up on their shoulders, singing the drunken anthem they'd made up and sung for each winner over the weeks:

> *There she goes, to the show*
> *Will she win? Heck if we know!*
> *But she'll give it her best, take a shot*
> *Against the losers, the rest of that lot!*
> *Walk to the launch pad, aim for the stars*
> *Don't close your eyes, You're Going to*
> *Mars!*

I find myself singing with them, carried along not only on their shoulders but their joy at the ridiculous-yet-somehow-inspiring event unfolding before us all. I can't wait to get through the gate.

I feel a tug at my t-shirt, and look down.

Voomvoom.

The throng puts me down, and I kneel down in front of him. "You take care of Jane. She needs you."

"I know. I will." And he hugs me, tighter than his little seven-year-old frame should be able to, and his body shudders. He's crying. I pull his face to mine, and kiss him on the cheek.

"I'll be back soon." Now I'm crying. "And then we'll go home."

I don't know why I said that. There is really no way he would ever be coming back with me to Fill City One, and if his home is the Honda, which I don't doubt, well, he isn't going back to that home either. But I meant what I said, and... it feels right. It feels like I'm telling the truth. I believe it.

His eyes light up at the thought, and he grins wide and skips back to his mother, beaming, repeating "voom voom!" Jane gives me a look that says *thanks for getting the kid's hopes up*, but then she puckers up her lips and blows me a kiss.

It's strange, I feel like I've been with this woman forever, this woman who calls herself my mother, that somehow the intervening years between the moment she fled and this moment have been filled with... something. Not just emptiness. I feel like simultaneously running into her arms and running away from her as fast as I can. But I just catch her kiss in my hand and put it in my pocket. I'll save it for later.

As I turn back to Ted, I'm beaming. One more chapter over. A new one beginning. I'm ready. Excited as hell.

"Before we let you in. Name."

"Paper." My hand shoots over my mouth.

"I don't need any papers. Just your name."

"Robin. Smith. Robin Smith. Robin Smith."

"Welcome, Robin Smith Robin Smith Robin Smith. DNA please."

I offer my hand, realizing it's wrapped in a bloody t-shirt sleeve, and offer the other instead. He pulls my index finger and scrapes it with a small gadget. "DNA... check. You are, in fact, Robin Smith."

The gates open, just enough for me to slip through, and close again, and the crowd continues to cheer from the other side as I receive my spacesuit. I turn and wave, and their cheering grows even louder, and I think: *Wow. They really like me!*

But the cheering is strangely loud. A little too loud.

To test a theory that's forming in my brain, I stop waving. And the cheering grows to a frenzy.

No. They aren't cheering for me. They're cheering for something else.

A white limousine stops right near the gate.

I can't see through the horde of people, and scalpers are surrounding the car, but it becomes clear someone is approaching the gate. With a dramatic five seconds left on the clock.

"Five!"

The person shows the scarab.

"Four!"

The box lights up green.

"Three!"

I can't even hear the person say their name from all the screaming and clapping.

"Two!"

DNA test.

"One!"

And the gate opens at the buzzer, declaring the end of the sweepstakes, to a crowd gone absolutely wild, all of them rushing towards me, and I get my first look at the twenty-sixth and final contestant on *You're Going to Mars!*

Aurora.

Wonderful.

Last year's runner-up on *America Sings!* – the impossibly-perfect, ultra-competitive, twenty-something brat-diva from Las Vegas, writer of the annoying mega-hit "Baby's Gone," and latest singer-with-one-name – is walking towards me. Or rather, stumbling. She's piss drunk, swaying on her feet, reaching for anything to support her. The crowd lurches toward us, right behind her, a line of security guards barely keeping them at bay, and camera flashes blind us both, and I can already read tomorrow's headline: "Aurora Is Going To Mars And Some Random Contestant Looks On In Disgust."

They hand her a spacesuit, and for a moment she looks at it as if it might be something useful to vomit in, but then she holds it up to the adoring masses. A spontaneous, drunken chorus of "Baby's Gone" begins. She loses her balance with that little maneuver, and I have to prop her up.

"Thanks."

Instead of saying you're welcome, I grunt.

From a side door, the producers lead out the other twenty-four winners, in a fairly-well choreographed photo op, to the military-esque-adventure-movie-soundtrack theme song and more cheers, and a total camera blitz. I actually recognize some of their faces, from the feed, and there are at least five or six celebrities in the bunch, looking more or less glamorous, even in their spacesuits.

I keep an eye on Aurora. Every time she sways, I poke her back to balance. She's pathetic, but it would be embarrassing for her to fall over drunk in front of a billion people on television.

Then she does.

And as she goes down, she grabs my t-shirt, and I go down with her, right on top of her in fact, to the roars of laughter and cheers and jeers from nearly every person under thirty-five on the planet.

She whispers, "Shit. Sorry."

"Get up. And if you throw up on me, I don't care if the entire galaxy is watching, I will hurt you."

The producers rush over, trying to make it look like this was all planned and perfectly normal, and a spotlight shines on the studio door, and Zach Larson himself marches out. Our generation's visionary and master showman, in his very own custom spacesuit, looks down at us trying to help the inebriated celebrity singer get to her feet, and a mischievous grin spreads across his face. Then he shouts into his microphone the words that will be the understatement of the millennium:

"Let the show begin!"

19

MARTHA

I expect Larson to show us to the luxury accommodations we've all seen on the commercials, and introduce us to our Team Leaders – the show will mimic a high-tech astronaut training program – but Ted and the other production managers instead herd the crowd out, shut the gate, and lead us through a maze of studio alleys to... a tarmac?

The camera crew is boarding an airplane, or something airplane-ish, right there in the middle of a TV lot. It's a large lot, the kind you could shoot huge action sequences in, but certainly not one long enough to use as a runway. Then again, this isn't an ordinary airplane. It looks like one giant wing, with a circular central area for the crew, and four massive engines, like nothing I've ever seen, some mix of jet and rocket engines, hanging from the wings in the rear, each now rotating back and forth independently, in what looks like a testing pattern.

Wow. AceSpace really pulled out all the stops. A giant, battleship-gray military aircraft, with *You're Going to Mars!* splashed in purple across the front. I wonder if they'll offer us champagne on board. I've never tasted champagne.

Our group of twenty-six marches down the carpet, yes, the classic red carpet from every celebrity runway ever, led by Zach Larson, cameras rolling, all of us in awe. A woman, pudgy to the point of stretching the fabric of her spacesuit, scratches her head. "Wait. Are we going to Mars *first?*"

The rest of us laugh, and the contestant next to her puts his hand on her shoulder. "Don't strain yourself, Claire. No, it's an X-93. Vertical takeoff. Prototype, first one I've ever seen. They're probably taking us out to the desert to see the Mars launch pad."

It's amazing how quickly perceptions are molded. From that first moment, I brand the woman, Claire, *out-to-lunch*, and the man next to her *know-it-all*. And looking around, I know it's wrong, but it's hard not to judge each of these books immediately by their covers: *athlete, stuck-up celebrity, actually normal, potential serial killer, friendly, cowboy swagger, that actor from Home Time, housewife*, et cetera. And of course, *brat-diva* – my hopefully very temporary companion Aurora, *America Sings!* runner-up, and now that I've met her, also *fall-over-drunk*.

I wonder what the others have branded me.

Larson walks over to *know-it-all* and shakes his hand. "Very good guess, Albert! But the X-93 is a government plane. Therefore it won't exist for another decade or two – if *ever*. This," he runs up to the craft and bows proudly next to the staircase, "is a little something AceSpace cooked up. As they say, if you want something done..."

And I can't help molding my instant impression of Zach Larson either: I like him. I thought that I'd have the opposite reaction on meeting this larger-than-life icon and media titan, that his disdain for rules, annoying quirks, way-too-self-assured attitude, and oh-so-over-the-top wealth would scrape like nails on a chalkboard. But there is something about him, the twinkle in his eye, of a young man, a boy really, in the body of a sixty-year-old.

Larson greets each of the contestants as they step onto the stairs, and Marina Delacosta, celebrity for no other reason than her father owns half of Italy and who, by the way, probably paid two million credits for her scarab, gives him a kiss on each cheek. "You arra coming Zach, yes?"

"No, my dear. I don't even know if this beast can fly."

Marina gulps, and Larson kisses her cheeks in return. "Have no fear, I've been on her several times, Marina. She's a dream. Like a mouthful of cotton candy. You're in for a treat. Your team leaders and I will be here when you get back." He grins. "*If* you get back."

Marina laughs nervously and climbs aboard.

As I push Aurora toward the stairs, she and I being last, Larson stops us. "Well, well. I see you two are fast friends."

I roll my eyes before I can stop myself, then blush. A plastic disc appears from somewhere in Larson's suit. "It's called a forty-five music record. My mother worked at a museum and used to sneak me in to play them all the time. I make my own now. This one's 'Baby's Gone.' Aurora dear, would you sign my copy?" He holds out the disc and a marker, and I literally have to guide Aurora's hand to the small center area of the disc and help her scribble her autograph. He just happens to have a copy of "Baby's Gone" in his pocket? I add *enigma* to my mental description of Zach Larson.

Aurora stumbles up the stairs, and as I follow, Larson stops me. "Thank you, ah..."

"Robin."

"Yes, Robin. Of course. Sometimes it takes a while for a name to stick." He looks down at my hand. "What happened here?"

"I fell. I'm an idiot."

"Let me have a look." And he takes my hand, gently unwrapping Voomvoom's makeshift bandage. "Nasty scrape. Let's see if I've got something here..." He reaches into several more pockets of his magic suit, and sure enough, pulls out what looks like a wizard's wand. "It's not what you think. You may have seen this on *Emergency Medic Alert*, but I've had my team miniaturize a MedBay wand into something pocket size." He slowly passes the wand over my hand, and I feel a strange tingle, some mix of burning and cooling, then warmth, like a cup of hot cocoa with marshmallows. I've actually never had a cup of hot cocoa with marshmallows, but from the reactions of the people in the commercials, I imagine this is what they're feeling. It's nice.

He takes out a little towelette, from yet another pocket, and wipes my palm clean. "See? Good as new." It's like a miracle. I've seen it on TV, of course, but the Fill Cities don't have medical tech like this, so it never seemed real. It's a shame. Miracles like this could do a lot of people a lot of good in the Fill Cities.

Larson leans in and whispers. "Now, tell me Robin, do you like rockets?"

What a strange question. If he knew me, he'd know I'm obsessed with rockets, and space travel. But he couldn't possibly have known. Yes, he's definitely an enigma. "Good guess, Mr. Larson. As a matter of fact I do."

"Zach. Please. From now on call me Zach. Well then, Robin, if you like rockets, you're going to love *Martha*."

"Martha?"

He pats the underside of the airplane-like thing. "I named her after my late mother. She's fast and feisty, just like Mom." Then he motions for my satchel. "May I take that for you? I can put it in your room. There's an area for small effects that's private and off-camera. You won't be needing it for the flight."

I clutch it to my body, probably a little too fast. "I... is it okay if I keep it with me?"

"Certainly. Just make sure it's secured. You might, ah, hit a wee little turbulence up there. Now, off you go."

"Mr. Larso- Zach... where are we going?"

He just smiles and walks back toward the studio, and I can hear him chuckle to himself. "I'll see you when you get back."

So I climb the stairs and board the plane-ish thing, close to the rear, and look around.

We are *not* getting champagne.

These are the barest-bones accommodations possible, with a positively military vibe. One big, gray, circular open area with a bench around the entire perimeter, rows of lights and buttons and rails along the ceiling, a door to the cockpit up front, and a couple of doors at the back. That's it. It's very unlike what I've seen so far, the schmaltzy signs and lights, the sets on the commercials, the red carpet. I wonder if this is on purpose, or if someone in charge of budgets finally put their foot down and said *enough, Mr. Larson.*

Ted greets us as the exit is sealed. "Ladies and gentlemen. Welcome aboard. Please pick a spot, any spot, I'll let you know when you need to buckle in. Enjoy the flight. An attendant will come by if you'd like water or a snack. You two, Aurora and..." he looks down at his tablet, "...Robin, if you two could change into your spacesuits in that little room in the back, thank you."

Claire raises her hand.

"Yes, ma'am?"

"Are we going to Mars?"

Ted laughs, and looked around. "One of you very definitely is going to Mars. But not for the moment. The spacesuits just help you look the part for TV. And you are, again?"

"Claire."

"Ah yes. Claire. Of course." He taps a note on his tablet. "Jerry, why don't we begin the interviews with Claire?"

Jerry, one of the cameramen, ambles over and kneels in front of Claire as she and Ted begin. Aurora and I change, and as I come back from the little room, I notice: we're already airborne. I didn't feel a thing. The engines are humming as if we're idling. Amazing. If the clouds weren't zooming past the windows, you'd swear we were still on the ground.

Claire, it turns out, is a twenty-three-year-old cashier from Ohio, who nearly threw out the winning scarab until her dog Ringo ferreted it out of the trash. She works at ZippieMart and plays Botech in a league on Saturdays. And she wants to go to Mars because what the heck, she's overweight and wants to get back in the shape she was in during high school. "Seize the day, am I right Ted?"

Albert is next to be interviewed, the one I branded *know-it-all*, and he doesn't disappoint. He's an electronics engineer, just thirty-one but racing up the corporate ladder, working for Oberon, building supercomputers. He times himself solving the *New York Times* crossword puzzle every morning. "Speaking of time, I don't have time to get married, but hey, if Mars makes me more attractive to the ladies, bonus." He is vigorous in his offer to help the crew if anything goes wrong on the flight. "I'm good with machines, you know." Ted and the crew smile and nod, as if to say *don't call us, we'll call you.*

Next is Mike Horner, the actor I recognized from *Home Time.* On the show Mike played the young son of an international spy who had never revealed to his family his true identity until the last episode of the last season. The show was a smash, and that last episode broke records. I remember watching it in our tiny little living room, all crammed in, screaming and crying and cheering for Mike and his TV dad. Anyway, the show set him up for bigger roles and even movies. He won't reveal how he got his hands on his scarab, but is absolutely determined to land the lead in the currently-two-years-out *Star Wars Fifteen: Jedi Once More* – and he thinks a trip to Mars will be the ultimate audition.

"Robin Smith."

I jerk back, surprised. I've prepared for this moment since they stuffed me into the armoire, making up my back story and repeating it over and over and over until I knew it backwards. And I repeat it again in my head quickly: I am Robin Smith, owner of a small farm in rural New Jersey. A sustenance farm really, chickens and goats and little fields of corn and soybean and squash, so I don't need to leave the property much. I live alone and watch a lot of TV, and that's my connection to the world (the watching a lot of TV part is true, for better or worse). Of course, that's possibly the most boring back story possible, it doesn't stand a chance if I'm going to win Likes with the global audience. So I've kept another part of my real past life in the story: that in my free time I build and program small rockets, and develop methane and other gas, liquid, and solid propellants. I guess I'm going for the *reclusive-hippie-girl-who-secretly-digs-science* angle. Is that even an angle?

But none of that story comes out of my mouth.

"So, Robin. Tell me a little about yourself. This'll be for what we call confessionals, or if you do something interesting later in the season, it's something we can call back to, like a dream."

"Well, I..."

Ted smiles and nods.

"I..."

He puts his hand on mine. "First time in front of a camera?"

I nod.

"Okay." He turns to Jerry and moves his finger across his throat, and the red light on Jerry's camera goes dark. "We'll find out more about you later then, Robin. Right now it's just you and me. Is it okay if I ask you yes or no questions?"

"Yes?"

"Good. You already answered one right. See? Easy. Now. Are you excited to be here?"

"Yes. Very. And nervous. Obviously."

"That's okay. And can you hold your breath for longer than three minutes?"

I raise an eyebrow.

"Sorry. These are just ice breakers. Don't think too much about your answers."

"No."

"Can you do more than twelve pull ups?"

"Yes."

"Have you ever been in an extremely stressful situation, say, a robbery, or a car crash, or running from a burning building, or being confined and escaping?"

Confined and escaping. "Definitely."

"Good. Do you have any mechanical, programming, or chemistry ability?"

"Yes. Yes. And yes."

It's Ted's turn to raise an eyebrow. He continues to tap on his tablet, being careful not to show me. "Okay, last question: is there anything interesting about you that we don't already know?"

I blurt out, "No!"

He pats my hand and turns to give Jerry the okay to move on, but I grab him by the collar and pull him close enough where I can whisper in his ear. "Yes."

He pulls back, enough to peer into my eyes, and I hope they say it all: that there is a forbidden past I can't tell him about, that I've just been chased through the streets of Los Angeles by a rogue toll monitor, been told a secret I can't believe, and that I'm supposed to be the one who goes to Mars, it's where I belong.

He smiles awkwardly and whispers back as he untangles my vice-grip fingers from his shirt. "I... think we have everything we, ah, need for the moment. Moving on..."

"Okay, folks. Please buckle your shoulder harnesses. It might get a little bumpy for a few minutes." We all watch out the large windows as the clouds drop away further and further below us. Suddenly we're pressed downward in our seats with incredible force.

Claire gasps. "What's happening? Ted? Ted! *Why aren't you answering me, Ted?!*"

Ted and the camera crew clip straps dangling from their vests and various gear onto steel bars running along the ceiling. "It's all right, Claire. Relax. Just a few more moments..."

The force, strangely smooth but extremely strong, vanishes.

Our bodies begin to lift off the benches, tugging at the shoulder harnesses.

We're weightless!

"Welcome to low Earth orbit, folks. Not really, we're only about a hundred miles up, but we're close. You can unbuckle now."

Low Earth orbit! One by one, contestants begin to release their bodies to the open space – and vomit. The camera crew groans and laughs, knowing this is priceless footage for the show, and exactly what Zach Larson wants. The towels and plastic sheathing over the cameras are no longer a mystery.

I think somehow, with my *Really Important Destiny* at stake, that I'll escape puking, so I unbuckle and let myself float, giddy – and immediately unload the contents of my stomach into the air. Whoops.

Aurora laughs at me, unfazed by the nebula of partially-digested food particles floating through the open compartment. She swats away a bit of my waste. "So. Who's throwing up on who?"

I must turn red, or look like another round might come shooting out of my mouth, because she turns me around and pushes me towards a window. "This might help. Look."

We grab the bars beneath the window nearest us and hold on, and look out together.

I immediately forget the flotsam in the cabin, and the nausea, and smile.

Space.

We're floating far enough above Earth to see the gentle curve of its horizon, and the infinite stars beyond.

Amazing. Beautiful.

The indescribably blue Earth is below us, its atmosphere almost glowing. And the pitch-black void above, dotted with more stars than can ever be counted. A tear escapes my eye and floats away.

Aurora fogs up the window with her breath, slurring her speech. "If I don't remember any of this tomorrow, will you remind me how gorgeous it is?"

I laugh and nod, and look down at our planet, so peaceful and clean, and truly awe inspiring. North America moves past as we fall gracefully around the planet. "That's where I'm from."

Aurora tries to follow my finger. "New York?"

"No. New Jersey."

"Wow. Me too. What city?"

My heart stops.

What are the chances? The very first person I meet on the set of *You're Going to Mars!* is from New Jersey? "Um. I thought I saw on *America Sings!* you were from Las Vegas."

She scrunches up her face. "That's the story. The 'Aurora' Story. And I do live in Vegas. But I've also lived in Florida, and Washington, and we even lived a couple of years on Oceana Twelve. Been all over. Kinda sucky life, if I'm being perfectly honest. Anyway, I left New Jersey when I was three, so I don't even know why I asked you which city. I don't remember a thing." She laughs. "Except my tricycle."

"I got a used tricycle when I was around two. Maybe it was yours."

"Red?"

"Of course."

"Well then it was definitely mine. You still have it?"

"Nah. It's deep in the fill by now."

She hiccups. "Deep in the fill? You sound like one of those Fill City people. You're funny."

Again my heart stops. I need to get better at *not* being Paper Farris, third-generation Filler, immediately. I am Robin. Robin Smith. Self-sufficient farmer and rocket hobbyist from rural New Jersey. "Do you mind me asking... what's a famous pop singer doing on *You're Going to Mars!*?"

She squints at me, like she's trying to determine whether she can tell me the truth. I guess I pass her brief, intoxicated test, because she leans in and lowers her voice. "My agent says it's the perfect promo." She peers around at the cameras, not pointed at us at the moment. Whispers. "I'm not supposed to win. Just make it far enough to promote the launch..." she chuckles at her own pun, "...get it? Launch? ... of my next album. *Rocket Girl*. But really? My secret reason?" She whispers even more softly into my ear. "I wanted to escape."

Huh? This girl, on top of the world, with freedoms I could only dream of, wants to escape? Escape *what*? My look of shock must be obvious, because she shakes her head, trying to focus. "Wow. Still drunk. Loose lips. You didn't hear any of that. Promise me. And you have to tell me something now, so we're even. A secret."

"Not a word. Promise." I look around, too, as if all eyes are on us. But everyone's busy either gawking out the windows, or clutching their stomachs and floating around looking for a bag or something to barf in. Can I trust this person? It's likely she won't even remember any of this. I could make up any "secret" I want. But there's something about her. She's revealed herself to me, almost immediately. She deserves the same. "You're not the only one, Aurora. I also needed to esca-"

"ALERT! ALERT! MALFUNCTION! PREPARE FOR EMERGENCY ACTION!"

We spin around to flashing red lights and a blaring siren. Panic spreads like fire in the open cabin, as the weightless bodies of the contestants bounce off each other, limbs reaching and writhing and grabbing, everyone looking for something to hold on to, something safe in the chaos. Claire screams at the top of her lungs and clutches poor Albert, who tries in vain to pry her loose. A man, Tanner, is smushing another woman's face, I think her name is Avery, against a window with his foot in an effort to push himself down to a safety harness. Several contestants are launching themselves toward Ted and the production crew, as if a bunch of cameramen could save them from a fiery death a hundred miles above Earth.

Aurora and I hold onto the bar beneath our window. I notice her body shaking, and she has her head tucked into her chest, like she's praying. She's afraid.

I put my arm around her. "Aurora. Take a deep breath. Look over at Ted and the crew."

She tentatively peeks at them. "Why? They're going to die too!"

"No. Notice how they're pretty calm? How they're still shooting, panning with the cameras? And that one next to Ted, he's holding back a smile. It's a little too perfect, don't you think?"

Confirming my theory – thank God – the alarm stops and the lights return to normal.

Aurora's body instantly relaxes, and she lets out a little snicker. "Sneaky sneaky."

An announcement comes from unseen speakers. "Sorry about that, ladies and gentlemen. My copilot must've – accidentally – pushed the wrong button up here in the cockpit! I apologize, and want to assure you everything's just absolutely fine. We'll be re-entering gravity in a few seconds, so if you could now find your seats and buckle in. Thank you."

The entire cabin seems to exhale, as bodies float gently to the floor, and nervous chuckles fill the space. We aren't going to die after all. Aurora buckles in and turns to me. "Pretty observant. If that was a test, you passed for not losing your cool."

"And you passed before for not losing your cookies."

She laughs. "Well, then I guess we're even."

It appears she's already forgotten our little "secrets" thing. Good. We look around, and it dawns on everyone that it all *was* a test, our first test. Several of the contestants whimper to themselves, three or four openly crying. One of the crew hands out towels for us to wipe ourselves off, and some kind of automatic vacuum scurries around, sucking up any waste that remains.

As *Martha* touches down a few minutes later, again with that most amazing, light touch, Aurora spies a camera trained on her. She unbuckles and shoots up standing, raising both hands in the air, tossing her head back and forth for maximum hair flip, and squeals, "Let's do that again!"

And Marina Delacosta throws up on her shoe.

20

WELCOME TO THE SHOW!

I magine taking your first space flight ever, and then being immediately paraded into a large television studio in front of an audience of several thousand, assaulted by giant, bright lights, all while wearing a stifling spacesuit partially covered in other people's regurgitated food.

If you can imagine that... *welcome to the show!*

I'm exhausted, alternately sweating, shivering, and nauseous, and Zach Larson greets us as if we've just taken a leisurely tour of an air-conditioned mall. "Here they are, ladies and gentlemen! The twenty-six contestants of *You're Going to Mars!*"

We march onstage in single file, smiling weakly and waving, to the theme song and the cheers of the crowd, who just watched our little low-orbit farce on massive projection screens in the theater. The contestant right in front of me, Baker, passes out, and has to be dragged backstage. Then another contestant. And another. By the time we take our seats around the mammoth circular table in the middle, with the huge AceSpace mission seal in the middle – a Red Scarab surrounded by stars – four contestants are gone. And a couple look like they're not far behind.

"Wonderful! Wonderful!" Larson sashays back and forth in front of us, applauding. "Our remaining contestants, congratulations on completing Stage One. Well..." he smiles coyly, looking directly into the camera, "...almost."

A woman two seats to my left raises her hand, limp, and whispers timidly into the microphone in front of her. "A- a-almost...?"

"Yes, my dear Addison. You see, the theme for Stage One is 'Endurance.' For the next twenty-one days, every day, to acclimate your body to the rigors of space travel, you'll be going on just a few more low-orbit flights."

"Just... a few?"

"Thirty."

Addison begins to cry. I think she might be relieving herself in her spacesuit, too.

"Addison, dear. If you, any of you actually, would like to leave the program at this point, I completely understand. Please raise your hand."

Addison, who already has her hand raised, points to it aggressively with her other hand, without losing a beat in her sobbing. The man next to her, Chris, raises his hand too, and doesn't even wait for a chaperone as he bolts off the stage, holding his hands in front of his mouth, his cheeks full of whatever was just in his belly a few moments ago. Larson walks over to Addison and gathers her up in his arms. "There there, Addison, Mars isn't for everyone. But here's a silver lining: you'll be going home with a lifetime subscription to Groupie Plus, ten thousand credits, and... you will be honored forever in the Wall of Heroes!"

He thrusts his hand out, gesturing to the area behind our

table. It instantly becomes opaque and glows bright, and lists the names of the six contestants, complete with their NASA-looking spacesuit photos, who are now "heroes." It's absurd, anyone can tell, and Zach Larson knows it, calling first-round-defeated reality show contestants "heroes," the whole thing is ridiculous, but he loves every second of it. It's his heartfelt homage to every lame, nonsensical show like it that has ever existed. And the feeling is contagious. I find myself rising from my seat and clapping wildly for Addison, and Chris, and the four other fallen "heroes," and I'm joined by my fellow – I don't know what to call them now – *not-yet-heroes?*

"Addison, dear. Do you like it?"

Between sobs, Addison squeaks out, "Are you kidding me? No."

Larson hands Addison off to a chaperone, and applauds her as she disappears off stage. "Very well. Onto the rules. Simple. You will live in this state-of-the-art facility for the next twelve weeks, with *zero* contact with the outside world, I repeat *zero* contact, your phones and such have already been collected. Last man or woman standing at the end of those twelve weeks wins a spot on the crew for the first manned mission to Mars in history! A seven-month, fully privately-funded mission to explore, test a bit of mining and farming and terraforming, and... who knows? Now, five teams of..." he counts the remaining contestants with his fingers, "... four will compete, accumulating points every day for reaching milestones. After each of three three-week Stages, the team with the fewest points will leave the competition in a two-hour live television special. Goodbye. In addition, Groupie subscribers around the globe will Like or Dislike you on a live feed twenty-four hours a day, and at the end of each stage the contestant with the fewest Likes, in addition to the lowest-scoring team, goes home. At Stage Four, we'll disband the two surviving teams and the remaining contestants will compete individually. Then, ultimately, the single contestant with the most points will join us on our historic voyage!" The stage dims, and he marches to the middle front, into a single spotlight, and extends his arms. As he does, more spotlights appear on either side. "Now folks... who would like to meet the Team Leaders, the crew of *High Heaven*?"

The audience goes wild cheering for the five god-like creatures who emerge from backstage. My clapping slows, then stops, as each of them in turn passes us and glares, a mixture of disdain and pity that makes my heart sink. The first is Red Team Leader. He'll be leading my team, according to a red spot glowing on the table in front of me. He takes a moment to scowl specifically at me, then shakes his head, then forces a smile and salutes as he turns to the audience. "Captain Daniels. Marine lieutenant, fifteen years. Purple Heart. NASA test pilot, AceSpace astronaut. Red Team Leader and Mission Commander."

Four more gods follow in succession, all AceSpace veterans, each as impressive as Captain Daniels: Reagan Malone, prior NASA Space Station Engineer, Green Team Leader; Dylan Garcia, A.I. developer, Yellow Team Leader; Drew Innes, PhD in physics and rocketry, Orange Team Leader; and Skylar Gaines, USAF fighter pilot with an MD and PhD in biology, Blue Team Leader. They bow in unison and exit the stage, once again scowling at us, I imagine going off to their dungeon lair to perfect the tortures they'll be subjecting us to over the next twelve weeks. Any remaining beliefs that this show will mimic a civilized, high-tech astronaut training program are gone. This is going to be boot camp.

"Now contestants... have a good night. You deserve the rest. And you'll need it, trust me. Fun, fun, fun!" We rise to follow the chaperones off stage, beyond exhausted, asleep on our feet, and I have the strong sense that the audience, and people around the world, are now making their bets, picking their winner and mentally discarding the losers. Larson seems to have the same thought, because as we pass him, he issues this dramatic challenge: "And finally, something to ponder in your dreams tonight, contestants... which one of you, and it will be just one, has what it takes? Which one of you, like the mythical scarab beetle of millennia past, will be reborn and usher in a rebirth for all mankind?" Then he lowers his voice, as if sharing a confidence. "And which one of you will bring back the secrets that Mars has yet to reveal?"

The secrets that Mars has yet to reveal.

I repeat his last thought over and over again, there's something about the way he said it, and as I'm led zombie-like toward my room, a question pops into my mind that sticks around like an itch that can't quite be scratched:

What does Zach Larson know?

21

THE LUXURIOUS ACCOMODATIONS

I dream they put us in small, cramped rooms with two bunks, top and bottom, no bathroom, and no windows. It smells in my dream, like stale food and something vaguely burning. It smells like home. Not in a good way.

As I begin to wake, though, eyes still puffy and shut, I stretch out my arms and legs on the big, beautiful bed I've seen in the commercials for the show, and smile, knowing that it was just a bad dream. In reality I'll be staying in a private, luxurious four-star-hotel room for the next twelve weeks, complete with a private bath and panoramic view of a park just outside the TV studio. I sit up and-

"OUCH!"

I hit my head.

I open my eyes to see what dared to interrupt my peaceful waking moments.

A bunk. Above me.

There are two bunks. And no bathroom. And no windows. If I reach out a little more I can touch both walls at once.

And it smells in here.

It wasn't just a bad dream.

My arms and legs are hanging off a smaller bed than I can believe a person can sleep on, even smaller than my bed at home. Maybe Voomvoom could sleep on this bed, it's bigger than the back seat of a car at least. Barely. As I stare up at the bottom of the top bunk, at the crossbar that probably made a permanent indentation in my forehead, I don't see any human limbs hanging over the edges, and silently thank God that at least the producers have spared me an annoying roommate, someone who would, in very small but constant ways, irritate the shit out of me until I volunteer myself off the show and disappear forever just like my mother. Yes, thank God, at least I'm alone.

"Hi."

I scream as a head peeks down from the top bunk, offering a hand to shake.

"Sorry. Oh, that's right. You just came in last night. You didn't know about this."

I tentatively take his hand and shake it. At least I think it's a "he." Its hair hangs down a foot, I can't see the face, and it's wearing some kind of bead bracelet. I look around, aghast. "What about... the big bed...? The park...?"

"The luxurious accommodations, right? Yeah, uh, for the commercials I think they were going for a *you-won't-believe-how-extravagant-this-is-going-to-be* thing. To get the celebrities interested? I don't know. But when we got here, I got here a week ago, they told us that was all bullshit, and we better get used to cramped quarters if we're going to Mars." He smiles. "It's not so bad when you start to see it from that perspective. Like part of training. Like what doesn't kill you makes you stronger kind of thing. Anyway, I'm Benji. Greenberg."

It's a he. Wonderful. I turn over and pull the blanket over my head. "And I'm going back to bed."

But my hope of falling asleep, to wake up to that other reality, the one with the big bed, is dashed immediately when someone bursts through the door.

Benji whispers from the top bunk. "By the way, the doors don't have locks. Nothing does. Good to know."

And the person who barged in shouts, "Have you seen this?!"

I instantly know who it is – Aurora. Well, *in-front-of-the-cameras* Aurora anyway.

A roll of toilet paper hangs from her finger. "Smith. Get up. Have you seen this shit? It's like a bad college dorm. I mean, come o-" and she interrupts herself with hysterical laughter.

I peek out from under the blanket. "What?"

"They put you with the nerd." She points to the top bunk. "That's rich."

"He's not a nerd." I don't know why I'm defending this Benji person, I've only known him for five seconds. But I don't like anyone being called names. "And what's wrong with being a nerd?"

"Oooh. I see. They set you up. Nerd couple. Cute." She bends over laughing.

I shoot to my feet, angry, but remember Nana's words: *Calm down. Solve the problem.* I take a deep breath. "Aurora. Is everything all right?"

"No. As a matter of fact it isn't. This place is a shithole, like we're in the army or something. Where's my private bathroom? I'm on my way to complain to Larson right now. He's a fucking liar. And I'm hungover, my head is about to explode, last night was a blur, so that doesn't help at al- hey…!"

"Hey?"

She leans in and whispers, looking around at the numerous unseen cameras that will record every second of our lives for the next three months. "Hey. Speaking of blurs. What did we talk about? Last night? On that space ship thing?"

I whisper back. "Um, nothing."

She pushes herself back, into the doorway. "Good. Because you're all sweet and innocent, and I like you, and maybe in a different life who knows, but... *you're going down.* Sorry. Just the way it has to be. I've got a competition to win." She flips her hair back and storms down the hallway, hunting Zach Larson.

Benji jumps off the top bunk and peeks his head out the doorway after her. "She seems nice."

"Were you here just now? Like four seconds ago?"

"Hey, isn't that the girl that won *America Sings*?"

"Runner up."

"Oh yeah. Runner up. So... you're friends?"

I rub my forehead where the crossbar smacked me. "I don't know."

22

PUSHUPS

Interview with Tanner Byron, contestant number 14, the oldest contestant on You're Going to Mars! *at 52 years old:*

"I've been running marathons since I was in college. I'm probably in better shape now than I've ever been. But it's not just the running. It's the beet juice. Do you have any idea how many micronutrients are in beet juice? The glutathione boost alone, I mean, blood pressure, cholesterol – it's pretty much the perfect food. Sure, my shit's bright red, but who sees that? Or *do* you guys see that? I hadn't thought, with all the cameras and everything. Oh, sorry, what, Mars? Yes of course, I can't wait to make it to Mars. Another giant step for mankind, right? Start a little beet farm in the greenhouse possibly. If I'm going off on the beet thing too much just let me know."

They've got us marching down the hall in our color-coded training suits, out to the Great Hall, a massive space complete with separate gym areas for each team, our communal dining space, a computer sandbox testing area, and a lounge. And, of course, more cameras than one could count.

"Hey."

It's Aurora. She sidles up next to me and brushes my shoulder. I notice the number patch on her shirt. "Aurora. You were the last one in. How did you get number one?"

"Because I'm number one."

"No really. I was the twenty-fifth one in, and mine says 'twenty-five.' You came in last."

She grins and puffs out her chest, showing off the big white oh-one. "Squeaky wheel. Larson is scared of me. It's the least he could do, that liar. Some poor sap Avery woke up with a twenty-six on her shirt. I saw her looking around, bewildered. It was pretty funny."

"Hilarious."

She leans in and whispers. "Hey. Guess what Captain Daniels' first name is."

I shrug. "I don't know. Rick? Jack? Something with a chiseled chin."

"It's Daniel."

"No."

"Yup. Daniel Daniels."

"Wow. I thought *my* mother was terrible."

"Right? But just so you know, I found out something else too. If you need some brownie points, call him 'DanDan.' He likes that. Puts a skip in his step."

"No way. Wait. Really?"

"Would I lie to you?"

We enter the Great Hall, each team heading over to its Team

Leader. Captain Dan Daniels – I'm still having a hard time with the name – looks at his watch. "You're late."

I take a quick glance up at the clock, next to a giant display with all our names on it. It's ten seconds past seven o'clock. We're *ten seconds* late. Somehow I think this tells me all I will ever need to know about Captain Daniels.

He barks, "Claire Soams."

Claire raises her hand.

"Put your hand down, Soams. Just say 'Present, sir.'"

"Present, sir." She bats her eyelashes at him.

"Is there something wrong with your eyes, Soams?"

"Um, no. Sorry, sir."

"Good. Mike Horner."

"Present, sir."

"Benji Greenberg."

"Present, sir."

"Robin Smith."

"Present, sir."

He looks down at his tablet again. "Smith. Not a very awe inspiring name, is it?"

"No sir. My mother couldn't come up with anything better, sir."

My teammates laugh – and immediately regret it. Daniels isn't laughing. "Well, well, I'm glad to see we're all in good spirits this morning. Let's celebrate by giving me fifty. All of you."

Benji raises his hand.

"Goldberg?"

"Greenberg. Fifty what, sir?"

Daniels jiggles Benji's twig-thin arms. "Fifty whatever you think you can handle. In your case, I wouldn't start with pushups."

It's comical, of course. I can maybe handle fifty pushups, so I start in. And Mike Horner, angling for that role on *Star Wars Fifteen*, is in top shape, he can probably do a couple of hundred without raising his heart rate. But Benji resorts to some form of situp-type thing I don't even recognize, he looks like he's having a seizure, and my last teammate, Claire – I almost start giggling. She's standing doing bicep curls. With no weights. Just curling her empty arms up and down, up and down, and counting. She spies me watching out of the corner of her eye, and winks. "Feel the burn. Do you feel it, Robin?"

"I feel the burn, Claire."

Daniels squats in front of me. "Did I ask you to talk?"

"No, sir. Sorry sir."

"Well you've earned twenty more, Smith. Keep it up."

"Hey, what about Claire? She was talki-"

"Thirty more. Want to try for forty?"

Oh well. It looks like he's making me the *example*. Fun.

Somewhere around thirty-five, a memory pops into my brain: when I was little, the three of us used to take turns sitting on Dad's back while he did pushups. You'd never know it from his hang-dog look and his spare tire, but he's amazingly strong. So we would take turns, and eventually all three of us would pile on, and he would eke out one or two more pushups, and collapse, then roll over and start wrestling all of us at once. We would win, naturally, the Farris Triple Team, but only because he let us win. Every time.

My family. I've never been apart from them, not for a single day, and now they might as well be 140 million miles away.

A tear mixes with my sweat and falls to the floor.

Daniels, still squatting in front of me, considers the tear. For a fleeting moment I think he feels compassion for the first time in his life, because he says, "Hey, Smith. You want to hear something inspiring?"

"Yes, sir. I would like to hear something inspiring."

"There've been more Smiths in space than any other name."

"Yes sir. Twenty-eight sir." I look up at him and grin. He raises an eyebrow. "Well look at you. You're actually right."

Hmm. He looks marginally pleased. Maybe it's time to rack up a few of those brownie points. "Thanks, DanDan."

His eyes widen and he growls. "What did you just call me?"

"Um, nothing, sir! I'm sorry! Aurora said-"

He kicks my arm out from under me, my face smacking into the sweaty, teary mat. "If you ever call me that again I will have you booted off this mission faster than a peanut butter sandwich runs away from a bear. Now keep doing pushups until you throw up."

I collapse around seventy-five, and flip over, exhausted, dry-heaving, staring up at the ceiling. My arms feel weaker than how Benji's must feel all the time. He, Claire, and Mike stand at attention, quiet as mice, trying to avoid becoming the next example. Daniels stands over my body on the floor, looking upside down into my face. I make a mental note to never believe anything Aurora tells me ever again.

A half hour later, my three teammates have joined me on the floor, panting, dry-heaving, wishing for death.

"Okay, people. Good warmup. Let's start your workout."

I groan, and Claire raises her hand tentatively. "S- s- start?"

And for the first and last time that day, Daniels smiles.

23

THE BIG BOARD

Endless hours and nonstop punishment later, we practically crawl on all fours with the other teams into the dining space. It's sadistic, putting the food right next to the gym, just a few impossible steps away, achingly out of reach. I want to cry, unsure if my body will carry me the remaining distance to its life-giving sustenance.

But it does. And I proceed to pile some of everything on my tray – no bologna sandwiches or blue food gel, thank you very much – steak, mac and cheese, roasted turkey panini, mocha chocolate pie, and countless other goodies hidden somewhere under the top layer of food, with butter, like mortar, holding it all together, as a cameraman behind the counter documents my gluttony for the world to see. I don't care.

We plop down, exhausted and hungry, at Red Table. The other team tables surround us, everyone equally ravenous, and the sound of livestock gorging at the trough fills the cavernous space.

Claire sets down her two plates – yes, two plates – and

strategizes where to start. "Oh my. This is even better than breakfast. How am I supposed to lose weight with twelve weeks of *this?*"

Mike Horner holds up a forkful of salad with the thinnest, see-through sliver of boiled chicken breast you've ever seen. Wow. That's restraint. "I guarantee they're weaning us off. By week twelve it'll be nothing but gray paste and protein pellets."

Claire grimaces at his thought, then looks down at her pie and rediscovers her joy. "Well, then *seize the day*, am I right? Seize it!" She licks her lips.

I'm already attacking my plate like it owes me money.

"Whoa. Robin. You ever eat before?"

I answer Benji with a mouth full of prime rib. "Sorry, it's just... this is sooo good... you haven't tasted my Nana's cooking. Or my mother's."

"I thought you lived on a farm. Alone."

"Um, yeah, uh, I mean way back when." *Change the subject.* "Hey, what's that?" I point up to the huge screen between the gym and the cafeteria, it must be thirty feet wide at least, above the lounge area with couches and beanbags. The screen lists our teams and our names with our contestant number. Another number next to each of our names fluctuates up and down.

"That's The Big Board."

"Oh, the one that says 'Big Board' on it in giant letters? Thanks. No, Benji, I meant what are those little numbers going up and down at the end?"

Mike Horner stands, as if he's giving a presentation. "They haven't told us yet, probably will at orientation tonight, but I've been keeping an eye on that second column of numbers next to our names. Watch this."

He peels his shirt off. Flexes his abs. And the number next to his name jumps from fifty thousand to fifty three thousand.

Claire claps. "Likes! It's the Likes!" She licks her fingers free of gravy and cheese, bounds up and stands next to Mike, hikes her shirt a little to show her midriff. Her number drops eight hundred.

She screams at the board. "Hey, come on! I'm working on it!" Her number regains two hundred. She smiles. "Sympathy Likes. I'll take it." Another hundred. She smiles again and winks at no one in particular. Another hundred. She giggles. Another hundred. She blows a kiss. Another hundred.

Benji surveys the space and all the contestants. "Wow. Incredible. I mean, I guess with that many people watching, every little thing we do will move the needle." He stands up, calmly, then shouts at the top of his lungs, "I LOVE THIS BEAUTIFUL COUNTRY! The U-S- of A!" And his number adds four thousand in a matter of seconds. He sits back down, grins, and folds his arms across his chest. "Boom."

Everyone swings around to see what the commotion is about. Within moments, there seems to be a general under-standing, because Marina Delacosta opens her training top to reveal a bikini and her Likes shoot through the roof. Mike ups her ante, shedding his training pants, and soon anyone with a body to show off is stripping, and Aurora is belting out "Baby's Gone," Lucy and Jayden from Orange Team are danc-ing, and a couple of Blue Team contestants are making out, it's complete mayhem, and the Likes are burning up.

I just sit there, with Benji, taking it all in. "I can't compete with that."

"Yeah. I'm playing the long game."

The numbers level off, and even start to dip, as if the

worldwide audience suddenly got bored with too much stimulation. Eventually, the cafeteria falls silent. Everyone sits down. I think we all realize at once that we're in a fishbowl in front of billions of people, twenty-four-seven, for the next three months. We better pace ourselves.

Aurora makes her way over to our table – I'm sure she only allowed herself a single grape for lunch – and addresses us, keeping an eye on The Big Board.

"Well, well. Red Team. I'm on the Green Team. Green means go. You know what red means, right? *Stop.* As in you might as well *stop* trying." She tilts her head just enough to see her numbers climb. Sticks her tongue out at us and grins.

"Actually, red is the color of Mars."

Benji and I say this exactly together. The nerdiest thing either of us could possibly say, and we say it simultaneously. I want to die.

But both our numbers shoot up, and Aurora's drops. She storms away in a huff. So I trot over to her, trying to shield us from the cameras, though I don't know if that's even possible here, and whisper, "Listen, you don't have to do the Mean Girl thing. I don't think that's you."

"Oh. Says the reality show expert and budding psychologist." She pats my shoulder. "Listen to the real expert, Smith. I'm just testing my Mean Girl persona today. See what works. Who knows? Tomorrow I might be an angel."

"Why not just... be yourself?"

She ruffles my spiky bleached crew cut, the first signs of brown growing in. "Look who's talking."

24

ROBENJI

Interview with Sophia Wheeler, contestant number eight, 48-year-old housewife from Tennessee:

"Honestly I don't know how I've even made it this far. My knees are killing me, I don't really like the space flights. And I miss my kids. My husband? Ha! Not so much. He's the main reason I'm sticking it out. He told me I I'd never be able to do it. Well, you know that's the best possible motivation, of course. I just keep picturing myself setting foot on Mars, looking up at the camera, and saying, 'Well, Bob? What are you telling your golf buddies now?' Then, of course, when I get home, we'll see how the dynamic changes. I might have him stay in the guest house. Oh, by the way, that's what I would spend all the money on. A big estate with a guest house. Bob can have the guest house. Like a permanent dog house. Are you watching, Bob?"

Day Ten.

I'm beginning to do pushups in my sleep. And of course, during virtually all of my waking hours. I've done more pushups than Dad has in his lifetime, I'm sure. I look down at my body, and even in my perpetually exhausted state, I have to smile. I'm becoming toned, stronger than I've ever been. The scale shows no weight loss, but clearly I'm losing fat and gaining muscle. It's grueling, the constant workouts of Stage One, "Endurance," but it's producing results.

We all feel it, the physical changes, even Claire. She's graduated to actual pushups, a few anyway, she's keeping up on the treadmills, and when she does her hilarious arm curls she now at least holds five pound weights in her hands. I imagine she might actually feel the burn, maybe the burn of a small candle anyway. Maybe.

Mike Horner was right, too: the food is changing. But not becoming paste and pellets. It's just getting... weird. It looks like real food, and it tastes fine, but there's something just a wee little different, like if someone here was introduced to one of my sisters, she'd look exactly like me, but something would just be... off.

Benji is easy to like, and thankfully didn't live down to my expectations of having a roommate. We're both "nerds," as Aurora helpfully reminds us as often as she can, so we share a common vocabulary. My tech is more rockets and astronomy, and his tech is more video games, but we both share a love of programming, and the sandbox terminals in the giant central space allow us to show off bits of D+ code. We've even co-developed a new return landing program for a rocket simulation.

"I fixed that last section for you, I think."

"Huh. Let me see." I pull his monitor over where I can see, and wouldn't you know? This gamer coffee barista with the bead bracelet from Ohio may have solved my years-old landing problem. "Wow. So you shrunk the dispersions here on the boostback burn, and grew them to counter atmospheric disturbances. I'm impressed, Benji."

He blushes anytime something like this happens, and the Likes go crazy on The Big Board. We know, it's obvious, that the world at large is dying to see romance blossom among the contestants. And there are intriguing things happening on both the Yellow and Blue teams. But Benji and I? Nah. He strikes me as particularly asexual, and just isn't my type, if I have a type at all. And now that this team thing is feeling a bit like family, it would be like getting involved with your brother. Ick. No thanks.

"So, the bracelet. Is that one of those Buddhism things, or just for looks?"

"I'm actually kind of into the Eastern thing. It's Buddhist prayer beads. You touch the beads to count your mantra."

"What's your mantra?"

"It's embarrassing."

"You don't want to tell me? Or it's actually the word 'embarrassing?'"

"I can't."

"You can. Come on."

"Gaba gaba ganeshi."

I giggle. "You're kidding."

He squirms. "Okay, I was actually sort of acutely high when I came up with it. But it just kind of became my default. It works though, seriously. Say it a couple of times slowly, while you're clearing your mind, and breathe in deeply before each time."

I try, sincerely, but after the first "Gaba gaba ganeshi" leaves my mouth, I can't stop laughing. I'm snorting. This is the opposite of meditating. I feel terrible.

"Aww, look. It's *Robenji*, coding and playing together. Adorable."

That is, of course, Aurora. She avoids the computer area of the lounge like it's a crime scene, but can't resist any opportunity to combine our names and try to make it stick with the other contestants: "Robenji." So far it hasn't stuck, thank God.

"Hey, Aurora. Why aren't you with Green Team?"

"I'm trying to avoid Marina. She thinks we're besties, because I can sing, and she can, I don't know, do whatever she does. Be glamorous. Strike a pose. Having me around is good for her Likes."

Benji stands up, smooths his training pants and his hair. "Uh, maybe I should go over there, you know, see if *my* presence helps her with Likes. I mean, look at this package. Am I a Like magnet or what?"

We laugh, and even Benji has to chuckle. Aurora pats him on the chest. "Nah, dude. You might want to stick with whatever this barista-Buddhist-nerd approach is and not go over there. Glamour Girl is busy learning a new skill. Look." She points to the far corner of the gym, where Marina lands a roundhouse kick to the throat of a sparring dummy, knocking its head loose. "Malone's teaching her kickboxing."

Benji gulps. "You're right. Barista-Buddhist-nerd approach sounds good. I'll stay right here with you guys. You guys are just fine."

"Oh, we're *just* fine?"

"That's not what I meant. Hey, listen... why did the chicken cross the road?"

Aurora rolls her eyes. "This better be good."

"Because it was being dragged by a coyote."

We both groan, and Aurora simply walks away.

I snicker. "Wow. If you're trying to impress her, it's working."

"Patience. Like I said, I'm playing the long game."

Claire trots over, fresh from a shower. "Hey. Um, I know she's on the Green Team, our mortal enemy thing and all, but I have adored Marina Delacosta *forever*. I have her perfume even. You think now would be a good time to go over there and introduce myself?"

Without hesitation, Benji and I look at each other and say, "Definitely."

So as Claire departs to risk a Marina Delacosta heel to her temple, she passes Ted, who's jogging across the expansive space towards us. "Robin. Hi. Mr. Larson would like to have a word with you."

I feel the blood leave my face. "Is... everything all right?"

"I'm sure. Probably something you forgot to sign."

We walk across the studio lot, past the tarmac, to the offices. I've never been inside the offices. Their building is a six-story black glass monolith that definitely doesn't invite you to go inside. It seems contradictory to me, that Zach Larson would choose to spend his days in something this ugly, something so opposite his personality. Shouldn't it look like the 2085 version of Santa's workshop? Or an exact replica of the square spaceship from *The Kronos Adventure*?

Inside is better. The windows are perfectly clear, like you're standing outside, and there are plants and trees everywhere. The logos of various companies Larson has either formed or acquired line the hallways. The elevator even has a tree in it – growing right through a hole in the floor, up through another hole in the ceiling, and it looks like out through the roof. Amazing. We get off on the sixth floor, more wide windows overlooking the tarmac. Zach Larson stands at the end of the hall, and when he spots us, practically runs to greet me. "Robin! Robin Smith! The numbers look good! They like you. Though your team could be doing better with points."

"Aurora's been reminding me."

He chuckles, and leaves Ted in the hall as he ushers me into his big corner office and closes the door. "Now, Robin. What do you think of the show so far?" He hands me a mint.

"Well, Mr. Larson, Zach, it's wonderful. It's a dream." I pop the candy into my mouth and look around. There's no way to tell if we're being filmed. Larson takes my cue. "Don't worry, Robin. There are no cameras in here. We're alone."

"Am I in trouble?"

He walks behind his desk and sits down, motioning for me to do the same. "Can I just tell you how much *I'm* enjoying the show? Immensely. Fun, fun, fun! I mean, it has its moments, like your friend Aurora can be a handful, demanding *number one* of all things, and there are various people making various demands, which," he snickers to himself, "won't be happening for the most part. Overall, though? Thrilled. Normal, deserving folks like yourself, mixing with equally-deserving actors, and singers, celebrities of all stripes, it's wonderful. Ratings are way beyond what we expected, and the advertisers are happy. Shoot, we could probably pay for this little trip to the red planet with just the ad revenue."

"I'm here... to talk about ad revenue?"

He grins, just a hint of a grin, and pulls a photo from his desk drawer, pushing it across for me to see. "No. I thought we'd talk about this."

I look down and practically choke on the mint.

It's a picture of my mother. In handcuffs. Giving the finger to the camera.

25

IT'S MY MOTHER.

"Who is that, Robin?"

"It's my mother. But I think you already knew that."

"Yes."

A clock ticks the seconds. The only sound in the room. I lose count after thirty.

"My contacts – I know quite a few people, you can imagine – gave me a little heads up. She was trying to steal a car. A very old one. My first instinct, of course, was to let the story play out in the press, create drama, heighten the intrigue. Nothing like a little piece of juicy news to boost ad spend." He takes back the photo and considers it. "But something told me, I don't know, maybe it was my own mother..."

"Martha."

He smiles. "...yes, Martha. This photo kind of looks like her, when she was alive. Feisty as hell."

More endless seconds pass. I pull the picture back in front of me. She doesn't look as upset as I think she would. More defiant. And her hands. Yes, she's giving the finger with her left hand. But she's making an "O" shape with her right hand. Is that another obscene gesture I'm not aware of? Or is she just acting insane as usual? Oh, who am I kidding? It's the latter.

"I'm sorry, Mr. Larson. Her name is Jane. She's..." and I twirl my finger in a circle next to my temple.

"Yes. I know. I know everything."

What? Adrenalin shoots through my veins and begs me to run. It takes everything I have to stay put. I death-grip the armrests on the chair, and grind the mint into little pieces in my mouth. "Ev- everything?"

"Yes. That your mother drove you from your farm in New Jersey. The tolls show DNA checks. That was quite a long drive."

"You're telling me." I laugh, and exhale like I imagine an armadillo must exhale after it narrowly escapes the wheels of a truck. Larson doesn't know the truth. Thank God.

"You seem very relieved, Robin. Is there more to the story?"

"No! No. No. That's everything. Is she...?"

"In jail? No. Like I said, I know quite a lot of people. One of those people left a door open in the right place at the right time. Seems her paperwork disappeared as well. She was reunited with the boy and disappeared."

"Mr. Larson, Zach, sir... I don't know what to say..."

"Say thank you."

"Thank you. Of course thank you. But... why?"

"I don't know. I like you, Robin. I think it might be unfair, even by my flexible standards, to see you depart this wonderful adventure so soon due to a little thing like a stolen car." He rises and scans the view from his window. "I've got a thing for underdogs. Now. Back to work, young lady."

I pry my hands from the armrests and get up to leave.

"Oh, Robin. One more thing."

"Yes, Mr.- ah, Zach?"

"Strike one."

26

SLIP-N-DIE

Interview with Suzie Q, number 22, winner of Season 41 of
Survive This:

"Yeah. They better watch out. All of 'em. Suzie Q's comin'
for 'em. I didn't survive eating crickets and snake meat for a
month to go down on some goofy obstacle course. I mean,
did you see me? On *Survive This*? I know you saw me, who
didn't see me? I lost thirty-seven pounds and got the fever.
But did that stop me? Nuh-uh. Or when they blindfolded
me and I had to climb down that cliff with my broke leg?
Nuh-uh. Ain't nothin' gonna stop me. That Albert dude's
smart, and if I'm bein' honest kinda cute, I'd take that for a
ride, but he ain't gonna stop me. Nothin's gonna stop me
from goin' to Mars. 'Specially not the Red Team. Have you
seen that Claire one try to get up the Climb?"

Tomorrow is the end of Stage One. Not saturated
enough with entertainment just watching us around
the clock, the global audience will be treated to a live, two-

hour Stage One finale television special, featuring a colossal obstacle course that will test our endurance and physical strength.

I need to focus. Each team is allowed just an hour today to run through it.

But all I can think about is Jane.

What the hell is she thinking? She wants me here, doesn't she? And she goes and gets herself *arrested*? Twenty-one years successfully dodging the authorities, staying under the radar, practicing her ninja invisibility while investigating her little conspiracy theories, and suddenly she gets sloppy? It doesn't make sense. She doesn't do things like that, at least that I know. But I don't know her well, not as well as-

"Robin!"

Captain Daniels reaches out to grab my hand, but it's too late.

I fall into the Alligator Pit.

As I look up at him, an animatronic alligator pretends to chomp on my arms. "Will we be running into alligators on Mars?"

Claire gasps. "I honestly didn't even think about that. Will we?"

Mike Horner glares. "Claire, be quiet." He and Daniels reach a hand down to me in the pit. Mike growls. "And *you* need to pay attention, Robin. I am *not* going home."

Daniels is pissed, as usual, but Mike is *very* pissed. Other than himself, I'm the most prepared for the physical challenge, so drifting off into la-la land, obsessing about my *dearly-departed-and-now-suddenly-not-quite-so-departed* mother is *not* being helpful. Benji and Claire can't be counted on to make it past the Slip-N-Die, so he needs me to be on my game. It's up to the two of us. I need to stop thinking about everything else except winning this thing.

First things first. "Okay. Captain Daniels. Mike. Let's start from the beginning one more time. If we can complete the course in under..." I do the math in my head, "...five and a half minutes, from what I've watched of the other teams, then Benji and Claire only have to make it to the Alligator Pit. They won't even have to finish, and I'm pretty sure we won't be last. We don't have to win. We just can't be last."

Daniels nods, and Mike pats Benji on the back. He still isn't happy, being saddled with two of the physically weaker contestants on the show, but Benji and Claire are giving it a hundred percent. We all know the deal. We all stay or leave together.

If you survey the obstacle course from above, as we did yesterday on our afternoon training flight, you'd say it can't be done in five and a half minutes. It's a gigantic zig-zag of ridiculous – and ridiculously difficult – tasks, most of which have nothing to do with Mars. Like the Alligator Pit. And the Truck Tire Roll. And the Slip-N-Die. If Zach Larson was going for equal parts physical endurance and wacky-looking humiliation, he nailed it. As Benji, Claire, and I watch Mike sprint through the first leg – the Quicksand Sprint – it's hard to stifle our giggles. But he makes it through several obstacles and approaches the Slip-N-Die.

"You're doing great, Mike! Just run across!"

"Just run across. Yeah. Easy just like that."

He's right. The Slip-N-Die is the farthest thing from easy. An arched panel ten feet in the air, the Slip-N-Die makes a serpentine path maybe twenty feet long. And it's covered in the most slippery substance I've ever felt, like oil on slowly melting ice. You either have to balance perfectly at the apex of the arch and tiptoe along its spine, or lay down, covering as much surface area with the lowest center of gravity possible, and slither along like a slug. Mike takes a deep breath, looks back at us, and grins. Then he takes a running start and jumps onto the panel, sliding like a surfer, angling his body to adjust for the wavelike shape of the path. By the time he falls, he's only three feet from the end, and his momentum carries him onto the exit mat.

Claire claps. "Oooh. I think I might try that."

"Please don't try that, Claire."

Daniels agrees. "You're not trying that, Soams."

Mike turns and bows. Then quickly takes to the thin ropes that hang over the Alligator Pit, pulling himself along through to the Truck Tire Roll. This mammoth device rolls truck tires towards you randomly, collecting them at the end and spitting them back at you. It requires jumping on top, from one to the other, against the crush of tires, toward the final obstacle: The Climb.

Four and a half minutes. He has a full minute to climb the thirty foot vertical rock wall. He does it in forty-five seconds. We cheer. Benji exhales. "Dude! You're my hero."

My trial isn't quite as elegant, but I finish. Five minutes, fifty seconds. *Damn.* I'll have to do better tomorrow.

Benji, as expected, makes it halfway through the Slip-N-Die and falls. He'll get enough progress points, even if he doesn't finish. Good.

"Okay, Claire. It's up to you. Don't worry about your time. You just have to get to the Alligator Pit. Take your time."

Claire hyperventilates for a few moments, psyching herself up, and tears across the Quicksand Sprint like a champ. "You got this, Claire! That's awesome!"

She smiles and launches onto the Swinging Rings with abandon.

Then misses the second ring. It smacks her in the face, and she falls into the trench below.

"Shit." She climbs out. "They'll turn off the flames tomorrow if somebody falls in, right?" She dusts off her training suit. "Well, how'd we do? We got a chance?"

Mike shakes his head. "What do you think, Claire? You made it through one obstacle. One."

"I know, I know. I'm sorry. I'll make it to the Alligator Pit. I promise, Mike. Here, let me do it one more time."

So Claire once again pumps herself up, sprints across the quicksand, vaults onto the rings, and... gets smacked in the face and falls.

Yes. We're screwed.

27

GOOD LUCK. YOU'LL NEED IT.

The next night, at eight, an audience of about a thousand greets us from huge temporary bleachers as we march onto the course, and another billion or so join us via TV. Larson has pulled out all the stops, once again, with floodlights, deafening rock music, fireworks, and even a flyby of *Martha*, the plane-ish thing, buzzing the crowd just feet above the makeshift arena.

The teams stand side-by-side with their Team Leaders: Red, Green, Yellow, Orange, and Blue.

One team will be leaving tonight.

Aurora sneers at us. "Good luck. You'll need it."

I wave back, and she winks.

Zach Larson takes to a platform set up in front of the first obstacle. "Ladies and Gentlemen. Welcome to the conclusion of Stage One: Endurance! Team Leaders. Are your teams ready for some fun?"

The team leaders shout their confirmation, though I detect a little hesitancy from Daniels. We've accumulated points during the past two weeks, for small milestones like pounds lost or distances run or weights lifted, but our team is second to last, even with Mike Horner leading the entire field of contestants, and our formidable individual Likes won't help our team total.

Larson raises a gun into the air. "The rule is simple: each contestant must enter the course alone, completing as many obstacles as fast as possible, gaining five points for each, and extra points for better time. There are enough points available for any team to come in first. Likewise, any team can fall to last and go home. Good luck!" He pulls the trigger and a flare shoots into the air, exploding into the five colors of our teams. The crowd ooohs.

Green Team is up first: Aurora, Marina Delacosta, Quinn Keller, and Albert Morse. Larson steps over with his microphone. "Green Team. You're currently in the lead. Who will be humiliat- I mean, master – this course first?" Marina raises her hand. "I will, Zach darling. Issa piece of pie."

The crowd laughs, and honestly I don't think a single one of us expects what happens next. The starting bell rings and the timer starts, and Marina's feet dance across the Quicksand Sprint, then leap onto and across the Swinging Rings like a gazelle. She lands on the mat with a flourish, to absolute silence. This heiress to a global fortune, who has never lifted a finger without some giant diamond on it, who has a staff to ensure she never breaks a sweat, just did that.

Her smile is the brightest and widest I've ever seen. She pretends to brush dust off her shoulder. "Well *amici*? Marina hassa some secrets up her sleeve, no?"

The audience, jolted out of their stupor, begins to cheer wildly for the New & Improved Marina Delacosta. She curtsies and dives into the Underwater Swim Tank, squirming her way – somehow elegantly – through the Mudder, and climbs aboard the Rover like she was working a lift back at the fill. By the time she reaches The Climb, the crowd is hoarse from screaming and every single contestant is picking their jaw up off the floor.

Marina scales thirty feet up The Climb like a spider, saunters over and pulls the chain that rings the finish line bell. Four minutes and ten seconds. Fifty-seven points. Wow.

She blows a kiss down to the crowd. "*Finito!*" The applause and cheers are deafening.

I turn to Benji. "She did that for you, you know."

"Which part? The blowing the kiss part?"

"The whole thing. She's trying to impress you."

"I don't know if I'm so impressed. You know, back in my day, we had to climb barefoot up a cliff twice that high on shards of glass to impress someone."

"You had feet?"

Benji laughs, and Claire smacks him in the arm. "Hey, while you guys are joking Miss Italy over here is dancing on our graves. Jesus, are they all going to be like that? What kind of drugs is she on? And does she have any extra?"

"Claire, your training pants are on backward." Mike is already pacing, watching his dream dissolve in front of his eyes.

But things get better – for us, anyway. Claire puts her pants on the right way, and several of the other contestants skid, flop, fall, get hit in the face with things, and more or less humiliate themselves. Jayden from Orange Team nearly decapitates himself on the Slip 'N Die. Avery Jacobs from Yellow Team somehow falls into the Swinging Rings pit before they can turn off the flames, and winds up running around the whole course in a panic, medics chasing her with fire extinguishers. She's fine, just a little singed, and the audience, and Zach Larson especially, love every moment of the pandemonium. I can hear Larson's advertising cash register cha-chinging.

Our team has drawn the shortest straw and is last to go. Despite the encouraging bad performances by other teams, we're still in third place. In order not to end up in last and wind up on Larson's ridiculous Wall of Heroes, both Mike and I have to finish the course in four minutes, and Benji and Claire have to at least make it to the Alligator Pit. Daniels barks at Mike. "You're up."

Mike girds himself, and tears through the course like a madman. The Blue Team, currently just ahead of us, starts shifting on their feet and wringing their hands. Mike clambers up The Climb, rings the bell, and looks over at the clock.

Three minutes and fifty seconds. Sixty-eight points.

The crowd erupts. There are no official records to break here, but if there were, Mike has smashed them. He looks down, scanning the crowd and the contestants. His eyes find Marina, and even at this distance, you can see him wink at her. The cameras, of course, pull in close on her face, showing her defiant scowl – but she can't hide a blush on her cheeks.

"Smith. You're next." Daniels pushes me toward the Quicksand Sprint. "Just do the same thing."

"Sure you don't want me to do it faster, sir?"

"You're hilarious, Smith."

Okay, Paper- Robin- whatever your name is at the moment: how bad do you want this?

The timer starts, and I dart across the quicksand, through the rings, and into the tank. So far so good. Into the Mudder, and-

Oh crap. I just lost a sneaker. Sucked right off my foot. No

time to go back. I slither my way out of the mud pit, pull off the other sneaker and make my way barefoot to the Rover, feeling for the first time every single pebble on the soles of my feet.

I race through the Rover – it's more like the lifts at home than a car, so I've quickly mastered this boulder-ridden section of the course – and take a running start onto the Slip-N-Die.

And my bare feet immediately fly out from under me, and I fall on my ass.

As my body slides down one side, I turn onto my belly and wait for my body to feel open air and failure.

But my toe finds a lip at the edge of the arc, and stops my slide.

Yes!

Just the slightest lip, it's barely there, but it's there. The audience goes hush, and holds its breath as I inch my way, toe by toe, to the end, falling off in a heap onto the exit mat. Cheers erupt, and I mouth a little "thank you" to whatever camera is in closeup, a thank-you to God, and to my family, for somehow granting my toes superhuman powers for a few moments.

The Alligator Pit proves no match for me, and I smile as I balance on the advancing truck tires, making my way toward The Climb.

But something's wrong with the machine throwing the tires, a small glitch creating larger gaps between the tires. It's totally unfair, I have to leap from tire to tire, no other contestant had to, I'm barely landing on each one in succession. But I can't whine about fairness. Not now. Now I just have to finish. I lunge at the last tire, and then to the awaiting platform.

And I hear a crunch.

Searing pain tears through my torso. I just broke a rib, at least one and maybe two, I'm sure of it.

I want to curl up in a ball and cry, it hurts so bad. Give up. But that's when I hear it:

"Get back in the saddle, kid."

It's Dad. I open my eyes, fully expecting him to be here, standing above me, like every other time I've fallen, arms out to help me up. But he's not here. And another feeling hits me, right where I just broke my rib, right in my gut, a feeling I've never had before:

I miss them. My family. Desperately.

Before this crazy show, I'd never been away from them, not for a day. Not for an hour. I *dreamed* of time to myself, of being alone for once, and now I'm here, utterly alone, and I have an incredible yearning for them. For Nana to put a warm compress on my boo-boo, and hum a tune until I can get to sleep. I ache to hear my Dad snoring on the recliner in the living room. I ache to see my sisters running around our little yard trying to catch chickens.

"Get back in the saddle, kid."

It's his voice again, and this time I raise my head and look around, it sounds so real. He's not there, but I have the overwhelming sensation that somehow he *is* here, yes, watching breathlessly on our crappy TV, cheering me on with Rock and Scissors and Nana. They're screaming for me to stop lying here and hurry the hell up. I can feel them pushing me, willing me to do better than I've ever done. Fueled with adrenalin, a feeling of invincibility washes over me, and I look thirty feet up at The Climb, and put the pain away somewhere deep, just for another minute, and get back in the saddle. Climbing hold by climbing hold, I pull myself up, as my rib cage begs me to give up, until I reach the top, roll over to the chain and pull.

Four minutes and forty-eight seconds. Sixty points.

Now I let myself curl up into a ball, wheezing, while the crowd cheers, and I cry like a baby, simultaneously trying to calculate if we still have a chance.

Maybe. If Benji and Claire make it past the Slip-N-Die, we can stay alive. Maybe.

They lead me back to our team's area, and a medical tech attends to me with a scanner.

"Hairline fracture of two ribs. Let's get you into the MedBay."

"No." I push him away. "I'm not leaving my team."

Daniels looks down at me. And for the first time since the day with the pushups, he smiles.

Benji's next, and he tries, he really does. But his Rover tumbles over a particularly large boulder, landing on its roof. Thank God he's safe, but he can't get the Rover righted. He's finished. Only twenty points.

Mike buries his face in his hands, sneaks a hesitant peek at the scoreboard, then turns to Claire. "You know what that means, right?"

"Please don't say it Mike. Please don't say it."

He doesn't have to say it. We all know.

Claire has to finish the entire course.

As Benji slumps back to us, guilty, like a dog who chewed a shoe, Mike does something very un-Mike-like, and places Claire's hands in his. "You can do this, Claire. There's more in there than you let the world see."

Claire seems to be part shocked at this intimacy, and

inspired by his words, and unleashes her inner champion at the ring of the starting bell. Now if there's something opposite Marina's elegant show before, this is it, it's awkward and lumbering and hilarious to watch, but Claire's determination is lighting up the Likes, and the crowd is going insane for its last contestant, and she is, in fact, making progress. Somehow, possibly again with almighty God and my family wishing it, Claire makes it past the Rover, and, sliding like a slug, across the Slip-N-Die, then the Alligator Pit, and miraculously, through the Truck Tire Roll. The cheers are deafening, it feels like the positive vibe of the audience alone could lift Claire up The Climb.

But she just stands there at its base. Bent over, hands on her knees, wheezing.

And crying.

She's done. Spent. Totally, completely empty.

She looks over at us, I don't know, maybe expecting us to say, "Don't worry, Claire, we didn't want to go to Mars anyway," but we just stare back at her, like "Any time you're ready, Claire."

I'm on the verge of tears again, too. I don't want to go home.

Come on, Claire. I don't belong here. I belong up there. I didn't risk my life getting this far just to fail. Please stop crying and do something.

There has to be a way. There's always a solution. There's alwa-

Wait.

An idea.

I put my hand on Mike's shoulder. "We're not going home."

Marching across the course, to the gasps and shouts of

the audience and the other contestants, I meet Claire at the base of The Climb and kneel, looking up into her eyes.

She blubbers over her sobs, embarrassed. "It's over, isn't it?"

I whisper, "We're not going home, Claire. Not today. Reach up for the first climbing hold."

"But... you're breaking the rules."

I grin. "And which rule is that?"

She searches her mind, I can see the gears turning, trying to recall the rule that says one contestant couldn't help another. "I just assumed..."

"Don't assume anything, Claire. Now reach up and grab that climbing hold."

She blows her nose in my shirt – gee, thanks Claire – and stretches and takes hold of the piece of hard rubber. "I... can't."

"You can, Claire." I lean down, put my shoulders under her ass, and push up. My ribs threaten to explode out of my body and a bolt of pain almost floors me. But Claire's foot wiggles around and finds its first hold. I push again, through the pain. Her foot reaches the next hold, this time a little more confident.

The shouts from the Blue Team, currently just ahead of us in points, grow louder. "She's cheating! Stop the competition!" But the cheers from the audience drown them out. "Claire! Claire! Claire!"

We're doing it. Claire is slowly but surely moving up the wall, her sobs reduced to sniffles, with me underneath pushing, emitting little whimpers of pain. She whispers down to me. "You poor thing, Robin. Are you okay?"

"Feeling the burn, Claire."

"Your poor ribs! Is there anything I can do? Shift my weight a certain way?"

"No. Just whatever you do, don't fart."

The cheers reach a crescendo as Claire claws her way to the summit, stands up, knees wobbling, and pulls the chain, ringing the finish line bell. She reaches down and pulls me up the final foot, and throws her arms around my neck, practically choking me, and sobs again, this time for joy. The points on the board show two hundred thirteen. We're ahead of last place by two points. And our Likes are increasing so fast it's just a blur.

The crowd claps and cheers, and sings together:

There she goes, to the show
Will she win? Heck if we know!
But she'll give it her best, take a shot
Against the losers, the rest of that lot!
Walk to the launch pad, aim for the stars
Don't close your eyes, You're Going to Mars!

It's sweet, and thrilling beyond the beyond, but as I dare sneak a glance over at Zach Larson, I'm positive he'll be shaking his head, and boot us from the competition for this flagrant disregard of the rules of his ridiculous game.

But he's grinning up at me.

And it strikes me: *of course he loves this*. Not only did this make the show even more exciting – people will sure as hell be arguing about it at work tomorrow – but hadn't he done the same thing to get to this point in life? Make up his own rules? Own the game? *Change the game itself* if he needed to?

The Blue Team's having none of it. They rush over to Larson, grousing and pointing, demanding our expulsion, or at least for a fair try at doing the same.

Larson shushes them and takes to the microphone, addressing us all. "Blue Team. All teams. Our audience. The people at home, all over the world. What you've witnessed may not seem fair. But it is *not* cheating. Our assumptions told us tonight's competition required a person, alone, to run the course. But the single rule states: 'Each contestant will *enter* the course alone.'" He flashes a sly grin. "It does *not* say anything about *finishing* the course alone." He twirls around, challenging the audience. "Now consider this: there may be a moment, on the voyage of *High Heaven*, when rules aren't enough. When fairness simply doesn't apply. When life is at stake. What's to be done then? Complain? Die because of some arbitrary rules? *No!* Our crew will have to ignore their assumptions, their preconceived notions of 'fairness,' and use every resource, every creative and unorthodox solution, to work together, to complete their mission. To stay alive." He points up at me. "I ask you all, who would you want in that moment?"

The crowd chants "Robin! Robin! Robin!" and I look down at the rest of my team, Benji and Mike, grinning wide, even Captain Daniels looks slightly proud-ish, and when I look back up to the Big Board to see us still in the game, I smush up Claire's cheeks and give her a big fat kiss, and we laugh and cry and raise our hands together into the air.

Second-to-last-place and two broken ribs never felt so good.

. . .

The Blue Team is added to the Wall of Heroes – though they don't go into the sunset quietly, in fact I think I hear the word "attorney" being shouted from the departing bus – and the Green Team, led by Aurora, receives Red Scarab medals just like on the Olympics. Larson even has an Olympic-style podium there for the first, second, and third place teams. While the show's anthem plays, though we're nowhere near the winners' podium, Claire, Benji, Mike, and myself hold hands, knowing we've won the night, and made it a step closer to Mars.

After the cheesy-but-awesome ceremony, Aurora saunters over, flashing her medal. "Hey Robenji. Shiny, huh?"

Benji reaches out and holds it up, examining it. "Aluminum with gold electroplate. This must've cost them at least three credits. Congratulations."

She snatches it back. "Oh hush." Turns to me. "Well, look who's making up her own rules now." And pokes me in the ribs. The searing pain feels like she stabbed me with a knife.

"OUCH! WHAT THE HELL?"

"Whoops. Just wanted to make sure you weren't faking it. I see you're not. Sorry."

I'd like to punch her in the face for that, but her apology actually sounds sincere, and punching people in the face on live TV isn't really my thing. "Uh, hey, congratulations, Aurora. You guys really knocked it out of the park."

"We did, didn't we?"

Marina Delacosta walks over too, and we exchange niceties, and as her and Mike flirt, I don't know why, my eyes sort of land on Aurora's shirt, on her number patch, the number One. Zero one. Oh one. Something about that number, it reminds me of something.

Oh my god.

My mother.

That picture of her being arrested. One hand in a circle. One hand giving the finger. Oh and one. Oh One.

My mother isn't getting sloppy. She got arrested *on purpose*. To have her picture taken. She knew one way or another I'd see it. And she's sending me a warning:

Watch out for Aurora.

Aurora taps my shoulder. "Watcha thinkin', sneaky?"

"Nothing."

28

I NEED TO GET BACK AND DESTROY EVERYTHING.

Interview with Eddie "Torch" Smith, least Likes at Stage One and latest addition to the Wall of Heroes:

"Nah, I'm not pissed I'm leaving. Hey. I got to go to space, sort of almost. That's pretty cool, right? And I got fifty thousand credits. I'm gonna use it to start a deli, I think I'm gonna call it Mars Deli. Mostly sandwiches with wicked cool names, like the 'Red Planet,' I think that's gonna be chicken parm with red sauce, some black olives, splash of sriracha. The 'Lander' is gonna have – get this – gold leaf foil on the roll. I'm gonna charge a thousand credits for that sandwich. You ever see that on TV, the really expensive sandwiches, they go viral and shit. It's gonna be sweet. What? What do I think of Robin Smith? Who's that? Oh, the one who pushed Claire up the rock thing? Yeah, she's awesome. Rule breaker. Great last name, of course, Smith, like me. Yeah, of course it would be cool to have another Smith be the first person on Mars. If she wins I'll name a sandwich after her. I'll call it 'The Smith.'"

I rush back from the MedBay. My ribs feel much better, strangely better. It's the second time I've experienced mainland medical technology, but it still feels like a miracle. A few passes with a large wand, a special electronic bandage, a night in one of their "tanks," and the pain virtually disappeared.

The rest of me, however, feels terrible. Panicked. I have to get back to my stuff. There are no locks anywhere, it was one of Larson's little tricks, ostensibly to promote "openness," but really to generate an *exciting-for-TV* level of paranoia, resentment, and hilarious "whoops!" moments when one contestant catches another in stages of undress, or on the toilet, or picking a zit, or having a fight, et cetera.

I wish I'd thought of it sooner: keeping *any* proof of my past life will put me in danger of being revealed as a resident of Fill City One, and that'll get me kicked off the show, and there goes my one chance at leaving this planet, and I don't even want to think about what it would mean for my safety. Or my family's. A shudder rolls up my spine as the name *Gitano* enters my mind. I've kept my belongings out of sight of the cameras, way back in one of my cubbies, but if Aurora starts snooping around...

I need to get back, and regardless of my nostalgia, destroy everything.

Except my baby sweater. I can't do that.

And I'm not sure about the poem. That's not incriminating, is it?

A sound.

There's no one else in the hallway, it's after curfew (at least officially). But I swear I heard something close to my left.

There. Again. Like a humming or something.

A door. Next to me. I never noticed. I put my ear up against it, and instantly the humming sound stops. I wait for a moment, as silent as possible. The humming starts again.

"Aurora?"

The humming stops.

"Aurora, is that you?"

Nothing.

Then in a flash the door swings in, an arm reaches out and jerks me inside. The door slams shut, and we're in blackness.

"Shhhh."

"Aurora, what are you doing?"

"I found a safe space."

"A safe space? Hey, can we turn on a light?"

"Whoops." She flicks her flashlight on, and a sharp beam of light blinds me. "Shit. Sorry." She redirects the flashlight up to the ceiling. We're in a tiny storage closet, surrounded by shelves and boxes. "Safe space. No cameras, no microphones. You can't tell anyone. Promise."

"Promise. Why were you humming?" I spy a notebook in her other hand as she sits down on an empty crate. "No. Let me guess. *Rocket Girl.*"

"Hey! How did you kno- ahh, the first flight, wasn't it? Loose lips."

I nod.

"I was pretty drunk. Well, thanks for not saying anything to anyone, very cool of you to keep my little secret. Oh, hey, speaking of drunk." She laughs and reaches behind her and holds up a bottle of something. "Tequila. Pull up a crate."

"Hey, I thought we weren't supposed to have any contact with the outside world? That was like the one rule."

"Listen to you, rule breaker. Here, take a swig."

"What's it taste like?"

"You've never had tequila? Cooped up alone on that little farm of yours? I'd think you'd be drowning yourself in tequila from the boredom." She slides a crate across the floor and passes me the bottle. "Here's to secrets."

I gulp a mouthful of the liquor, way too much it turns out, and it burns like jet fuel sliding down my throat. "OUCH! WHAT THE HELL?!"

"Shhhh!" She laughs. "And take it easy, leave some for me."

"Gross. You can have the rest."

"Yeah. Five minutes from now you'll be grabbing it back, I promise."

Sure enough, five minutes later, a little warm disorientation is creating a perma-smile on my face, and my fingers involuntarily reach out for the bottle. "So Aurora... do you still *not* want to win?"

"Wow. I told you a lot on that flight, didn't I?"

"Yeah."

"Whatever. The plan was to get out mid-way, and release the album just as the *High Heaven* was starting its voyage. But now, it's happening again. I can feel it. The rage. I'm too competitive."

"Uh, you think?"

She laughs. "When I stood on that stage next to Tucker, they made me congratulate him for winning *America Sings!*, but really I could've ripped his throat out right there in front of a billion people. I just wanted to win. Whatever it took. There's nothing worse than second place. I don't even care about the prize. Just the winning. You know what I mean?"

"Not really. I want the prize. I want to go to Mars more than anything else."

"I guess that's the normal person response. Or the normal nerd person response anyway. So why do nerds want to go to Mars?"

"Well, I can't speak for all nerds, but there's this feeling I have, I've never told anyone..."

She pushes the bottle at me. "Go on..."

"Where I come from never felt like home. Like maybe Mars would feel more like home."

"What, like you're family's a nightmare?"

"No, no, nothing like that. They're wonderful. I just..." I trail off. The booze is threatening to open the vault.

She nudges my knee. "Where *did* you come from?"

I think of my mother and her warning. "It's, ah, complicated." Turn my flashlight to her notebook. "So, whatcha working on?"

"Complicated. I get it." She takes another swig from the bottle. "I'm working on the title song." She clears her throat and sings:

> *"Rocket Girl / I'm goin' far*
> *Gotta leave now / Sail through the stars*
> *If you look real hard / I'm that dot in the*
> *   black*
> *Will you be waitin' / If I ever get back?*
> *Will you be waitin' / If I ever get back?"*

I don't know why, something's definitely wrong with my damn tear ducts in the past two weeks, because I find myself, yet again, wiping back wetness from my cheeks.

"Awww, Robin. You like it."

"Yes. I like it very much. But I think that's the tequila talking."

She smacks my knee. "Ha! You sound like my two sisters."

I think I gasp, because she raises an eyebrow. "What? Can't imagine me having sisters?"

"No. I mean yes. I mean, it's funny. I... have two sisters too."

"Huh. Maybe that's why we're here together. Surrogate sisters."

She raises the bottle, takes a sip, and hands it to me. And we laugh, and sing, and compare notes on the other contestants, and talk about our dreams.

Like sisters.

Some vague cloud of time later, I shuffle into my room, buzzed, smiling. It's a good feeling, almost like having a little family with me, way out here in the artificial world of a Burbank television studio. I half-remember about checking my belongings, giggling to myself at how paranoid I had been. I really was becoming my mother there for a second. *Ha!* And to think she was giving me some silly signal through a police photograph? That is absolutely nuts.

I pull my satchel from its cubby, more from nostalgia than fear, and turn on my little reading light. It'll be nice to mix this feeling I'm having with some concrete memories of the people I've left behind. The contents spill onto my bed, and I grin. Sure enough, everything is there. The Zach Larson poster. The braid of hair. The poem. Of course, my baby sweater. I pull it to my face and inhale the past, the smell of the fire, but also of my whole life. And yes, even my mother's Get-Out-Of-Jail-Free card is there, reminding me that although she's certifiably insane, she cares about me deeply. Yes, it's all there, as I expected.

Wait.

No.

Something's missing.

It takes a few seconds, in my semi-incapacitated state, to search my memory for what it is. It has something to do with them all: Nana, Dad, Rock, Scissors, Duggie, and, I think, even Tom Bradlin-

Oh no.

The photo.

Greetings from Fill City One. Wish you were here!

Panicked and suddenly sober, I dig my hands into the depths of the satchel. Nothing. Shuffle the items around on my bed. *Nothing.* Bolt around our little room, banging into things and turning on all the lights, searching, searching. Nothing.

"Mmmrrphh...? Robin...? That you...?"

"It's okay, Benji. Go back to sleep."

But it's not okay. It's anything but okay. I search everywhere. Under the bed. Behind the drawers. Still nothing. I sit down, hands shaking, and face two possibilities:

Either I lost the photo, which is entirely possible, so much has happened to this satchel in the past few weeks, or...

Aurora took the photo.

And she knows.

She knows my secret.

And she'll do anything to win.

29

STAGE TWO

Interview with Marina Delacosta, contestant number 9, daughter of owner of half of Italy, Franco Delacosta

"*Si.* Yes. We are taking a little trip this morning. Ted thought he would surprise me, but I am up at four already! Every day I do this now. I'm-a very excited. I have to admit, this experience, my Papa thought it would be good for me, for his princess to spread her wings, like a swan, I don't know if that's the correct saying, forgive me, but I did not want to go. I say to Papa, I say, "Papa! You cannot make me! Mars? Are you *insano*?" And he says, "*Per me, principessa. Solo questa volta. Just this once. Per Papà. Per favore.* Please." And I make-a him buy me a yacht, a very big one, maybe the biggest, I don't know. And I come on the show. And you know what? He was right. I am a new woman. Maybe woman for the first time. I am strong. I feel invincible. I don't need the yacht no longer. I can have it *all.* What? Who? Mike Horner? *Si.* Yes. I know who he is. He seems like a nice man. I barely know him. Why? What did you see?"

I have all the time in the world to obsess about last night, about Aurora and the photo, as Ted wakes me up at four a.m. along with the other remaining contestants, and herds us onto two transports for a long and secret mystery ride to Stage Two.

I also have all the time in the world to deeply experience my first ever, head-splitting hangover. In my stifling spacesuit, on a moving transport, over bumpy highways (or at least they feel like bumpy highways to me), every pebble and divot, for miles and miles, the windows clouded so we can't see where we're headed. I have to ask Benji to get up so many times to run to the bathroom he finally just sighs. "You take the aisle seat."

"Sorry, Benji. Ugh. Aurora is such a bad influence."

"I could use some bad influence."

"Trust me. You don't want to be feeling the way I'm feeling right now."

"How'd she sneak booze into the compound?"

"Are you really surprised Aurora found a way to sneak booze into the compound?"

Benji shrugs. "Hey, want to hear a chicken joke?"

I shrug back. "No."

"So there's a kid, and he says, 'Mommy, how do they know whether an egg will be eaten, or hatch and become a chick?' The mom smiles and pats his head. 'Honey, the farmer looks carefully and knows. He sends the ones we eat to the supermarket, and saves the ones that hatch.' The kid coughs, and out pops a chick. The chick wipes itself off and shouts, 'Yeah, well that idiot farmer needs a new pair of fucking glasses!'"

I chuckle a little, it's the first positive feeling I've had all morning. "Thanks dude."

"Hey, by the way, we haven't talked since you were in MedBay. Great job with the Claire thing in the Stage One finale. Man, Blue Team was *pissed*. I'm going to go out on a limb here and say that the teams'll be throwing the rules out the window from now on. Good work. You're like a chaos agent."

"Thank you?"

"It's half a compliment, so sure, you can say thank you." He reaches into his pocket and pulls out a phone. "Take this, for example."

I immediately scan around for cameras. "Hey! Zero access! We're not allowed to have phones! How the hell did you get your hands on a phone?"

"See? You're a chaos agent. You started it. You have anyone you want to call?"

"Um. No." And as Benji ducks down in his seat and illicitly call his friends, I wish I could tell him the truth. That I'd want to call my mother first, and find out if she's watching the show and if she saw Aurora sneaking around my room, and if it showed she left with anything. Then I'd want to call my sisters, and tell them I love them dearly, and that as exciting as all this is, right now I miss the shit out of them and would rather be sitting around binge watching shows we've seen a thousand times, or cooking breakfast with them, French toast with little pieces of eggshell left in on Dad's pieces so we could hear him crunch into it and roll his eyes. Then of course, I'd want to call Dad, and tell him all the things I'm not sure I've said enough. And Nana, definitely Nana, I'd love to let her dote on me on the phone for a while.

"Hey, look." Benji's pointing out the front window onto

the horizon. The digital clouding on the windows slowly dissipates, revealing a barren desert dotted with red boulders and caves, and nothing else. But there's a shape, off in the distance, a man-made shape that interrupts the natural surroundings.

A dome.

We all crowd to the front of the transport, oohing and aahing at the mammoth structure getting larger as we approach. Though I'm not sure why any of us should be surprised at its size, given Zach Larson's penchant for huge, oversized everything.

As its details emerge, I notice that the dome is actually a container for several smaller domes. And it isn't tall like a skyscraper, but more like a big blister on the skin of the desert. In fact, if there are support beams, they're invisible at this distance, and the whole thing is crystal clear, so it has the impossibly delicate appearance of a soap bubble.

It's maybe a hundred yards in diameter, with about ten sub-domes in a circle inside. In the direct center, a slightly taller sub-dome contains what looked like a forest, or fruit trees.

Claire claps. "We're going to simulate living on Mars! I get the bottom bunk, Mike."

"Claire, dear, I'm sorry. Once again, you're almost correct, but not quite."

It's the disembodied voice of Zach Larson, who hasn't joined us on our little junket into the desert. It's just us contestants, no team leaders either. We all peer around for cameras, though I don't know why, they could be anywhere.

"You see, you won't be simulating *living* on Mars, you'll be simulating..."

Everyone knows some twist is coming, it's so Larson, but

his perfect timing is a little off, because seconds turn into minutes, and the suspense grates on our tired nerves. Lucy from Orange Team shouts out, "Simulating *what*, Larson?" and then softer, "Showboater."

"I heard that, Lucy." Larson chuckles. "Sorry for the delay. Okay, here we go. Take two. You see, contestants, you won't be simulating *living* on Mars ..."

The transport turns from its straight-on approach, veering to the dome's left side, changing our perspective, revealing something new.

"...you'll be simulating *building* on Mars."

Directly behind the first dome is a second, a miniature version, hidden from our approach until now. But this dome has no structures inside, just palettes of panels, tubes, tanks, plants in sealed containers, and I imagine about fifty million screws.

"Welcome to Stage Two: Erection."

Every one of us lets out a groan, as I'm sure every person watching around the world does, and Zach's voice even giggles knowingly.

Quinn shakes his head. "He's a child."

"Thank you, Quinn. I'll take that as a compliment. Now let's get to it, shall we? Fun, fun, fun! All right, the rule, again just one: erect the MDV, or Mars Domed Village, using the adjacent finished example and full instructions included as a guide. Teams will receive points for each module, Red and Yellow Teams working on air/water/food, Orange Team on mining, and Green Team on terraforming. This is a half-size replica of the village one lucky winner will be helping to build on Mars, and this one is simplified for non-experts. You have three weeks to get all systems operational and complete the task. Now, if you would, exit the transport, fasten your helmet securely, confirm your breathing apparatus is active, and step into the smaller dome."

"Did he say breathing apparatus?"

No answer from Larson.

Slowly our contingent of fifteen remaining contestants steps off the two transports, scanning around like ducklings without their mother, clipping on our helmets.

Marina calls out to the open air, her radio signal audible inside all our helmets. "Zach, darling. When willa Ted and the team leaders be joining us?"

I think I hear a laugh somewhere far away, and moments later, the transports silently reverse course and leave.

Albert points to the smaller dome. "They're inside already. Waiting for us."

Like sheep we follow Albert to a shape vaguely like a doorway. It's a digital display, and above it, words flash in blue light: PLEASE PROCEED THROUGH THE MEMBRANE.

Claire elbows me. "Proceed through the membrane. Sounds kinky."

Confidently striding into the dome, Albert is swallowed whole by what looks like clear jelly, as we watch in awe. He turns and motions the rest of us to follow. I step forward. It's funny how much your body can tell you *not* to do something. I'm literally pushing my body forward against its will, while it tells me not to walk into what looks like a wall. The substance is maybe a couple of inches thick, and on the way through, something like electricity tickles everywhere the wall touches my spacesuit. My body instinctively steps backward, away from the perceived danger, and I feel a strong resistance. Immovable. I can't retreat a millimeter. Somehow Larson has created a gigantic self-healing, one-way membrane. Incredible. But if this is the way *in*, where's the way *out*?

I step inside, shaking off the strange electric feeling, surveying the interior of this technological wonder, and yet again, have to hand it to Larson. This looks exactly like the Martian landscape, rocky and red. I shuffle over to one of the palettes of materials, running a gloved finger through a quarter-inch of red dust. He definitely sweats the details.

Once we're all inside, Tanner looks left, right. "Hey, where's Albert?"

Albert peeks out from behind another palette, palms up.

"Hey, Albert. You said Ted and the team leaders were inside."

"I... assumed they were in here. I thought I saw something moving. Among the palettes."

"You're an idiot."

"It was a safe assumption."

"Obviously not safe enough. Now what?"

"We wait. Claire, what do you think you're doing?"

"Getting out of this stupid suit." Her hands reach up to unclasp her helmet locks. As she disengages them, a little "whoosh" sound comes from inside, and her eyes widen in horror, and she falls to the ground, gasping for breath, clutching her throat.

"Claire!" Mike and Suzie Q jump on her flailing body, fighting to reseal the helmet. Ultimately, Mike has to pin her arms down while Suzie Q reengages the lock. Claire draws in air desperately for a few seconds, and finally settles down. "Jesus Christ! Larson's trying to kill us!"

Albert flaps his arms, to calm us I guess, though it looks more like he's trying to take flight, and he addresses the group. "People. Number one, it's obviously a vacuum in here. Don't be stupid. No offense, Claire. Number two, Larson's not trying to kill us. And number three, we wait for our team leaders. Period."

"How long?"

"Until they get here."

I glance down at my spacesuit's armband readout, and have a flash of certainty: Ted and his camera crews aren't coming. Our team leaders aren't coming. Larson isn't coming.

No one is coming.

We're alone.

And we have an hour of oxygen left.

WE'RE TRAPPED.

W e're trapped. And the irony suddenly strikes me: I just spent my entire life trapped in Fill City One, dreaming about escaping its walls. And when I finally do, I wind up here. Trapped. I actually laugh.

Claire hits me. "You're laughing while Larson's trying to kill us!"

Albert waves her down. "No. Claire, calm the hell down. There is no way Larson is going to let us die in here. There are hidden cameras everywhere. He'd be killing us live in front of billions of people. Forget about the cruelty for a second. Think about the liability. And the fact that he'd be prosecuted on fifteen counts of murder. Well, at least negligent homicide."

Suzie Q waddles over and squeezes him. "Mmmm-mmm. See? My Albert's not an idiot. I knew there was a reason I liked you. You smart." Her helmet faceplate bangs into his, and she considers it for a second. "Wait. How are you so sure?"

"Because. Like you said." He points to his helmet. "Smart."

"But *how* sure are you he won't let us die?"

"One hundred percent."

"Then prove it. Prove that he won't take it too far. Take it off. The helmet."

For a moment terror paralyzes me. I like Larson, but how far would he go to make this thing real? Albert's right, of course, there's no way he could let us die. Right? If he couldn't, how close would he let us get? Like poor Claire. She could have died in seconds. Where was her help going to come from? How close to death would he let Albert come? Albert seems to be having the same thought, as his fingers slide up to his helmet tentatively, then back down again.

"A hundred percent, huh. I didn't think so. Tanner was right. You a fool." She kicks some dust up at him. "You off the list. Hear that, Albert? You don't get a piece of Suzie Q ever, got it? Okay, who's really in charge here? Or you folks want Suzie Q to lead the way?"

Aurora pipes up helpfully. "Okay, if you insist, I'll do it. I am the most technical-slash-engineering-slash-sciency-what-ever type in this motley group. Clearly. So everybody, just start putting shit together. Now."

"No. Imma tell you all what to do," Marina says.

"NO. We wait for the team leaders. They're coming."

"No they're not."

"Yes they are."

While the rest of them quibble, I just shake my head, make my way out to one of the lifts, and climb into the cab. *Ahhh.* Just like mine back home. Well, except that this one is electric, not methane, and pristine and perfect, not ancient, grimy, and begging for me to put it out of its misery. I start it up and tap the com. "Available options."

Without any static – *hallelujah!* – the crisp, clear voice speaks. "Destination. System settings. Help. Custom modules. You may speak in natural language, Robin Smith."

Wow. This really is nothing like the Fill City lifts. Natural language. Voice ID. Nice. I mute my com so only the cab can hear me. "Can you, um, heads up display the module layout and instructions for breathable air, and autodrive to the correct palettes?"

"Affirmative." The windshield in front of me lights up with diagrams, animations, and selectable buttons. Impressive. Okay, so Larson left us in the lurch. But he gave us everything we need to survive and complete the task. In my new understanding of fair, that seems fair.

I spend a few minutes familiarizing myself, then drive the lift over to the group.

Aurora barks at me. "Hey Robin. Who said you could take one of those?"

"She's a chaos agent."

"Shut up, Benji."

I lean out of the cab and unmute the com. "Okay, I don't care who's in charge of what. But here's how I see it. We can either spend the next..." I look down at my arm display "... forty-two minutes making noise, then run out of oxygen, then test our *would-Larson-really-kill-us?* theory. Or we can set up the first module, which I *highly, highly* recommend be breathable air, and then we won't have to test the *would-Larson-really-kill-us?* theory. There are four more lifts, I think Mike, Sophia, and Quinn climb into them, I've seen you on the Rovers in the obstacle course, don't worry, they accept natural language instructions. You guys follow me. Albert, you take the lead on the building site, you're not an idiot or a fool, you're the smartest engineer we've got. Aurora-"

Tanner interrupts. "What about the teams? Shouldn't we stick to our teams?"

"Good question. I say let's ask again in forty-two minutes. Everyone okay with that?"

The fourteen souls stranded with me under this dome collectively shrug, which I take as a yes. Aurora approaches my lift. "Hey, bossy pants. Don't call out my name like I'm your subordinate. Who voted you the leader? You don't get to tell me what to do."

"Believe me. I know."

"But if I did want to contribute, if I was to be gracious enough to participate, what should I do?"

I reach into the lift's toolbox and toss her a drill driver. "Start putting shit together."

31

START PUTTING SHIT TOGETHER.

Ten minutes. That's all we have left.

I'm amazed, actually, at how this collection of the worst possible candidates, celebrities and housewives and baristas and salesmen and singers, and a Filler of all people, has almost put together a working B.A.G. – Breathable Air Generator – module. Zach Larson's private engineering team has made something seemingly impossible almost plug and play.

Almost.

"Albert! What's going on with that compressor valve? We need to connect the thermal dissociator over here." Everyone is either fastening something together, lifting something, tapping madly on tablets, or at least running around trying to look busy.

"Hey! This is like putting together a five-thousand-piece puzzle in forty-two minutes. Blindfolded! Give me a second!"

While we wait the eternal seconds for Albert, Aurora turns to me. "Not that I'll retain this, but how the hell does this thing work?"

I take a deep breath. I can barely understand it myself. "Okay. Mars has an atmosphere that's mostly carbon dioxide, and Larson has duplicated that here in the outer dome. We're not in a vacuum, like Albert thought. We're in Mars atmosphere. This thing we're all standing around uses an electrode boundary to liberate an oxygen atom from the atmosphere's CO_2." She raises her hand, but I cut her off. "Don't ask, I have no idea. It just works. But this thermal dissociator has to go here, and then we have to power on and wait five minutes for it to pump enough oxygen into the dome. It's going to be close."

"I knew all that. I was just testing you." She nudges me and grins.

"Hey, can I ask you a question?"

"Sure."

"Have... you been snooping around my room?"

I know it's ballsy to ask, and I don't know what to expect, maybe a look of terror, or an indignant smirk, or for her to slap me. But she just smiles, like I was asking her to pass the salt.

"Why? Do you have something to hide?"

"No."

"Good. Then my answer's the same. No."

I make a mental note: Aurora is way too good at this. I'll have to try another tack.

Albert taps the top of the machine. "Robin. Okay, we're done. Connect the dissociator."

I connect and tighten the unit. "Start it up!"

The unit begins humming, and I look down at my armband. Four minutes of oxygen left. We need five minutes to start up. Crap.

"Okay everybody. Either these suits give us a little extra at the end, or we're going to be holding our breath for about a minute after they run out. Start breathing as shallowly as possible."

I have never seen fifteen people so silent and serious, as we stand facing each other around this huge machine, taking little sips of air, listening to it hum. Sweat is dripping from our foreheads. Every second is grueling.

I remember the night in the armoire, in the back of the truck, not suffocating, but roasting in my own personal oven. There was a moment where I let go, it's such a strange feeling, letting go of your life. I'm having that exact feeling again. It's not such a bad feeling, really. Surrender. It starts off with a relaxing exhalation, then a white light starts to-

"Hey." I feel a slap on my face.

Then I hear a woman's voice. "Well. Don't you look pathetic?"

"Mm... Mom...?"

"Guess again."

I open my eyes.

It's Aurora.

She has my helmet in her hands. Everything else is blue. "I never told you. On Oceana Twelve, I was on the freediving team. I can hold my breath for five minutes. Is there anything *you* haven't told me?"

"You... saved my life..."

"Are you kidding? I saved *everybody's* life. Larson owes me one. A big one. And I better get a zillion Likes for this." She lifts me up to a sitting position, and there we all are, sitting up against the Breathable Air Generator, huddled under a blue tarp, helmets off, groggy. But breathing.

Tanner taps his temple. "Putting that tarp over the output feed, concentrating the oxygen under here, dragging

all of us under? I thought Albert was smart. You're a genius."

"Aww, don't make me blush." She plops down right in the middle of us and lowers her voice. "Listen, I know you're all very woozy, and maybe that's unfair because it works in my favor, but let me ask anyway. Now who do you think should be leader for Stage Two?"

Every finger points at her.

"That's better. Now you..." She lifts me up and my knees threaten to give out.

"Yes, boss?"

She hands me back the drill driver. "Start putting shit together."

32

THE PIT

The light on the B.A.G. turns amber, then green.

Slowly lifting the tarp, we tentatively take our first steps out into the main dome.

We can breathe freely. *Ahhh.*

And then the smell assaults me, punches me in the gut and I fall to my knees, gagging, trying desperately to retain the contents of my stomach.

It's the exact smell I remember, that exact mixture of methane and sulfur. It floods my brain with a memory so real it seems to be happening all over again: our trip to The Pit.

Rock, Scissors and I had grabbed our little bags with egg salad sandwiches and skipped school, and spent the day hiking all the way there. It was the first time we'd ever done something like that, sneaking away without permission. *What a thrill!* We were smart enough, even at nine or ten, to bring refurbished gas masks. You'd think it would look odd to anyone along the way, watching little triplet girls skipping down the street with gas masks on. But Fill City – I know now by comparison with the "real" world – was filled with odd sights like this, so we were hardly noticed.

When we got there, to The Pit, I felt a strange mixture of awe and disappointment. It was certainly gargantuan, a mammoth circular hole in the ground, the largest rotating arm I've ever seen, rotating slowly, ever so slowly, mixing and fermenting the mysterious contents that would become Ferti-Food. But I don't know. I guess I had expected more. Like barely contained wildfires, or that the sludge might sprout tentacles, trying to escape, with a life of its own, or that black clouds, complete with lightning and thunder, would permanently hover over the spot, cursing it forever, like something out of Dante's *Inferno*.

We sat between two trucks, watching the mesmerizing rotation of the arm, all of us suddenly realizing how starving we were. But there was a problem we hadn't worked out ahead of time: how do you eat lunch with a gas mask on? After much debate, we decided it would be possible to quickly unlatch our masks and, while holding our breath, munch a few bites of egg salad, then slip the mask back on, and repeat.

And it worked.

At first.

But we quickly learned that holding your breath and eating were mutually exclusive, you can't really do both, not entirely, and soon the Unadulterated Stench of Hell was penetrating our nostrils and we were running, screaming, vomiting inside and outside our masks, all the way home.

The next time Nana made egg salad, she witnessed a first: we simply wouldn't eat it. None of us. But instead of forcing it down our throats – it was food, after all, a blessing not everyone could afford – she eyed us over, one by one, and seemed to lift the thoughts from our brains, learn our whole illicit story just by observing our quivering lips, watery eyes, suppressed gagging, and fingers pinching our noses closed. Instead, she told us of a family tradition that went back as far as she could remember, that each child was allowed one food they weren't required to eat, a single choice, and without hesitation we shouted together, "Egg salad!" and we never saw it again. Side note: if Dad ever wondered why egg salad disappeared off the family menu forever, he didn't let on. I suspect he didn't like it to begin with and was glad for the reprieve.

"Whoa. Robin. You okay?"

"Yeah. Thanks Benji. Just remembering something."

"Looks like a fond memory. Here, grab my hand, get up. I think we need your help with Dear Leader."

"You don't smell that?"

"What?"

I sniff. "That."

"Um. I guess it's faintly funky. Not really. Listen, we've got bigger problems."

Aurora is barking vague orders, but it's leading to lots of aimless shuffling and not much else. I take a few deep breaths, forcing myself to acclimate to the aroma (that no one else seems to have a problem with?), and sidle up behind her, whispering, "Shelter domes."

She swirls around, annoyed.

I whisper again. "Fun Mars fact: it's comfortable now, during the day, but tonight, if Larson has created a proper simulation, it'll go down to minus a hundred degrees."

Still annoyed. "And you know that how? Oh, that's right. You're a nerd. So?"

"So... the shelter domes are the only structures with heat."

She turns back to the others. "Okay, I've decided. Shelter domes first. Everybody knows that, come on, people! Now on the double! And stick with your teammates. The board is back."

I look up, shielding my eyes from the sun, and yes, The Big Board has returned, this time as a digital display on the inside of the dome, maybe fifteen feet above our heads. Four teams remain: Red, Green, Yellow, and Orange. Our points and Likes have been reset to zero, but it appears we've each been given ten points for our communal effort at staying alive. And Aurora now leads the Likes, not surprisingly, by a wide margin. "So, Albert. You still think Larson would've saved us? Albert? Hey, where's Albert?"

"He's over there."

Off about twenty-five yards, near where we came in, sits Albert, rocking back and forth, knees tucked up against his chest, leaning against the interior wall of the dome. He's got a neighbor, too, Avery Jacobs, it's almost cute how they're rocking in rhythm, except that it's obvious they're shell-shocked. Avery even has a little drool hanging from her lip.

Slowly I approach, and sit between them. Sniff the air. "Hey. You guys smell that?"

Silence.

"Albert. Come on. Talk."

"A little funky. Not bad. Listen, I'm done. I'm tapping out."

"You can't do that."

"Shit, yes, I can do that. Stage One was fun. This? Larson is a freaking lunatic. I was wrong. He doesn't care if we die. I think he might even want some of us to die."

I rest my hand on his shoulder and laugh. "No. You were right the first time. He's not going to let us die. I think he knew Aurora had that trick in her back pocket."

"How?"

"It's Larson. I don't know. But he's not an idiot. Or a negligent homicide-er. I think we're safe. We have to trust that he knows our limits and how far to push. We have to trust each other, the stuff we don't know about each other, things that will help when we don't expect it."

"That sounds like a load of horse shit."

And actually, even as it was coming out of my mouth, I thought it sounded a little fecal, too.

"Agreed. But listen. What makes better TV? Safe and sound, or life and death? Fake danger, or real danger? Or at least *perceived* real danger?"

He nods.

"Good. So are you going to let a little danger keep you from chasing the most amazing adventure in the history of our species?"

"Yes."

"Come on. You really going to just sit here until Stage Two is over?"

He hesitates. "Yes."

"Ugh. How about if you come back I'll set you up with Suzie Q over there. She's obviously got it bad for you."

"How about I'll come back if you promise to *never ever* do that. In fact, if you promise to keep her away from me maybe I'll come back. Far away. I'm serious."

"Deal." I extend my hand. He hesitates again. Finally shakes on it. "Great, Albert. Now help me with Avery."

We get up and dust ourselves off, Albert's still a little shaky, and we reach down for Avery's arms. She jerks them away. "Nnn... nnnn... nnn..."

I look into her eyes. She's somewhere really far off. "Avery? You in there?"

Her hollow stare is my answer. And she's blowing little snot bubbles. I think that's a bad sign.

Aurora's suddenly at my side. "What gives?"

"Avery. She's toast."

Aurora steps back, looks up and around. "Hey. Larson. I know you're watching. We've got a casualty. Come and get her."

Nothing. No response.

"Didn't think so. Well, one less contestant to worry about when it hits a hundred below tonight."

I punch her in the arm. "You don't mean that."

"Try me."

I ignore her. "Okay. Albert, we'll leave her here for the moment, construct the MedBay dome first, and come back and move her in."

For a traditional shelter, you'd build the structure first, then fill it with utilities and furniture. For the MedBay, the process is reversed: first we assemble the interior – medical scanning equipment, heating unit, water, the connection to the CPU for the membrane – and then we build the structure outside it all. Well, we don't build the outside, exactly. It's printed – we just set up the printing unit. It's an incredible sight, watching the unit roll in ever-higher circles, painting the air with clear, I don't know, plastic? Gel? It's like watching an igloo being built, but by a robot. On Mars. And not of ice. Okay, it looks nothing like an igloo being built. Anyway, if you look close, you can see just a hint of circuitry running throughout the material. No superstructure. Just the simple parabolic shape, the surface tension holding it together, and the combined outside and inside pressure maintaining the shape and the thickness. The size of a large camping tent, this dome looks just as flimsy. But when I put my weight against it, I'm amazed at its strength – like a soap bubble made out of clear titanium.

While I lean against it, I tap through the manual for a little more on this miracle substance and, more important, how we're supposed to enter. It's called PPMM – Powered Polymer Matrix Membrane – actually a weave of clear nano-threads, some carrying electric current, some carrying information, all held together with powered van der Waals forces, the same molecular attraction that allows geckos to stick to glass. Larson is calling the PPMM in his manuals a "smart surface," allowing things to exit or enter based on instructions to the CPU, down to the molecular level, and intelligently healing itself after something – like a human body – breaches its surface.

Benji knocks on the surface. "Okay, so how do we get in? Do I clap twice?" *Clap clap.* "Open sesame."

"No, wait... oh yes, over there at the bottom. Tap that little red light with your foot. But not ye-"

He taps it, and before I can complete, "yet!" the light turns green and I fall through the membrane onto my back.

"Thanks."

The teams get faster with each dome, and we manage to complete the four sleep shelter domes and two backup domes before uncontrollable shivers tell us it's time to quit and get warm. We're exhausted, happy to call it an early night and get a cozy twelve hours of zees.

But it doesn't exactly go that way.

I don't know if it's one of Larson's little tricks, or if there's something wonky with the domes, or if it takes time for the thermostats to regulate, but the temperature is swinging wildly, from oppressively hot to ice cold every couple of hours, so our entire night is an awkward group dance of stripping down to our underwear, then bundling up into our spacesuits and blankets, and repeating the process.

To make matters worse, the digital privacy screening built into the PPMMs is acting up too, so more than once we find ourselves staring at the other teams, and them at us, in the middle of taking our clothes off, or tripping over each other, or relieving ourselves in the outhouse dome.

"*Psst.* Hey Robin, where's Mike?"

"Go to sleep, Benji. He's in the outhouse."

"I was just there. He's not there."

"So? What are you, his nanny? Go to sleep."

On cue, the privacy screening glitches out again, and our domes are perfectly clear.

"Oh, wait. I found him."

"Good for yo- oh my God."

At the end of the two rows of sleep domes, in plain view of all teams, is Mike Horner, on a cot in one of the backup domes, in his birthday suit.

With Marina Delacosta.

Benji laughs. "Either the thermostat in there is on its blistering hot phase, or they're..."

"Do they not know we can see them?"

"I think they're a little preoccupied."

Claire holds her fingers up to her eyes. "I shouldn't look." She spreads her fingers just a little. Just enough.

"God, look at their Likes." A quick glance at The Big Board shows Mike and Marina's numbers growing fast, so fast they look like they're going to burn a hole in the PPMM.

Maybe they noticed the numbers animating, or more likely felt the eyes of thirteen contestants on them, and heard somehow, even through the soundproof domes, our laughter and shouts, because they suddenly look up, scramble for a sheet, and cover themselves, like an ostrich with its head in the sand, hoping no one notices the two-body-shaped lump on a cot in one of the backup domes.

I look over to the MedBay, and wouldn't you know, even Avery is giggling.

Silver lining.

A few minutes later, Mike retreats to our dome. "Stupid privacy screening. Dammit. How much did you guys see?"

Benji yawns. "What are you talking about? Were you gone?"

I yawn too. "Yeah, Mike, be quiet. We're trying to sleep."

Mike harrumphs. "Wait. Come on. Really? You didn't see? Did everyone miss that?"

"Missed what? Go to bed. You're a pain in the ass."

"Huh." So Mike, a little more relaxed now, climbs back into his little cot, clearly relieved.

A minute or two later, just before Mike nods off to sleep, Claire whispers into his ear and pokes his rear.

"Nice tattoo."

33

BEETS

"Beets!"

The rest of us are trying our hardest not to talk about Mike and Marina's little tryst last night, but Tanner Byron couldn't care less, he's sincerely freaking out about three young beet plants he found in among the food generation supplies. "Beets!" He hands one to Claire.

"Beets? Oh. I thought you said butts. As in, 'I was thinking of getting a tattoo on my butt.'"

"Shut up, Claire." Mike is digging through the next crate, soybeans. But he's got a little smile on, he's trying not to show it but it's there, and Marina marches right into the farming dome and plants a wet one on him. "Attention, fellow contestants. You know what? I-a don't care. You saw what you saw. Issa not a secret anymore. I am between relationship, have no children, as is Michael, so there issa no problem. You gotta problem, speak to my fist. I mean, speak to me first. And there is no rule against any of this. Is there, Robin?"

Oh, great. I guess I'm the expert on rules now, or lack of

rules, having trashed them on the last round and made up my own. Robin "Rule Breaker" Smith. Wonderful. "Do what you want. I don't care. But can you leave now? We've got two weeks to plant and successfully grow this stuff. Red and Yellow teams only. You're supposed to be out there setting up the terraforming experiment. Go. Away. Vamoose."

"Vamoose? Is not Italian. You trying to speak Italian?"

"No. It's just something my Nana says."

"Aww. That's a cute." She pecks me on the cheek, then grabs Mike by the collar and pulls him up into an embrace that would make a stripper blush. He sighs – I am not exaggerating – like a damsel in an old movie, and falls into her kiss. She leaves. Dramatically. (Is there any other way?)

Suzie Q harrumphs. "You think Albert got that in him? Pull a girl into his arms like that?"

"What are we growing in here, mistletoe?" Claire says.

Tanner laughs. "It's the *wa* and the *ma*."

"You smokin' them beet leaves, Tanner?"

"No, I lived in Japan for a number of years. Their perception of spaces is much different. To them, a space itself can foster relationships and affect interactions. The *wa* and the *ma*. In this case, they would say 'Confinement brings us closer.'"

Claire smirks. "That sounds like an ad for a prison."

"Ha! No, it's true. This space is forcing us to confront each other closely, in almost primitive ways, like cave dwellers, and I suppose that's stimulating some *amore*. I wouldn't be surprised if we see more of that kind of activity in the coming days. And beets, they're high in nitrates you know, they help vasodilation, increased blood flow to the-"

"Enough, enough. You're driving me crazy, beet man."

Claire swats him with both hands, and waves them in front of her face like she's having a hot flash. "Back to work."

And so we carry on setting up the hydroponics, and the aeroponics, hanging our little plants delicately from their harnesses, and as I mix the Martian soil blend for the traditional ground farming tests, I can't get it out of my head: *confinement brings us closer.* Tanner, kneeling next to me, smiles and inserts a beet plant into the hole I've just dug. I lower my voice. "Hey Tanner. Did you live in a confined space in Japan?"

"Yes, with a family in Tokyo. It was fascinating. I found these families who live in very small spaces to be extremely close, fiercely loyal. Each member feels less an individual, and more an extension of a larger unit. They form very strong bonds. I imagine it must be quite the opposite for you, living alone on a large farm."

"Um, yeah."

He notices a tear appearing on my cheek, wipes it away. "Sorry. You miss home?"

I draw in a sharp breath. "No." Then, "I don't know."

I'm having that longing again. I can hardly bear it, I want to reach out and embrace my sisters, and Dad, and Nana, and never let them go. Take them with me to my home on Mars. Build a little confined space for us up there, a little place to grow our own food, and make our own air, and, and... be free.

Someday.

Claire was joking about the mistletoe, and who knows if Tanner ever really learned anything about Japanese philosophy, but they both wind up being right. Over the next week, as we tend to our farm and experiments, the tight living arrangements and close work quarters seem to be having a hormonal effect on some of the contestants. Not me, thank God. I'm just enjoying the steady pace of progress, lack of emergencies, and-

"Robin! Emergency!"

34

HAMBURGER

"Hey boss. What's u– eewww…" A quick glance behind Aurora tells me everything I need to know: Jayden, the really quiet one on the Orange team, has his arm pinned in one of the gears on the mining excavator-feeder that grinds anything we dig up into analyzable powder. I can't see beyond the gear, there's blood mixed with the drill lubricant all over the place, so there could be a whole lower arm and hand in there, salvageable, or it could be a couple of pounds of ground meat. My bet is ground meat.

Aurora leans into my ear, whispers. "Look. You know I'm faking this whole thing. But Jayden's hurt. Bad. I can't fake this shit. Everyone's flipping out. Help?"

She's right about the flipping out. It's like a coop full of chickens just saw a fox stroll in.

"Okay. Everyone calm down. Nana's right: Calm down. Solve the problem."

"Nana?"

"Sorry. Something she says. Albert, give me the brief."

"I- I- Nnn-"

"Oh, boy. Okay, Lucy, give me the brief."

"The feeder was jammed with a rock. Jayden stopped it, reached in, but somehow it turned back on. We stopped it immediately, but his hand got sucked in."

Claire faints. One down.

"You couldn't reverse it?"

"The reverse shorted out I think. Won't work."

"Will it turn forward?"

Jayden shouts, "You want to turn it forward? My arm is in there!"

"Listen. If it's like a broken lift, we can trick it into thinking it's going forward, even though the gear is turning backward. Does it have an audible interface?"

"No, Visual only. Panel-based."

"Crap." I move to face the input panel. "Okay. Settings... good. There's a command line option. Albert, you think you can dig into the settings deep enough, search for gear rotation?"

"Nnn..."

"Albert! Snap out of it man. I need you. Can you do it?"

"I... can try."

"You better."

I turn to Jayden. "How are you holding up, buddy?"

He spits out through his teeth, "My arm is in the mining feeder. Is that a rhetorical question?"

"Now, if this works, Jayden, your arm's going to come out the way it went in, and that's not all good news. Right now the gear is so clamped down on you it's stanching any bleeding. But as soon as you're free you're probably going to go off like a geyser." Sophia faints. Two down. "We'll tourniquet at your shoulder, that'll help, but just letting you know."

"Thanks?"

"You're welcome. Would you rather be awake or asleep?"

"Another rhetorical question."

"Okay, Aurora, go into the MedBay, find the propofol. Get it and a syringe, stat."

"Stat?"

"I watch a lot of TV. Go."

Albert calls from the other side. "Got it. Found the line of code. I think."

"Good. Can you set the forward rotation to a negative number?"

"I think."

"Don't think. Just do. On my count, commit the edit and recompile."

Albert nods.

"Five."

Lucy faints. Three down.

"Four."

Aurora jabs Jayden with the needle. He's out in an instant.

"Three."

I put my arms under Jayden's shoulder. Aurora supports his other shoulder.

"Two."

Benji runs over and kicks the MedBay dome open for us. Avery jumps off the bed and cowers by a cabinet.

"One."

Albert stutters, "On one, or on go?"

"Just go!"

Albert commits, the machine thinks for a moment, and then the gear grinds backward. We pull Jayden out in a spray of blood.

Albert faints. Four down.

I pause, for just a millisecond, to admire the human body.

It's an amazing machine, and actually much more flexible and resilient than we think. Take Jayden's arm, for example. To look at that mining gear, you'd expect hamburger to come spitting back out. But the whole arm, in one piece, reappears. It's broken in – oh God – at least fifteen places, and there's so much blood I can't see where the cuts are, but it's whole. Amazing.

I pull the tourniquet even tighter and we haul ass to the MedBay dome, plop him on the table, and the miracle machine goes to work – immediately sucking his arm into a sleeve, like a balloon around the whole thing, but clear, so we can watch it washing his wounds, stitching his lacerations, setting his bones, waving the wand thing, re-infusing him with his own lost blood.

"Whew."

Aurora looks down at our shirts, covered in blood and drill lubricant. "That is *not* gonna come out." And we start laughing, and share a hug, and then start crying, releasing all the freakout that had bottled up inside us. "Thanks, Robin."

"Don't thank me, Aurora. Thank this miracle machine."

In answer, the machine beeps. "Chance of full recovery. Ninety-nine-point-three percent. Time to recovery. Eighteen days."

"See? What *can't* this thing do?"

The machine beeps again. "Update. There seems to be a problem."

"Oh, for Christ's sake. It was a rhetorical question."

Another beep. "Mister Jayden Freid is showing signs of epileptic seizure and cardiac arrest."

Jayden's body is convulsing. "MedBay – do something!"

"Negative. Mobile MedBay not equipped for arrhythmias caused by temporal lobe epilepsy, as this condition is present only in point-zero-two percent of humans, and not included on Mister Jayden Freid's medical report. Please schedule immediate transfer to full MedBay facility."

"Transfer?!"

"Yes."

"We can't do that! We're in a freaking dome! In the middle of nowhere!" Think. Think. Think. I look around at the faces staring at Aurora and me. What the hell are we going to do? Who knows even the slightest thing about MedBays? Albert? Sophia? Tanner? Benji?

Wait. Benji.

"Benji. Your phone! Give me your phone!"

"What phone? Me? We're not allowed phones. Remember, zero access. I don't have a-"

"No time! The phone from the bus!"

Benji runs back to our shelter dome, reaches under his cot, pulls out a pair of underwear, and tucked inside is the phone. He dashes back and hands it to me.

"Gross, Benji."

"You want the phone or not?"

"Ick. It smells. I'm not kidding." I tap out a number. "Uh, hello?"

"Good afternoon. Groupie Studios. How may I direct your call?"

"Zach Larson."

The woman on the other end tries not to, but she chuckles. "Is there a department you'd like to be directed to?"

"Zach Larson. Now."

"I can take a message."

"Put him on. Now!"

"I'm sorry. Mr. Larson has a staff-"

"It's Robin Smith. You got a TV there? Look at it right now."

I'm giving the finger to the Big Board, assuming there's a camera up there. "See that? That's me, talking to you, live, in front of a billion people."

"I'll put him on."

"Thank you."

Larson's on the line faster than a bolt of lightning. "How did you get a phone in there?"

"That's your first question?! We've got a little problem, Zach!"

Aurora nudges me. "Gee, you guys are on a first name basis?"

"He told me to call him Za- it doesn't matter! Zach, Jayden's in trouble!"

"I have eyes."

"Then DO something!"

Before I even finish saying the words, four people, at least I think they're people, they're in head-to-toe white quarantine suits, push past me. They grab the top of the MedBay bed and silently, perfectly, rush in unison out of the MedBay and out of sight with Jayden, toward the other, larger dome, without a word.

Avery Jacobs calls after them. "Hey! What about me?"

A fifth quarantine suit guy, who I hadn't even noticed, turns to her. Shrugs.

Wait. The phone. I hear Larson's voice. "Robin. Are you still there?"

"Y- y- yes?"

"This call was unnecessary. Do you really think I would let you die?"

The fifth suit guy puts his hand out, wordlessly but clearly demanding the phone. I hand it over. And as he grabs the phone from my hand and snaps it in two, in that moment before it dies, I faintly hear Larson's voice:

"Strike two."

35

YOU'RE PLAYING WITH FIRE.

"What the hell was that?"

Aurora's pacing, furious. It's just her and me, she demanded we be alone in the MedBay. Even Avery is gone. Aurora is scary when she's angry. Why am I even in here?

"Aurora, Larson didn't know."

"Didn't know what?"

"The temporal lobe epilepsy or whatever it's called. It wasn't on Jayden's medical report. He either lied, or nobody caught it. Larson didn't know. Couldn't have anticipated it. He anticipates everything."

"Look at you, advocating for Larson. Whatever. It's good to know our saviors in white suits are right next door, but he's still playing with our lives. That's bullshit. This is supposed to be fun. You know, 'fun, fun, fun'?"

"I hear you, Aurora. But this is serious training. Think about it: one of us is going to Mars. Not winning a recording contract."

She glares. "Low blow, Smith. If that's even your last name."

I take a step back. "What the hell is that supposed to mean?"

"Nothing. Whatever."

"Okay, listen, obviously we're stressed, close quarters and near-death experiences and all."

"And Avery. She annoys the shit out of me. Have I told you that?"

"A bunch of times. Hey, where is she?"

"Over there. Banging on the wall nearest the other dome. Trying to get them to rescue her. You better go get her."

As I head out, I put my hand on her shoulder. "Hey. I'm sorry. Are we okay?"

"Whatever. I guess. Sure." Then she looks right through me. "I just really don't like being played with. Like, *really*. You're playing with fire if you're playing with Aurora."

Oh, God. I have to tell her the truth. Now. Her eyes are burning holes into my soul.

No. Wait. Let her calm down first. Later. I'll tell her later. After I get Avery.

By the time I reach Avery, her palms are red from slapping them feebly against the dome's wall. "Please... please... come back..."

"Avery. There's nothing wrong with you. They're not coming back. It's time to come home."

"I'm tapping out. Please."

"I don't think you get to tap out on this stage. We're stuck with each other for the next five days, unless you want to get your arm stuck in a mining machine. But don't get any ideas. Forget I said that. Come on." I take her hand and lead her back to MedBay. On the way she trips and falls. "Avery, come on. You're making this harder than it needs to b-"

Huh. She tripped on a wrench. Who's leaving wrenches

laying around? This isn't like we're in some ramshackle shed out back of Nana's trailer with two-bit tools lying wherever. This wrench alone probably cost a thousand credits, and every single screw has been accounted for. Hmm. But I guess we're just regular people, like the kid who forgets her drink overnight on the dresser, leaving a nice, permanent moisture ring in the wood and nearly giving Dad a coronary (in case it wasn't obvious, I'm that kid). I pick the wrench and Avery up and head back to MedBay.

36

SECRET WEAPON

Aside from almost dying of oxygen depletion, and watching Jayden be devoured by a mining machine, and occasionally wiping drool from Avery's lip, I'm really enjoying this stage. I wouldn't say that out loud, of course, as some of the contestants clearly have the *what-the-hell-have-I-gotten-myself-into?* face on pretty much all the time now. I wouldn't be surprised if some of them volunteer off the show after this stage. Avery being first in line, of course.

Not me. I'm actually getting my nerd on learning about farming on Mars. For example: did you know that Martian soil has all the macro- and micronutrients needed to support plant growth, including nitrogen, calcium, iron, even boron? And there could be a limitless water supply? Regions of ice stretch across Mars, some of it just below the surface, waiting to be converted to liquid water. And the beets? Boy, Tanner could tell you more than you ever need or want to know about beets on Mars.

Aurora also seems to be enjoying herself. After her *I'm-going-to-kill-Larson* moment, she threw herself into the work, channeling her rage into an impressive terraforming experiment. In a separate sub-dome, she and her team added enough gases to warm up a large patch of ice, melting it and releasing its carbon dioxide, further heating up and thickening the atmosphere in the sub-dome, creating a cycle of warming. Then they introduced microbes to see which ones could survive and synthesize the chemicals necessary to support life. It's just an experiment, but an incredible peek into what we might be able to do up there on the Red Planet.

"So Aurora, you're into microbes now, huh?"

"Don't tell anyone. And I won't tell anyone how much you like beets."

"Deal."

"Anyway, it's really the *telling-other-people-what-to-do* part that I like."

"I see that."

"And the winning."

"Hey. You haven't won yet."

She laughs and points over at the mining machine. "Come on. Orange team's done, they're still cleaning Jayden's blood off the mining unit. They haven't scored a point in days. And you guys, Red and Yellow? Soybeans and potatoes? Be still my heart."

"We've got a secret weapon."

"Who? Benji? Your string beans are more impressive than Benji."

"No. You'll see."

37

THIS IS GOING TO BE SOME FINALE.

The end of the third week. I've grown accustomed to the smell that no one else seemed to notice in the first place. Our veggies have flourished and grown enough to get us points on the Big Board tonight. No one else has been hurt, the thermostats have been regulating just fine, and the privacy screening – thankfully – has shielded us from each other's less sharable activities. I find myself whistling as we approach the large table and chairs out in the open, next to the MedBay. It's the finale of Stage Two, and as Aurora said, I think it's a good bet that we're safe, and that the poor Orange Team is going home: Jayden (who I assume is alive but I have no idea), and Lucy and the silent one, I think her name is Emma (the only truly intact members of Orange Team).

Aurora greets me. "I didn't even know you could whistle. Hey, you want a guest appearance on *Rocket Girl?* I could write you in a whistling part."

I sit down next to Aurora and whisper back. "Sure. But you'll have to wait for me here on Earth until I get back from Mars."

She laughs. "We'll see who's waiting for who, Nerd Girl."

The table has been set for a feast. As part of the instructions for the farming teams, we were to prepare a meal for everyone during the finale. I, of course, insisted I be left out of the cooking – I would have gotten us even less points than Orange Team. Instead, behind me marches in the rest of the Red and Yellow teams, each holding a steaming platter. And bringing up the rear, Suzie Q.

"Psst. Look. Our secret weapon."

Aurora smirks. "Ha! Her? You think she'll get you more- oh my God. Food."

At Suzie Q's command, the teams unveil their platters, and the air around us is filled with the aromas of real, actual, honest-to-goodness food. Delicious-looking food. Pesto with gnocchi. Mushroom risotto with kale. Roasted fingerling potatoes, cauliflower, and – you guessed it – beets. It turns out Suzie Q, in a previous life, was a cook at a busy hole-in-the-wall barbecue joint for years down in her native Alabama, cooking recipes handed down for generations and making up her own. Benji opens a bin we found in the food stores but hadn't told the others about, a surprise left by Zach Larson. He lifts out four bottles of wine. Then four more.

"Wine!"

"To the chef!"

Suzie Q takes a deep bow while the contestant rush to fill their glasses and taste their first alcohol in weeks. "You're welcome, folks. See, barbecue is my thing, don't do vegan, it's like a curse word where I come from, but I made do. Thank God for the spices and cheese they left us. Put allota love in these here. Whatcha all think?"

The entire table, including Avery, rises in a standing

ovation. Albert raises his glass in a toast. "To Suzie Q. Our savior!"

Really, Suzie Q could've put anything in front of them in place of protein bars and food paste we've been eating here, or that mysterious food-like stuff they've been feeding us back at the studio, she could plop a big bowl of boiled potatoes and a salt shaker down, and they would've cheered like she scored a touchdown in the Super Bowl. But she really has outdone herself, and I even find Albert sneaking a little wink and a nod over in her direction. She bats her eyelashes.

Oh boy, this is going to be some finale.

We finish eating, every crumb of Suzie Q's apple crisp, and waddle, buzzed, over to the terraform dome for Aurora's presentation. Mike and Marina hold hands, of course, are their hands ever *not* intertwined now? And Suzie Q sidles up to Albert, and he doesn't step away this time. I wonder if this is what it felt like to be at the old drive-in movies. I suddenly feel the space next to me extremely empty.

Aurora, now in her spacesuit, flips her hair a little, locks her helmet in place, steps into the terraforming dome, and begins her show. "In 1836, Charles Darwin visited Ascension Island, a barren volcanic outgrowth between South America and Africa, and vowed to create a lush preserve. Through trial and error, new plants took hold, and eventually, now two hundred and fifty years later, Ascension Island is a paradise, a beautiful, cloudy forest."

She spreads her arms, and a light shines on a little seedling, barely an inch tall, next to a small pool of water, in a sub-dome in the middle, maybe three feet diameter by three feet high. "In just three weeks, we were able to alter the gas content in this sub-dome, and create a stable, oxygen-rich environment. Enough to grow this teeny-weeny plant." She locks her legs straight and starts to sing:

> *Life, from nothing / From just the hope*
> *Of a few driven people / Who believed*
> *Precarious, fragile / Just like us*
> *On hope and faith conceived*

For a moment, the competition slips away, and we look around at each other, and I think we'd all like to go to Mars together. I'd even take Avery with us.

"Hey. So where are the points?"

Huh. Benji's right. Up above, the Big Board is clicking away with the Likes, but the points have stalled for days. "Isn't this it? Isn't the stage over?"

In answer, as Aurora finishes her song, the Board flashes a note across its top: *Please return to the dining table, and each contestant retrieve a tablet.*

So we make our way back and sit around the big table. Aurora unclicks her helmet and plops it among the dirty plates. Claire motions to the mess. "Maybe we're supposed to do the dishes first?"

But our tablets wake up and sync, and Zach Larson's voice fills the dome: "Congratulations! You've completed your tasks. Ah, with the notable exception of the mining team. You'll be happy to know Jayden is recuperating nicely, and Avery, dear, we've been watching you closely, and the good news is you're fine. Apparently the experts are fairly certain you're faking it."

Avery slumps in her chair and scowls. "Pffft!"

"In any case, someone asked about points. For Stage Two, we're going to do something a little different." A list of all the other contestants appears on my tablet. "You're going to give points... to each other."

We peer around at each other. So much for the camaraderie we were feeling a minute ago. This is war. First, we'll give ourselves and own team members the highest scores-

Larson interrupts my thought. "I know what you're thinking. But you're only allowed to award points to contestants on other teams."

Hmmm. What to do? Aurora, for example: I should give her a zero, right? She's clearly the strongest contestant, a far cry from the drunk singer I thought she was, and what she lacks in technical know-how she more than makes up for in sheer competitive tenacity. If I'm going to Mars, she's the one to get rid of. If everyone else is thinking the same thing, there's a chance...

Wait! Listen to me! What's happening to me? Yes, I would do anything to get on this mission, but... anything?

No.

I will not cheat. Yes, it's true, I kind of made up my own rules in Stage One. But... I don't know, I was lifting someone up then. Literally lifting Claire's ass up that rock. It felt like I was giving. This time I would be dragging someone down. Taking. It's a fine line, but whatever. This doesn't feel right.

I give Aurora the maximum twenty points. She deserves it.

We sit in silence, tapping away, watching the tallies on the Big Board. It doesn't take long, but it feels like forever. Regardless of our performance, contestants could, at least theoretically, send any team home. But as the numbers slow down, then stop, it's clear everyone's been basically objective, and there are no surprises.

Except one.

38

SECOND PLACE

I have to look twice at the board. To make sure my eyes are
working.

I have two hundred ten points. I'm in the lead.

Aurora has two hundred three.

I beat her.

It doesn't matter, really, both our teams, Red and Green,
as well as Yellow, will advance to Stage Three. Poor Orange
Team, as expected, will go home. And Sophia got the fewest
Likes, so she can now build that doghouse for her ungrateful
husband. But I let out a little yelp of excitement anyway. I
can't help it. Aurora glares at me. She's fuming. "But- but- I
sang to you guys!" She's up now, pacing back and forth,
pointing everywhere. "She... dug some holes in the ground!
Big deal!"

Benji raises his hands. "Whoa. You dug holes, too. And
what's the difference? Both our teams made it. Calm down,
Aurora."

"Calm down? I'll tell you what the difference is. I saved
your lives!"

"What's wrong with you, Aurora? You came in second place. Big deal."

Uh-oh.

He said the words. *Second place.* This is bad. Very bad.

I have just put Aurora, runner-up on *America Sings*, into *second place.* For the second time in her life. I cringe as Mike opens his mouth. "Listen, Aurora, you're awesome, and you're both into the next stage, but just for the sake of argument, between just the two of you, who do you think is more qualified for this Mars mission? Robin, whose hobby is rockets, or you – a singer?"

Aurora looks like she just got kicked in the stomach. And then a rage rises in her face, a blistering rage I haven't seen yet.

Oh no.

"*Robin?!* You think that's her real name?"

Yup. Here we go.

Benji jumps out of his chair to my defense. Admirable. "Yes! Robin! What the hell are you talking about?"

Admirable, yes, but I already know it's too late. Aurora reaches into a pocket of her suit, and I'm not surprised when I see the photo of myself, surrounded by my family. *Greetings from Fill City One! Wish you were here!* She shoves it in my face, then slowly turns so each person and the cameras can see clearly. "Robin Smith? Really?"

It is done.

Shock on each of their faces. "You're... a Filler?"

I can't speak. I can't breathe. Tears stream down my face. I look up at Aurora. "...why?..."

She stares down at me with a strange expression, filled with rage and pity and... something else. She's holding herself back from crying. "You lied to me... I gave you so many chances to come clean... I wanted you to... I begged you to... do you have any idea how many times I've been lied to?"

"I'm so sorry. I just needed to escape. Like you."

"We could've... I... loved you."

And then the lights go out.

39

LIKE A SISTER, YOU IDIOTS!

I n the dark there are gasps and murmurs, and I think I
hear Claire stifle a giggle.

Aurora pounds her helmet on the table. "Like a *sister*, you
idiots! I loved her like a *sister*! What's wrong with you people?
Is that all you can think about in here? You know you can
love someone like that, without getting all hormonal, for
crying out loud. God. Now will somebody turn on the damn
lights?"

I'm numb, closing my eyes against the reality of what just
happened, but I sense people scrambling for flashlights,
heading for the CPU to find out what's going on.

I just sit there, alone, paralyzed, in the blackness. I can't
remember anything ever feeling this dark, maybe before I
was born, in my mother's womb. Before I started.

And now I'm over already.

I'm going deep into the fill. There's no way the Gitanos
will let me live after this. Daring to break their cardinal law in
front of the entire world.

Aurora just signed my death sentence.

I hear a sniffle. I open my eyes. It's her. I'm not alone. She's still here.

"I'm a dead woman, Aurora."

The sniffle stops.

"Yes, I lied to you Aurora. I lied to everyone. I had to change my name, my whole story, just to make it here. Do you know what the Gitanos do to people like me?"

"Gitanos. Don't know who you're talking about. Is that another lie?"

"The people who control Fill City. You step out of line like this, they make you disappear. Gone. Into the fill. So thanks for that."

"Don't try to turn this around on me. You should have told me the truth."

"I wanted to. I almost did, many times. You should know that, somewhere inside you I think you do. I don't like lying. Lying isn't who I am."

"Really. Then who are you?"

"I'm..." But I have no answer. I've come so far, been reborn into something new... but what? Am I still me, Paper Farris? Am I still a Filler? Or am I someone that's grown comfortable putting on a mask, the mask of Robin Smith? Or am I somewhere in the middle, like my hair now, bleach blonde tips and dark brown roots?

Who the hell am I?

I don't have time to answer. Mike and Albert rush back. "Something's up. And it's not just us. It's the main dome."

We rush over to see our team leaders, and more of those quarantine suit guys, wildly waving their arms from behind the wall of the main dome, about ten yards away. What the heck? Where were all these people hiding? It's like a clown car over there.

And then from behind them emerges a man with a message on a tablet.

It's Zach Larson.

He presses the tablet against the wall, and its message reads: *Put your spacesuits on. Now.*

40

SABOTAGE

I pick up a tablet to write back, and Aurora grabs it from me. "No. Let me."

She taps out: *What the fuck, Larson? Is this another one of your tricks?*

Larson does not smile, or chuckle, or roll his eyes. He's dead serious. I've never seen him with that look on his fa- *wait.* "What the hell is Larson doing in that dome?"

"I guess he's been living in there for three weeks, spying on us and waiting for us to kill or maim ourselves – which we did – so he could play God. Yeah, I'm talking about you, Larson. Are you hearing this, Larson?" She taps the wall.

He shakes his head. His tablet reads: *No com link. No power. No tricks. Put on your suits.*

Why?

PPMM reversed in both domes. Losing air fast.

Shut it down.

Can't. Locked out.

Aurora taps furiously. *Locked out? Shut it ALL down! YOU made this, idiot!* She jabs a finger at him twice for emphasis.

Larson hangs his head. Taps out one more message: *Sabotage.*

Holy shit.

That single word sends us all back to being a coop full of freaked-out chickens, falling over each other to rush back to our shelter domes to get our spacesuits and an extra hour of oxygen.

But I can't get into my dome.

I shout across to the others. "Hey! Can anyone get in?"

"No!"

It's pitch black, we have no power, our oxygen is running out – again, that's twice but who's counting – we can't get to our spacesuits, and the very last thing the viewers around the world saw before their TVs went blank was Aurora exposing me as a Filler.

This finale could be going slightly better.

We run back to the wall and I tap a message: *Power out. Why domes still active and not letting us in?*

Larson, now in full suit with helmet, types back: *PPMM like inertial drive – without power, retains current state indefinitely for safety. Someone reversed airflow, then cut power. Backup generators cut too. We're locked out. Put on suits!*

Can't! Suits in shelter domes!

Larson makes another face I haven't seen yet, the *I-can't-believe-I-didn't-think-of-that* face. Apparently in the main dome they had a separate locker or something for their suits, because all of them have theirs on, and they forgot that we kept ours in our shelter domes. Geniuses. The only one with a suit on is Aurora from her terraforming presentation, which decidedly doesn't help the rest of us. Larson turns to Captain

Daniels and a couple of other techs and they debate something.

May be hardware/software intrusion, Larson messages. *A.I. virus. On daughterboard or such. Robin. Can you find it?*

"Wasn't he watching? You're not Robin. Duh."

"Not the time, Aurora!" I tap back, *In the CPU?*

Larson nods.

Albert and Benji and I make our way to the back of the CPU, and I remember: *the wrench.* Someone *was* here! But how did the cameras not see them? How did the CPU not know? I lay down, scooch in under the unit, looking up at the underside of the CPU shell, and sure enough: three bolts missing. The access panel above me is being held in by just one bolt. Whoever did this was in a rush. "Benji! Get me the half inch wrench!"

He's back in an instant. "Albert. Get under here with me." I unbolt the panel, and a world of technology beyond my comprehension stares me in the face. "I have no idea what I'm looking for." Albert points to the rows of mother boards. "If it's a daughterboard, it'll look like a puzzle piece out of place, maybe hanging off by a wire - there!"

He reaches in and touches it lightly. "I'm going to pluck it out."

"Are you telling me that because you hope I have a better idea?"

"I'm getting light-headed."

"Stop talking and take the damn thing out, Albert."

He's right though. My eyes are starting to get a little wonky, and I have to shake my head to clear it. Our air is running out faster than I thought. "Hurry."

"I already did it." He shows me the culprit, a tiny circuit board, yes, about the size of a puzzle piece. "So. Now what?"

I slide back out – hitting my head, because of course – and run, a little woozy now, back to the wall. We hold out the little puzzle piece and shout, "Now what?"

More furious silent debate in the other dome. Then Larson turns to me, and I swear to God... he shrugs. His message: *Thought it might stop the virus.*

"*Thought* it might? You're kidding me!" I grab the tablet from Aurora, for a moment wondering at the coincidence of her being the only one with a suit on, but quickly shaking the thought off. "Aurora. Clip your helmet on, you'll have plenty of air, then grab everyone and do that tarp thing again with the B.A.G. and the outlet vent. If you grab one of the lifts, they have their own power source. You can connect the leads from the battery to the B.A.G. to restore its power at least for a few minutes, you know how, right?" She just stands there, sort of stunned, I guess she doesn't have a snappy sarcastic rageful response ready.

"*You know how, right?!*"

She bolts, shouting at the others and getting the tarp ready.

I type out a message to Larson: *What if I try sudden electric current to PPMM?*

Possible. But PPMM in rigid state. Only letting out oxygen molecules. Nothing else can penetrate.

Nothing, huh? I don't even bother to write back.

He's obviously never seen what lift forks can do at forty miles an hour.

I run over to the nearest lift, thanking God it has its own power. "Wake up."

"How may I help you, Robin Smith?"

I almost laugh. The lift hadn't gotten the memo yet. "Is

there a way to route power into the forks themselves? Electrify them?"

Hesitation. "No."

"Damn."

"I do not know what *damn* means, Robin Smith."

"It means I'm probably going to electrocute myself." I hop out of the cab and rip open the battery panel. It's massive, with several positive and negative leads. Hop back in the cab. "Heads up display the least necessary wiring. I need two lengths, ten feet."

"Least necessary?"

"I don't know. Interior lighting. Anything."

The lift highlights the wiring diagram for the interior lighting. I duck under the dash, prying open the plastic panels, and start ripping wires out. Better hurry. Breathing is getting harder. I can't see straight.

"Robin Smith, that wire was not part of the wiring for..." Silence.

"Whoops." Oh well. No time to get the A.I. back online. I grab a screwdriver and rubber gloves out of the toolbox, go around to the side, attach a wire to each battery lead, then – extremely slowly and delicately – loosen a screw on each fork housing and fasten the wire.

I have created a monster. Anything that touches these forks will be instantly electrocuted.

I smile to myself, because this isn't the first time I've done this exact thing. When we were sixteen or so, Duggie and I were learning about electrostatic induction – well, I was learning about it and Duggie was nodding his head between naps – and we – I – decided to make a lift into a giant capacitor to see if we could light up fluorescent bulbs between the forks. It worked, but it also caused a minor explosion – Fill

City security called it major but no one died or even got hurt, so really? – landing Duggie and me suspension and a month of docked pay, and a forced part time job repairing the lifts for the rest of my life. But it was worth it to see Duggie's yelps of glee and singed eyebrows. I liked to think Nana was actually impressed, because instead of grounding me for fifty years, she just muttered, "Teenagers!" and took away my TV privileges for a week. But *America Sings!* was on that night, we loved watching it together, and she couldn't help herself, and we wound up cheering on Esther Jones into the finals and eating way too much popcorn. Nana can be such a pushover.

Whoa. Focus, Paper. You're getting lightheaded. And don't touch anything metal.

I gingerly climb into the cab, moving the lift into place as far from the point of contact I want as possible. It's not a straight run, and the A.I.'s down, so I can't just send it at full speed and jump out. I'll have to steer this thing until the last moment and try to make a dramatic leap to safety. Or die. I'm probably going to die.

I punch the dash to maximum, and the lift builds up to twenty, thirty, then forty miles an hour. I only have seconds to say a silent prayer before it hits the wall. I say I'm sorry to everyone, my family for putting their lives in danger, to Aurora for letting her believe I was someone I'm not, to my mother, for I don't know what, but I feel I owe her an apology too. To everyone I've deceived with this whole charade. Please, everyone, forgive me. I've learned my lesson. A little late, admittedly, but I learned it.

I exhale, and feel much better.

And realize that I have about three nanoseconds to jump.

I leap from the cab of the lift, watching in slow motion as it smashes into the wall of PPMM, spectacularly, but crumpling like a sheet of tin foil. Crap. Larson was right. Even a lift at forty miles an hour can't pierce this stuff.

Wait. A little flash.

It did pierce the wall. Just enough.

And then an explosion, like a bolt of lightning, rips through the sky above me. The entire dome flashes white hot, blinding me.

Darkness.

Then another sound: the rush of air into the space, and... something like a million crystals falling from the heavens.

No, wait. It *is* a million crystals falling from the heavens! Little chunks of PPMM are about to kill me! I have just enough time to curl up into a ball, protecting my head, when I'm pelted with the equivalent of a full hailstorm in a matter of seconds. I picture the infinite small bruises I'll have tomorrow morning over my entire body.

But I'll be alive tomorrow morning. Damn that feels good.

I breathe the air in deep, feeling the rush of a new life, and kiss the red dust on the ground. I hear footsteps, and Claire asks, "Is she alive?"

I turn over and grin at them all. "I'm alive." Then I remember the moments before all this, when the world learned who I really was, and the Gitanos' collective jaws dropped to the floor, and they cocked their handguns, and I frown. "For the moment."

Benji reaches out his hand. "Let's go help the others."

"I'm sorry, Benji. All of you. I hope you can forgive me."

Benji nods. "I can't speak for everyone, but we're not dead. You did that. That counts for something."

Mike shakes his head. "No. Sorry, Robin. Or whatever your name is. It's not enough." He walks away, toward the other dome. Claire follows him, whispering, "A Filler? That's so strange."

And Aurora follows them both, silent.

After a little while alone, I walk to the other dome, little chunks of PPMM crunching underfoot. Zach Larson, behind the main dome's wall, in full spacesuit, holds up his tablet: *Do you know how much that dome cost?*

I honestly can't tell if he's trying to make light of the situation. He doesn't smile, or wink, or nod, but his eyes are telling me something. If I had to put it into words, my guess is that they're saying, "You lied to me. And we have a sabotage problem. But you kept a bunch of people from dying on my watch, and I won't be going to jail for multiple counts of negligent homicide, so thanks for that."

Three transports finally arrive, and a backup-backup generator crew rushes off one of them. Within minutes, the main dome is powered back on, and its hostages are set free.

Ted and his cameraman run over as Larson slips through the PPMM membrane and unlatches his helmet. "Mr. Larson! What happened?!"

"That thing is on, correct?" He points to the camera's little red light. Ted nods.

"Good. This young woman has something to say."

"I do?"

Ted fidgets. "Sir. People are watching. Like, a historic number of people. Shouldn't you be-"

"Give her a microphone." He turns to me. "You have some explaining to do."

Ted hands me a mic.

The world is watching.

"I- I- I'm... sorry." I try to hand the mic back to Larson. He pushes it in back in front of my face.

I want to ask for forgiveness a thousand times. But suddenly, guilt isn't what I feel most. Something else is rising in me. Some other feeling I've never had.

"Yes. I am sorry. Sorry that I lied to get on this show. My name is not Robin Smith. Actually, technically it is Robin, but my Nana– well, that's a completely different story." My throat constricts. It doesn't want the next words to come out. But I force them. "My name is Paper. Paper Farris."

I take a deep breath and look over at Aurora. "I needed to escape who I am to be here. But I am finished trying to escape, trying to become someone I am not." Tears begin to stream down my cheeks. "Who am I? I am... a Filler. A third-generation Filler from Fill City One." I take one step closer to the camera and stare straight into its eye. The strange feeling begins to burn in my chest like a fire, and now I know what it is: PRIDE.

"Yes. I am Paper Farris. I am a Filler. And I am proud. Proud of myself. Proud of my family. Proud of my people, the people of the Fill Cities, hard-working, loyal, and generous people who provide the fuel for this country and eliminate its waste. These people, who you don't know, who you may look down on, who don't have a voice, these people... are my family."

Where did that come from?

Alien words coming from my mouth. But they feel right. Like I'm telling the truth. *Finally.* In my mind, I reach through the camera into my family's living room and hug all of them at once. Everyone in Fill City. In all the Fill Cities. My mother and Voomvoom. I hug them all.

I look up, now back in my actual reality. It's dark and silent. No one cheers. I can literally hear crickets off in the distance. Did anyone hear me?

Larson gently takes back the microphone, beams into the camera. "Well, there you have it, ladies and gentlemen! What a night! Tune in tomorrow, as the three remaining teams begin competing in Stage Three: Back to School!"

Ted cuts the camera, and Larson lowers his voice. "My office. Tomorrow morning."

He walks away, towards the third transport, and I can hear him say the words even though he doesn't: *Strike three.*

41

TRUST ME.

"Well. You made quite a splash last night. Bravo on that speech."

"I'm sorry, Mr. Larson."

He pats me on the shoulder. "Zach." Then moves to the window and looks out onto the studio lot. The morning light is pouring in, but it feels darker than last time. "You can stop saying you're sorry. Thirty times in one conversation is enough. The person who should be sorry is the one who sabotaged the domes with that A.I. virus. The person who wants this mission to fail. That person will be very sorry."

"So I can stay?"

"No. Now it's my turn to apologize. I'm sorry, Robin. Paper. You cannot stay. I honestly wish you could. Did you see the ratings last night? Oh dear Lord. It was another record. Shattered. You're a star. And your Likes. I can hardly keep track."

"But it's *your* show. *Your* rules. Just tell everyone I can stay."

"No. Listen, I couldn't care less if you broke one of my rules. Any of my rules. You know that. I'm much more interested in finding out who threatened our lives. But you broke one of your *own* rules. You're a citizen of Fill City One, Paper, and must abide by their laws. The Gitanos have already asked to retrieve you. They have a car waiting at the garage, in fact. The federal government has extradition agreements with the Fill Cities. I make my own rules, yes, but I don't break federal laws. There's nothing I can do."

A sudden desperation grips me. I look around for a secret exit. "Can't you help me escape then? Go into hiding? Like my mother? Please?"

"I'm going to ask you to trust me. No."

"No?"

"No. I don't think Meal-In-A-Bags and dodging toll monitors suits you."

"What?" I explode from my chair and grab his collar. "What are you talking about? What do you know? How could you possibly know that?"

He considers me for a long moment, pushes me gently away, smooths his shirt, and taps the tips of his fingers together. "Yes. It's time you knew. You're not the only one with secrets." Sits back down. From a drawer he pulls a Red Scarab, and places it on the desk between us. He presses the head.

Nothing.

"Oh for Pete's sake." He smacks the scarab on the desk twice and presses the head again, and the wing covers spring open. "Now... what do you see?"

"Is this a trick question?"

He grins. "You're on to me. Yes. The real question is what *don't* you see?" He gently lifts the left wing cover, with increasing pressure, until it snaps off. Hands it to me. *"Now* what do you see?"

A chip. There's the teeniest little computer chip on the inside of the wing cover, barely visible. And an even teenier antenna. "You heard..."

"Everything. Not just you. All the winners."

"That's how you knew about Aurora, you had that record disc already made. You knew about my rockets. My mother. Fill City..."

"Yes."

"How can you justify that?"

"My rules, Paper. My conscience is clean. I needed to know about all of you. Everything I could."

"Why?"

"Isn't it obvious? This is a mission to Mars, Paper. Not a television show. How can I know one of you isn't something dangerous – like a saboteur?"

"One of us?"

He shrugs. "Whoever did this was extremely crafty. Not to worry. It won't happen again. I've made the necessary security upgrades and we're reviewing all the footage, though that will take quite some time." He gets up again, as if he wants me to rise so I can leave.

"So that's it? We're done here?"

"You're not listening. I asked you to trust me."

"If you let me out that door, I'll be in the fill before you can order breakfast."

"I already had breakfast."

"Smart ass."

"Paper. Listen to me. Do you think I did this show for the money? I could fund this mission a few times over. No. I did this to get our great country excited about exploration again. To give them something to believe in. And some*one* to believe in. An underdog. Someone who came from nothing, who shares their dreams, and fears, and guilt, and hope. And I think they've found her."

"He said as he let her be taken away by mobsters. Nice speech, Zach."

He sighs. Reaches under his desk and lifts out my satchel. Hands it to me. Then hands me a small, thin rectangle.

"My Get-Out-Of-Jail-Free Card. Great. My mother's insane, you know."

"I actually like her. From what I've heard anyway. Reminds me of-"

"Martha."

He smiles at me now, looking like Dad, that smile that knows I'm going to be okay, that the road might be bumpy, but at the end of the day, I'll curl up with my blanket in a warm, dry space somewhere, and wherever I am, for that moment, I can call it home, because he'll always be there with me.

"That's my Dad's smile. It's annoying."

He laughs. "Sorry. Now, I can't see what's on here." He points to the card. "It's DNA coded. When I tried to read it, it notified me I'd need Gitano family DNA to gain access. That's very complicated stuff, DNA coding. There are only a handful of people who could swing this. Insane or not, it seems your mother has some talented friends."

"Wonderful. She can bring them to my unmarked grave."

Larson stands, comes around to my side of the desk, and kneels. "I am letting you go. Only because I know this isn't goodbye."

I don't know what comes over me, I reach around his shoulders, and sob silently into his neck. "I'm afraid."

"Life is scary. I know. I'll tell you all about it someday. But do you really think I would let you die?"

42

FILL R UP

W ell, this isn't what I expected.

I don't know why I expected a normal, official looking transport, like a police or security vehicle, waiting for me on the top of Groupie Studios' private garage. I should have known better. The Gitanos, as I've said, could never shake the "mobster" mystique, so instead of something normal and official, they've sent me a glossy black stretch limousine with a custom license plate that reads "FILL R UP." Of course.

I've seen this before.

Rock came running into my chemistry class – fifth grade? – totally disregarding the teacher's admonishments. "Paper! Paper! Look! Out the window!"

The entire class rushed to see, and we peered down on that rarest of rare birds:

A Gitano.

Sighting a Gitano in the wild was so rare, in fact, that the teachers stopped yelling and got worried looks on their faces.

The limousine, black and long, opened its window just a

crack, a wisp of smoke escaping. The principal shuffled over to it and leaned in hesitantly, then nodded so many times I thought his neck was broken. Then the car's door creaked open, and a leg stepped out. An entire black suit emerged. We gasped.

It's funny that we gasped, because the person stepping out of the limousine could've been anyone. There was nothing unique or special about him, other than the limousine and the suit, and that he was clean. Not particularly tall or short. Or thin or fat. Or hairy or bald, or handsome or ugly. But there was one thing: his presence.

The man walked with such a confident and menacing presence, people involuntarily behaved like magnets of the same pole, repelled a few steps back as he passed them. He disappeared under the entrance awning, smiling, and we waited for what seemed like a year, without a single sound – hushed for probably the first time in our student careers – until finally the man emerged again, this time with a companion.

Mister Ellington. One of the history teachers.

"Where's Mister Ellington going, Mrs. Weiner?"

We couldn't take our eyes off the Gitano, so we couldn't see the stricken look on her face. We only heard a little whimper.

"Maybe he's getting a promotion, Mrs. Weiner?"

"Y- y- yes. That might be it."

And we never saw Mr. Ellington again.

I return to the present just as a skinny young man in a black suit steps into the sun, shielding his eyes. It's funny: cars haven't needed drivers in over fifty years, but my mother insists on driving herself, and the Gitanos insist on having someone sit in the front seat, even though all they do is tap a few buttons. It's just for the show, the insecure display of power. We live in a strange world. Whatever.

The man walks to the back and taps a little button.

A double-door opens and a cloud of cigar smoke billows out.

A voice from inside: "Get in."

I can't see in, it's so dark. I imagine Satan himself is inviting me into his mobile version of Hell.

There's no point in any other course of action, if I run I'm positive I'll wind up with a bullet in my back, so I surrender to my fate. I climb in, immediately assaulted by the smell of bad cologne, bourbon, and cigar smoke. Black leather is everywhere. A finger points to the seat next to the TV, I suppose so the limousine's sole passenger can watch *You're Going to Mars!* and his prey at the same time.

There's a gun on the seat opposite me, next to a very large man. It's nine o'clock in the morning and he's drinking bourbon and smoking cigars. And though it's ice cold in here, a thin sheet of sweat slicks his bald head. He breathes heavily between puffs and drinks. Basically, the picture of perfect health.

"Close the door, Angel. You're letting all the goddamn heat in."

Angel's been looking at me, distracted. He hurriedly slams the doors and rushes back to his seat. The privacy screen slides up. The car starts moving, descending the ramps, out past the paparazzi and the fans, into the real world beyond.

I'm shaking with fear, but this scene, I've watched it so

many times, I involuntarily laugh. "Could this be any more like *GoodFellas*?"

"What?"

"The movie. One of the oldies."

"Oh, yeah. The one where everybody gets whacked."

"That one."

"Yeah. I could shove an ice pick into the back of your neck. Would that make it even more like *GoodFellas* for you?" Leo puts his fist to the back of his own neck to demonstrate.

Sweat breaks out on my forehead even though it's zero degrees in here. "I withdraw the question."

"Good. Now, little Farris. You were great on that show, like the thing with that Claire, pushing her ass up the rock wall, jeez I almost laughed my balls off, but... there's nothing we we need from you, there's nothing you can offer us in exchange for your life, so I'm sorry kid, but it's into the fill for y-"

Angel taps on the glass. Lowers the privacy screen. "Leo. Um, sir."

"What? I was just doin' my pre-execution speech!"

"I'm sorry sir. But you should turn on the TV."

"Now? Angel, you're killin' me over here." Leo bends over – I swear almost having a heart attack with the strain – and turns on the TV next to me. I don't dare bend forward to look back and see the screen, as I have an allergy to ice picks and guns. But I can hear a voice.

It's Larson.

"...and they have taken one of our own, a fellow contestant, for no other reason than a sixty-five-year-old contract dictates she can never leave her place of birth. Yes, the person we knew as Robin was someone else: Paper Farris. She did not tell the truth. But... wouldn't you do the same? To exercise your basic human rights? To follow your dream? For a chance to live... free?"

I visualize him waving his fists, stirring up a crowd into a frenzy, and then I hear it: cheering. I don't know how he does it. Somehow, he's assembled an audience of thousands into Groupie Studios. He has once again spun nothing into gold, raising a ridiculous reality show into some form of national statement, some newsworthy moment to highlight human rights. If I were more cynical, I would dismiss it as self-promotion. But there's something sincere about it. Maybe I'm not the only one who feels it.

"...you've seen the footage. Her daring rescue of team-mates and competitors alike under the dome. She didn't discriminate... why should we? She deserves a second chance, does she not? And so I call on our friends, the Gitanos, to make this exception, in the name of human decency, in the name of good will, to allow a fellow human being, like the rest of us in all ways and different in none, to participate in the dream of going to Mars. To allow the people of the Fill Cities to join us in cheering the advance-ment of our human species! I ask you, our friends, to bring Paper back."

Aww. Larson. My knight in shining armor. At least he tried.

Leo smashes the off button. "Oh, give me a fuckin' break. Big deal. Whiner's gonna whine. Boo-hoo. Now where was I?" He turns to me, with a totally inappropriate level of glee in his eyes. But I'm holding out the Get-Out-Of-Jail-Free Card like a half-inch-by-two-inch shield, and I almost laugh at how ridiculous it is, how tiny it suddenly seems, especially compared to the immensity of Leo, and I know more certainly, as he promised, that I'll soon be sleeping somewhere with a dirt blanket, permanently.

He crosses his eyes to focus on the card. "What? A stick of gum? No thanks. I'm not allowed to do sugar."

I muster as much courage as I can, though I'm absolutely sure I sound more like a mouse than a lion: "Read it."

He rolls his eyes, then chuckles maniacally, then coughs, like Bradline might, signaling an oncoming brain aneurism, or a chunk of lung might pop out of his mouth. He finally catches his breath, pats his sweaty forehead with a pink handkerchief. "You're lucky, Farris. I'm in a good mood this morning. Let's take a look-see."

He has to reach over again to where the TV is – wow, he's actually getting some exercise this morning, *work those abs, Leo* – and inserts the card into a slot. The screen flashes to life. I can't see what's on it, but I can see Leo's expression change from *slightly-annoyed-amusement* to *slightly-annoyed-confusion*. "Huh. Computer, override login access, audible code LEO-ONE-TWO-THREE-FOUR- FIVE."

"Really? That's your audible code?"

"Shut up, kid. And if you tell anyone that I'll kill you."

"Now you're giving me options?"

But before he can make good on his promises, or just smack me for being snarky, the computer responds, and I could swear even it's a little afraid of Leo. "I'm sorry. Card DNA encoded. Gitano DNA required for login. Please place your finger on the pad."

Leo doesn't even bother to lean forward. I guess two crunches a day is enough. He decides to go back to being amused, I imagine realizing somewhere deep down that a single additional moment of stress in his life might be the last straw and trigger a massive coronary.

"Okay Farris. Your little card trick's pretty fancy. Gotta admit." He hands me back the card and motions for me to hand it up to Angel. Man, Leo *really* doesn't like to move any more than he has to. "Take us to Phoenix, Angel. Make it snappy. We gotta see Gene." He turns back to me. "Whoopdee-do. You bought yourself a few hours. Happy?"

"You're not a Gitano?"

He laughs. "Oh, no. I'm sweet as peach pie compared to a Gitano. Wait 'til you meet Gene."

43

THE SMOKING GITANO

T he car stops.

We're in the middle of nowhere. Desert on all sides. Even with the near total blackout of the window tinting, the day outside looks bright and blistering hot. "Why are we stopping?"

Leo leans to one side and farts. "Heh. Look at you. In a rush to get to the fill."

Angel activates the privacy screen, and while it slides up I chance a look to him. He has a sort of guilty half-smile on, and quietly mouths, "Sorry." I guess he's had his share of Leo farts. I'm on my own.

So we idle awkwardly for a few minutes, now just Leo and me, and I fantasize about bolting from the car, just to escape his nauseating mixture of aromas. Believe it or not, he makes me miss the Everpresent Stink.

"They're here."

Another identical long black limousine pulls alongside us coming from the other direction. Angel pops out and skitters over to it. The back window cracks open an inch, and sure enough, a wisp of smoke escapes. Angel nods, and slips the card to an unseen hand.

A few minutes later, on the intercom: "Leo, good work. You showed admirable restraint. We'll arrange disposal later."

Good work? All he did was *not kill me*!

The other limousine lurches onto the side of the road, u-turning and sending up a cloud of orange dust, then speeding away. We follow. And before long, I see it:

Fill City Seven.

Just like the others, with thirty-foot walls and pipes sprouting out like arteries, sending urgently-needed nutrients to the rest of the body, the mainland. No. Now they seem more like long fingers, jabbing and gripping the land, keeping it under its control. As we approach, the endless line of trucks pulls aside and lets us proceed. My palms are sweaty. Mars seems way more than 140 million miles away, and a friendly face even farther.

Directly inside the walls there's a tunnel to the right, just big enough for the limousines, leading underground. We enter the darkness. My ears pop.

A small room. Windowless. Cinder block construction, no effort to make it look welcoming – of course, I mean why would they want to make a torture-slash-execution chamber welcoming? I'm alone. I don't even know how many hours or days pass until I hear a knock on the door.

"I'm a little busy. Can you come back later?"

The door opens, as if by itself, and a body is thrown in. Oh my God! A dead body!

No. It's breathing. Zip-cuffed wrists and ankles, a burlap

bag over its head. I approach the bag and touch it, and the poor creature screams.

I scream back. "Aaaaahh! It's okay! It's okay! I'm not with them! I'm trapped in here too!"

The head whips around inside the bag and goes silent. Without seeing the face, I could swear the bag looks at me like... it recognizes me.

I pull it off.

It's my mother.

"JANE!" I throw my arms around her and she groans in pain. "Jane, what the hell are you doing here?!"

"I'm here to save you. Can't you tell?"

I laugh and cry, and have a million questions. But first: "How?!"

"The Get-Out-Of-Jail-Free Card. The first thing it does when it's popped in is send out a beacon signal. I followed you here. The rescue part isn't going exactly as planned, I'll admit. By the way, you look pathetic."

"I should be the one saying that." I pull her face close. She's bleeding from the lip and the nose, and already one of her eyes is blackening. "Oh Lord, you're a mess. Wait! What about Voomvoom?!"

"Shhh! Don't worry. He's safe. My friend Molly finally relented and took the bugger. He's like an anchor, you know."

"You're terrible."

"Hey. I'm here, aren't I?"

"Great. So we can be next door neighbors in the fill."

"Look, nobody's going into the fill. That beacon signal was just the first line of attack. Any good rescue plan has multiple lines, multiple possible approaches to maximize success. The second line of attack? They should be finding out about that doozy right... about..."

Seconds pass. Too many. "Right about what? Right about now? What's the doozy? Nothing's happening. Right about... now?"

"Jeez. Give it a minute. I'm not perfect you know."

"Did you just actually say that? They must've kicked something loose in your head."

She ignores me. "Shhh. Right about..."

A loud shout outside the door. It clicks open.

"Now."

A woman marches in, taking a momentary break from yelling at Angel and the other henchmen around her, and fixes her cold gaze on us. She takes a deep drag of her cigarette, repeats some mantra I can't make out, and her rage recedes a little, roiling just beneath the surface, as the smoke escapes her nostrils.

"Well, well, Jane. I'm Gene. Oh God, Jane, Gene, that's going to get annoying fast. I'll just call you Farris."

I raise my hand. I don't know why. "What about me?"

"Not that this'll take that long, but okay, hello Paper."

Jane coughs. "It's Pepper."

I turn to her. "Really, Jane? Still?"

"What?"

"Never mind." I turn to the woman. "You're a Gitano?" I guess I expected someone much more like Leo to come in and do the deed. This woman is tall, severe, but elegant, with a pinstriped black skirt and high heels. Her hair is perfect. She even has lipstick on. The only thing she's missing is one of those little extension poles for her cigarette. Women like her don't plunge ice picks into people's necks, they can't even manage stealing Dalmatian puppies. I hope.

She sneers. "You were expecting...?"

"Nothing. Nobody."

"Good, you brat. You can shut up. Now, Farris, I've just learned the true nature of your little card. My, you've been a busy bee." She leans down and slaps Jane hard across the face. "This girl and you, you little maggots, have broken contracts *your families signed,* and left one of the Fill Cities. We have *contractual rights* to take you back. Yes, *federal law* demands it. But you dare to intimidate me? Blackmail me? For doing what's legal and right?"

Another line of blood trickles down Jane's chin. "Fuck you. Yes."

She slaps Jane again. "Look at you. So proud."

"You bet your ass I'm proud. You know how many years it took me to make that?"

She goes to slap Jane again, and Angel makes a strange movement, accidentally putting himself slightly in the way, catching the slap on his own face. "Get out of the way, Angel! God, if you weren't a Gitano I'd have you in the fill a hundred times by now."

"Sorry, ma'am. I was going to uncuff her."

"Now? You're in the way, as usual." She pushes him aside and gears up for another blow.

I lunge forward and another one of her goons grabs me. "Stop hitting my mother! And is someone going to tell me what the hell you two are talking about?"

Jane whispers to me, half embarrassed, half cocky. "Your hobby was rockets. Mine was the Dead Body Database."

"The Dead *what?*"

"I'll let our gracious host Miss Gitano tell you all about it. I'm sure she'd love to."

Gene Gitano's rage threatens to boil over. She swallows

hard, puffs, repeats her mantra. She says it low, but I can hear it this time, I think it's "Pretty Bubbles." I'm dying to ask her why a Gitano would have a mantra like that, instead of something like "Breaking Bones," but she cuts me off before I can ask. "Problem. This is a problem. We can't have this. Pops will lose his mind."

"Pops?"

"I said shut up, girl. I was talking to myself. Your mother here, she's created quite a problem for us. I'm thinking. I like to think out loud. Ugh. It would be so much easier if I could just get you two into the fill and go get lunch."

My mother laughs. "See? She can't kill us."

"Oh, don't jump to conclusions. I'm just thinking through the logistics."

I stand up and stamp my feet, throwing my absolute best little spoiled kid brat tantrum. "Someone is going to tell me what the hell a Dead Body Database is!"

The Gitano steps in to strike me but stops. "Hmm. No. You know what? You're right. I'll let your mother tell you, that sometimes helps me think. Talk through the problem. Listen and talk, listen and talk. Thank you for the suggestion, Paper."

"You're welcome." *At least you're remembering your manners, Paper.*

Jane motions for me to come back down to her. "I've been working on the Dead Body Database since I was fifteen. Pinpointing the exact location – latitude, longitude, and depth – and DNA-coded identity of every person they've killed and buried in Fill City One. Well, not everyone, but lots."

"God, that's a morbid hobby."

"It started more as a memorial. Like a permanent record,

honoring the unknowns. But very quickly I knew it was something more. After I found Senator Brooks."

"*Senator Brooks?* The former Air Force captain who pushed through the *Inquisitor* Mars rover mission?"

"Bingo. They said he died on a glacier in Alaska. Never found the body. But I did." She struggles to her feet, still cuffed tight together, and approaches Gene Gitano in little jumps. "They buried Senators." Jump. "Activists." Jump. "Scientists." Jump. "The President!"

"Enough!" Gene Gitano turns away from her, tapping her chin, thinking, thinking.

President Sherman? The first astronaut to be elected President of the United States? The father of the second Space Race? He was one of my heroes. Disappeared on a hike right outside of Camp David, despite the presence of his full detachment of Secret Service. Gone. Forever. *They did this?*

"Jane? Why didn't you release this database earlier? Shine a light on this? It could've helped you expose them, and find out more about the compound."

Gene Gitano whips around. "Excuse me?"

Jane coughs again. "Kid. Ixnay on the ompound-kay!"

I move closer to hear better. "What?"

"*Ixnay* on the *ompound-kay!*"

"Are you having a stroke?"

"It's pig Latin! Jeez, you're supposed to be the smart one."

"What the hell is pig Latin? Did you make that up too?"

Gene Gitano shoves us apart. "Really, Paper? Even I know pig Latin. She said to shut up about the compound. Now, what *compound* are we talking about? I'd really like to know."

Jane glares at me, this wasn't supposed to be the time for her big reveal, I guess she wasn't ready, but the ball is rolling down the hill at full speed now, this is the moment it all comes out. "Gene Gitano, I know what your family has done. Killed and corrupted, for decades, to cover up a compound, an element found by a Mars rover, I don't know why, but you even tried to kill Zach Larson and the contestants on that show to stop a private mission from exposing you and your trash. I wanted Pepper here to find the element first, get up there and prove it for the whole world to see, but I guess we'll have to go with what we have and do it now. You're going down." She juts her chin out defiantly.

Gene Gitano looks sort of constipated for a moment, like she can't decide whether to kill us personally on the spot, or have one of her goons do it while she flicks ashes on us, or just let us rot in this room for the next few weeks until we expire. But she starts to laugh. And laugh. Heartily.

"Whoo! That is *rich!*" She walks over to me, whirling her finger in a circle by her temple, whispering in my ear. "I feel sorry for you." Then she takes a step back, composes herself, lights another cigarette, crushing the old one under her toe. "Thanks for the laugh, Farris. I haven't laughed like that in I can't remember when. Wow. Laughter feels good. You're so funny – especially the part about *You're Going to Mars!* I mean, you really think that was *us?*" A giggle. "Have you been watching the show? It's clearly that Aurora girl. She'd do anything to win. Even kill the rest of them."

I protest. "No way. That's ridiculous."

"Naive, little Farris. You didn't see her sneaking around in your room. Everyone's room. She'd do anything. And the spacesuit she just happened to have on? Please. It's like she's wearing a neon sign that says 'It's me.'"

"See, Pepper? I told you. Watch out for that Aurora."

"You *were* trying to tell me through that police photo!"

"Of course. You think I would ever get arrested by accident?"

Gene Gitano continues, tapping her chin. "Or maybe it's that Claire one. Just stupid looking enough. Smart as a fox underneath. Sometimes that's how they produce these shows."

Jane and I both shake our heads and say together, "Claire? Now *that's* crazy."

"It's obvious. She seems innocent, dumb as a rock, but those are the ones you have to watch out for. Or maybe, I don't know, after watching that last episode, maybe it's Avery – wait – back to the point."

"Which was?"

"You're accusing us of murder, to cover up an imaginary compound, containing an imaginary element, so that we can take over the world?"

"Not take over the world. I didn't say that."

"Whatever. Close enough. Do you realize how absolutely ludicrous that sounds?"

And once again, I have to look at my mother that way, that way that admits she actually is insane, and like it or not, I kind of have to agree with Gene, the smoking Gitano.

Jane glares at me. "Why are you looking at me like that? You agreeing with this Gitano witch?"

"No." But I am. Oh boy. The guilt burns like fire.

Gitano turns and heads for the door. She's had enough chit-chat. Nods to the goon holding my arm. "Crazy, criminal Farrises. To the fill with them."

Jane says calmly, "You don't want to do that."

"Oh, Jesus Christ. Now what, Farris?"

"There's a dead-man's switch. We've all been implanted," she points under her armpit, "with these. If any Farris family member dies, or has it removed, it'll stop transmitting, and the Dead Body Database will immediately be published across the net, on every available server in every country in the world. Harlon, Rock, Pepper, Scissors, any of them."

I look under my armpit, down my sleeve. Sure enough, a tiny scar, right in the fold. I never noticed. "How the hell did you even do that- *hey, hold on...* you didn't say Nana."

She looks blankly at me.

"You. Didn't. Say. Nana."

She shrugs.

"You're terrible!"

"She's ninety-seven! And I only had six units! You know how expensive those things are?"

Gene Gitano throws down her cigarette. "Stop! Stop! I can't listen to you two bicker anymore. Jesus. Paper, you had to grow up with that?"

"No. She abandoned us."

"Oh, right. Lucky you."

"Hey!"

"STOP! Let's say I dispose of you two anyway. And your whole family. Which I'm inclined to do, especially at the moment, yes, you're pissing me off that much. So you release this Dead Body Database. It's all untrue anyway, make-believe fluff, maybe needs just a little cover-up on a couple of the details. We make some more enemies, maybe one or two of us – not me, God no – go to tennis prison for a few years. Then it's over. Forgotten, like all the other bogus news stories ever in the history of the world. All your efforts, wasted on a magic trick that pulls a big bag of nothing out of a top hat." She laughs again. "A month later, it'll all be back to normal, like it is at this very moment, with hundreds of thousands of

Fill City workers pumping out Turbo like it was any other day, happy with their lives, content as they've ever been, and-"

Another goon steps into the room. "Miss Gitano, ma'am. There's a problem."

She glares at him. A solid ten seconds passes. "A dramatic pause? Honestly? What are you waiting for?"

"Sorry ma'am. There's an uprising. Work stoppage."

"Ugh. Am I the only one in here with a brain?" She proceeds, sing-song, "Enact protocol seventeen, make an example, put down the ones who are acting up-"

"We can't, ma'am."

"Excuse me?"

"We can't, ma'am."

"*Why?*"

"Because they're *all* acting up, ma'am. Everywhere. All the Fill Cities. They've all gone on strike."

44

GOOD COP

I t could be worse.

While Gene Gitano decides what to do with us, and her and this Pops person figure out how to deal with a global strike, I expect them to make us sleep on the concrete, defecate on the floor in the corner, and catch rats and spiders for food. But as the days pass, they've let Angel put down an air mattress, and give us snacks and water, and escort us to the bathroom (you can barely call it that but it's better than the corner of our cell). I suspect they're doing a good-cop-bad-cop thing from the old shows, with Angel as the good cop, but I don't care. I'm alive and not dying of dehydration, or having cigarettes burned into my arms.

They even let him bring in a TV.

"Angel, that's too much. Come on. Are you playing good cop? You must be."

"Huh?"

"You know. Where you're nice to us and eventually you get us to incriminate ourselves."

"Incriminate yourselves? You've already shown all your

cards I'm pretty sure. The Dead Body Database? The Martian Element Theory?"

"Good point. So you're being nice to us why?"

He just tosses the remote to me. *"You're Going to Mars!* is on three." And leaves.

Jane grabs the remote and presses three. "He likes you."

"God, what are you, my mother? Oh."

"I can tell. Harlon used to get that look on his face before we started dating." She winks at me.

"Please. Jane. We're waiting for them to take us out in burlap sacks and bury us alive, and you're talking about one of the bad guys crushing on me?"

"Bad, good, right, wrong. Love is a weird thing. It doesn't care. It wants what it wants."

"Wow. That was deep. You made that up?"

"Nah. Read it in *People Magazine* a long time ago."

"What's *People Magazine*?"

She ignores me and points to the screen. "Oooh. Look. Stage Three: Back to School."

The TV has a running ticker across the bottom of the remaining contestants and their scores: Aurora, Marina Delacosta, Mike Horner, Claire Soams, Benji Greenberg, Avery Jacobs, Tanner Hiroki, Suzie Q, Albert Morse, Quinn Keller, and myself. Aww. Larson has kept me in the lineup, ever the optimist – albeit with a question mark superimposed over my face. Interestingly, although I'm not scoring any points, Larson has allowed viewers to continue awarding me Likes, and I'm ahead of everyone, including Aurora. By a lot. She must be *pissed*. In the current scene they're in an emergency room, standing around a patient, all in scrubs. Skylar Gaines, Team Leader of the departed Blue Team, is pointing to the patient's legs, both broken and pointing out in unnatural directions. I imagine every single person in the world cringing at once. "All right, teams. Mister Davis here has had a little construction accident involving a three-story fall. Before the MedBay sleeves can get to work we'll have to set these breaks. Volunteers?"

On cue, Claire faints, and the rest take a step back. Tanner holds his hand up to his mouth and turns green. Aurora, on the other hand, flips her hair a little and squeals, "Let me at 'em!" She wrenches one leg with Skylar as poor Mister Davis screams.

Jane nudges me. "See? I told you that Aurora was a bad seed. Look at that bloodlust."

"Come on. You don't see the whole thing with Aurora. I have. I think she's actually very nice, and authentic. If you really knew her you'd like her."

"Nah, I think that Gitano witch was right about her. How do you know she didn't try to sabotage Stage Two?"

"I just know."

"You just know it couldn't have been the only one left with a spacesuit. Really." She shakes her head, pats me on the knee. "In any case, I'm proud of you. Some of that stuff you figured out in that stage, with the lift and the domes? Chip off the old block."

"Great. Before you know it I'll be formulating Meal-in-a-Bags."

"I'm pretty sure the plural would be Meals-in-a-Bag. The 's' on Meals."

"What are you a grammar expert now?"

Without hesitation, as if she'd been waiting to say it her whole life, she says, "I'm your mother. Correcting your grammar is my job."

I want to say "maybe if you didn't jump ship five minutes

after I was born I wouldn't be making grammar mistakes now" but I just say "okay" and enjoy the warm feeling of actually having a mother-like person, even if it is the last thing I feel before I die.

The broadcast is interrupted.

"Breaking news: in a stunning development, the Phillips Administration has declared a federal state of emergency, implementing mandatory rationing of all fuel consumption in the wake of the global strike of Fill City workers."

My mother and I gape at each other as the news continues. It seems there have been daily protests, counter protests, and counter counter protests erupting everywhere, demanding my return to the show, and new contracts for the workers, and calls for resumption of Turbo production as the global economy begins to be affected, and even proposals for the immediate de-privatization of WasteWay's properties. Meanwhile, legislators on Capitol Hill seem paralyzed to make headway, as relationships with WasteWay leadership continue to thwart minority party efforts to effect change. (Translation: Congress has its pockets too full to move.) The images on the screen are amazing, if alarming: throngs of people, tear gas, hoses, mounted police. I spot a sign that says, "LET PAPER PLAY!", and another saying, "Where is Paper Farris?" and a third with "We are all Paper!" Another one reads, "Give us our Paperback!"

Jane laughs. "Paperback. Get it? Clever buggers!"

Huh. Maybe Larson was right. Maybe his little crusade to keep me alive is working. And maybe my mother's outrageous Dead Body Database will help.

The door opens. Gene Gitano. A wicked smile. "Hello, ladies."

...or maybe none of it will work and we're going to die.

45

TENNIS PRISON

She looks around at the various items in the room, then the TV set. "Talk about tennis prison." She yells out into the hallway, "Angel! Get in here!"

Angel scrambles, practically tumbling over himself, into the room.

"Are you responsible for this?"

"I'm sorry, ma'am. You- you told me to make them comfortable."

She rolls her eyes. "I meant comfortable as in *just-this-side-of-a-painful-death* comfortable, not *air-mattress-and-television* comfortable. There's a bag of Cheetos over there for Christ's sake. Regardless. It's over."

My hearts stops. This is where we perish.

"Farris. Young one, not old shriveled up one."

"Hey!"

"Shut up, Farris. Paper, you, get up."

I rise, my knees knocking. Gene Gitano lights a cigarette. "You can go."

"Huh?"

"You heard me. Go. Get out of here. You and your mother and that Larson idiot make a perfect team. What a shitstorm you've created. But it's all fake news, it'll blow over, we'll survive, as we always do. I only have two conditions."

I glare at her without answering.

"If you say one word about any of this, she's in the fill. Try me. One word and Jane's in the fill."

"You're not... letting her go too?"

Gitano snickers. "Hey Jane, you're right. She's not the smart one, is she? No, we're not letting your mother go anywhere. When you're a citizen of Fill City, that's for life, honey, unless you're the ninth generation. But don't worry, we'll let you live together when you lose that stupid show. Right here in good old Fill City Seven. For the remainder of your days." She actually cocks her head back and laughs, like a movie villain.

"Second condition. You get those Fillers back to work. I don't care how you and that Larson idiot do it. You get them back to work, or she's in the fill."

I run to her. "Jane! I'll get the Fillers back to work. Then I'll lose. On purpose. I'll probably lose anyway. I'll be back in a couple of weeks."

She grips my arms. Stern. "No. You are *not* losing. You are going to Mars. And you are finding whatever is up there. And you are telling the world. You will do that. Not just for you. For *ME*. Do you understand?"

I nod. I understand. "But, their word means nothing. How do I know they won't hurt you? Or kil...?"

Angel steps between us all, and risking a beating from his boss, leans in close, so close his lips are touching my ear, and he whispers, in the softest whisper you can imagine, "I'll take care of her."

And I don't know, his unexpected and brave compassion, mixed with this terrible goodbye, something happens, and I grab Angel by the collar and pull his face to mine, and suddenly we're kissing, more passionately than I've ever kissed anyone, it feels like I'm giving him my whole heart, and we're sharing a promise, a promise that he'll give most of my heart to my mother but also keep some of my heart for himself. Because there is something about him that I trust. Something about him that... I don't know. Mom was right. Or *People Magazine.* Love is a weird thing. It wants what it wants.

He sighs. "Wow."

Jane smiles and winks at me. "That's how it starts."

46

THE LARGEST UMBRELLA I'VE EVER SEEN

I can hear the wipers slapping back and forth on the windshield, but the privacy screen's been up the whole ride, so I can't see if it's Angel up front. Although I can't imagine they'd let him be anywhere near me, after my dramatic stunt back there in Fill City Seven. Leo is in his usual spot, across from me, and suddenly I'm certain he lives in this car, I've never seen him outside it. I imagine them bringing him all his meals in here, and taking away his chamber pot every morning, and maybe wiping under his armpits once in a while to keep the stench bearable.

"What are you looking at, Farris?"

"Nothing. Sorry."

He kicks me shin. "Did I tell you to talk?"

"Ow! Yes. You asked me a question."

Leo just turns and looks out the window, no longer amused by me, or more likely deeply disappointed he didn't get to personally toss the first shovelful of dirt onto my grave, so instead he contemplates the rain with a quizzical look on his face. Apparently they never get rain out here in Los

Angeles anymore, so when it does happen people don't quite know what to make of it. He peers through it, like a sailor with a brass telescope searching across stormy seas – but really nothing like that, because come on, it's Leo – and he eyes a figure across the garage roof, alone and unarmed.

"Time to go home to daddy."

I don't know why those words piss me the hell off, but they do. "He's not my father."

"Shut up." He cracks the window and yells. "Larson! Come and get her!"

The figure walks towards the car, under the largest umbrella in the world, you could have a picnic under that umbrella, of course it's comically oversized, because the approaching figure is Zach Larson, coming to rescue me. I don't get shining armor, but I do get a giant umbrella. At least I won't get wet.

Larson raps on the glass. "Robin. Paper. Are you all right?"

Leo taps a button and the double doors open. Larson reaches in and takes my hand, and our eyes meet. "I'm all right, Zach." As he pulls me out of the car, halfway, Leo lunges forward a little – because there's no way he's making a full lunge – and grabs my other hand, as if he and Larson are about to play a game of tug-o-war with me.

"Not so fast. Now you listen close, Larson."

"Let her go. *Now.*"

I guess Leo's not used to being addressed like this, because he pulls me back and growls, "What, you think you're a big man?"

"I'm not half the man you are, Leo."

"How do you know my name?"

"I know a lot of things."

"Fucking smarmy asshole."

"Big man fucking smarmy asshole to you, Leo."

Leo's head looks like it's about to explode, his free hand is arguing with itself whether to reach for the gun and shoot us both dead, but it thinks the better of it and hands control back to Leo's brain. "You listen close, Larson."

"You already said that."

"Fuck you. Now, you and her get the Fillers back to work, all of 'em. That's the deal."

I can't tell whether Larson is glaring at Leo, or sort of pitying him, or about to laugh at him. "Deal."

Leo lets go of my hand, disgusted, and I go tumbling into Larson's arms. The limousine screeches off in the rain, and before it skids down the first ramp I can hear Leo laugh and yell, "Have a nice trip, Farris!"

I let Larson's arm stay around my shoulder, it feels familiar and comforting, like I'm home and Dad is putting a blanket around us while we take cover from a sudden storm.

"You think this umbrella's big enough?"

Larson laughs. "I have a bigger one, if you can believe it."

"I can."

He twirls it around, and hums a tune I feel like I've heard before. He's smiling and practically skipping with me, splashing in the little puddles like it was the most beautiful day of the year. "See Paper? I told you it wasn't goodbye."

"Yeah. You were right. As usual." A drop falls on my ear, it can't be rain, this umbrella is easily keeping a five foot diameter dry, so I look up again and spy wetness in Larson's eyes. Aww. He's such a sap. "Thank you, Zach. It's good to be back."

"I'm glad you're back, Paper. Truly." He stops and faces me. "Now... are you ready to get back in the saddle?"

God, he couldn't sound more like my father if he tried,

and like Dad, Larson really doesn't want a verbal answer, he wants action, wants me to prove it, so I take his hand and put down the umbrella, and we skip through the puddles like a couple of school kids, humming his little tune, laughing up at the gray, getting drenched in the rain.

47

THERE IS NO WAY THIS IS GOING TO WORK.

There is *no way* this is going to work.

Saying a few words on air, some platitudes about working together for a better future? And the Fillers are just going to magically return to their jobs? Come on.

But Larson insists, and clips on my lapel mic and walks out of his office, leaving me alone with a cameraman and a little red light. As he closes the door he says plainly, "Just tell the truth."

I clear my throat and stare right into the lens.

The truth.

"I, uh, want to thank the Gitanos. They could have punished me, and I think all us Fillers know what that means, but they hesitated. They listened. They wanted to understand what this means to you. And I think they do understand, I represent some of the frustrations of having lives not completely under our own control. The Gitanos want me to let you know that they hear you loud and clear. They've agreed to let me continue in this competition, provided Mister Larson and the other contestants approve, as a sign of good will, as a promise from them that this is only the first step in making the improvements you're so desperate for. In exchange, they've asked for you to return to work, to take this next important step alongside them. You return to work, and I return to the competition. To win. Not for me. To win for us."

The camera's light turns off.

I hang my head.

No. It wasn't the truth.

Not a word.

The Gitanos are a terrible bunch, who don't give a flying fuck about the welfare of us Fillers. But as the lies floated out of my mouth, I also made a silent promise to my people: yes, I need to continue this deception, but before it's all over, I'll find the truth, whatever it is, and I'll bring it home to you. There's no going back, for me, or for you. I will push this boulder forward. I mentally cross my heart and hope to die before I give up on this promise.

It works.

I don't know how. I guess I might have said the words with enough conviction, or more likely the people of the Fill Cities deciphered my code and heard my unspoken promise, and they return to work, a little grudgingly, and the world lets out a sigh of relief, and the pipelines open up, and the protests dwindle and disappear, along with the giant piles of garbage that had been rotting on the streets. I let out a sigh too, that Jane and my family are safe, for a moment at least. I've held up my part of the bargain, and have to trust the Gitanos' word (which I don't), or at least have to trust that Angel will find a way to protect them (which I do).

Angel.

It's crazy. I can't stop thinking about him. *Why?* He's a Gitano, for God's sake! And he's comically skinny, way too skinny for me, and *blonde*. I dated a boy with blonde hair once when I was fifteen or so, and I'll just say it was like my history with egg salad: before, I had no strong opinion, but after? – *ick*. I've decided this must be the Stockholm syndrome, where I fall for my captor out of desperation and dependence. That has to be it. The part where his lips tickled my ear, and sent a shiver through my body, or the fact that after a few good looks I found him strikingly handsome, or when we kissed and my brain momentarily short-circuited – those are all just manifestations of the syndrome. Making matters worse, too much time has passed since I've been with someone, so my romantic immune system must be compromised. I spend so much time with Duggie, I think he's either a repellant to other men, or they assume I'm romantically involved with him. And so I am vulnerable to this insidious kind of illness.

But Angel. There is something about him...

"Paper. You were in the middle of a question and you drifted off."

"Oh. Sorry, Zach. Where was I?"

"The scarab. Your mother. Some other words in no particular order. Word salad."

"Oh. Right. Sorry. So... you heard everything through the scarab."

"That's not a question."

"Did you hear my mother talk about this element thing? On Mars?"

He nods but doesn't speak.

"The Gitanos laughed at her. And I... it's awful... I couldn't say I didn't agree with them. Your take?"

He shrugs. Poker face.

"You think she's crazy."

He turns and stops me. "I don't think there is a mysterious new element hiding on Mars, no. I think the secrets waiting to be revealed are much more pragmatic, perhaps a deep vein of something extremely valuable, say, rhodium. Mining, scientific technologies, even tourism. The economic potential is enormous. And perhaps governments don't want a private citizen invading their turf. Possibly they'd even covertly sabotage a mission for it. People have died for much less, even in this country. But to think that a brand new element, unknown to man, has been kept a secret for seventy-five years? It would be the most sensational cover-up in history. So improbable that I'd have to say it approaches impossible."

He sees the crestfallen look in my eyes and frowns.

"BUT... I'm putting on a reality game show called *You're Going to Mars!*, and you're driving electrified lifts into impenetrable domes at full speed, so – who are the crazy ones?" He crosses his eyes and sticks his tongue out to make me smile. Then he continues walking me towards the Great Hall.

"And who knows? People have said for years I'm not to be believed. They could be right."

48

DEAD MAN WALKING

Interview with Aurora, contestant number one, runner up on last season's America Sings!:

"How do I feel about Paper, a.k.a. Robin, coming back? Isn't it obvious? She lied to us, she can't be trusted, and you know just once I'd like Larson to stick by some rules, this show is a damned free-for-all, just once he should put his foot down, and ship her off for good. I mean, don't get me wrong, I'm glad she's not, you know, whatever, I wouldn't want anything terrible to happen to her, underneath all the lies she's actually a pretty sweet person. I meant what I said back there, during that whole shit-show of Stage Two, it's embarrassing but it's true, I said it. She could've been like a sister, you know, together at the low moments, throwing back a shot or two just for kicks, or three or four, celebrating the high moments, sharing secrets, lifting each other up. Is that too much to ask? A little honesty for once in my life? A shoulder to cry on? Shit, no, stop. I'm not making any sense. Delete that."

I step into the Great Hall.

It's been transformed for Stage Three: Back to School into a pseudo-university setting, with separate spaces for labs, and computers, and equipment, and a massive simulation unit that will allow us to learn the ins and outs of the ship making mankind's maiden in-person voyage to Mars, the *High Heaven*. The remaining three teams are at what looks like a chemistry lab, and Drew Innes, former Orange Team Leader, appears to be the teacher for this portion of the stage.

The door closes behind me with a dull thud and the chatter and clinking of beakers stops.

Silence. Ten pairs of eyes fix on me.

I tread gingerly over to Red Team's table, feeling like I'm being led to the electric chair, even a little surprised I don't hear someone say "dead man walking." A quick glance up to The Big Board shows they've already completed the medical portion of this stage without me, so we're way behind both other teams. When I pass in front of my teammates, their frowns say it all: *thanks, whatever your name is.*

Drew returns to his lecture. "Excellent, Yellow Team. Fifteen points. All right, now the next process..."

I sit down, and realize not only am I facing Green Team's table, but I'm directly across from Aurora. She smiles and whispers, "Oh. You're not dead."

"You sound thrilled."

"Is it that obvious?" The smile stays plastered to her face, I pretty sure it's one of her evil ones. She shrugs. "Not that it matters. You're going home this Stage for sure. You know how many points your team will need to catch u-" She squints at me. "*Hold... on... a... second...*"

I look left and right, point to my chest. "What? Me?"

"Yeah. You." She gets up, walks over and sniffs the air around me. "You're... you've *met somebody!*"

Everyone turns in their chairs. I immediately turn bright red. "You can *smell* that?"

"No. The sniffing was just for effect. So it's true then. I knew it. Ha!"

"No it's not! Well. I don't know."

"You were supposed to be dying or tortured or something, and you find *romance?* I was actually feeling sorry for you, Paper Farris. I actually felt guilt. For the first time in my life."

"No, please, please, you should still be feeling sorry for me, and very guilty, no I don't mean that, I mean it's not like I planned it or-"

"Stop stumbling over yourself. I get it. So who's the lucky one? Another tortured prisoner?"

I motion for her to bring me her ear and I whisper his name.

And she erupts in howls of laughter so loud the cameramen need to swat their headphones off to avoid breaking their eardrums.

"Oh. Yeah. That'll end well!"

I have to respect Aurora. She just tells it like it is. I simply can't argue. She's right. I'm falling for a Gitano. That says it all, doesn't it? One hundred percent guaranteed disaster, ending probably in death for everyone involved. Aurora saunters back to her chair, smiling in the knowledge that she has certainly bested me this time. For good. For life. Well, the short life I have left.

I look for a little comfort from Claire. "Hey. Miss me?"

Claire is trying very hard not to look at me. And not doing a very good job.

"Claire. Come on. It's me."

"Oh. Were you looking at me?"

"Claire!"

"Robin- ah, Paper. You have to understand. I grew up hearing that Fillers were different. Small. A greenish tint to their skin. Stuff like that. My whole life."

"Do I look green?"

She eyes me over a little, looks close at my face. "No. Of course not." Then from somewhere deep she pulls out a little of that Claire compassion I know she's got, reaches out a hand and puts it on mine, a bit tentatively. "Listen, it might take some getting used to. You're from another world."

"Fill Cities aren't another world. They're all over the country. Other countries too."

"What's it like? In one of those?"

"Well, first thing that comes to mind, there's a smell, we call it the Everpresent Stink. And the work is hard, and dirty. And all our data is screened and scrubbed, so the net is slow to non-existent. And the food is, well, you can imagine. And I've never had a vacation of course. And if you step out of line..." I slice my finger across my throat. "Maybe you're right, Claire. Maybe it is another world."

"I'm sorry. It sounds like hell."

The word "hell" stings a little, and reminds me that there is more to the story, I'm hiding the good parts, maybe looking for maximum pity. "No, wait Claire. Sorry. It's not just that. There's more. In Fill City One all the families are very close. My sisters are my best friends, and my Dad, and my Nana is still alive at ninety-seven, so much for the health risks of living in a garbage dump, right? And we get a few channels of satellite TV included in our pay, and all the methane we can burn."

She's looking kind of awkwardly at me, like "all right,

dear, if you say so," but I'm on a roll and I can't stop. "And the best part? When a wind blows away the Everpresent Stink for a little while, and the haze parts, and the whole family climbs up one of the higher fills and looks up at the blue sky, and we have a picnic, maybe it's late Spring before the heat really starts cooking the fill, and we throw around a frisbee with the neighbors. It's me and Rock and Scissors versus the Connors, and it's like we know each other's movements before they happen, so of course we win and the Connors laugh and say, 'someday we'll beat the Farris Triple Team.' And when you smile it's pure and it's full of joy, because for that little itty-bitty moment, that's all there is."

I come to my senses feeling wetness on my chin, a tear running down my face. I'm embarrassed. Before I can wipe it on my sleeve, though, Aurora tosses me a box of the little lab cloths from her station. "Sounds nice."

"It is."

She reaches into her pocket, then leans to me and hands me the photo she stole from my cubby. "Here. I kept it to pretend it was my family for a little while."

"Why?"

"Wow. You still don't get it, do you?"

Drew, who's been trying to ignore the fact that he's lost control of his class, smacks his hand on the lab table. "Ahem. Paper Farris. Care to share your amazing stories with the class?"

"Well, if you'd like me to-"

"I was being sarcastic. You've disrupted the lecture long enough. And you've got a *lot* of catching up to do, young lady."

Wow. Drew is really playing up the high school teacher act for the cameras. I guess he's got to, as I can't imagine high school chemistry being the blistering hot entertainment the global audience is clamoring for. When Drew turns back to his holographic projection of a carbon dioxide molecule, I nudge Benji and whisper. "Hey. Chemistry class? I mean, you and I find this fascinating, but isn't it deadly boring TV?"

"Nah. They figure out ways to liven it up. Avery blew off two of her fingers on Wednesday."

I sneak a peek at Avery, who wiggles a little hello with her fingers, two of which are blueish and in splints, presumably reattached at the MedBay. The movement makes her wince and she tucks them back into her lap.

"By the way, Hi. My name is Benji. Benji Greenberg. You are?"

"Come on, I'm sorry, Benji. You know how sorry I am."

He nudges me back. "I'm kidding. It's good to have you back. You're all clear with me. It's Aurora you have to worry about. She is *pissed*."

"No kidding."

"Hey, why did the drug addict cross the road?"

"I'm guessing this has something to do with a chicken."

"Because there was a chicken on the other side selling crack."

"You're terrible."

"Hey, so... Paper? That's kind of a strange name."

Drew pairs us off for the lab experiment, we're going to recreate the Sabatier process, synthesizing methane from hydrogen and carbon dioxide, and I'm with Benji, so while we prepare ourselves to lose some fingers, I tell him the story, and he thinks it's cute, and by the time we've prepared the mixed catalyst bed, he's back to being a hundred percent the Benji I knew, and I'm like fifty percent the friend he knew and fifty percent the friend he just met. I'll take it.

I can imagine the good viewers at home taking a well-deserved nap during this class, but personally I find the fuel discussion riveting. When the *High Heaven* launches, it'll remain in orbit for a week, getting all the systems ready and refilling the fuel tanks. But there's a physical limitation to how much fuel the rocket can carry, so Larson knew once on Mars, he'd have to utilize materials on the Martian surface to generate fuel for the return trip to Earth. The answer? Methane. Mars' atmosphere contains an abundance of carbon dioxide, and plenty of water trapped in ice just below the surface. By utilizing a mixed catalyst bed and a reverse water gas shift reactor, we can produce enough methane to refill the tanks when we're done with our experiments, and get home. So the *High Heaven*'s rocket engines, fifty-six of them, draw a liquid methane/oxygen mix, rather than the traditional oxygen/kerosene/hydrogen mixes.

I smile to myself, realizing that my little rocket experiments back home, using methane-based propellant, had more in common with the rocket I may be riding in than I thought. Maybe they weren't failures after all.

"Yes, Paper?"

"Huh?"

Drew points to my raised hand. "I assume you have a question."

Crap. Why did I have my hand up? "Um, oh, yes, I was thinking, if we make more methane than needed and pyrolyze the excess of it into carbon and hydrogen, we could recycle the hydrogen back into the reactor to produce more methane and water. Just a thought."

Drew scowls at me, then stops and looks off. He scribbles something on his notepad. Turns back to me and nods.

"Good. Very good. Wow. That's actually... I'll have to talk to Mister Larson about that. Twenty points for Red Team."

Benji, Claire, and even Mike reach over and give me a little fist bump. Aurora raises an eyebrow. "Pyrolyze? Is that even a word? Brown noser."

And that's when Avery sets herself on fire.

49

WHAT KIND OF NAME IS PAPER ANYWAY?

Interview with Avery Jacobs, contestant number twenty-six, back in MedBay (again):

"I think I have it figured out. It's a curse. This show is a curse. Every time I try to leave, they bring me back. I'm like Prometheus, rolling the stupid boulder up the hill for eternit- oh, that's Sisyphus? Well I'm like Sisyphus then, though I can't understand why people would want to see that. Sadists. And every time I tell them to stop liking me, they do it even more just out of spite. See? Look over at the board. They're going crazy. And when I cry it goes up even faster. I've tried to stop crying. I'm holding it all in now. You haven't seen me cry this whole week, have you? I'm trying to get zero points this stage, negative points if that's possible, maybe that'll offset the Likes. I'm going home if it kills me. Now if you'll excuse me, I think my skin graft is ready."

S tage Three, Day Seventeen.

I've learned so much from this show. Of course the obvious, physical fitness, space flight, terraforming, physics, chemistry, everything one of us will need to be a contributing member of the crew that goes to Mars. But what's equally fascinating is learning how television works. Like, I never really noticed how some of my favorite shows, *We're Watching You*, for example, have virtually nothing going on, but audiences are glued to them for the mishaps, and the conflict, and the gossip, and of course, the sex. And Larson appears to be following these reality show best practices. For example: in this stage, Larson put Mike Horner in Suzie Q's room, and Albert in Marina Delacosta's room, just to see what would happen. Of course it resulted in a lot of late night room switching, some petty but very loud accusations, generally a whole lot of blurred, flesh-colored areas of the TV screen – and a spike in ratings and a crapload of Likes. Down the hall, on the other hand, nerd watchers had finally given up on Benji and me hooking up, which does the exact opposite for ratings. So guess who Larson moved me into a room with?

Right. I don't even have to answer.

She's been cold, aloof, angry, nice, bitchy, compassionate, but mostly just pissed that Stage Three is right up my alley and not hers. And that's pretty much every night.

"Aurora, come on. You've got Albert on your team. He'll carry all of you."

She yells from the top bunk. "Shut up. Was I talking to you?"

"You were talking, and saying my name."

"I was talking about wanting to rip up paper into little pieces. I wasn't talking about you."

"That is *not* funny."

"What kind of a name is Paper anyway?"

Once again, I get to tell my favorite story, Aurora allows it, although she's grunting and harrumphing through it, like she can't wait for it to be over so she can continue grousing about me. But then: "Your mom left you?"

"Yeah. The first line of my favorite story, the story of my life, is how my mother left us."

"Mm-hmm. I have the same first line. But it was my father."

I don't know whether to say anything. I don't.

"He left us when I was two. Me and my mom. Alone in New Jersey. Mostly lies since. I don't know what's true."

"Hey. I thought you said you had two sisters."

"And I thought you were a sustenance farmer who lived alone with her chickens."

"Fair."

"No. I was messing with your head about the sisters thing. I don't have any sisters. I always thought that would be cool, though. Singing into our hair brushes together and talking about our favorite bands."

"And braid circles."

"What the hell is a braid circle?"

I hop off my bunk and – tentatively – motion for her to sit next to me on the floor. "We don't have a third, but..." and as she sits down at my knees, back facing me, I take a few little bunches of her hair and begin to fold them. "Rock likes the Fishtail, and Scissors likes the Four Strand, and my favorite is the Farris Waterfall."

"You can braid that thing on top of your head?"

"It used to be very long, down past our butts, all three of us. Then my Dad had the genius idea of cutting mine off and bleaching it for the show. He said that way I'd never get found out. Boy, that worked out."

She turns to face me, undoing my work, looking grave. "I'm sorry I did what I did, Paper Farris."

"No. It's better this way. I hated being Robin Smith. I hated being someone I'm not. I should thank you."

"Shirley Schneider."

I squint and tilt my head like a confused dog.

"That's who I really am. Shirley Schneider. Don't laugh."

"Um, you're talking to someone named Paper."

"Good point. Yeah, Shirley and Sally Schneider, if you can believe it, bouncing from state to state with the Air Force, she was in logistics or something, they wouldn't let her stay put. She got me a nanny that happened to be into singing, so something like four hundred competitions later, we write 'Baby's Gone,' and I show up on *America Sings!* and everybody lives happily ever after. Whoopdie-doo."

"I'm... sorry."

"Nah. Look at the two of us. We're here aren't we? Best shape of our lives, well-fed, we're on an adventure, and we both have somebody somewhere that loves us."

"I miss them. Terribly."

"Yeah. Mom's not so soft and cuddly, but same." She reaches out and tugs a patch of my hair. "We should really get rid of those ridiculous bleach tips. Unless you're going for a pop-diva look like me."

"No. You can have pop-diva. It's all yours. I'll get the scissors."

I move to rise, but she grabs my hand and pulls me back down.

"Wait. First... can I... hug you? Nothing weird. I promise."

"Um, sure. Of course."

She reaches over and embraces me, and it reminds me so much of Rock and Scissors, it's like a gift, it transports me home, and I ask myself how I could ever have doubted Aurora, underneath all the flash and the snark she's just like my sisters.

We sit like that for a while, and she whispers, "This is nice."

The little doubt pokes me again. "Um, can I ask you a question, Aurora?"

"Sure."

"Back in Stage Two, when you wound up with the only spacesuit... I never got to ask you... that was just a coincidence, right?"

"Of course. Why?"

"Nothing. Forget it."

She pushes back, peering deep into my eyes. "Would you ask your sister that?"

50

THE BUTTER WOMAN

Well, the mystery of the *ever-so-slightly-off* food we've been eating since week three has finally been solved.

It's called Food Printing, and it's our next class in Stage Three.

And I love it.

Food has held a strange place in my life in Fill City One. One would think with our living conditions and lack of anything but the most basic food rations, we'd find other things to obsess over. But the opposite was true: every Sunday afternoon we could manage, we'd watch cooking shows from the mainland together, groaning at the delights being prepared and dreaming of their taste on our tongues.

"Now would you look at that! Oh, my Lord, have you ever seen that much butter?"

"Nana, remember that time we had butter on our pancakes? Can we do that next weekend?"

She held the three of us a little tighter, like a hen readjusting her clutch of eggs. "Hmm. I believe I could call in a favor with Jack. I bet if we each wrote Jack a little letter saying something we liked about him, we'd find some butter in our rations this week."

And so we wrote to Jack, the grocery manager, and here's what my letter said: "Dear Mister Jack, You are my favorite person in the whole world. Aside from Nana, and Daddy, and Rock, and Scissors, and maybe two of my friends. Or three. You are my favorite right after those people. We would like to have a pancake party next Sunday, and do you know what goes really well on pancakes? Yes, butter goes really well on pancakes. And I hear that you are the man to call for butter. The very best man. The butter man!"

Nana loved my letter, and Jack apparently did too, because we had enough butter in our rations that week not only for pancakes, but to make the chicken and goat and mashed potatoes all taste a little dreamier. *Mmmm.* Butter. Jack liked the letter so much, in fact, he insisted Nana call him The Butter Man, and before long, that was his name throughout Fill City One.

And now *I'm* The Butter Man. Well, The Butter Woman.

We've each been given some time, after training, with the Food Printer, and I have, of course, decided to perfect my butter. Almost-butter.

The food printer on *High Heaven* will create food for the crew from twelve basic ingredients stored in bulk – proteins, carbohydrates, fats, and minerals, along with some aesthetics like colors and fibers and spices. Much like the printing unit that creates the PPMM of the domes, this machine paints food from the plate up, almost molecule-by-molecule. For me, it answers the question, "How do you get a tech geek to actually like cooking?"

The others have created passable steaks, seafood, pasta,

even vegetables like – yes – beets. But they've been going broad, not deep. Their creations will go down better than pastes and pellets on the long journey to Mars, but like the foods we've been eating for weeks here, they'll never pass for the real thing. I, on the other hand, have spent my time obsessively tweaking and tweaking the ingredients, like a mathematician, to create the most accurate possible simulation of just one thing.

Benji nudges my elbow. "That's an awful lot of butter, Paper."

"Hey. I have a thing, okay?" I take out some spoons and point to the giant dollop of yellowish heaven. "You want to try?"

The rest of them approach, tentatively, and Drew smacks his lips. "Damn. Wow. I can't believe that's not butter. Mike, go get your lobster and let's dip some. Lobster with butter. Red Team, ten points."

Aurora and Marina *tsk*. "Come on, it's just butter." But then they taste it. "Oh."

We're catching up. Our team is only twenty points behind-

The doors to the Great Hall slam open.

Zach Larson marches in.

"Turn off the cameras."

Without missing a beat, ever the pro, Ted barks into his headset, "Run the new romance backstories in 3... 2... 1..." Nods to Zach.

"Good. Teams. Change of plans."

We shouldn't be surprised there's a change of plans, it is Zach Larson after all, but we're surprised nonetheless. Drew approaches him. "Zach. Is everything all right?"

"I'm sorry to say, no. The Senate just introduced a bill.

The Off-World Biocontamination Act." Our hands shoot up with a million questions, but he waves them down. "Yes, it's crazy. Basically, they're saying it's unlawful to have humans, with all our bacteria, potentially contaminating other planets."

Drew shakes his head. "But we've been to the Moon. And every piece of equipment currently on Mars has been handled by humans. And our hardware is the cleanest ever."

"Doesn't matter. They're trying to stop us from going. Something's up. If it passes, by this weekend the FBI and Homeland Security will raid us, and shut the whole thing down. Now, I have a senator friend or two, but there's only so much they can do…" He looks directly at me. "Someone *really* doesn't want us to go."

I move to him and whisper, "The… element?"

He leans down, whispers back. "No. More like what I was talking about. A turf war."

Claire stamps her foot. "So that's it? It's over?"

"Over? Heavens no, Claire! Onto the good news. I've moved Stage Three's finale to tomorrow evening, and we'll begin Stage Four the following morning."

Ted raises his pen and points. "But, sir… Stage Four is in the simulator here… right? What's the difference? What's to prevent them from raiding us and shutting down the simulator?"

"Simulator?" He laughs. "Think fun, fun, fun, Ted! Why simulate, when we can-"

"Sir. Please don't say it."

"Ted. Make it happen. In two days, we start Stage Four: *Launch.*"

Ted's mouth drops open and his pen hits the floor.

51

PAPER 2.0

Wow. Okay. A lot to juggle:

1. The federal government suddenly wants to take down this private space mission, which has been years, maybe decades in the planning, one week after I return from a near-death experience with everyone's favorite mobsters, the Gitanos.

2. We're launching into space to beat the vote on their Off-World Biocontamination Act. In forty-eight hours, after the game-show-like finale of Stage Three, the remaining contestants will launch into space and compete from the actual *High Heaven* instead of a simulator. If we don't beat the vote, and still try to launch, we will probably all go to jail.

3. My family, and Jane, are in potential mortal danger.

4. The contestants are questionably okay with my return, some more so, and some very obviously less so. Aurora, predictably, swings wildly between the two.

5. I am falling in love with a Gitano.

6. Someone with inside access to the show has tried to

sabotage the whole thing, willing to kill us all, for unknown reasons. And that person or persons are still at large.

So... why am I smiling?

There must be something wrong with me.

Somewhere along the line, somewhere among the small and large disasters that have consistently taken place since finding the scarab, something happened. I became something different.

But you know what? Maybe that's... not a bad thing. My old self, Paper 1.0, thought life inside Fill City One was hard. The work was most definitely grueling, and nothing came easy. But in a way, that made me soft. Naive. I had just the area within the thirty-foot walls to worry about, and it was easy to say, "If I ever get out," not knowing just what would begin to happen the moment I did.

But now I'm Paper 2.0, diving into the deep end of the real world, and I find that I'm able – after a little flailing and splashing and near-drowning – to swim. And you know what? I like swimming. Yes. I like pushing forward. I like the idea that this is the farthest thing from easy, that trying to make it to Mars is kicking the crap out of me, making me prove it to myself and the world over and over again how bad I want it. I'm beginning to like the idea, at last, that I am some form of representative for my people, that my life being on the line is not just about me, but about all of them, even the mainlanders.

Yes, maybe it's all that – or maybe I've just gone batshit crazy like my mother.

"God. Will you shut the hell up?" Aurora barks.

I open my eyes. "Yikes. Was I saying that out loud?"

"You were whimpering and thrashing around and laughing, and kissing your own hand and whispering 'Angel,' and murmuring something about life, love, and freedom. God, you are so annoying. Come on. We've got a transport coming for Larson's game show, and I need this last hour of sleep to regenerate my brain."

"You need a lot more than an hour."

She jumps down from the top bunk. "Wise ass." Grabs her pillow and smacks me with it.

And yes, we have an actual, *straight-from-the-movies* pillow fight, feathers exploding into the air, and I'm certain the Likes are going through the roof out on the Big Board, I mean, two women having a pillow fight on live TV? But I don't care, it's fun as hell. We finally fall in a heap on the floor.

Aurora sighs. "You ready to go down, Farris?"

"Take your best shot, Schneider."

52

OLD SCHOOL GAME SHOW

I didn't know Zach had this in him. Of course, he's the consummate showman, proven again and again, as well as being the consummate businessman, in fact the world's first trillionaire. He makes it look easy. All of it.

But this?

He stands there, in front of us, in a bow tie and a seersucker suit, his silver hair slicked back against his head, and a wall of categories behind him. Zach Larson has morphed into an old-school game show host. Complete with index cards and a microphone.

"Well, well, contestants! Here we are, at the finale of Stage Three: Back to School. I'd like to invite you to take your places before the board."

We step up to our individual podiums, grouped into three colors, our remaining Red, Green, and Yellow teams. The whole thing would be strange enough, but we're not standing in just any outdoor arena – the entire set and massive bleachers have been set up in the shadow of the *High Heaven*, right here on the launch pad in the middle of the desert in

Arizona, the main dome from Stage Two visible in the distance. We gasped when we first landed here and stepped off *Martha*, craning our necks to take in the gargantuan rocket that stretched into the sky. The largest rocket ever constructed, nearly twice the size of the Saturn Five rockets that brought the first astronauts to the Moon, its base is a cluster of fifty-six engines, each of which could swallow *Martha* whole. A rush of awe had filled me, looking at this giant thing, a thing that showed in physical reality the potential of the human race, what we could accomplish if we worked together, the best minds and the best hands, weaving possibly the most intricate machine in the history of man, and proving beyond any doubt that we deserved to be here, and to knock on the door of other worlds.

But now the behemoth ship is being used for something just slightly sillier: the Stage Three game board is being projected onto it. This board, I'm told, is modeled after an ancient TV game show called *Jeopardy*, apparently the longest running show of all time in its day. (*Survive This!*, a reboot of the ancient *Survivor*, being the current holder of that record, with an astounding forty-two straight seasons.) On the board are five columns of point amounts, from ten through fifty, under category headings including Medical, Chemistry, Engineering, Space, and Mars. Looking past the board to the wild crowd, I once more truly appreciate Larson's genius. At first I thought all this was just a ploy to bring in boatloads of advertising revenue – which it most certainly has – but as the show takes shape I see he's doing a lot more: he's educating the people around the world about Mars; reigniting their fire for exploration and discovery; and reminding them that the drought of human space exploration – not a single manned mission to another world has taken place since 1973, over a hundred years ago – is finally coming to an end. Zach Larson is getting them ready to break out of their isolation, their Earth-centric haze, and reach past our limitations, to some new potential.

Or he's just really good at making money and likes to hear himself talk. Either one.

Mike Horner nudges me. "Psst."

Mike hasn't talked to me since I returned, he's really gone out of his way to avoid me, and other than that one little fist bump back in class we haven't interacted at all. "I'm sorry, Mike."

"You already said that. Listen, I've got a thing about honesty and loyalty. Can't change it, I'm sorry. I'm working on it. But I wanted to let you know, I realize you've been through a lot, I respect that, so you're still invited."

"Invited?"

He just smiles. "Shh. It's starting."

Larson puts his hands in the air to raucous applause. "Ready for some fun, fun, fun, folks? Rules are easy. First one to smack their buzzer answers the question for points. They then control the board, choosing the next topic and point amount. When the board is complete, I'll ask a final question on which you can wager up to your team's entire three-week total. The two teams with the most points will proceed to Stage Four. The teams will then disband and each contestant will compete individually for the coveted spot on the crew of *High Heaven*." He turns to the audience. "Now, no helping them please - that would be cheating!" He winks, and the thousands of fans in attendance laugh and jeer, as they all know at this point "rules" is an overrated word, and life is more fun when they're broken.

"Ready, contestants? I'll go first. Mars for ten points. How many moons does Mars have, and what are their names?"

Avery slams down her hand and her podium lights up. *Bwonk!*

"Yes, Avery?"

"Dog shit."

"Avery, come now, this is a family show."

"Dog feces."

"That's better. Still not right, though. Negative ten points for Yellow Team. Anyone have the correct answer?"

Aurora buzzes in. "Two moons. Phobos and Deimos."

"That's correct, Aurora! Ten points for Green Team. The board is yours."

"I'll take Medical for twenty points."

"All right: What is the itchy skin condition *tinea pedis* better known as?"

Avery slams her hand down again.

"Yes, Avery?"

"Dog shit. I mean, dog feces."

"You're trying to lose this game for some reason, Avery, aren't you?"

"Some reason? Don't play coy, Larson. I'm on to you. You've cursed me!"

Avery's Likes start rising like crazy. She hears the ticking, looks up at the board and cringes, holding back the tsunami of tears waiting behind her eyes. "Come on, Larson, say it. You've cursed me."

"I have not cursed you, my dear Avery. I'll admit that your... misadventures haven't exactly been detrimental to our ratings, but I wish no ill upon you, of course, and look forward to having you aboard *High Heaven*. Negative ten points for Yellow Team. Anyone else?"

Albert buzzes in. "Athlete's foot."

"Very good, Albert! *Tinea pedis* is, in fact, athlete's foot. Ten points for Green Team. Now, for two extra points, Albert, can you tell me: if athletes get athlete's foot, what do astronauts get?"

Albert furrows his brow, boy this is one serious question, until Larson turns to the crowd with an inviting wave and they shout, in unison, "Mistletoe!"

Larson laughs. "Hey! I said no cheating!" But his wink tells them not to pay him any mind.

"All right, Albert. Your board."

"Chemistry for ten."

"Excellent choice. Name two liquid hydrocarbons."

Avery slams her hand down. Again. And again. Her "dog feces" act goes on for a few more questions, until her buzzer mysteriously malfunctions, and she's left continuously slamming the poor thing with both palms. No longer able to hold back the weeks of tears, she blubbers into her hands, then covers her ears to stop hearing the chatter of infinite Likes being added to her name.

Suddenly, Larson does the unexpected (yes, somehow he can still surprise): he stops the show. A single spotlight shines on him, and a second shines on Avery, and the rest is blackness and silence. Larson whispers, "Avery... can you tell me what you want? Your wildest dream? It's not going to Mars, is it?"

She looks up, embarrassed and red and blotchy, eye makeup smearing all over her face. Shakes her head.

"Then, what is it?"

She shakes her head again.

"Come, come, Avery. I want to know."

"Kittens. And puppies. Okay? I've always wanted to own a pet shop. Are you satisfied?"

"Would you be surprised, Avery, if I had already guessed that?" And instantly the lights return, and the set is swarming with kittens and puppies, coming in from all directions, each with a yellow bow to match Avery's training suit. The crowd is stunned for just a moment, and then *ooohs* and *aaaahs* and cheers erupt from them as they pick up the animals and cuddle them, and the entire arena dissolves into good-natured chaos. Larson himself reaches down and gently cups a kitten and a puppy in each hand, walks over to Avery, and offers them to her.

She sniffs. "I... I don't know what to say."

"Say yes."

Now she can't say anything, the tears are really gushing, mixing with snot and a little drool, but it's happy snot and drool, and she nods and accepts the gift, steps from behind her podium and embraces Larson and her new little animal friends, and all is forgiven.

"Yes, Avery. We've rented you a storefront back in Seattle, and have you all ready for business. We've even come up with a name: Take Me To Your Owner. Get it? Like aliens?" The crowd groans as he holds up the sign Ted just handed him, showing a UFO with puppies bounding down the gang plank into their new owners' arms. "Now. I would like you to stay. At least through tonight's game. Do you think you could do that for me?"

Avery nods enthusiastically, and wipes her nose on her sleeve. "Can I keep these little guys here?"

"Certainly. As for the rest, Ted, won't you please corral them all up and get them over to the incinerator?"

Avery sputters. I think she swallowed her tongue.

"I'm kidding, *kidding!* No, of course they'll all be waiting for you when you get home. Now where was I? Oh yes, Medical for thirty: the parasite *Cryptosporidiosis* may be found in what common substance?"

We all stare at Larson. *Huh? We never covered this.*

"Avery, perhaps?" And he winks at her.

She gingerly buzzes in, clearly afraid Larson may be pulling the rug out from under her, damning her with another curse, she's totally unsure, but the twinkle in his eye gives her the courage to say it:

"Dog feces?"

"That is correct, Avery!" And the crowd erupts in laughter and cheers again, and we all wonder at Zach Larson's ability to pull moments like this out of his ass on the fly. It's simply amazing.

The rest of the show isn't quite as chaotic, but the extremely close score does have the audience here and around the world on the edge of their seats. Red, Green, and Yellow are all within ten points of each other, and the last question allows us to bet our total if we want.

Larson grins. "Very good, very good, contestants! You've clearly done your homework. And congratulations to our Team Leaders for getting some of this to sink in!" A spotlight shines on the five *High Heaven* astronauts, with ever-stoic-looking Daniels nodding politely and folding his arms, and the rest waving like they just can't wait to end this lunacy and get to the actual mission.

"All right. The final question. All teams bet up to their full point balance upon hearing the category, then answer when I call on you. This is for all the marbles, my friends. One team will go home. The rest of you? Stage Four: Launch. And here is the category: Minerals. Place your wager now."

Benji, Claire, and Mike whip their heads around to me. "Well?"

I hesitate. Seconds pass. "Hey, why only *me* on this?"

Blank stares. Claire actually laughs. "That's a rhetorical question, right?"

"Okay. Whatever. Bet the house, Benji. All of it. We have to assume both teams are going to get it right and bet it all, so it's the only way to stay in the game. Don't worry. I got this."

Larson interrupts the teams' murmuring. "All right, friends, please put your stylus down. Now the question: What Martian mineral is needed for the magnetite-wustite redox cycle for an alternative method of producing oxygen?"

The countdown music starts. And... oh my God. I'm blank. Nothing. We didn't cover this. Or if we did, I was daydreaming about Angel, or about launching into space aboard the *High Heaven*, or walking across the landscape of Mars, the crunch of crystals beneath my fee- *wait. Crystals.* Oh yes. I've got this. I grin and nod to my teammates.

The countdown stops, and Larson raises his arms. "Please put your tablets down. Now first, Yellow Team, you're bringing up the rear with two hundred forty-five points. Your answer?"

Tanner taps Yellow Team's tablet, and their answer appears on the big board:

Dog Feces.

Even Larson can't control himself and laughs. "Well, I suppose if you weren't confident in the category, there was only one way to go. Bravo, Yellow Team. Now, how much did you wager?"

Tanner taps again: *Zero.*

"Smart. Very smart. You've retained your score of two-forty-five. Now, Green Team? You're behind Red Team by just five points with two-fifty."

Marina taps her tablet, and shouts, "Issa hematite."

Oh my God.

She's right. I know it. Before Larson even nods his head.

And I was wrong.

"And we betta all two hundred fifty points."

They blew us out of the water. And Yellow bet zero. And we have the wrong answer. And we bet everything.

It's over.

We're going home.

Benji reluctantly taps the tablet with our answer: "Tridymite."

"Oooh. I'm sorry, Red Team. Oh dear. Your wager?"

I grab Benji's hand to stop him from tapping. Is there any way I can undo this? Like if we don't show our answer, we don't lose? I contemplate taking the tablet and breaking it in two. Please. It can't be true. It can't be true. We came so close. I thought I was right, I was certain, and I wound up being wrong. Again.

I let go of Benji's hand, and close my eyes, and hang my head.

And hear cheering.

Huh?

I open one eye. People are on their feet, roaring their approval. I open my other eye and turn to Benji. He's grinning wryly at me. "I had a hunch. You flinched. And you're welcome."

Larson claps. "You bet nine points! That lowers your total to two hundred forty-six, but it's still enough to stay in second place. Green Team and Red Team, you're proceeding to Stage Four!"

I reach up and kiss Benji on the cheek. "Thanks for not listening to me."

"What did you say?"

"Wise ass." I punch him in the shoulder, and we hug, and we all hug, all three teams, even Yellow Team, through their tears. I think through all the craziness, we did get to like each other, maybe even become some weird, dysfunctional family-like thing. I hug Tanner, who mentions something about an organic farm, although honestly I tune him out as soon as I hear the word "beet." And Suzie Q, who will somehow have to live without her obsession Albert while we take a trip into orbit for the next three weeks. I even give a fist bump to Quinn Keller, who's going home with the least Likes, and who I honestly don't remember saying a single word to this whole time. And of course, last but not least, I hug Avery.

"Well, Paper. I guess you won't miss me."

"I will."

"Come on."

"No seriously, Avery, I don't know. I will. I never had a lot of..."

We share a smile and she says, "Friends."

"Yeah. And back home, you'd fit right in."

Aurora walks over. "Avery, Avery. I'd shake your hand but I don't want to pull your fingers off."

Avery lowers her gaze and walks away. I kick her foot. "Aurora, you have such a way with people."

"Whatever. I just came over here to congratulate you."

"Wow. Really?"

"No. I actually wanted to gloat. I beat you. Na nana na na na."

"Yup. That's more like it."

We fist bump, and Larson taps his microphone. "Contestants. I hate to interrupt your heartfelt goodbyes, but we need to take our places."

"Take our places? For what?"

Larson motions for Mike Horner and Marina Delacosta to approach him. "For the wedding, of course."

53

YES, THERE IS A WEDDING.

Yes, there is a wedding after the game show. At the launch pad of the largest rocket ever built.

And as bizarre as it sounds, it really is so sweet.

The sun is setting, it couldn't be any more flawless really, and Larson bends down so Ted can place a robe over his suit. Zach Larson, now Justice of The Peace and Wedding Presider. I think we're all done being surprised.

Mike has changed as well, into an all-too-perfect tuxedo, and we all wait, as is customary, for the bride to appear, knowing full well that Larson has gone over the top once again, and we're not disappointed when Marina parades back out, in a gown with a train long enough to reach all the way back to Los Angeles, and a veil with tiny lights flickering in it, like a constellation of stars in the heavens. The women in the audience sigh collectively, and I've never seen so many camera flashes. It's like a royal wedding. I'm not kidding.

Zach walks them through the mini service, and they exchange rings, and Marina now has an even bigger ring on her finger than she used to, you can probably see it from space, I imagine them closing the mine this diamond came from, knowing it couldn't possibly offer up a single karat more after this giant rock emerged from it.

"Now. Do you, Mike Horner, take Marina Delacosta to be your wife, to have and to hold, from this moment forward, through time and space, until you pass to the great beyond?"

Mike smiles a smile that breaks a billion hearts. "I do."

"And do you, Marina, take Mike to be your husband, for all time and through all trials, from the top of each mountain to the depth of each valley, for as long as the universe itself breathes life?"

She beams, and a tear threatens to ruin her perfect eye makeup. "I do."

And they kiss, THE kiss, the kiss that weakens knees around the world, the kiss that will be written about for years, and of course – not a soul on Earth is caught off-guard at this – Larson nods to Ted, and fireworks fill the sky behind the *High Heaven*.

And for a moment, sincerely and with no exaggeration, I can feel the entire planet, each and every soul, sigh just a little, and smile, and let a little romantic love sweep them off their feet, and believe just for that moment that this is what it all comes down to, isn't it? The moment we give ourselves to someone, fully, leaving nothing of ourselves, and we find that somehow we're even more for that gift.

Aurora puts her arm around me. "Stop crying, Farris. You're embarrassing."

"I'm not crying. You're crying."

"Whatever. Hold my champagne."

And she swaggers over to the newlyweds, bows, then

turns to face the audience, and grabs a mic from Ted. "I'd like to say these two are my friends, but as you know folks, they're my sworn mortal enemies." Laughs ripple through the audience. "But look at them. Cute overload. Cuteness Threat Level Eleven. So yeah, I had to write them a little something." The music starts, and Aurora sings:

> *Cuore, Il mio cuore,*
> *My heart is yours,*
> *Il tuo é mio,*
> *Together we start,*
> *Nessuno puó separare,*
> *Forever, sempre, my love, mi amore.*

I have no idea what half of it means, but it's beautiful, and as Aurora leads a chant of the last "mi amore," over and over with the swaying crowd, Marina's parents rush down from their dais and embrace her, and then embrace Mike and Marina, and it's not hard to imagine Signore Delacosta writing a check for a cajillion dollars to Larson for giving his daughter the wedding of the millennium.

Once the music has faded, the crowd calmed, and all the tears shed, Larson whispers to us, "My friends, the vote on the Off-World Biocontamination Act is scheduled for tomorrow afternoon. We really should get some sleep to get an early start, to avoid a surprise visit from friendly federal agents."

Mike takes Marina's hand. "Zach. We're not coming."

"Oh dear. But... Mars..."

"Mars is a big deal. Yes. But this," he looks into Marina's eyes, "it's bigger."

I think my heart just exploded. Can you imagine someone saying something like that to you?

Marina kisses Larson on both cheeks. "Goodbye, Zach darling. Mike issa right. I don't need Mars no longer. I have found something better. My own strength." She pulls Mike into an embrace. "And my love."

54

THE BIGGEST DAY

In just a few hours, the sun will rise on the biggest day of my life.

A day that marks the beginning of mankind's rebirth into something new. A species that someday will count Earth as just one of its homes.

Zach has given me permission to walk here, alone, around the base of the massive *High Heaven* rocket, in the wee hours before our flight. The launch pad is mind-bogglingly large, the size of six football fields, it seems even larger now that the stage and bleachers are gone. Now I can see, beyond the pad, brush and trees thriving, even in the face of the occasional five thousand degree flames of liftoff.

I walk to them, along a double chain-link, barbed-wire fence, to get beyond the harsh lights on the launch pad and see some stars.

There. Almost directly overhead, Polaris. Below it, Ursa Minor and Ursa Major. They've always been there for me, permanent and comforting, and tonight, something different: I feel like they're inviting me. They can't wait to greet me.

I remember teaching, or trying to teach anyway, the stars and constellations to Rock and Scissors, late at night, when the Fill was quiet except for the hiss of the methane lamps. We were born in September, Rock just before midnight on the twenty-third, so she was a Virgo, and then myself and Scissors just after midnight on the twenty-fourth, both of us being Libras, and I used to show them both constellations whenever the haze parted with a midnight breeze. According to the serious-but-ridiculous astrology book we found, our astrological signs meant Rock was "modest and shy" – *totally* wrong – and "overcritical and harsh," which was spot on (although she was harshly critical of that description). And that meant Scissors and I, as Libras, were "diplomatic and urbane," whatever that meant, and "idealistic." I liked that last one. Yes. Idealistic. Not Scissors so much, but me definitely. I always liked to look to an ideal future, I don't know why, to dream about what a future might look like, with people on other planets, exploring space, not just stewing here on Earth, no, we could escape the gravity of this life, and reach our potential. I really believed it. I still do. Scissors just liked the idea that "libra" translated to "book" in Albanian, and of course books are made out of paper, which she found funny. I preferred the Zulu translation of libra: "free." That had a nice ring to it.

Thinking of them, all of them, and looking up at the little points of light, inviting me but so very far away, suddenly I feel very alone.

"Pssst."

. . .

I jump out of my skin. *"Who the hell is that?!"*

"Angel."

"Angel?! What the-?"

"Shhh! I'm sorry. But I had to see you."

He climbs the first ten foot fence, draping a cloak over the barbed wire, then on to the second. Drops to the ground, dusting himself off, and faces me.

"How...?!"

"I've been following you. On the show, and..." He points to his armpit, "...that thing your mother implanted-"

"Oh my God! My mother! Is she-?"

"Shhh. They're okay. I snuck your Mom out, we picked up Voomvoom, and we're in hiding. We're safe."

"Then... my family...!"

"Shhh! Don't worry. Gene and Pops are spooked. Even with me AWOL and your Mom gone, that Dead Body thing and the strike has them spooked, and the Fillers are back to work, so your family will be safe for a little while. I'm working on a longer-term fix, too. I came here because I just had to... I had to say goodbye."

I run up to him, practically tackling him, and smush my face so hard against his I think we both chip a tooth. I whisper scream, "Angel! You're my guardian ange- oh- that's weird."

"Yeah. The name's a little on the nose, isn't it? Funny, I grew up afraid it would become an ironic name, like Angel, the Gitano who killed the most people ever. You know, like Tiny is the biggest guy you've ever seen."

I pull back, for the first time realizing I may be in the arms of a murderer. "Have you ever...?"

"Killed anyone?" He laughs. "No. They have to keep me around, I'm a full-blooded Gitano after all, but I'm not cut out for any of it. I had to rough up a guy once and I threw up. It was a mess. The guy actually felt bad for me. He handed me a towel. That's when I knew." He takes my hand and we walk. "I knew that couldn't be my life. Leo, Tiny, John, Marie, Gene, Pops, all of them, all the same. Life is cheap to them. I knew I was different. Life means... *something* to me. I won't live that life anymore."

Images flash into my mind, Angel tapping on the privacy screen in the limousine, stepping awkwardly in front of Gene Gitano. "You interrupted Leo in the car for me. And you took that slap for my mother on purpose. Didn't you?"

He smiles sheepishly. "I was going for subtle."

I squeeze his hand. "It was brave. Very brave. Thank you."

He stops and turns to face me. "I'm the one that should be thanking you. You guys gave me the reason to finally do it. Now I'm free."

I shake my head. "Don't get ahead of yourself. The lifestyle of my mother, which it looks like you've adopted, is not free."

He thinks for a minute. Kneels in the brush, then pulls me down to lay at his side. We look up at the stars together. "It feels free to me."

I probably have a thousand deer ticks on me now, hungry for blood, but I don't care. I'm lying here in the weeds with the man I... whatever... with an angel, sent not by God, but by of all people the Gitanos, to watch over my mother and my family. The leaves and grass tickle and embrace me, and I do feel safe again, and not alone anymore, and yes, free. I look over at him, and I can feel a stupid grin growing on my face, the uncontrollable perma-grin of a girl falling in love. Maybe it's just the wedding, I don't know, and right now I don't care. And either I'm imagining it, making this vision a little too perfect, or I'm actually smelling it.

"Can you smell that?"

"Yes. Lavender. The exact opposite of Leo's farts."

We both giggle, uncontrollably, up at the stars. He turns his head to me. "Tell me about Mars. All I know for sure is it doesn't have animatronic alligators."

"It does. That part is true. They're nasty."

He nudges my elbow. Reaches down to hold my hand. "Come on. Really. I want to know where you're headed."

"Well, I'm not headed there unless I win. For the next three weeks we'll still be competing, in orbit, and only one of us wins the actual voyage to Mars. But if I do win, I'll be traveling the following three months aboard this ship" – I point up to the top of the massive rocket rising above us – "the *High Heaven*. Not the bottom part, the booster, that'll come back down and land here. Then, a week before we get to Mars, we'll position a magnetic dipole shield at the Lagrange Point, to create an artificial magnetosphere and protect the planet from solar wind and radiation – which will give us a big head start on future missions, and terraforming. Then we'll land near Columbia Hills, a range of low hills inside the Gusev crater, there's an escarpment there with plenty of ice just below the surface. Lots of data from previous rover missions, so it's well-mapped and safe. It'll take a week to print the main dome, then we'll spend three weeks setting up the fuel and oxygen production, the farm, and the mining, and the terraforming tests. Then we'll travel for another three months home."

He's counting on his fingers. "Seven months. That's a long time."

"You don't want to spend that much time alone with my

mother. I understand. Believe me. Has she offered you one of her meal bag things yet?"

"No, that's not it. Although she is a handful."

"Don't worry. It'll be the fastest months of our lives. Promise. I can't wait. Imagine it, Angel. We're finally going to reach another planet. Take the first baby steps to being a multi-planet species. I can't think of a better hope for the future."

I realize he's gently kissing my hand, and inch by inch up my arm. I laugh. "I wouldn't think talking about magnetospheres and terraforming is exactly what you'd consider romantic."

"It's your voice, Paper. You could be listing parts from a transport manual, it doesn't matter. I love listening to your voice. Hearing you talk about the future. And watching your mouth move while you tell me your dreams. You have a beautiful mouth." He reaches over and touches his lips to mine. "Listen, I know Mars is a big deal. But this? For me? It's bigger." And he pulls me into his arms, dramatically, and I laugh, and I think of Marina Delacosta and Mike Horner, and it makes me smile, and I surrender.

55

LAUNCH

I t's just like you would imagine, and nothing like you could ever imagine.

The large elevator – a pond full of animatronic alligators could fit in here – glides up effortlessly, approaching the tippy top of the *High Heaven*, above us nearly three hundred and fifty feet from the ground. I look down at Benji's hand as he absently rubs the beads on his bracelet.

Ted lifts his tablet. "Everyone here? Robin Smi- ah, Paper Farris."

"Here."

"Aurora."

I whisper, "You mean Miss Schneider?"

"Shhh. Shut up. Here."

"Mike Horner- whoops."

"Yup. Gone. Fell in love. Love kills your common sense."

"Okay, yes, that's right. Good for them." Ted continues his checklist, with Claire and Benji the other remaining Red Team members, and Albert the surviving Green Team member.

Just five contestants have made it to Stage Four.

The crew, the ones with the actual jobs and necessary skills, repeat "Here" as their names are called: Captain Daniels, looking as sternly as ever out the windows, watching Mission Control get smaller beneath us. Then Reagan Malone, Dylan Garcia, Drew Innes, and Skylar Gaines, all with the best posture I've ever seen, gleaming in their shiny new spacesuits, helmets at their hips, ready for action.

Five contestants. Five crew.

And Zach Larson.

I nudge his arm. "Not for nothing Zach, but walking the launch pad last night, your security around the perimeter is pretty lax."

"Oh, is it really?" And he grins and winks at me.

Shit.

I should've known.

"Don't worry, Paper. We blurred out the appropriate bits before we posted it to Groupie."

"You didn't."

Larson shrugs, but before he can answer, Aurora crosses to the space between us. "Hey Larson. I thought you were staying home. You know, the big guy behind the scenes. You never even came up in *Martha* with us."

"I apologize. I thought it went without saying that I was coming. You think I'd spend ten billion dollars on this and not go myself?" He points down. "Take a look at these feet, Aurora."

"So? They're feet."

"These feet are going to be the first feet to step on another planet." He looks up, squints into the distance. "Uh oh. Uninvited guests."

Off to the south, barely visible, a caravan of black trucks, like ants, is throwing up little clouds of dust as it snakes its way down Route 88 to the launch site's entrance.

"Ted?"

The headset squawks into Ted's ear. "Yes sir. The vote went through. Seven hours early. Mission Control is being instructed to shut down the launch."

"Damn, they voted early, sneaky bastards. Tell them we will do no such thing. Countdown?"

"One hour thirteen minutes."

"Let's make it thirteen minutes."

"Sir!"

I don't know why Ted even said that, he's never won a single argument with Larson and he certainly isn't going to start now. Instead, he whisper-shouts into his headset, and all our stomachs tighten into knots.

"No one throw up. I forbid you."

The elevator reaches the gangplank and halts with a little clunk, and Zach practically pushes us all, running, towards the doorway to the main cabin of *High Heaven*. "Come, come, children, don't want to be late for school!"

Three of the crew stop short in the middle. Daniels, Reagan, and Dylan. Reagan pleads, "Sir. If they've voted, this is illegal. We can't..."

Zach turns back but doesn't stop. "We can. We will. Come."

Reagan and Dylan hang their heads, and retreat to the elevator. They're not coming. They're staying here on Earth. Damn. Daniels growls, "You're going, Zach? No matter what?"

"I'm going, Dan, no matter what. This is it."

Daniels shakes his head, looking angry that he has to decide between the country and service he's known all his life, the U. S. of A., or his friend and employer for the last five years. He looks between Larson and the two crew apparently staying behind. I can't imagine the thoughts screaming in his head.

He steels his jaw. "Hurry. In."

Larson gives the hint of a smile and pats him on the back as he enters the hatch. Ted, standing just outside, addresses us just like a mother might do with her kids on the first day of kindergarten. "I'm leaving. But I'll be watching you! There are seventy-three cameras on board. Don't do anything I wouldn't do!" And he turns and dashes back to the elevator to catch up with Reagan and Dylan.

The team is moving fast, obviously faster than they had planned, and we don't have time to admire the incredible interior of this ship. Daniels barks, "Secure the hatch! Start the systems checks! Contestants buckle in!"

The engines have been idling for hours, just in case, so we're ready. The five of us contestants, and three remaining crew, and Larson, climb into our chairs, awkward, now lying on our backs, looking up out the front window at the cloudless blue above us. The rumble beneath us is unnerving.

I have the sudden, panicked feeling that I want to go home.

To get the hell out of here, and feel the ground under my feet, and appreciate the knowns, even if they're bad knowns, the solid dirt, Nana's terrible dinners, the bad TV, playing with my little rockets... wait.

Rockets.

I have to laugh. I've imagined myself, more times than I can remember, a little miniature me, being inside those tiny homemade rockets as they shot up into the sky, whooping with excitement, and flying free. For years I have imagined that.

And look at me now.

Here I am.

The thing I had imagined is real. I am going to shoot up into the sky. I *am* going home.

My cheeks tighten into an involuntary smile, and my fear dissolves, its void filled instead with anticipation and adrenalin. I look over at Aurora, sitting in the seat beside me. She looks like she might be having the same thrill-slash-terror moment. I reach out my hand, and she takes it without looking, still staring wide-eyed out the window, afraid, and I whisper to her, "Hey. Look who's the Rocket Girl." And her hand shakes a little less, and her lip curls up just a bit at the edge.

All systems check out, and shouting echoes through the cabin and over the speakers.

Ted's voice sounds nervous. He's finally lost his cool. "Sir. They're at the gate. They have papers."

"I don't care if they have bazookas. Don't let them in."

We watch on monitors throughout the cockpit, and see that the team of federal agents is now past the verbal arguing phase and is forcing their way into the main compound.

"Sir?"

"I have eyes, Ted. Bolt the doors. Start the countdown."

"T-minus one minute thirty-seven seconds."

The thunderous growling three hundred fifty feet down reminds us: we're sitting on enough explosive fuel to literally shoot us past the Moon. Aurora and I are practically strangling each other's hands. Albert is silently making the sign of the cross. Benji is furiously fumbling with his beads and whisper-shouting "Gaba gaba ganeshi" over and over. Claire grips her armrests madly and says to no one in particular, "Oh, Lord. I think I just peed."

"T-minus one minute."

Now the federal agents are inside the control room, and there's a scuffle. The agents in suits step back, replaced with agents in black tactical gear, pointing guns at the poor computer nerds who never in their lives asked for anything like this. The monitor shows them scrambling like mad to disable their controls, but the gun-toting agents pull them from their posts and sit down in their seats, banging away, trying to stop us. The lead agent – I presume because he's got the suit *and* a gun, and he's the only one with a red tie – sticks his face into one of the cameras.

"Larson! If you don't shut this thing down in the next thirty seconds, you're breaking federal law. You'll be fugitives!"

Larson snickers. "Space Fugitives. I like that. Sounds like another show. Ted, will you jot that down for later?" He turns his head and says, as calmly as possible with fifty-six engines preparing to erupt like fifty-six volcanoes, "Crew and contestants. My friends. I did not think it would come to this. But it has. I have forced you into this situation, and as long as my hand is on this master control, I am essentially kidnapping you. So I'd like each of you, I insist, actually, in order to avoid arrest or worse, to speak clearly into one of the cameras, the following: 'I, state your name, am the unwilling victim of Zach Larson's illegal voyage to Mars. Once I reach Earth orbit, instead of competing for the following three weeks, I will end my participation immediately and take one of the lifeboats back home."

Silence.

It takes an eternity, but one by one, we shake our heads, and grin at each other, and truly understand how far we've come: this is no longer a silly competition. Each of us has gone through nine weeks of hell, learning that this isn't a trillionaire's folly, or a little girl's dream, or a path to fame and fortune, although it is all those things, too. No, this is *big*. *Really* big. The word "big" can't even do it justice. It's probably the biggest thing we've ever tried to do as a species, right up there with the wheel or plumbing. And we are, each of us, part of it. So we are not going home, not a single one of us, not before we get a chance to shoot out of orbit, to Mars, and see how far we can take the human race. Alas, four of us will go home before the actual voyage to Mars, but not for giving up. Screw that.

"Ten seconds."

Larson grins too. "Well then. Let's see what all the fuss is about, shall we?"

"Eight seconds."

Aurora's grip threatens to break my fingers. "Is this happening?"

I nod. "Yes. But don't worry. You'll get to go home before the Mars part."

She laughs. "We'll see."

"Four seconds."

There's a flash in the control room and the monitors go blank.

"Mister Larson! Sir!"

"Can't stop it now, Dan! Three! Two! One! Lift off!"

The cabin begins to shake like a house being torn off its foundations by a tornado. Then a force, like none I've ever felt, like an immense ocean wave, pushes us up into the blue, and I'm pinned to the back of my seat. I gasp at the great weight on my chest, the oppressive force of gravity trying desperately to keep me here on Earth, and I begin to cry, but not from the pain or the fear – from joy, the joy of fulfilling that little girl's wish, of becoming the thing I had dreamed of.

I did it, little Paper! I did it! I made it!

Tears stream down my face as blue turns to black in mere seconds, and we pass the point that *Martha* had taken us, low Earth orbit, hurtling towards our high-elliptical orbit thousands of miles farther. Where *Martha* felt like a modest jump, this feels like a giant leap, a *real* space flight, where the curve of the horizon is sharper, you can even begin to see Earth as a sphere floating in space, and there's a sense that the slightest little push will break us free from its pull and send us on to Mars. As the thrust abates, my body floats against the harness, and the sun shines through the front window into my eyes, warming my face. I exhale. *Ahhh.*

Little Paper can stop dreaming. She's arrived.

Zach turns to us. "Not many men and women have been this far from Earth. You should be proud."

And I am proud. Beaming with pride actually, and grateful to every single person who helped me get this far: my whole family, my mother included, and Benji, and DanDan, and Zach Larson, and Angel, and yes, even Aurora. I look over at her.

"Why are you looking at me like that, Farris? Are you going to puke on me again?"

"No. Look at us. We did it."

56

AGENT BURKE

Daniels scowls at us and turns to Larson. "Sir. We're receiving a transmission. They've opened the com-link. It's on channel five."

"Push it to all the monitors. Every channel. I want everyone to see and hear it."

The monitors spring back to life. There are bodies on the floor of the control room.

Larson lunges toward one of the cameras in the cockpit. "Oh, my God, what have you-"

The agent with the red tie speaks. "Relax, Larson. They're just stunned."

"They better be all right! Or else!"

"Or else what?"

Larson looks over at a status screen. Calms himself. "You know, groups of people can be a very powerful thing. And there are over a billion people watching this, Agent..."

"Burke." He waves at the billion viewers. "Hiya folks. Oh, about the show. That's why I called. The minute we figure out how you're keeping that streaming link live, it's going down.

Permanently. Your whole operation is in violation of the Off-World Biocontamination Act."

Larson smiles. He knows he's got a good team. A completely decentralized team. The show isn't going down any time soon. "Yes. About that. Why is what we're doing illegal exactly?"

Burke reads from his phone. "Section two ex-nine: As a human mission, you are considered very likely to cause forward contamination via multicellular life on another celestial body, considered unnecessarily harmful by the United States Government. Thus, you are instructed to abort this mission, and return to Earth now."

"Why didn't the legislators simply ask to review our hardware and protocols? We're cleaner than any manned mission in history."

"I am not tasked with knowing the answer to that question. Abort now."

"Why does the U.S. Government not want us to go to Mars, Agent Burke?"

"As a human mission, you are considered-"

"No. *Really* why?"

Silence.

Claire pushes her face into the camera. "Yeah, government man. Why are you picking on Zach? You're a big fat meanie!"

Zach gently pushes her away. "Claire, thank you for your enthusiasm. Commendable. But I'll take it from here." He turns back to the camera. "Agent Burke, I know you can't answer that question. And likely you have no idea. So, I'd like to switch this to a private channel in my quarters, and speak to someone who might know a bit more than you, no offense. To negotiate the release of the Mission Control personnel, and immunity for the crew of this ship. This is not their fight. They have done no wrong. Perhaps you can ring Senator Jameson for me?"

Agent Burke flinches. "No."

"Pretty please?"

"No."

"Let me remind you again. There are over a billion people watching you, Agent Burke. I have nothing to hide. Do you?"

Agent Burke reaches up and the monitors go blank.

57

ON LIVE TELEVISION?!

"I have a senator to call. In the meantime, please," Larson points around and smiles wide, "enjoy."

With nothing for us *unskilled-and-in-the-way* contestants to do while we approach the refill tanker, we take our first real look at the interior of *High Heaven*'s main cabin. It is enormous, larger than half a football field wrapped into a tube. And absolutely beautiful. Imagine entering a high-class arcade – I'm not sure if that's an oxymoron, but that's what it reminds me of – with wood paneling, intimate, warm lighting, seating areas, video games, dining areas, a small theater even. Yes, wood. In a space ship. I'm sure it's not real wood, and we're floating so I can't tell what it would be like to walk on it as a floor, but the way it surrounds us, lining the cylindrical shape of the cabin, creates a surprisingly cozy feeling. Aside from the cockpit at the very front, there seems to be an intentional lack of buttons and controls, like Larson really wanted it to feel like a home away from home. It works.

On his way past us, he hands me a bag of small rubber balls. "First to a hundred wins."

"What do I do with these?"

He points above us, and I have to remind myself that there is no up, or down, there are no floors or ceilings. It's disorienting for a moment, then I float up to discover a game board set into one of the walls, with five concentric holes, each with a point value.

"It's skee-ball without the gravity. Here, let me show you." Larson plucks one of the balls from the bag, squints, and tosses it gently toward the board. It floats into the second ring, a little vacuum sucks it in, and a *ding!* indicates twenty points.

An unfamiliar, disembodied woman's voice startles me. "Twenty points. Excellent, Zach. You're getting better."

Claire yelps and spins her head. "Who the hell is that?"

Zach chuckles. "Oh. Where are my manners? That's Martha. I know, the name is a little over the top. She's nothing like my mother. She'll be our guide of sorts, an A.I. like the ones in the lifts back in Stage Two, but considerably more powerful. Don't worry, though, she doesn't have a personality per se, so there won't be any computer uprisings on this trip. Isn't that right, Martha?"

"That's correct, Zach. Zero percent chance of me taking over the ship and killing you all."

We laugh, it was funny, but Martha didn't mean it to be. Did she? The five of us look at each other, thinking the same thing: you hear a human voice, so you instinctively project onto it human qualities, like a sense of humor, or a veiled threat. It's hard not to. So every time you interact with an A.I., you have to consciously remind yourself that it's just a machine, just a really long line of code, an algorithm housed in a box somewhere. Isn't it?

"Thank you Martha. Now, will you give our guests, the

five contestants, a tour of the rest of the ship? I have a bit of negotiating to do."

"Certainly, Zach. Paper, Benji, Claire, Aurora, and Albert, please follow the lighted path."

So while Larson debates with the authorities just how many lawyers he'll need when we get back, Martha introduces us to the MedBay, and the "kitchen," in quotes, and the gym, and finally, our cabins. There are, incredibly, forty cabins on this ship, each capable of housing two crew, for a total of eighty people on board. Larson is clearly thinking ahead – decades ahead. For this voyage, though, there are so few of us we'll each get a tiny, double-bunk cabin to ourselves – twice as much room as we'd gotten back in the studio, though it'll still feel just like a crowded elevator. In place of gravity, the rooms have vacuums, to hold us onto the bed, for example, or to hold toiletries while we bathe.

As we return floating via the second hallway, we pass Larson's captain's quarters. I half expect full paneling, a few bottles of rum, perhaps a peg leg leaning up against the wall, or a parrot perched on a post next to his writing desk. He's the captain of a pirate ship now, after all. But no, it's exactly like ours, albeit slightly larger, with a few more gizmos at his disposal. And no cameras.

He's yelling. "*...and you're going to let them blow us up on LIVE TELEVISION?!*" He slams his fist down on the panel, ending the call.

Then he turns, noticing us. Forces an exhalation, smooths his silver hair. After a moment, smiles.

"Ah. Perfect timing. Won't you come in?"

It takes a few minutes for Larson's hands to stop shaking from rage, and for him to tell us what he knows. Despite the best efforts of his two senator friends, this is all he was able to negotiate: if, within a week, anyone aborts the mission, they will not be prosecuted, including Larson himself.

"We are, as you know, on a highly elliptical orbit, with an apogee of nearly fifteen thousand miles from Earth. The perigee, or nearest point of orbit, is just under a thousand miles, which we will reach in seven days. Just within range of the government's satellite anti-missile systems."

Claire stutters, "They would k- k- *kill* us?"

"They're bluffing. Of course they wouldn't kill us." He taps his chin. "I don't think."

"You don't *think?!*"

"Sorry. Bad joke. No, I'm absolutely certain they wouldn't kill us. They know murdering innocent citizens on live TV isn't a possibility. And they're already stretching the poor Constitution to its ripping point. No, they don't want us to go, however they *definitely* don't want a revolution. It's an idle threat. But..."

"Oh my God, there's a *but*. We're all going to die."

Larson laughs. "We're not all going to die, Claire. Just you."

"That's not funny!"

"Sorry. In any case, just to be on the safe side, I've decided, instead of one and a half orbits, taking three weeks, we will break free and head to Mars after the first half orbit, in seven days, coming close enough to release the lifeboats for our departing heroes – yes, you'll be included in the final installation of the Wall of Heroes – and we'll use Earth's gravity to give us a nice push as we engage our own engines for the voyage to Mars."

Benji says what we're all thinking: "So at some point we're

still going to be close enough for them to shoot us out of the sky."

"Well, we wouldn't come out of the sky. We would explode, atomized into teeny little pieces, floating outward forever."

"Nice."

"Listen, all. It's not going to happen. I'll bet you a billion credits. Trust me."

Claire covers her face with her hands. "Great. He just said 'trust me.'"

Albert shakes his head. "I don't get it. The sabotage attempt in Stage Two. Now this. Why?"

"I think the government was happy with their little monopoly on Mars, however lazy they were about it. This private mission threatens to open up economic opportunities that they won't be able to control. So now they're getting desperate. Which means the rewards of our trip must be greater than we'd thought. Mining, terraforming, colonization, tourism even. Imagine it. We're talking about multiple trillion-dollar industries."

Aurora pulls herself over to the window, looking out into the black. "You're already a trillionaire."

Larson shrugs and smiles. "It's not really about the money. It's about risk and reward."

I float over to his ear and whisper, "Maybe this element thing...?"

He pushes me away. "For the last time, it is NOT some imaginary, undiscovered element, Paper!"

I gasp. He's never spoken to me like that.

"I'm sorry. I'm sorry, Paper. But the evidence simply doesn't support the theory. I did quite a bit of research after we last spoke about it. There is nothing. *Nothing.* I would know. Face it. Your mother is-" and he clenches his teeth.

He doesn't have to say it.

Crazy. Delusional. Total nut job. It's true, but my ears get hot with anger anyway. "Oh, yeah, Zach? Well at least I have a mother."

He steels his gaze on me, a glare I haven't yet seen either. "I'll give you a moment to think that one over."

"Oh, God. Zach, I'm sorry."

Benji raises his hand. "Uh, what the hell are you two talking about?"

Larson smiles, waves his hands in the air. "Nothing, nothing. Just the rant of an old man. Listen, tensions are running a bit high, and I completely understand. Why don't we all retreat to the main cabin? We have a week to complete what would normally take three."

As we float out of his cabin, he tugs my ankle, holding me back, and whispers ominously into my ear, "Strike four."

"Strike four? There are only three strikes. You know, if you're still using the baseball metaphor."

"Oh. I was never much of a baseball fan. Regardless, I'm trying to be ominous."

"You're not doing a very good job."

"You're right. Let me try a different tack: in case you haven't noticed, I've been quite the cheerleader for you. The viewers love you. I believe you've got the right stuff. To win. I don't want you to ruin it by becoming... ah..."

"Like my mother?"

I flick his fingers away from my suit and float away.

58

A RIP IN YOUR SUIT

I don't have time to stay angry at Larson. We've got just six days before we reach the perigee, or nearest point to Earth, where we jettison the losing contestants and then slingshot out to Mars. We'll barely have time to complete flight dynamics, emergency measures, and our current challenge: spacewalks (or as Captain Daniels insists on calling it, extravehicular activity). We've been docked with the tanker for about twenty-four hours, the refueling is going fine, but Daniels is simulating a coupling problem that can only be fixed by actually going outside on a tether with a toolbox, and while we're out there we'll be performing maintenance and replacing one of the thermal covers.

"Oooh. This is scary. I don't know..."

"Get out of the way, Claire." Aurora pushes her aside in the narrow airlock and jumps out the hatch like she's skydiving, letting the tether out with no tension, floating away from us into space. "Wheee!"

I've got to hand it to her, she's taken to the weightless

thing, ever since our first flight aboard *Martha*, like a natural. She turns and waves. "Come on, scaredy-cat."

Albert gives Claire a little push, and Claire tumbles head over feet, screaming into our coms, "Help! I'm lost in space!" Aurora catches her in a bear hug, her helmet facing straight at Claire's ass. "Thank God I can't smell right now. Come on Claire, you're on a tether. Turn yourself around and let's go fix some shit, girl."

Eventually we all make our way out the hatch, the five of us and Daniels.

And it takes my breath away.

Outside the confines of the ship, it's just us and... nothing. Space. The Earth floats fifteen thousand miles away, indescribably stunning, and the Sun even farther, simple and beautiful, and off in the distance, innumerable points of light, twinkling. I had expected this to feel like falling or speeding, as we're traveling thousands of miles per hour, but it's more like, I don't know, just *being*. I know that's a strange word, but it's the only way to describe it. There are no forces acting on me, no gravity, no propulsion, and nothing confining me, other than the spacesuit. It feels completely... free.

"It's wonderful."

Daniels squawks over the com. "No chit-chat. We've got jobs to do, people, out and back in. Extra time is extra danger. And what is the number one danger?"

We all respond, he's drilled it into our heads for hours, "Rips."

"That's right. A rip in your suit and it's game over. There are sharp edges out here everywhere. Be extremely careful."

And so, with Daniels' buzz kill, we begin our slow caravan across the surface of the ship, toward the refill tanker couplings.

About halfway there, I get an itch on my nose. The kind of itch that doesn't ask to be scratched, it demands. "Captain Daniels, sir?"

"What, Smith? Farris?"

"My nose, it's-"

"Itchy? Yeah, that happens. Forgot to tell you. Suck it up."

Jeez. Someone needs to tell DanDan he doesn't need to be such a dick all the time.

The couplings aren't hard to work, really, but the suits, with their internal oxygen pressure, make every pinch and grab and turn a little harder than I expected. My fingertips and forearms are going to be crazy sore later. "Benji, can you hand me that fifteen millimeter wrench?"

He unclips the wrench from his belt ring and clips it to mine. But he doesn't test the clip, and lets go, and it wasn't set, so the wrench slips through both of our fingers. "Oops." It clinks off my helmet and shoots into the beyond.

Immediately, like some kind of space grasshopper, Daniels pushes off from the side of the ship, letting his tether extend out completely. He snatches the wrench from its trajectory with the very tips of his fingers. "You *idiots!*" He reels himself in. "Do you have any idea what a piece of floating debris that large could do to this ship? Or the tanker? The tanker *full of fuel?* Do you?"

Benji and I both reply, "Sorry."

"Sorry will get you killed."

I don't know, what do you say to that? Sorry again? We say nothing.

He clips the wrench onto my belt ring. Whacks it into my

palm. "Ten points off for both of you. Consider yourselves lucky."

"Why are you so angry?"

"Excuse me, Goldberg? Look at what you two just-"

"No. I mean the whole time. The whole show. Like always angry. And it's Greenberg."

"What is this, a therapy session? Gee doc, it all started back in the womb... get back to work, Goldberg. And shut your pie hole."

The thermal cover and the other maintenance tasks proceed without incident, and four hours later, we're on our way back into the ship. Daniels pushes himself past me to get the hatch open. "Stay." So the five of us wait there for him, in a line toward the opening, me taking up the rear. "Okay, one by one, inside."

Albert floats in first, followed by Benji and Claire, and Aurora, and when it's my turn – I can't move. I try to turn, but I can't see what I'm stuck on, it's at my lower back, must be right where the tether is connected. Something is snagged. I give it a little tug – the slightest little pull, barely any force, and I hear it: "PPPSSSHHHHHHHHHH!"

Oh my God. The oxygen is rushing out of my suit.

A rip.

I flail my arms and legs, I don't know why, my panic reflex is working just fine but that's not what I need right now, and I realize my situation is even worse: my tether isn't connected. It must've been torn free. I look into the airlock as I float away, with what I'm sure must be a comical look of surprise and terror on my face, this totally isn't how I would have predicted I was going to die.

Oh, well. I made it this far. Goodbye, guys.

And then there she is.

Like a rocket, Aurora is shooting out at me, arms out. Her tether reaches its limit, and we're both waving our arms like a couple of school kids slap-fighting each other, desperate, and finally she gets a hold of my helmet handle, and pulls me into her arms. With her free hand, she rips a piece off the roll of PPMM tape we each have on our belts, like a mini, self-contained version of the dome substance that fixes rips. The leaks slows, but doesn't stop.

"Don't worry, Paper. I've got you."

I answer with a whimper, trying desperately to hold my breath and not die.

She understands. "You're welcome. And thanks for the extra points."

We finally get into the air lock and seal and pressurize the space. I'm heaving, soaking wet with sweat, helmet off, looking around at five concerned faces, scratching my nose.

Aurora points at Daniels. "Where the hell were you, DanDan?"

"Hey. There were five of you in front of me in this tiny airlock. I was behind all of you. You took your time getting out to her, by the way. And if you call me DanDan one more time..."

Aurora laughs. "Sure. Whatever you say." Then she looks over at me and laughs again. "You're such a klutz."

And you know what? I would normally agree. I'll admit, I have been known on rare occasions – all right, pretty frequently – to lose my footing, or grab the wrong thing at the wrong time, or snag my clothes on the most random nail in the wall – but not this time. I was extremely careful, just like Daniels told us. I watched every single step.

I'm not sure this was me. A terrifying thought.

Suddenly an even more terrifying thought shoots into my brain: *You know who else is irrationally paranoid, right Paper? Yes, your mother. The transformation is almost complete. You're almost your mother.*

59

THE IDEA PHILANDERER

Interview with Claire Soams, contestant number 21, one of five remaining contestants aboard High Heaven:

"Ted, I can hear you but I can't see yo- oh, that's better. Now the best part about being up here? I don't weigh anything! There aren't any scales, but if there were... zero pounds! Suck it, Rebecca Donegan! She was the homecoming queen, by the way, that insufferable bitch. I could live in space just for that sweet revenge. But seriously, this space thing is growing on me, it's like an adventure every day, even with DanDan – *oh sorry, can you edit that out Ted so he doesn't hear it? – Captain Daniels,* being so tough on all of us. I think Paper mostly, I don't know if it's one of those things where he's treating the one he wants to succeed the worst to make her stronger or something. Whatever. You know, between you and me Ted, don't put this on air either, he is kind of cute, in a hard-ass way, isn't he? Oh, don't look at me like that, Ted. Mike Horner's gone, taken, and Albert and Benji, well, they're Albert and Benji, but Dan... I could do worse. After this is all over, picture it: big, strong ex-astronaut and me, with a pension and two good-looking kids, and a white picket fence and all the trimmings. I'm already imagining going back to my boss at ZippieMart and telling him to shove it. Now shush, don't post this or stream it or whatever, this is all between just you and me. Oh, this is live? Well dammit to Hell, Ted."

We're all sitting – or, more accurately, being vacuum-sucked back into chairs – in the dining area, eating. The printed food is serviceable, but I can tell we're all imagining something a little more tasty and real. As I spread butter – yes, my just-shy-of-realistic butter – on a less-than-realistic roll, Larson regales us with another old glory-days story about creating this company or that, and – *wait* – is Claire making eyes at Daniels? *She is!* He's either oblivious, or he's purposely avoiding her glances, concentrating instead on making sure his meatloaf doesn't float away from him. It's crazy, I mean, Claire and DanDan? They're such polar opposites. But then I stop and remember that I'm falling for a Gitano, and we're not exactly from the same side of the tracks. So I ponder Claire and Daniels with a new set of eyes, and you know what? *Why not.* I decide to help her out. "Captain Daniels. Are you married?"

"I don't talk about personal matters, Farris."

Aurora flicks a pea at him. "Come on, DanDan. It's not against the rules."

The pea bounces off his eyebrow and he glares at her. "It's not DanDan, dammit. But yes. Married. Happily. With three beautiful kids. A fourth on the way. I don't like to talk about personal matters. Next subject. Tomorrow is flight dynamics, we should review the preparation."

Claire sighs, then gives me the laser eyes, as if to say, *Gee, thanks for helping, Paper, and ruining my little fantasy.* Then she turns, in steps, to Albert, then Benji, and I might be imagining it, but she seems to be sizing them up, and coming to the conclusion that neither of them is worth the effort. I catch her eye, giving her a little "I'm sorry" look, point my chin at Larson, and mouth the words *what about him?*

She actually scoffs out loud, drawing surprised looks from everyone at the table, then takes a bite of her meatloaf and chews on it, and my secret suggestion, for a few moments. "Hmm. Zach. What about you? Ever been married?"

"No, Claire, I'm afraid I haven't met anyone as wonderful as you."

She blushes immediately, and fans her face. "Come on, stop kidding me like that."

"I'm sorry. The truth is, you are wonderful, Claire, truly, but I have always been, forgive the cliché, married to my work. An analogy: I meet an idea, I fall in love with her, and then together we have children, in the form of companies and products and services. And when I see my children grow up, I meet another idea, and fall in love, and the process starts over again."

Benji joins in. "So, you cheat on your idea wives. You're like an idea philanderer."

"Perhaps not the best analogy."

"Who was the first? Idea, I mean."

"Oh, Benji my boy, that goes back a long way, doesn't it? Let's see... I had an idea, when I was quite young, that I could create an invisible suit." He stares past us, almost wistfully.

"And did you?"

"I was very good with math, and the technology was

nascent, I tried very hard, but it would be a number of years before I could escape via different means."

"Escape?"

Larson waves his hands in the air. "Did I say escape? Forgive me. This old man must be getting space dementia. I meant to say *vanish*. You see, I was obsessed with magic at a young age, and of course, central to that idea is making things disappear. Eventually, I succeeded."

He turns off the suction from his seat and rises, floating away, down and around the hallway towards his cabin. He peeks his eyes back, just a little, and says, "See?" And disappears for the night, leaving just the echoes of his laughter in our ears.

And it strikes me, and maybe all of us, that for all the stories, all the background we've gotten over the past nine-plus weeks, Zach Larson is still such an enigma, a bottomless pit. No one really knows how deep it goes or where it leads. Claire reflects my thought: "Hmm. What a mysterious man."

Then, of course, she adds the most Claire-like question possible: "Is it okay if I say I'm suddenly hot for Zach Larson?"

60

GOODNIGHT, MARTHA.

"I'll be leaving now. Please remember to turn me back on."

Martha the A.I. says this with no emphasis, she always says exactly what she means and no more, but there is something undeniably un-machine-like about her statements, a certain wit and an ever-so-subtle overbearing maternal presence. Larson insists she – it? – has no personality, but it's not just my imagination; Martha knows she is taking care of us and thinks she is our mother. As an example, my conversation with her yesterday:

"Martha, start the treadmill, put me on the 45-minute hills course."

"Certainly. But you haven't eaten."

"I know. It's not mandatory though, right?"

"Of course not. I am here only to provide advice for maximum exercise benefit and optimal health. You may choose not to follow that advice. Starting hills course in five, four, three-"

"Stop. Forget it. Now I feel guilty. Okay Martha, I'll eat first. What do you have?"

"Normally I would suggest a banana, or a fruit smoothie, however if you'd like to exercise without a waiting period, perhaps just three ounces of food gel-"

"Oh, God no."

"I'm sorry. Is there a problem with the ship's food gel I should be aware of?"

"No. It just makes me think of my mother."

Silence. I suppose that statement didn't require a response, but Martha's silence fills the gym. Awkward.

"Ugh. Okay, Martha. Three ounces of food gel."

"An excellent choice, Paper."

"Wait, what color is it?"

"It can be any color you wish."

"Good. Anything but blue."

As I slurp my orange food gel, I can feel Martha dying to say, "See? Now isn't it better when you listen to your mother?"

We're turning off Martha temporarily to run through Emergency Measures. With an A.I. controlling virtually all systems on the ship, it's easy to get complacent and forget that a simple electrical failure, or a fire, or God forbid a hack, could disable Martha completely and leave us drifting in space, wondering, "Okay, now what the hell do we do?"

"Goodnight, Martha." Larson flips up his button cover, turns to Daniels, and nods. Daniels flips up his button cover. "Three, two, one." And they simultaneously press the two manual override buttons to Martha's controls. Immediately the ship goes dim, and red backup lights throb. A speaker – not Martha's voice – announces, "A.I. not responding. Life Support and Term Sleep systems not monitored. Propulsion systems not monitored. Solar Array systems not monitored. Refrigeration systems not monitored. Navigation systems-"

"All right, all right. We heard you." Larson cuts the audio, leaves his captain's chair and hands out plastic cards to each of us. "As we've reviewed folks. Without Martha, the ship still functions, but more like the involuntary functions of a human body: breathing, digestion, baseline computing. The rest is manual. Here are your tasks. Contestants, as always you'll be receiving points for correct and positive actions, and negative points for mistakes. Which, I might point out at this stage of our journey, could prove fatal. So please," he grins as if it could never ever possibly happen, "no mistakes."

Aurora immediately grabs my arm and pushes me toward the fuel tank area. "You heard him klutz. Don't kill us all."

We're working in pairs for redundancy, and Larson has specifically paired me with Aurora for a little extra drama. As we check all the propellant systems and make small manual adjustments to this and that, I look up at the camera near our post. "Hey Aurora, I've gotten so used to the cameras, I forget that there are more or less a billion people watching us right now. Everything we do."

"Even more incentive not to kill us all, Farris."

"Come on, that's not fair."

"I know. But it bumps my Likes up every time I give you shit."

"What if there were no Likes, nobody watching even. What would you do then?"

"I'd still probably give you shit."

"That's what I thought."

She points at the various virtual gauges on the wall of this tiny corridor. "So, tell me what we're doing here, boss."

"Well, from what I understand, Martha is constantly

keeping track of the propellant tanks for levels, mix, stability, pressure, and calculating the ship's trajectory and distance, and life support, based on all those variables. Without her, one of the other crew would have a full-time job back here. Like we're doing right now."

"Life support? I thought DanDan and Benji were doing that."

"They're monitoring that system, yes. But the fuel is the key. The primary system. The solar array will provide power during the interplanetary stage, but the fuel gets us up, over, down, and back to Earth. Without fuel, nothing else works."

"So we're the most important two people on the ship right now."

"That goes without saying. Twenty points for us."

"Oh, so you're handing out points now?"

"From one most important person on this ship to another, I hereby grant you twenty points."

"And I, Aurora, grant you, Paper Farris, nineteen points."

"Nineteen. Of course."

"Of course."

Suddenly, a crash.

Shouting.

"Uh, oh."

61

DON'T YOU TRUST ME?

We rush back, as fast as we can float and push ourselves along with railings, to the main cabin, expecting to find life support offline or a gash in the ship's hull.

Instead we find Larson and Drew between Daniels and Benji, keeping them apart.

"You little weasel!" Daniels is swinging. "Let me at him!"

Benji's hands are in the air. "What the fuck is wrong with you, Daniels? I touched one knob!"

"And almost got us killed!"

Benji pleads. "Mister Larson, Zach. I don't know what Daniels is talking about. Life Support is fine. I didn't even touch anything there! I was running the Term Sleep system through a test. That's it."

Daniels turns even more red. "Exactly! Sir, he's twiddling with a system that shouldn't be touched. One malfunction in Term Sleep and we could be sleeping forever. Idiot!" He takes another swing at Benji, and accidentally clips Larson's jaw.

Everyone freezes, floating silently in place.

Larson grabs Daniels' collar, calmly but firmly. "Stand *down*, Captain Daniels." Daniels lowers his gaze, floating backward. "I apologize, sir. To you, not to him."

Larson's glare softens. "Dan, what's wrong? This is not like you."

He shakes his head. "Sir. With all due respect, you've known since Day One that I didn't like this... contest thing... letting unskilled civilians get anywhere near proprietary and dangerous equipment like Term Sleep. It's idio–" He stops himself. Silence.

"Say it, Dan."

"It's idiotic."

"Dan, you've been working for me for five years. That's a lot of flights, a lot of tests. We've been through much together. Don't you trust me?"

Daniels' hesitation seems to go on forever. Then he whispers, "Yes."

"Well, in any case, I stand as accused, somewhat of an idiot. I accept that. But I didn't expect to have five contestants on board with us, the timing, I think you'll agree, was out of my hands. I will ask you to continue to trust me, for just one more day, until all but one contestant is left on board, the other four returning to Earth on the lifeboats. If you can't stomach that, working with one contestant for our journey to Mars, I'll have to ask you to leave with the four tomorrow."

Daniels looks as if he's been slapped, Larson questioning his dedication to the mission like that. He almost looks sad. I feel bad for him. But my pity stops as soon as he opens his mouth: "I'm in. But Greenberg and Aurora, if it's one of you two, this is going to be a loooong trip. You're going to wish you lost."

Aurora snaps, "Huh? What the hell did I do, DanDan?"

"Other than disrespect me every time you open your filthy mouth? And flip your ridiculous, empty head around-"

"How dare you!" And she launches off the wall at him.

I try to hold her ankle back, but I get a smack in the face, and that gets my blood boiling, so I'm off to tackle her. Benji joins Larson and Drew in holding back Daniels, and before you know it, multiple faces are getting punched, including poor Claire, and she's crying now, and the cabin looks like a bar room brawl, and Larson finally has to shout at the top of his lungs, "ENOUGH!!" and he sends us all to our cabins without dinner and locks our doors.

A few minutes later, the lights return to their normal brightness.

"Do you require any first aid, Paper?"

"No, Martha."

"I would offer to review the *High Heaven* flight manual with you, but there is no section on physical fighting. It was deemed such a remote possibility it wasn't even included in the manual. I think we can agree, however, that physical fighting on board this ship is both unproductive and potentially dangerous, and should be immediately discontinued."

"Yes, mother. I assume you're giving everyone the same lecture?"

"Yes. And my name is Martha."

62

THE GRAND FINALE

"Welcome, citizens of Earth, to the grand finale of *You're Going to Mars!* And here they are..."

It's like a perp lineup on one of those old cop shows. All of us guilty as hell, paraded in front of the cameras, Benji sporting a black eye and Claire a swollen lip. DanDan, off-camera to the right, is looking at turns disgusted and repentant, and while Larson chats it up happily with the worldwide audience at home, as if the entire crew hadn't just broken every rule of civility aboard *High Heaven*, Aurora and I are whisper-shouting at each other.

"You smacked me!"

"You were trying to stop me!"

"Yes! From punching Daniels in the face! Of course I was trying to stop you! You're welcome!"

"You should have been *defending* me! How many times do I have to save your life to get a little respect?"

"That's totally unfair. And I've saved your life too."

"Whatever. Okay, yes. True. But still."

"So, no apology?"

"What? I'm the one that deserves an apology! You distracted me, and look what happened!" Aurora turns her head, revealing a patch of hair that's a little thinner than the rest, where Daniels tore out a clump in his rage.

"Eww. I'm sorry."

"Wow. That was easy." She smooths the hair over the thin part. "I'm... sorry too." She puts her hand out. "Friends?"

"Sure. Not for long, though. You're about to go home. I'll call you when I get back from Mars."

"Not so fast, Rocket Girl." She pushes me out of formation, and Benji has to grab me to keep me from floating off camera.

Larson glances back at us, not missing a beat. "...the contestants, and you at home, haven't seen their compiled scores yet. Martha's been tabulating them from the crew's awarded points as well as successful tasks and, ah, deductions for *mistakes*." He looks back again, and I'm expecting *strike five*, or whatever strike we're up to, but he truly seems to have forgiven and forgotten, and winks at us, but he also seems a bit sad to say goodbye to some of the people he's forged friendships with over the past ten weeks. What's missing from his face is any trace of fear, any hint to the people at home that as we approach the closest point to Earth on our way around, there is the very real possibility that something sent by the government with blow us out of the sky. Or into teeny little pieces shooting outward forever.

"And so, Martha, will you do us the honor, and announce the fourth runner up?"

"Certainly, Zach. The fourth runner up is... Albert Morse."

Ugh. I can't say I'm surprised, for Albert, as smart as he is, didn't exactly shine on this stage. I suspect he secretly wanted to explore his love-hate thing with Suzie Q instead. And on cue, as if to confirm my suspicion, the monitors cut to a live feed of Suzie Q. She's giddy. "Ooooh, Albert! You comin' home now! I'm sad for you, sorry you didn't win, honey-bunch, but man-o-man I been waitin' on you! What did you do to me, you mysterious man you? You got me turned all inside out! Ha!"

We all laugh, and Albert sneaks a smile, another little betrayal of his poor performance this week. Awww. He really wanted instead to go home to Suzie Q, didn't he? Once again, *People Magazine* is right and love proves to be a weird, powerful thing.

He floats over to all of us, with little hugs, me last, and whispers right into my ear, "Good luck."

"I haven't won yet."

"Yes, you have." And he kisses me on the cheek and smiles. "Wish me luck with Suzie. I have a feeling I'm going to need it." I chuckle and nod and wish him luck. He floats off to Skylar, who's manning the lifeboat down the second hallway.

Larson gives him a hearty handshake on the way. "Albert! You've done well, my boy. As fourth runner up, you'll find half a million credits in your account when you return home, that should keep you and our wonderful Suzie Q occupied for a while, and of course, you've earned a lifetime subscription to Groupie Gold."

"Do I get on the Wall of Heroes?"

Larson laughs. "Of course! How could I forget? Ted?"

The monitor cuts to Ted in the hidden control room. He nods, and the monitor is filled with all the contestants who've failed – *I mean, 'become heroes'* – before us, now including Albert.

"Martha, it's time now for our third runner up."

"Certainly, Zach. The third runner up is... Claire Soams."

Claire bursts into tears instantly, releasing ten weeks of angst and joy and physical torture and the thrills of winning, and the pride of knowing she's come much, much further than anyone had thought she would.

Larson is actually wiping away tears. "Claire, Claire, Claire. What can I say?"

"Don't say anything." She hurtles across the few feet between them, and smushes her face against his, trying to see how far she can get her tongue down his throat.

"Mmmppphhhggghhh!" Larson is struggling to say something, or scream, but her mouth is really glued to his face. Claire's been looking for love this entire time, and dammit she's not going home without at least a little taste.

She finally comes up for air, giving Larson an opportunity to peel her off and get a safe arm's length between them. "Well! That's something to remember!" Then he leans over, taking a huge risk if you ask me, and pecks her gently on the cheek. "You are a gem, Claire."

She blushes and waves her hands. "I will always love you, Zach Larson."

Wow. She just realized she loved him yesterday and today she's making a lifelong vow? But it's cute, so cute, and everyone sighs and laughs, and we all have to admire Claire's enduring ability to, in her own words, "Seize the day!"

We each get a sloppy Claire hug and kiss, and as she drifts off to Skylar, crying, disappearing into the hallway forever, I notice it.

She has her flight pants on backwards.

. . .

"Well, Martha. We almost didn't make it out of this without another wedding, did we?"

"There was a point-zero-zero-zero-zero-six percent chance of marital union between you and Claire Soams."

"I won't even ask how you calculated that, Martha. Now, moving on: our second runner up?"

Certainly, Zach. The second runner up is... Benji Greenberg."

I turn to my roommate, my buddy from the first moment he hung his head from the top bunk, the one who instantly forgave me for pretending to be someone I wasn't, the fellow nerd who fixed my rocket landing problem. My friend. The tears really start now, it feels like the moment I left Fill City One and my sisters, like some part of me was being wrenched free and left behind. I rush to him and pull him into my arms. "Benji."

"Paper. It's okay. You won't be alone." I feel him wrap something around my wrist.

"Your prayer bracelet! No, I can't-"

"Please. It was three credits. I have like five more at home. Now," he turns the bracelet softly around, "remember, when you need to, turn it and use the beads to count your mantra."

I whisper, "I don't have a mantra."

He smiles. "Yes you do."

And we whisper the words together: "Gaba gaba ganeshi."

It's the nerdiest thing ever, our shared mantra, and we both laugh like idiots, but I don't care – it's perfect. I hold him tight, trying not to let him float away, laughing and crying. "Don't leave, Benji. Who'll save me from DanDan?"

Aurora finally pulls us apart. "Hey, Robenji. Enough.

Leave some of this stud muffin to me." And she gives him a dramatic kiss, it's like a kiss from a music video, I'm sure sending Benji's poor heart into palpitations, and he drifts of out of view with a dreamy grin on his face.

Goodbye, Benji.

Off to the Wall of Heroes for you.

Daniels looks relieved. One less young punk for him to deal with. But Larson seems sincerely sad, he's down to...

Aurora. And me.

It's hard to describe how I feel. On the one hand, I've never felt closer to my destiny. Where I belong. I can feel the sand of Mars beneath my feet already. I can see the dome rising in a Martian sunrise. I can hear the gears of machinery building a new life on a new world for humanity. And I can sense that I'm here, in this place, at this time, to find whatever secrets lay beneath its surface.

But on the other hand, I think... Aurora deserves this more. She's more honest. More courageous. Better in just about every way than me. Sure, I'm smart, I can run circles around her in a discussion of chemistry or engineering, but is that what matters? Or does it matter more that in just ten weeks, she's revealed more about me than I even knew about myself? Or does it matter more that she'll selflessly dive out of an airlock into the void of space, determined not to let anything bad happen to me?

I will never forget her face at that moment.

The face of love.

The face of giving more of yourself than you expect in return. Of inviting someone into a broom closet to share a song. The face of someone that knows when you need a laugh. Or a shoulder. Or to talk in the dark. Or when you need to be saved.

I have two sisters. Rock. Scissors.

And now I have a third. Aurora.

It's time I gave more than I expect in return. God, I can't believe I'm saying this, but... I hope I lose.

I look over to her, and she catches my glance, and she makes a face at me and whispers, "You know what I'm thinking, right Paper?"

"Yes. That you can't wait to beat my ass."

"Ha! No. I'm thinking second place is kind of my thing. It's my jam. I'm going to make it one of the songs on the album. 'Second Place.' I've finally embraced it, Paper. I don't need it any more. Thank you. Sincerely."

"Wow."

Now I really don't know what the hell to think.

Larson, meanwhile, is at the apex of his showmanship, dramatically drawing this out, squeezing the very last drops of entertainment – and as a by-product, ad revenue – in this finale. He turns away from the cameras, to us, and his look says it all: that the two contestants he and the global audience have not-so-secretly been rooting for, twenty-four hours a day for ten weeks, are the two that are left.

He grins. "Hmm. Aurora and Paper Farris. Who would've guessed?"

Daniels can't hide his disdain. "Not me."

Aurora takes a swipe. "Funny, DanDan."

Daniels fights with himself to remain on the sideline instead of lunging at Aurora. Larson just smiles calmly. "Okay, settle down. Now... the moment we've all been waiting for. One of you, and it will be just one, will be reborn like the mythical scarab beetle of millennia past, and usher in a rebirth for all mankind. And bring back the secrets that Mars has yet to reveal!" He waves his arms, reminding me strangely of Nana and her little scarab routine. "Martha, drumroll please. And the winner is...?"

"I can't provide that information."

"You- you *can't?*"

"I cannot. Because there is a tie."

63

TIED

Oh my God.
Tied.

Aurora and I burst out laughing.

"Come, come, settle down," says Zach. "There must be some kind of mistake, Martha. I thought the points system didn't allow for a tie?"

"There was a point-zero-zero-three percent chance of a tie."

Aurora pats Larson on the shoulder. "Don't be too hard on yourself. That's higher odds than you getting married to Claire."

He laughs. "Have no fear. We've anticipated any outcome. In this case, we'll simply go to the Likes, and let them decide." He glances over one of the small screens near the main camera. "My. Would you look at those?" The Like Counter is burning up, clicking faster than I've ever seen it. "Martha, can you give us some live stats?"

"Certainly, Zach. We are receiving nearly two million Likes per minute. The previous record, set by the high-speed car chase of actor Aidan Bailey and the Los Angeles Police in 2077, was one-point-four million. And the show, Zach..."

"Yes?"

"Officially this is the most watched television broadcast stream in history."

Larson's eyes well up. He's done it. Not stroke his own ego, though that was part of it surely, but no. He's gotten the entire world interested in our journey. Our journey as a species to another world. They're believers now, all of them. They can't wait to see us succeed, and forge ahead in the spirit of discovery. (Either that, or they've tuned in to see if we get blown out of the sky by the U.S. Government.)

I reach over and grab his elbow. "Zach. You did it."

"We."

He puts his arms around both of us and grins wide at the camera. "It's been my honor and privilege to be your host, fellow Earthlings. And now you, mainlanders and Fillers, people of every stripe and walk of life, will decide who joins me on this journey, with a simple tap of a button." He holds us a little tighter. "I welcome the winner of *You're Going to Mars!*, with the most Likes, in three... two... one...

And the monitors go black.

64

DID YOU MISS ME, LARSON?

The monitors spring back to life, but instead of the Likes Counter, they're showing a face.

Agent Burke.

"Did you miss me, Larson?" He waves to the camera. "You're crafty, Larson, I can't even imagine how much it cost to get that encrypted communications array up and running, but we found it. We found it all, all the nooks and crannies. We're shutting you down. If you dare to continue on this mission, you'll be completely blind. No coms to Earth. For the entire trip. Nothing."

"You can't!"

"Watch me. You have five minutes to get everyone on a lifeboat, Larson. Goodbye."

The monitors go black one final time.

"Skylar," Larson shouts into a com, "get ready to release the lifeboat." He turns to us. "Well, Paper, Aurora, we may never know who truly won the show. There is only one thing to do."

We say it together: "We're not going home."

He laughs. "That's not what I was going to say. I was going to say I think we have room for *two*." The light twinkles in his eyes.

"You have *both* won *You're Going to Mars!*"

It seems a little small, this celebration, without a single person on Earth watching; the Fillers didn't get to see their representative take the main stage. I imagine they'll be speculating about who won for weeks, or months even, assuming we make it back. With Skylar out at the lifeboat hatch, our only audience right now is Captain Daniels and Drew Innes. And Martha, I guess. She says, "Congratulations, Paper Farris. Congratulation, Aurora." Daniels claps half-heartedly, sneering at Aurora, and gives Skylar the command to release the lifeboat.

Out of the front window, we can see a mini-ship darting across space, arcing toward Earth, beginning to glow in the heat of the atmosphere.

Skylar returns to the main cabin, and Zach motions us to our chairs. "Now. We won't be able to communicate with Earth, at least until Martha can find us another satellite to hijack. But we've got everything we need for the trip. They thought they could stop us with a little blackout? That's what we were supposed to be so scared of? Ha! I told y-"

"Zach! Incoming!" Daniels is tapping his radar, as if he doesn't believe what he's seeing.

Larson looks out the window. "My God. They weren't bluffing."

These missiles, or whatever they are, streak past the ship. I want to jump out of the way, like I used to when my rocket experiments would return to Earth and try to kill me. But I'm strapped in, the harness strangling me, helpless. Two missiles, I think. They explode out of range of my sight through the front window.

Zach exhales. "Ah. A warning shot. See? I knew they wouldn't really-"

"Two more, sir!"

Martha speaks, and I don't think I'm imagining a little panic in her voice. "Zach. Ninety-nine-point-three percent chance of a direct hit by at least one of the two incoming devices."

"I suppose I should stop making presumptions now. Martha, please evade."

"Evasive maneuvers commencing."

The thrusters ignite, and the ship rocks, creaking, clearly not designed to pitch and roll like a fighter jet. I look at Daniels' hands, gripping his joystick for dear life- *wait*. Is he steering *against* Martha? Larson notices too. "Dan! What are you doing?!"

Gritting his teeth against the strain, Daniels shouts, "Going to manual! I've got a thousand more flight hours than Martha!" He throws the *High Heaven* into a yaw-roll combination, increasing the thrust.

Oh, yes. I'm definitely going to throw up now.

The two missiles pass so close to the front window that if they were going slower I could read the lettering on the side. Daniels is clearly indulging his darkest murder-suicide fantasy.

The missiles explode, much closer this time, and the *High Heaven* shudders like that old shed at home during a thunderstorm.

Did I say throw up? I meant die. I'm definitely going to die now.

THE DREAM

I'm about to dream.

In exactly ten seconds, according to Martha.

It's an interesting feeling, that twilight between waking and sleeping and dreaming, here in the Term Sleep chamber. It's cold, very cold, but warm at the same time, and memories and imaginings mingle in a confusing soup.

I do remember the missiles as I drift off, that was real, we didn't die after all, although the fear on all our faces was most certainly the look people have right before they perish. Daniels narrowly avoided a direct hit, and in a single combination righted the ship and sent us slingshotting out of orbit and towards Mars. I remember looking squarely into his eyes and wondering what he felt right then. Relief? Pride? Was he thinking about his kids? Was he angry at Larson? All of the above? But all he said was, "Quit looking at me, Farris," so I guess that was that.

It's getting hard to focus, only a few seconds left.

These Term Sleep chambers, three in each crew cabin, weren't necessary for this voyage, it's only three months until we reach Mars. But Larson is thinking very far ahead. He imagines voyages in the coming years far beyond Mars, where some form of hibernation will be required, lowering all metabolic processes to a minimum to protect crews from radiation, muscle atrophy, and bone loss, and to keep costs down, and of course, the biggest benefit if you ask me: to prevent people trapped for long periods in a confined space from killing each other.

As my body approaches 89 degrees, the cold and shaking is replaced with a strange calm. I remember Larson telling us they didn't design Term Sleep to include dreaming, that it should have felt more like anesthesia, where one moment you're awake, and the next moment you're awake again but it's months later. However, in all the testing, and they've been testing it for years, they've found vivid dreaming to be part of the experience. Larson's psychologists hypothesized that humans might *need* the dreams, to...

Nana.

Is this real?

She's a young woman, toiling away in a greenhouse, tending to tobacco seedlings. She spies me in the doorway. I'm shaking. "Come! Come! You'll catch your death of cold out there!"

I'm next to her now. She hands me a dumpling on a plate. "Hungry?"

"Ah, no, I'll pass."

"You've always liked my dumplings before."

Okay, this is definitely not real. I'm dreaming.

Now she's showing me how to prepare the little tobacco plants for transplantation into the fields.

"Tanner would love this."

"Who's Tanner?"

"Oh. Just a guy. You don't know him."

She pats my hand. "It's only a couple of weeks yet, after the frost, the machines will dig the holes of course, and take care of the rest, but this part needs the human touch. It's the most important part. They're becoming."

"Becoming?"

She picks up a tiny seed, I can barely see it on the tip of her finger, and whispers, "This is just a dream. It needs to become real." Pointing to a large plant in the corner with huge leaves, she hurries over, pulling me along, and plucks a small pod from the plant, placing it in my palm. "And then back home again." She squeezes my hand closed, and when I open it, the pod has burst and hundreds of seeds spill out. She grins and looks around the greenhouse. "I wonder if I'll have children someday?"

"You do have a child. Harlon. And three grandchildren. Rock, Paper, and Scissors."

She laughs. "Like the hand game? Ooh, let's play."

So she knows the game after all. At least in my dream. Funny.

Her hand shoots out as Rock and I cover it with Paper.

She smiles. "You are Paper."

"I am."

She makes Scissors with her other hand, and I see the three of us, and then we're there, in the kitchen in the trailer, three triplet toddlers, tugging on Nana's housecoat, we're all claiming to have boo-boos on our knees. She scoops us up all at once, and plops us on the counter, and turns to get the Band-Aids. She turns back, and one by one, places a Band-Aid on our imaginary injuries and kisses them. I'm looking down at her hair, and it's strange, I don't remember it being so dark. Then she looks up from my knee, and I know why.

"Mom?"

"Yes, Pepper?"

"Oh, for crying out loud, you can't even get my name right in my dream?"

66

TESLA

"Wakey wakey. Eggs and bakey."

Is this still a dream?

Tap. Tap. Tap.

No. It's Larson. Tapping on my Term Sleep chamber. Ugh. I hold up my fingers. Five more minutes. Please. Where's the damn snooze button on this thing?

"Paper. Paper. Time to wake up."

He's unlatched the cover to the coffin-like enclosure, and is feeling my hands. They're ice cold. My body is shivering from head to toe. No, not *my* body, it feels like someone else's body. Strange.

"I- I- I- I- f- f- f- f- f-ree- free- zz-"

"Don't talk. Here, let's get you out of there." He's pulling me – or this other body I'm residing in for the moment – and putting a big silver blanket around it. Almost immediately, my shaking starts to subside, and my limbs begins to feel like my own. Okay, I'm me. So far so good.

"You were moaning, Paper. It sounded like you were arguing with someone."

"Y- Y- Y- Yeah. That's about right."

I look around, as if something will show me the passage of time, like a tree in the middle of my cabin with the leaves turning color. Nothing. I could have been asleep for an hour. Or a week. Or the three months we were supposed to sleep. Or a million years if something went wrong.

"How long...?"

"Exactly on time. Well, a little early actually. I wanted to show you something."

I float, groggy, following Larson, through two hallways, to one of the storage bays. I haven't been in here yet, this is where all the massive equipment for the domes and experiments lies in wait. Seems like a strange place to have our first post-Term-Sleep team meeting.

He punches in a code and the doors slide open.

And there it is.

A cherry red 2008 Tesla Roadster convertible.

"Holy cow. It's real."

"I thought you might know about her."

"Of course I know. The legend, anyway." Way back in 2018 there was a man named Musk, with big plans for Mars (very much like Larson I suddenly realize), who sent into Mars orbit a test ship, including, according to the tales, his car, a cherry-red Tesla Roadster. It was never confirmed, or if it was the private records were long gone, so only the hardest-core star watchers even knew about the story, from trolling conspiracy UFO and Mars landing sites. Not that I'm saying I've ever done that, but, okay, whatever, yes I've done a whole lot of that.

"Zach. Be honest. That car is the real reason for this whole thing. The show. The mission."

He laughs. "Absolutely!" Floats around to the driver's seat

and pulls himself in, buckles up, turns the steering wheel left and right. "Actually, I just won a wager. A rather large one. So lucrative I couldn't resist having Martha reel her in. Come, sit."

I float into the passenger seat, and we look out the front windshield at the magnetic dipole shield components that'll be installed shortly by the team- *hmmm.* I shake off the last of my grogginess and look around, and for the first time notice it.

"Zach. Why are we the only ones awake?"

67

HOW MUCH DO YOU TRUST AURORA?

Larson reaches over and buckles me in. "How much do you trust Aurora?"

"Well, I was beginning to trust her like a sister, until you just said that."

"I'm sorry. I don't want to ruin your budding friendship. Forget I said anything." He reaches to unbuckle me. I swat his hand away. "Like I'm going to forget you just said that."

"Very well. As you know, there was a very sophisticated sabotage attempt during Stage Two of the show. I can't be too careful."

"And you think it's *Aurora?*"

"No. No. Of course not."

"Of course not. She *won*, Zach. She made it. What the hell reason would she have to sabotage this voyage?"

"Please listen. We are all susceptible to outside influences. Powers that can sway us into making decisions we wouldn't normally make. Actions we wouldn't normally take. For reasons we might not even understand. It happens. And as I've taken stock, of all of us, including myself, I understand we all have moments away from the cameras. Moments that aren't accounted for. It's natural, even on a heavily monitored television show. Everyone on this ship has them. But Aurora has more. Many more. Plus entire evenings that can't be accounted for during the show."

"Tequila."

"Excuse me?"

"She snuck tequila – don't ask me how, she's a magician – into the studio, and would hide out in a storage closet and write songs. I was even in there one night with her. I'm not kidding. That's the truth."

Larson's face visibly brightens, and he exhales deeply. "Thank God. That's what I was hoping to hear from you. A logical explanation. Now we can wake the others. Excellent. So you trust her."

"A hundred percent." I must still be groggy, because it feels like someone else is saying the words.

68

MARS

I can almost reach out and touch it. Hold it in my hands. Mars. Like a little red ball, wanting to play catch.

We're on a spacewalk again, all of us except Larson and Skylar, I'd like to think that our presence out here is crucial, but really we're just standing by while Martha deploys the cluster of magnetic field generators and an inflatable container that will create a magnetic shield in a stable orbit between Mars and the Sun. If anything goes wrong I can't see how we could possibly save this complicated contraption, there are a million wires and panels and ways to tear a nice big oxygen-sucking hole in your spacesuit, and we'd probably all wind up as corpses floating in a loose orbit around the planet forever. But Larson insists, and Martha agrees, so we're here. The dipole shield will deflect high energy solar particles, which strip the atmosphere away, enough to allow the planet to slowly restore it. Then, theoretically at least, some of the oceans will return, the greenhouse gases will multiply, and with some other terraforming tweaks we might be able to live on Mars. Theoretically. Eventually. Not in my lifetime, or my children's lifetime, maybe my grandchildren's. Maybe someday a Farris will call Mars home.

I wonder what they'll be like. Will they be like me? Is that a good thing? Will they be like Dad, with his soft-spoken strength and mischievous glint in his eye, or like Nana, always seeing silver linings and giving without ever expecting anything in return? Or will they be like my mother? And would that be as bad as I think? Probably. I hope they get Rock's and Voomvoom's dimples.

I wonder if they'll be like Angel.

"Farris! Stop daydreaming and hand me that wrench. And don't go flinging it into space like last time."

God, you'd think DanDan's sour attitude would turn around, here of all places, at the doorstep of the breathtakingly beautiful Red Planet, but it's gotten worse. It must be the ever-present pebble in his boot that is Aurora, his arch enemy, not me, but he treats everyone except Larson with pretty much equal disdain. I keep trying to give him the benefit of the doubt, like Tom Bradline, who eventually got an Official Paper Farris Positive Appraisal, but I'm sorry to say the jury is handing me at this moment the verdict on Daniels: he's kind of an asshole. I hope my grandchildren aren't like him.

Martha interjects in our coms. "You can all come inside. The deployment is a success. Captain Daniels, I can take care of that last connection. Paper, hold on to that wrench." Aww. Martha's watching out for me. She's a sweetheart.

We return to the ship, and before our next sleep cycle, we're already on approach for landing. Martha, alas, hasn't had any luck restoring coms with Earth. Larson and her agree the government must've temporarily jammed all signals coming from our direction, so any satellites or land stations trying to communicate would just get static. He's hopeful that Ted, ever-dependable Ted, will figure something out (if he's not already rocking back and forth whimpering to himself in a federal prison cell somewhere).

"Keep trying, Martha."

"Of course, Zach."

The good news is that we don't technically need coms with Earth to do anything here on Mars – no telemetry, computing power for attitude control system, power, propulsion, nothing. Larson really just wants to be able to livestream his historic footsteps onto the first planet other than Earth human feet have landed, and I can't blame him. He's finally gotten everyone – and I mean *everyone* – excited about this voyage, this incredible step for humankind – and now no one will even see it? I feel bad for him.

But my little pity party for Larson only lasts a minute, as the excitement of what we're about to do starts shooting adrenalin through my body. We're hopped up, strapped in, Aurora and I next to each other, out of the way of the real crew, while the *High Heaven* gently circles the planet for a few more minutes. The solar arrays have been stored, we have plenty of fuel, and we're ready. All systems go.

Aurora nudges my arm. "Hey, pssst. I never got to ask you."

"How you managed to get this far? I have no idea."

"No, wise ass. What did you dream about? On the way here."

"Oh. My family. It was nice. Very warm and fuzzy. Then my mother. Not so warm and fuzzy. She's annoying, even in my dreams."

"I dreamed about this."

"This, like the whole show and voyage and everything?"

"No. Like this exact moment. Us, sitting here, looking out at Mars, having this exact conversation. And then we landed in the dream, and the next thing I know I'm running, as fast as I can, away from the ship, towards something, trying to suck air into my lungs. I ran for three damn months in that dream. It was exhausting. I can't remember what I was running to... oh."

I turn to her. "What?"

"I just remembered."

"And?"

"I can't tell you."

"Well, now you have to."

"I can't. It's going to sound weird."

"Just about everything you say sounds weird. Try me."

She scrunches up her face, embarrassed. "I was running to... you."

"You had a huge piece of fake cheesecake right before we went to sleep, didn't you?"

"Come on, Paper. I'm being serious. That's weird, isn't it? The whole running thing."

"Sure. But it sounds better than dreaming about my mother for eighty-five days."

"I thought we were out for ninety days."

"Right. Duh. Ninety. I'm an idiot."

"You are. Hey, remember that first flight, on *Martha* the plane thing?"

"Of course. I threw up on you."

She laughs. "That too. But something, I don't know, like the dream... I'm sorry if this sounds even more weird, I feel like I've sort of been running to you ever since that first night."

"Uh-oh. Are you going to break into song? Is this when you start belting out your new single, 'Running to You'?'"

"Hey, I like that! Can I use that? Hey, Martha, can you make a note? 'Running to You,' words and music by Aurora. Title by Paper Farris."

"Noted, Aurora. I will remind you on the return trip. Please secure yourselves. Descent will begin in ten seconds."

Martha tilts the ship a few degrees as we drift, automatically tweaking the radial thrusters to keep our heat shield directed at the thin atmosphere. Daniels reaches for his joystick and looks over at Larson, clearly pleading. "Sir?"

Larson smiles. "Dan, please. Call me Zach. And yes, you may take us down manually."

Daniels contorts his face, I think it hurts for him to actually smile, but he does, he's beaming actually, and he confidently transitions into manual flight mode, using Martha for guidance but retaining full control.

The ship's temperature increases from the friction of the atmosphere, just enough to make it uncomfortable and introduce the bowel-evacuating thought that there is every chance this will not work, with close to forty-thousand failure points, and that the first people on Mars will be dead people. I wonder if my family has bought a little box for me at the Fill City One mausoleum just in case.

I've only been to the mausoleum once, right after PopPop died. I was too young to get it, the permanence of it, I remember looking at the little door wondering how PopPop would live in there, it was way too small, and there weren't even any air holes. And then he just never came back, and when I asked where he was Nana said, looking up with mist in her eyes, "Heaven," and that was it: I wanted to go to Heaven to visit PopPop, to bring him home so Nana would never be sad again. So I built levers first, like little see-saws, heaving the heaviest rocks I could carry onto one end, and hurling myself a staggering three inches into the air. Catapults were next, though after my first test with a stray dog as pilot, catapults were immediately banned. (The dog survived, and we took him in, and we named him "Gimpy.") Then, by the time I was constructing rockets, the memory of PopPop had become foggy and distant, leaving only the compulsion, the obsession with flying up and out, getting away from it all, into the heavens. I have never shaken it.

I wipe a tear from my cheek as I watch Captain Daniels bring the *High Heaven* about, nearly 180 degrees, with our engines now facing down, and us looking up into what is starting to look like a sky, almost blue. We're falling nearly five miles per second, a feeling both exhilarating and terrifying at the same time, until Daniels engages the engines and we begin to decelerate.

I look over at the monitors, afraid to see some unexpected boulder in our way, but the landing site has been meticulously planned, flat and clean. Daniels makes little micro-adjustments on our way down, gracefully balancing gravity, thrust, and crosswind, until we're mere inches from the Martian surface.

Clunk.

Psssshhhhhh.

Silence.

We look around at each other, uncertain. We've trained for this, all of us, even the two completely incompetent TV show contestants, but somehow it doesn't seem real. Have we...?

Martha breaks the silence. "Captain Daniels, you have successfully landed the *High Heaven* on Mars."

We erupt in cheers and hooting – "WE DID IT! WE DID IT! *WE DID IT!*" I spy Daniels mopping his face with his sleeve, turning away but it's plain to see he's crying, I hope it's tears of joy because he *just manually landed a freaking spaceship on Mars.*

Larson unbuckles himself, and the others follow, and floors emerge – yes, fake wood – for us to stand on, and everything tilts to adjust for the gravity. Me? I'm hanging by my seat belt, it's tangled into my flight suit. Somehow no one is surprised.

Drew rescues me, and I flop to the floor. Wow. This gravity thing, which I really thought I loved, having lived with it my entire life, isn't so great after all. Or in the words of Aurora, who's sitting next to me rubbing her temples: "Gravity blows." Once we had left Earth three months ago, the feeling of weightlessness was actually liberating and fun. I didn't expect to like it so much, and I didn't expect to hate this feeling of coming back to Earth – I mean Mars – so much.

Luckily, with the Term Sleep and our Martha-mandated exercise regimens, muscle and bone degradation isn't an issue, so we're up on our feet in minutes, making our adjustments more mental than physical. Daniels is marching around like he does this every Saturday morning, barking orders and flipping switches and turning dials.

Larson reaches out two hands for Aurora and me, and lifts us up. I'm amazed at how strong he is for sixty, until I remember that Mars' gravity is only a third of Earth. It's not like the moon, just a sixth of Earth's gravity, where you can bound around in huge leaps across a small crater, but it's enough to give the appearance of superhuman strength.

Here we are, standing at the top of a 350-foot rocket, celebrating, and suddenly I can't believe I never asked: "So... how do we get down?"

Daniels actually grins at this, and Larson laughs. "Ah, yes! Aurora and Paper, follow me."

We descend one of the ladders – which during our voyage was a hallway – into one of the large storage bays. As Martha seals the door behind the five of us – Drew will remain behind on the ship for now – we climb into spacesuits and lock our helmets on.

"Everyone thumbs up? Ready? Okay, Martha, let's see you flex those biceps."

"Certainly, Zach." Instantly a tremendous door opens up on the side of *High Heaven*, revealing Mars' great outdoors in its red, rocky glory, and a rush of outside air almost floors us. A gigantic arm unfolds and extends from the ceiling of the storage bay, and on the way to the opening, picks up a metal cage, with room for one. There are more cameras clamped onto this cage than anyone would ever need, even in an historic moment like this, it looks like it's being attacked by a swarm of black plastic eyes. Martha's arm extends the cage just outside the opening, hanging out over the Martian surface. Its door clinks open.

"Zach. Mars awaits."

Zach Larson has been waiting for this moment for a loooonnng time. His excitement, always bubbling right up to the surface, is overflowing. He's jumping up and down in his spacesuit, like a kid, little yelps escaping his mouth, high-fiving us, pumping his fists. He bounds forward, impatient, putting his hand on the door to the cage.

And he stops.

Turning around, with a twinkle in his eye, he clears his throat. "You know, it's been over a hundred years. Things have changed. This time let's make it one small step for a man *and* a woman. I think I've got room in here for one of you."

He's looking at Aurora and I.

"No, no, no, Zach. This is your thing. Remember. Billions of dollars. A decade of planning. Don't get sappy. You don't have to do the gender equality thing right now. We understand. Really. This is your trip."

"I won't hear of it. I've already made up my mind. But I can't bear to decide which one of you should come. You'll have to decide yourselves."

Aurora turns to me, and I can see that complicated look she always gets wash over her, like she can't stand being second in anything, it's worse than death, but I'm like her surrogate sister, so she's torn, but there really is no right or wrong in this situation, so why shouldn't it be her? She grins at me. "There's only one way to do this: Rock, Paper, Scissors."

I smile back and say, "Okay. Shoot."

She juts out her hand, in the shape of Rock, knowing, of course, that my hand would form Paper. I whisper, "Paper covers Rock."

She winks at me. "I know." Then pats me on the back, maybe a bit too enthusiastically. "Now don't go doing something stupid like falling out of that cage on your ass. You'll embarrass humankind for all eternity."

"It's one step."

"I know."

So I squeeze into the one-man cage with Larson, and he's all smiles and tail wagging and he can't wait to get down to the surface. As soon as the door locks, he lowers the arm's cable as fast as possible, ten feet per second, making me dizzy.

"Paper, I haven't felt this exhilarated since... I've *never* felt this exhilarated!" He's taking in deep breaths, like he's breathing the fresh spring air of Mars, viewing in the full panorama afforded us in this little cage. "It's beautiful, isn't it?"

"Even more than I imagined."

Psssshhhhh. The cage stops.

We're here.

About to take perhaps the biggest step any human has ever taken. Another planet! A future home!

Larson unlocks the door and swings it open. "I would say ladies first, but honestly that would be pushing it. Let's do this together, shall we? Three, two, one, go..."

The doorway is meant for one, but we're both pretty lean, so I'm thinking we can make it out together. At the same time, though, my foot is reaching out, and it's thinking we're about *eight* inches from the surface, when in reality we're about *twelve* inches from the surface. So in order not to fall, I instinctively turn my body, grabbing Larson, whose surprised look almost makes me laugh, almost, and we tumble out of the cage.

And the very first human imprints on another planet are Larson's shoulder and my ass.

"Oops."

"Well. That was graceful."

Larson gets to his feet, dusts himself off, and lifts me.

I look up, the three hundred or so feet to the *High Heaven*'s open door, and hear Aurora in my com:

"Didn't I just say not to do that?"

69

THE PRODIGAL DAUGHTER

There was never any doubt, really, that I would feel at home here. I've been visualizing it for so long, so many years, seen so much rover footage, that I recognize the ground under my feet, the yellowish-brownish-blueish sky, the Columbia Hills outside this Gusev crater. This rock I'm holding. The glare of the sun in my helmet. It's like coming home.

No, wait.

It's *familiar.*

But not like coming home at all.

There's another feeling, if I'm being completely honest, that I didn't expect. After the thrill and joy of our first steps on Mars (I'm officially calling them steps from now on if that's okay), after the rush of unloading all the gear that will become permanent fixtures here, I find myself remembering a story for the first time in a long time, the story of the prodigal son, who set out to get away from it all, to make the world his own, but lost it all, and found that only by coming home did he own anything, and finally know where he belonged. And who he really was.

I smile, at the irony, knowing that I had to come this far, 140 million miles, to realize that I'll only truly become who I am by going home. That's where I belong. It makes me laugh. I can't stop laughing. Images of Nana, kissing my hand, and Dad sticking out his pot belly, and Rock and Scissors throwing a deck of cards into the air and laughing, and Jane, looking over and winking at me with a blue tube sticking out of her nose, and Voomvoom caressing the Red Scarab with a little smile on his face, and Angel, sweet Angel, looking deep into my eyes with his puppy-love grin. I remember the photo, the one they slipped me in my armoire coffin, the one Aurora used to reveal me to the world, and I take it out of my suit's zip pocket, tracing the faces with my gloved finger. Look at them all, and Duggie, staring off into space. And Bradline, beet red, annoying as always, but about to save my life. These people, these crazy people, are my home. Who I am. I'm bending over laughing, I can't stop.

Aurora kicks my boot. "What's with you? Space dementia setting in already?"

"No. I think I just grew up."

"Ewww. You threw up? In your helmet?"

"No. I *grew* up."

"Oh. Let me know how that works out. Maybe I'll give it a go at some point." She hands me a solar panel. "Until then, stop daydreaming and connect this. And the twelve-thousand other ones we have to get done before lunch."

70

DRILL

Remarkably, a day on Mars is roughly the equivalent of a day on Earth – as opposed to Mercury, for example, whose days are almost 59 Earth days long – so we can use familiar language to mark our progress, like "yesterday we finished setting up the power cabling" and "tomorrow we'll take one of the rovers out to the ridge," and we can enjoy the relative normalcy of eating together at dusk, and sleeping at night.

Today, Day Seven, marks the day the dome should be completed. Funny. Seven days of creation. I'm pretty sure Larson didn't do that on purpose, but if you accused him of playing God, he wouldn't totally disagree, and he'd chuckle at the comparison. Although unlike God, Larson wouldn't let us rest on the seventh day. There's solid month of work to do. No weekends, slackers.

We watch, Larson and I, as the printing unit rolls in a hundred yard circle, painting the air with the PPMM. It rises with the nearly complete domed wall, inch by inch, sucked onto its surface with Van der Waals forces and computerized magic. Meanwhile, we've completed setting up the mining drill, as it doesn't need its own dome, just battery power for the moment. It's made up of three parts: the actual drill, the excavator-feeder – that's the part poor Jayden got his arm eaten by – and the sample analyzer. The drill's been boring into this little patch of soil and rock seventy-five yards away from the dome, humming efficiently. It's already at thirty feet, deeper than any of the rover drills ever on Mars.

Larson smiles at the glistening dome and points to his com. "By tomorrow, we'll be standing on the surface of Mars without these helmets on, talking to each other like native Martians. How about that?"

"Darn. I was just getting to enjoy continuously re-breathing my own body odor."

Aurora snickers over the com, "Great. Tomorrow we'll all be able to smell you."

I keep forgetting that everyone can hear everyone else, most of the time anyway, through our shared helmet coms. I peer over from the drill to see where they are. Daniels isn't in sight, he must be on the ship. Aurora's still over at the power production facility, a huge field of eight hundred solar panels, patiently connecting about a million miles of dust blowers. She appears to be waving at me, so I wave back, but then I realize she's giving me the finger.

Skylar and Drew are in a rover, still scouting the perfect spot for fuel production. I can see the teeny vehicle off in the distance, speeding along and kicking up the limitless dust this planet seems to produce. There are plenty of adequate sites for fuel production, closer by, but since we're not sched-uled to start production until next week anyway, they've decided to spend a little extra time, as our little home here is, at least theoretically, scheduled to become a permanent facility. For a moment I consider that this "perfect spot" search is really just a ruse to get some alone time. Hmmm.

"Skylar. Drew. You guys there?"

No answer. They've gone to private coms. Am I smart or what? *Those two!*

"Couldn't they have just sent out the heli-drones?"

Larson looks down at me and grins.

"God, why does everyone within a five-hundred-yard radius of you get so amorous?"

"It's people, Paper. I just put people together. The rest simply happens."

"It's funny though. You never got married."

"I've had my loves. Someday I'll tell you all about the- step back, Paper!"

I look down. There's moisture on the drill. The brown, viscous lubricant is bubbling up from the surface, approaching my boot. "Damn, the lubricant's leaking! Stop the drill!"

Larson taps the control panel and the humming stops. Taps a few more times. "Diagnostics running, and... Huh. All looks good. Martha, are you reading this?"

"Yes, Zach. All subsystems appear to be working correctly. No leaks."

"Huh."

"You may proceed at will."

Larson looks down then up at me. "Must've gotten some extra lubricant onto the bit when we were setting it up. Paper, I'm going to start it up again." He turns on the drill, and almost immediately more of the lubricant starts bubbling out, then, *psssshhhh!*

"We've hit a gas pocket. I'm going to back it out."

The drill rises out quickly, and we both gape at the hole.

406 | ROB DIRCKS

Because it's not a hole anymore. It's a puddle.

The hole is filled with liquid.

"That is *not* lubricant."

I lean down to get a closer look. "Water? Some kind of methane mixture? I can't smell with the helmet on."

Larson hands me down a flask. "Water's my guess. Amazing! Here, fill this. We'll have Martha do a test." I submerge the flask into the substance. It's thicker than just water, more like a thin oil, and hand it back to him. He taps a little out into a small covered tray on the top of the sample analyzer, and pushes a button to activate the combination of mass spectrometer, gas chromatograph, and laser spectrometer. Puts the flask into his zip pocket. We wait. "Martha. You get that?"

"Zach, can you clear out the tray and put in another sample?"

"Uh, sure." He wipes out the tray, taps in another. We wait again.

"Martha. You get that? Come dear, what's going on?"

"Sorry, this sample took longer than expected. Carbon, hydrogen, methane, as expected, but there is an anomaly."

We whip our heads around and stare at each other. "Did she say *anomaly?*"

"Yes, Paper. There is no record of an element with this particular mass and profile. It's an anomaly."

I fall to my knees and whisper: "Mom. You were right."

Another strange feeling washes over me, looking down at this puddle of something that wasn't supposed to exist, something my mother was willing to risk her life for. Suddenly all the pieces of the puzzle, everything I've gone through since Nana found the Red Scarab, click into place in a single moment.

I weep.

Larson kneels next to me, a hand on my shoulder. "I was wrong. Your mother wasn't crazy."

"No, she's definitely crazy." I laugh. "Just not about this."

Yes, Jane was right all along: the Gitanos and WasteWay, for decades, have killed and corrupted our government to cover up the existence of this element. They tried to sabotage this mission. They coerced the senators and congressmen they owned to enact the Off-World Biocontamination Act. They nearly blew us into little red spatter in space. But... *why?* What made this substance something that WasteWay would want to bury?

Martha, as if reading my mind, answers into my com. "Zach and Paper. Based on preliminary computations, that substance is analogous to methane, but a highly-concentrated variant. With some hardware modifications, I believe that flask could power our trip home."

Larson stands up, hitting his head on a corner of the sample analyzer, falling back to the ground, on his ass, laughing. "The flask? It's eight ounces! Are you serious, Martha?"

"I am always serious, Zach."

He turns over, now on his belly, his helmet inches from the little pool of the substance, and I join him, staring it at it like a well full of gold. He's giggling. "Paper! Do you have any idea what this means?"

"It's practically free energy!" I dip my glove tip in and pull it out, a few drops on my finger. "This much could heat a home for a year. It would put WasteWay out of business. No wonder they never wanted it found." I rub it into the soil and hang my head. "I want Jane to know. I want them all to know. But our radio's blacked out, and God knows if we'll even be allowed to land back on Earth."

He pats my hand. "Fear not, young Paper. We'll be home in no time, safely on Earth before you know it. Martha dear, in light of this discovery, I'd like to accelerate our departure. Eliminate the terraforming and farm experiments, halt the mining tests, and recalculate our departure date."

Silence.

"Martha? Hello?"

Nothing.

"Hmm. I guess-" and Larson lets out a groan. Before I can even look over to him, I feel the blade rip through my space-suit and enter the flesh near my lower back, sending a white hot bolt of pain through my body. I don't even have to look to know blood is spurting out of me.

The weight of another person. On me.

Trying to kill me.

Aurora?

Was my mother right about her, too?

I had entertained the idea, here and there, but I never really thought she had it in her, or had the motivation to destroy something so completely, just to claim herself a victor. Was she crazy, in a much more dangerous and destruc-tive way than my mother? Had she been hiding something dark and twisted from me this whole time, like I had hidden my true self from her? Was all the talk about sisterhood, all the affection, all the laughs, a lie? Could Aurora possibly be an unhinged lunatic, trying to kill me?

I turn against the power of her body on mine. I must see her face before I die. To know the truth, once and for all. My body is almost too weak, already losing oxygen and blood, but I turn my head enough, and against the glare of the sun in my helmet, I can see the silhouette of a hand with a knife, about to strike again, and I can just make out the face in the helmet above me.

"You?"

71

YOU?

"**D**anDan?"

He puts his full weight on me again, pinning my arms with his legs. He's wailing, tears obscuring his faceplate, full of rage and sadness, like a man watching his own funeral. "You should have left it in the ground! You should have left it in the ground! You should have left it in the grou-"

Something hits him sharp across the helmet, cutting short his tirade, knocking him unconscious immediately. He falls off me.

A new silhouette replaces Daniels, standing against the bright sun, holding a dented solar panel.

Aurora.

I hear her voice in my com. "I never liked him."

I wheeze back, "...the tape..."

"Oh, right." She grabs the roll of PPMM tape, tears off a couple of inches, and pushes her hand through the opening in my suit, pressing the tape against my wound. Immediately, the nano circuitry goes to work, sealing the gash and stopping the bleeding. I'll find out later whether I still have a working liver, or kidney, or whatever organ is currently screaming inside me. Without hesitating, Aurora places another patch of tape across the tear in my suit, and within moments, my gasping turns back to something like breathing.

Aurora's hovering over Larson now. "Damn. He's got multiple wounds. His suit is shredded!"

"Get him in the bag!"

I can stand, though I almost pass out, and hand her the bag, an instant-inflate lifesaving device that every work position has. She quickly rolls it out, shoves Larson on top, throws a roll of tape on him, and pulls the cord. The bag inflates, seals, and pumps oxygen in. We can't even tell if Larson is still alive, there's so much blood. Aurora jams her hands in the emergency arm holes in the bag and starts covering him with tape, anywhere she thinks he might have been cut. "God, he's so pale."

"Let's get them both back to the ship. Martha, get the crane ready."

Silence.

"Martha!" Nothing. "Damn. Daniels must've cut her off. I hope he didn't do anything crazy."

"Like try to kill two people on Mars?"

"Right. We should assume the worst. Let's go. We can operate the crane manually."

So Aurora drags Larson, in his bag, and I drag Daniels, still unconscious but now hogtied with some line, toward the platform that will take us up into the *High Heaven*.

I turn to her while we plod along, as fast as we can, the pain in my side begging me to stop. "I'm sorry."

"What are you sorry for? This asshole almost killed you. He may have killed Larson."

"I... thought... just for a second... not entirely seriously... that it might have been..." I whisper, "you?"

She stops. Drops the bag and poor Larson with a thud, puts her hands on her hips. "You really think I would KILL anyone?! You think I'm a KILLER?! I'm a SINGER, you idiot!"

I just look down.

"God, Paper, really, how many times do I have to prove it to you before you trust me? Before you believe me?" She jabs a finger into my chest, and I almost fall. "I love you, you stupid moron."

We roll Daniels and Larson on the platform, and I tap the manual controls. The cable begins to retract and we begin our rapid ascent to the bay opening in *High Heaven*.

Tears stream down my face. "If Zach dies... and Martha's disconnected... how are we going to..." I'm really sobbing now, panicked.

Aurora pulls my helmet up so our eyes meet. "Hey. Stop. We're going to be fine. You know how I know? Because I TRUST YOU. You are the smartest person I've ever met. You're like super-solution-woman. See? That's called *trust.* You should try it sometime."

I throw myself at her, nearly knocking us both off the platform, and embrace her, my body shuddering.

She puts her arms around me. "It's all right. All right. I understand. I wasn't actually Miss Forthcoming in the beginning of this whole thing either. And it took me a long time to trust you after Stage Two. And you've got that mother abandonment thing going on, not to psychoanalyze you too much, but no wonder you've got trust issues. And the whole Fill City thing? Jeez, is there anyone from there that *isn't* nuts? It's just like I've been sayi-"

"Shut up. Just shut up."

And she does shut up, finally, and holds me a little tighter. It feels good.

After a few moments, she turns her head, looking down and out across the crater, at the rover way in the distance, now heading our way. "Oh, look who finally decided to join us – Drewlar. Shit, they're in for a surprise."

"Drewlar?"

"The name combo thing. Drew plus Skylar equals *Drewlar*. I'm trying it out."

"I don't like it."

"I don't like you slobbering on me like a freaked-out toddler while we're trying to save Larson's life either."

"Touché."

72

IT'S OVER.

I'm in the MedBay, enclosed in the north full-body pod. Martha's completely offline, as we feared, but the medical systems, like all other systems, are designed to function without her guidance. It's just a lot more of a pain in the ass. Or in my case, a pain in the kidney.

Actually, I can't feel a thing from my lower back down, thank God, the pod's injected me with some kind of spinal epidural, but I can certainly *see* what's going on, and I wish I couldn't – at the moment there's a damaged kidney dangling an inch above my body, dripping blood. I turn my head and vomit, expecting Martha to say something maternal and slightly annoyed, but the pod simply sucks my waste into an unseen receptacle.

"Why am I awake?!"

The MedBay voice – not Martha's soothing voice, but the more robotic one I remember from Stage Two – says, "Unable to parse the meaning of this question."

"I command you to, uh, put patient under general anesthesia."

"Patient shows risk factors for malignant hyperthermia. General anesthesia discouraged."

"I don't care if it's discouraged! Give patient general anesthesia! Or put patient in Term Sleep!"

The MedBay pod just continues its work in silence, knowing who's actually boss in this situation. It is going to save my life the correct way, whether I like it or not.

Meanwhile, I can hear Aurora out in the main cabin. She's yelling. And Daniels. Bound to a chair. He's crying.

"Listen to you, DanDan. You're such a fucking baby."

"It's over. I'm not talking. It doesn't matter."

"I don't care! I want to know everything! NOW!" She slaps him.

I can't see them, I can only visualize what's happening, but I don't believe Daniels has ever been slapped by a woman, so he's temporarily shocked into silence and his sobbing halts. "You want to know? *You really want to know?! They were going to kill my whole family!*"

"The mobsters."

He nods.

"Continue."

"No."

"Listen, you asshole. I know you think it's over for you. But I'm standing here right in front of you, alive. I am not giving up. It's not over for me. For the rest of us. So quit it, right now, and tell me everything. Imagine I'm your daughter. Your youngest daughter."

Damn. Aurora really knows how to get to people. Daniels starts crying again. Through his sobs, he manages to croak out little bits of information. "...the closer Larson got, the more desperate they got... at first, they tried to bribe me to derail this or that system, thinking Larson would eventually just give up. I wouldn't bite. Then... Stage Two..."

"You. You sabotaged the domes."

"I didn't want to do it! But they were done with bribes. Now they were sending me pictures of my kids leaving school. My wife sleeping. From inside my goddamned bedroom!"

Aurora slams something against something else. "So, kill us instead of your family, huh. Seems fair."

He blubbers some more.

"Stop. Stop. Keep going. So they knew about this element thing?"

"I don't know the details. They said if I heard or saw anything about a mining discovery, anything unexpected, I had to kill the mission immediately, the whole thing, destroy everything, or else they would..." he's back to sobbing, "...kill my Janey and my beautiful kids. It's over. I'll never see them again."

Oh, God. His wife's name is Jane. I didn't need to hear that.

"How much did you destroy, Dan?"

"It's over."

This time it sounds like a punch. I think I hear him spit and a tooth clink onto the floor.

That's exactly when I hear Drew and Skylar enter the cabin. "What the fuck is going on?"

"Oh. You two back already from your little love junket? Wonderful."

"What the fuck is going on?!"

"Well, while you two were turning off your coms and doing whatever you were doing, Larson and Paper discovered a new element, apparently some kind of super fuel, then

Captain DanDan here decided to kill everyone, but he didn't get the chance because I knocked him out with a solar panel, which by the way are very lightweight for being so strong, I'm impressed, and now I'm trying to find out just how fucked we are, like are we stranded permanently on Mars fucked? So yeah, you basically missed the good parts."

I imagine Skylar rushing over and kneeling next to Daniels, she's pleading. "What is happening, Dan? No! Tell us it isn't true! It can't be!"

But his silence gives her a different answer.

She's freaking out. "Why?! *Why?!*"

Aurora interrupts. "No, no, no. Been there. I'll tell you later. I'm currently trying to get to the part where we find out if we die on this dusty, red, piece-of-shit planet. DanDan - how much did you destroy?"

His voice sounds totally resigned now. "Martha's infected. Gone. I dumped the fuel, the food, and the reserve oxygen. We're not going back. We're not staying here. No one will ever know. It's over."

Aurora screams in frustration. "Okay, you two start figuring shit out. Do whatever you have to do with him." Then I hear shuffling, and suddenly she's staring down at me. "Hey." She looks down at my entrails. "Jeez, that's disgusting. They didn't put you under for this?"

"No. Apparently I have a marker for malignant hyperther-"

"Later. So I just got Daniels to unload everything, and-"

"I heard."

"And?"

"And what?"

"And what's your plan?"

"Well, first I was going to see if I live, Aurora."

"Let's assume that."

"Aww. You really do trust me. And then, I was going to start praying like hell Larson lives."

"Let's assume that, too."

"And then I was going to ask Larson what the hell to do."

We both look over to Larson, in the south MedBay pod. He's unconscious, and I can see various wands and needles and scalpels and sutures frantically poking and sewing. He still looks so pale, his breathing very shallow. Suddenly he taps the plastic shield and turns to us and I practically jump out of my pod, he looks like he's come back from the dead, like a Mars zombie from an old movie. Oh God.

Aurora lowers her head, looking grave, and whispers, "You better start praying like hell."

73

I HAVE ONE MORE SECRET.

"I have a story to tell you..."

"No, Zach. That's what happens right before something really bad happens. You tell a story. I don't want to hear your story. Tell me when we get home. I'm serious."

"...Aurora, dear...Can you give us a moment...?"

Aurora reluctantly leaves the MedBay, leaving Larson and I trapped in our individual MedBay pods, looking through plastic at each other. Both our procedures have finished, and I'm feeling astonishingly better, ready to roll almost, but the way Larson looks, I don't think he could say the same, not even close. His eyes have lost their twinkle, and his skin looks like a dead frog's. Immediately my eyes begin to well up. "No, Zach."

"Listen to me, Paper. I am a practical man. The display near my torso is showing something I'd rather not share, so I'd like to get this story out as quickly as possible. Please don't interrupt."

I nod, and I feel a wave of sadness pushing up my throat. I swallow hard.

"I have one more secret I haven't yet shared."

"Another secret? Why am I not surprised?"

He smiles weakly. "No interruptions. Now, I've been rooting for you since the beginning, I think you know that. But it's not just because you were an underdog, though I sincerely do like an underdog. It's because..." now he's choking back tears, he's having a hard time saying the words, and I can't explain, but I know the truth before the words leave his mouth:

"I am a Filler, too."

I gasp, and want to reach out to him, and hold him, a fellow Filler, and strangle him, for never telling me.

"My life was not an easy one. I was alone, and my caretakers... let's just say my well-being wasn't their top priority. And so I vowed to escape, and never look back. To disappear. And I did."

He wipes his eyes.

"I became someone new. My own person. I found Martha, and she took me in, my surrogate mother, my *real* family, and raised me to be the man I was to become. And true to my word, I never looked back, *never*..." he points at me, "until you."

"Why- why didn't you tell me?"

"I... don't know." He laughs, and its costs him – he winces in pain. "I like to think I know everything. When I knew that you were coming, I thought the right thing to do was to hide my secret, protect it even more. But then I met you. That first time, passing the mini MedBay wand over your little cut, that look in your eyes, of amazement, at the unlimited possibilities of a world outside Fill City, combined with your obvious desire to escape – and I was smitten. I had met, for the first time in my new life, someone who truly understood where I began. Strangely, I felt like I was coming home."

His hands start shaking. "There isn't much time now. I will get to the point, and you must allow me to be sentimental. I have never had a family of my own, but you have become a surrogate daughter of sorts for these few months, and I am blessed for it. You are a very special woman, Paper. In gratitude, I had arranged before we left, should anything happen to me-"

"Don't say it. Don't say it, Zach."

"That you be granted my shares in all the corporations of my estate. My mother is long gone. *You*, Paper, are my family."

"No. I don't want it."

"It's too late. You will go further than I ever did with it. Use it, and this new element we've discovered, and I can't even imagine what you'll do. My days of... becoming... have come to an end. Yours are just beginning."

"No! Zach, we're trapped here! I need you!"

"That's a nice thought. But really? You never needed me. Not as much as I needed you."

"That's not what I'm talking about! We need to get home!" I'm shouting and crying, and slamming my fists against the pod dome.

"Paper. You will get home. I'm sure of it. You have Drew, and Skylar, and Aurora, and yes, even Dan. He's a good man, caught up in something terrible."

"No! This isn't happening! Martha! Aurora! Somebody! Help!"

Larson's breathing gets shallower still, and he begins to cough. Blood. "...oh... one more thing..."

I can hardly see through my tears, and this stupid plastic dome, but I watch helplessly as his eyes close one last time.

"...if Martha wakes up... tell her I said goodbye..."

. . .

Several silent minutes pass.

Then a sound.

Like a beep.

Then a voice, "Zach..."

The voice sounds so full of mourning, beyond sad, but it can't possibly, because the voice is Martha.

"Martha!"

"Zach Larson is deceased. Time of death oh-four-thirteen hours, GMT Earth time."

They're just words. And she's just a few lines of code. But I can hear her artificial heart breaking.

"Martha. He told me to say goodbye."

She hesitates for a short eternity. "Thank you for telling me that, Paper."

"Are you... okay?"

"I am at ninety-three percent normal operating health. I have eradicated the virus Captain Daniels inserted into my code, taking one hour and three minutes longer than the time I had estimated. I am sorry for the delay."

"Sorry? Holy cow, please don't be sorry. I'm thrilled to hear your voice!"

"And you are also at ninety-three percent normal operating health. A coincidence. Zach enjoys when I note coincidences. *Enjoyed.* Would you like me to continue noting coincidences?"

"I prefer silver linings."

"You will have to teach me what silver linings are."

"Of course."

"Until then, I will await your next instructions."

"Me? Shouldn't it be... oh... I'm third in command? That doesn't sound right."

"It is the protocol defined by Zach, before this mission began. Full leadership belongs to you now, Paper Farris. What would you like to do?"

I look over at Zach. "Let's bring him home."

74

SAUSAGE LINKS

I insisted on packaging up Zach's body into the cherry red Tesla Roadster convertible. He looks so peaceful there, and I'm positive it's exactly the way he'd have wanted to leave the mortal plane, riding a kick-ass car through space. I plan on burying him in it, too. I'm also positive that this decision has left my fellow crew members saying to themselves, "Larson put that nut in charge? What could be worse?"

Well, as it turns out, plenty. It turns out Daniels' little *turn-off-all-the-lights-on-the-way-out* trick has left us with zero fuel, zero water, no food production capability, no farming equipment or plants, a broken water-oxygen processor, and only twenty-four hours of reserve oxygen in backup tanks. Even if we could figure out how to retrofit the fuel system to accommodate this new element thing, either 1) we run out of oxygen before we can complete something workable here on Mars, or 2) we run out of oxygen if we leave now and try to make it home. Basically, there is no scenario where we don't die clutching our throats, gasping for those last few molecules of breathable air. A pleasant thought.

We're sitting around the dining table with old-school paper and markers, scribbling aimlessly like a kindergarten class without a teacher. I keep drawing the ship's two fuel tanks and lots of question marks. I glance over to Aurora. She's drawing a Care Bear.

"That's helpful."

"I used to draw them when I was five. It's soothing. Hey, it's better than that explosion of kindergarten creativity you've got going on. What is that, sausage links?"

"No, dummy. It's the fuel tan-" *Explosion.* Did she just say *explosion?* "Aurora, you're a genius."

"What, that I knew you were drawing sausage links? Or my Care Bear?"

"Okay, listen up guys. We've got two tanks, the bottom one here reserved for methane and the top one here for oxygen, connected – I suppose – like sausage links. The contents are mixed to create the fuel we used to get here. Now, if we can use the bottom tank for the new fuel, this element – God, we need a name for that – and it doesn't need to be mixed with anything, we can isolate the top tank to store the water to fuel the backup oxygen electrolysis generator."

Drew sighs. "To store what water? Daniels dumped everything. We have no water."

"Not yet. That's where the *bomb* comes in."

Aurora laughs. "Okay, I was on the fence when you strapped Larson into the convertible, but now it's official: you have space dementia. Somebody lock her in the back cabin with Daniels."

Drew curls his lip into the beginning of a smile. "No. That large ice patch. North about three miles. *Boom.* We gather and store the ice in the top fuel tank. Ten points for red team."

"Exactly. And thank you. I'm sure those points will come

in handy as we narrowly escape death to get the hell off Mars."

Skylar raises her hand. "But... we don't have a bomb. No explosives."

Drew grabs the flask in the middle of the table, nods to me, and hands it to her. "Now we do."

And so the next twelve hours become a mad rush to solve our four big problems:

1. Water

First we create a bomb, using just a wee bit of Marsonium – that's the name we've given the new element, which is actually a gas, but exists here on Mars in a liquid compound with methane, carbon, and hydrogen. It's a crude bomb, like a stick of dynamite from an ancient western movie, it looks ridiculous, taped together with this and that, electronics thrown together in an hour, but according to Martha, it should do the trick.

Second, we drive out to the ice patch with the bomb and see what happens. Drew and Skylar have volunteered for this task, possibly to spend their last possible alone time together, saying weepy, smoochy goodbyes. Whatever. I'm just kind of glad it's them and not me. Aurora and I watch through the open bay door as they get smaller and smaller into the distance on the rover.

"You think they really love each other?"

"Hell no. In case you haven't noticed, it's pretty slim pickins here on Mars. Larson's- well, you know. And Daniels,

I mean come on. So Drew starts looking pretty attractive by default."

"I don't know. He'd have to be the last man on- oh. Right."

I point. "Hey, here they come."

Drew and Skylar are racing back in the rover like a bat out of hell, trying to outrun the detonation. And then...

Wow.

A light, brighter than any I've ever seen, blinds us and the shock wave throws us back on our asses.

Clink. Clink. Clink. Clink. Clink. Clink.

"What the hell is that sound? Paper, what the hell is going on?"

I have to laugh. We're witnessing yet another first. "It's a hailstorm. On Mars."

Chunks of ice, from teeny, pebble-size to spare-tire-size, are clanking against the hull of the *High Heaven*. Drew and Skylar are dodging the larger chunks on their way back, reminding me of the way my mother drives. There is enough ice out in that field right now to fill every skating rink in America.

Okay, first problem solved: water.

2. Fuel

Thank God for Martha. While Drew and Skylar – I almost caught myself saying Drewlar – are out collecting the ice and hauling it aboard, Martha and I are working on the adjustments to the fuel systems. And she's doing most of the work.

"We will have to separate the Marsonium from the other elements in the compound. I will guide you through the process, using the thermal-electric distillation unit."

"You're the best, Martha."

"You are assisting."

Martha's all business as usual, but I can't help it, I'm always trying to see if there's more under the hood. "Do you miss him?"

"If by 'miss' you mean yearn for a person's presence after an absence, no I do not miss anything or anyone."

"Even Zach?"

There's a pause, I don't know if I imagine these things, continually anthropomorphizing Martha, projecting humanity and personality on to her, but it feels like a pause to me.

"No."

"Really? Come on."

"You will find the main burner in that left compartment. Be careful, Paper, to keep the Marsonium far away from combustion at this point, or you may die in a fiery explosion."

"But you'd miss me, right?"

"No."

"Fine." I'm pissed, I mean Martha's super-intelligent, but she can't even throw me a bone and say yes? We work on the distillation process, then on releasing the gas into the bottom tank, then on the fuel line adjustments. We work in silence. When we're done, and everything's working and ready, I imagine she feels guilty, because she says, "Paper. May I tell you about my programming?"

"Whatever. I guess."

"At my level of calculation ability, approaching but still very far from what you call consciousness, there is an effect, with no word for it yet, an effect that results from our very similar thought processes, humans and I. The people I work with become... familiar, identifiable and relatable in a unique way. A file, if you will, is created, not with factual details about the person, but with more subjective, subtle information. It would be difficult for me to even show you this information in a way that would make sense. When that person ceases to work with me, the file is no longer needed, so I delete it. In its place, there is a temporary void."

Awww. She does miss him.

A smile to myself, and a tear makes its way down to my chin.

3. Oxygen

The backup oxygen electrolysis generator is working fine, I guess Daniels only had so much time to sabotage as much of the voyage as possible, he couldn't think of everything. So we fill the top tank with ice, using up four precious hours, melt the water, retrofit a connection from the generator down to the tank, start up the generator, cross our fingers, and...

It works.

Huh. It's funny. I'm so used to things going wrong, and now we've got three things working in a row. I look up, to Heaven I guess, thinking the preposterous thought that maybe Larson is looking down on us, helping us out, and I fall to my knees and start bawling.

Aurora bends down next to me. "Hey, Paper. It worked."

"I know. I just... is he really gone?"

"Wow. You really connected with him, huh?"

"He was a Fil... he was a friend. No, like family, almost. My heart hurts, Aurora. I keep expecting him to jump out, like it was all a trick, and yell, "Fun, fun fun!" and that's the real ending to *You're Going to Mars!*, and we all have a good laugh, and he breaks some kind of ratings record, and he gets a ticker tape parade down Broadway. Or he comes out and says, 'Strike five.' Did you know he had no idea how many strikes there were in baseball?"

"Uh..."

"Aurora. Really?"

"Not exactly a fan of the ball with bases game. It's worse than watching golf. I'm thinking three, though."

"Yes. It's three strikes. Like three strikes and you're out. It's a metaphor for running out of luck."

"So, how many strikes have we got? Are we running out?"

"Actually, if we can solve the last problem, it's a home run."

"What's a home run?"

75

FOOD

FOOD. That's the last of the big four problems.

We have fuel. Check. We have oxygen. Check. We have water. Check.

So what's the rush?

Well, Daniels not only destroyed the farming resources, and introduced all our plants to the Martian atmosphere, killing them all, but he also dumped the bulk food ingredients – which made quite the colorful streak of sludge running down the side of the *High Heaven* – leaving us with only the packaged food reserves.

Enough food for one person.

Even if we stretch rationing to the limit, only one person could survive for only two months.

Skylar raises her hand. "Can I just state the obvious? We can't stay here. We'll have nothing to eat."

Aurora mumbles something.

"What, Aurora?"

"We could eat Larson."

"Oh my God. That is absolutely the most horrible thing you've ever said."

"Hey, we're brainstorming. There's no bad idea in a brainstorming session."

"Yes there is. That's it. That is the ultimate bad idea. Can we agree that we're not going to extend our lives through cannibalism?"

Drew and Skylar nod. Aurora shrugs.

"Good. Obviously we have to leave. As soon as possible. Skylar, you mentioned Term Sleep?"

"Yes. With Term Sleep, I think we're fine. Minimum nutrition requirements would use up half the food stores, leaving us awake for a day or two after launch, and up to a week when we approach Earth. I think we'll need that time to figure out whether the government will even allow us to land."

Ugh. That thought again. That we might pull this whole thing off, just to be blown up into little bits a few miles above home.

Zach Larson, if you're up there somewhere, I could use one last favor.

76

ITCHING TO GET HOME

"Three... two... one..."

The thrust is incredible. Not only does Mars have lighter gravity, reducing the power necessary to escape it, but man, do we have *power*. This Marsonium stuff is like nothing I've ever seen. Like nothing anyone's ever seen.

Goodbye, Mars.

Except for a few containers of the new element, we've left everything behind: the nearly finished dome, solar array, mining gear, the rover. Hopefully there'll be another private mission, another group of starry-eyed visionaries who'll pick up where we left off and take us a few steps farther. I feel sad, in a way, not completing it, but really? Ever since the discovery of the mystery element, and especially with Zach's death, I've been itching to get home. My real home.

"Martha. How's the new fuel system?"

"Within operating parameters. Five percent hotter than estimated."

"Is that significant?"

"Nominal."

We're being pushed back into our headrests, our cheeks smushing against our jaws, and somewhere in storage I imagine Zach Larson whooping and waving his arms out the window of his convertible.

Just in case, we've got full spacesuits on, although if even the slightest thing goes wrong with the fuel or the oxygen production, we might as well have wrapped ourselves in toilet paper. Daniels is already in Term Sleep, and if all goes well we'll be joining him shortly.

"I hope everyone's feeling sleepy."

Aurora groans. "Can we pick different dreams this time? No more running. I'm exhausted."

"Tell me about it. You don't have to dream about my mother."

"Good afternoon, Pepper."

I open my eyes.

It's Jane. She's driving a tractor trailer, I'm sure it's filled with brie-colored armoires, and I'm in the passenger seat. She likes to say "good afternoon" when I wake up any time after dawn, like it's a flaw waking up at a reasonable hour like normal people. Wait - this is feeling extremely real. Is it real?

"Here." She hands me a sandwich. "Roast beef."

Nope. It's a dream.

"Thank you." And suddenly I remember. "Jane. Mom. You were right."

"I'm always right."

"I mean about the element. Everything. WasteWay and the government were hiding the data. For decades."

"You're acting so surprised. I told you that months ago."

"I know, but... I didn't believe you."

She smiles at me, a foreign smile for her face, quite maternal actually. "Have you ever heard the story of the prodigal son?"

"Yes! I was just thinking about it the other day. It's about the boy who leaves home but realizes he belonged back there all along."

"Right kid. Wrong story."

"Excuse me?"

"The story's about the boy who leaves home and loses it all and has to come groveling back."

"Well that's just sad. I like my version better."

"You're missing the point. The point is that it's *all* our stories. We think we know everything, but we never really know our place, until we go off on our own, and we lose it all."

I look at her, confused.

"Come on. I thought you were the smart one. Listen: until we're stripped of everything, we know nothing. And then we learn it for ourselves, and that brings us home." She grins. "Hey, this is going to be a long trip. You want a meal-in-a-bag?"

I wave it off and hold up my roast beef. "I may know nothing, but I know I don't want one of those."

"Suit yourself." She begins to snake the tube, pink this time, up and over her ear, and into her nose. It's no less gross in my dreams. Then she looks over, smiles again.

And begins choking.

"Pepper! Pepper! There's a leak! There's a leak!"

I can feel my heart racing, but I can't reach out to help her. I'm paralyzed.

Something's wrong. This doesn't feel like a dream.

"Paper. Paper."

I open my eyes.

The inside of the Term Sleep pod. *Hmm.* Are we there already?

"Paper. Paper."

"*...huh?.... Martha?...*"

"I'm sorry to wake you so early. But there's a leak."

77

THE LEAK

Martha guides me, still groggy, to the spot Aurora and I had been, monitoring the fuel systems during the emergency drill.

But this time it's definitely not a drill. As I look through the large, thick window into the tanks chamber, red lights are flashing, gauges are blinking, something is hissing. It feels like the end of the world.

And I'm alone.

It's just me, Martha did the only thing she could, if she woke everyone the food would run out and we'd all die anyway. And she's already alerted me, in her *oh-so-personable* way, that by doing this I might be taking one for the team. A big one. The permanent one. Great.

"Okay, what am I looking at?"

"Inside the chamber, the bottom tank. Seven-point-three inches from the coupling, there is a seam. A microscopic breach has appeared in that seam, leaking at a rate of two-point-six cubic inches per minute. It is safe now, but will reach explosive limit in eighteen minutes if not attended to."

"Gee, that's all? What's the bad news?"

"We obviously cannot use a blow torch to repair the seam. This ship and its occupants would explode into small pieces approximately fifty microns in diameter."

"Nice. Any good news?"

"There is a solution, and that is why I have awakened you. There is a ninety-one percent possibility that a length of PPMM tape, over an equal length of PPMM epoxy putty, will seal the leak sufficiently."

"Why do I feel like I'm waiting for the 'but...'?"

"Quite astute, Paper. You will have to hold the epoxy putty and tape in place, with a minimum pressure of one pound per square inch, until it is fully cured. Do not worry though. It is a fast-curing material."

"Fast-curing. Good. How many minutes?"

"Two hundred and four."

"That's not minutes! That's hours! Like over three hours!"

"Earlier materials took seven hours to cure. You'll be applying pressure for less than half that time."

"Remember what I told you about silver linings? *That's* a silver lining, Martha."

So I haul ass into my suit and into the chamber. Wow. It is HOT in here. The engines are still over a hundred feet below me, but I feel like they're blowing directly in my face. I suddenly realize Martha could've woken any one of us up for this job, it's not particularly technical, I'm just wadding up some putty and holding it on a leak for three plus hours.

"Hey, Martha. Why did you have to pick me for this? Seems kind of unfair."

And I remember Zach's words, way back on the

obstacle course: *there may be a moment, on the voyage of* High Heaven, *when fairness simply doesn't apply. When life is at stake. What's to be done then? Complain?* He was talking about me, of course, changing the game myself, breaking the rules to get up here in the first place. How did he know it would be me in the end? I whisper back to Martha, "Forget I asked."

"Asked what?"

"Wise ass."

I wish I could say it was more impressive, this act of bravery and sacrifice, ensuring this discovery makes it back to Earth and changes everything, but it really is just wadding up a ball of epoxy-putty, putting a piece of tape over it, and smushing it against the hole I can't see in the seam, putting constant pressure on it.

"Martha, can you give me a countdown clock or something at least? A timer?"

"Certainly, Paper. In exactly two hundred one minutes, the small display to your right will either light up red, showing that the seal has failed, and that this ship and its occupants will explode into small pieces approximately fifty micro-"

"I heard you the first time. And what if it's green?"

"The opposite. You will live. You will go home."

It's been an hour.

I've never tried to put pressure on something for an hour. My hands are killing me.

But I guess that's better than this leak killing us all.

"Paper. I have news."

"If it's that this stuff is cured already and I can go back to sleep, bring it on. Anything else, keep it to yourself, it's just more bad news."

"Certainly. I will not tell you."

I float in silence for a minute, trying to uncramp my hands. "Well, now you *have* to tell me."

"The quantum radio has received a signal. From Earth."

"EARTH?!"

"Yes. Would you like me to open up a channel? Simultaneous entangled communications at this distance will only be audio, there isn't enough bandwidth for video."

"Yes! Yes! Of course!"

There's a little click in my helmet com, then static, then... "-can you hear me, *High Heaven*? Transmitting at one-point-"

"Ted!"

"Paper? Paper Farris?"

"Yes! Ted!"

"Confirming entangled connection. Paper, our telemetry is showing you're in flight, on a trajectory toward Earth. Why aren't you on Mars? What's wrong?"

"Holy cow. Where do you want me to start?"

I tell him everything, about the discovery, and Zach, and Daniels, and he tells me quite a story, too: incredibly, the Dead Body Database had been published, on servers around the world, and people in large numbers began to take to the streets, demanding answers, and demanding that the Off-World Biocontamination Act be repealed to allow us to come home. It hadn't been repealed, but the government granted a stay to appease the hordes of protestors. Ted and team were allowed back in business in Mission Control.

We're coming home.

If we survive.

"Ted. I almost forgot. Can you get someone out to Captain Daniels' family, quickly, get them into hiding temporarily until this is all figured out?"

"Already on it."

"What? How?"

"Some guy named Angel. He had a tip."

"Angel! Is he there?"

"No. There was a woman who delivered the tip from him. She insisted on getting in, talking to you. We didn't let her in, she seemed dangerous and unstable. We kicked her out. She wouldn't leave, she's outside the perimeter, parked in some old car. For three days now."

Yep. That's my mother.

"Ted! Go get her! I need to speak with her!"

"Pepper?"

God, the wrong name never sounded so good.

"Mom."

"You must be thinking of someone else. You usually call me Jane."

"You were right, Mom."

"I'm always right."

I laugh. It's just like the dream. "Martha's downloading all the analysis to Ted right now. Jane, Mom, it's incredible. Marsonium, that's the name we gave it, it's got some other-worldly properties. When it burns, it produces something like ten thousand times the power of methane. This would've put WasteWay out of business. That's why they were hiding it. Trying to bury it. You were right all along, Mom."

No response. And then I hear it. For the first time. My mother is crying.

"I... did it for you and your sisters, Paper."

"You must be thinking of someone else. You usually call me Pepper."

She laughs. "I love you, my baby." And then after a little while, "You did it."

"We." I take a deep breath. "And I love you too, Mom." I look at the timer. An hour and fifteen minutes left. "Well, we *might* have done it. I'm in a little pickle right here. I'll know in a little over an hour if we're ever going to see each other again." Now I'm crying too. "Mom... I don't want to die. I want to live. And I want to come home."

"Don't be stupid. You're not going to die. And I'm not going anywhere. I'll stay right here with you. The whole time. Now, why don't you tell me all about it, your great adventure? I want all the details. Gimmee gimmee."

"Where should I start?"

"Tell me everything. From the beginning."

I look at the display. That's an awfully long story to try to fit into an hour and fifteen minutes. And then, once again, I wonder if that light is going to flash red or green. But strangely, this time the thought doesn't frighten me. Whether I live or die, my Mom will be with me, and Zach Larson, and I will have made the difference I was meant to, for the Fillers, and for everyone, and they'll all live forever in my heart, even if that heart is blown into little 50-micron diameter pieces.

I've become who I am. I've made it home.

78

THE LIGHT FLASHED GREEN.

T HE LIGHT FLASHED GREEN. I don't remember much else, just that I let out a little sigh of relief, I didn't even have enough energy to scream "I'M ALIVE!!!," and I returned, somehow, sweaty and exhausted and hands cramped into useless little knobs, to my Term Sleep pod, and Martha tucked me in and told me once again that I would be dreaming in ten seconds.

As I stand here now, looking at the bookshelf in the living room of my newish trailer next to Nana's, I still feel like I'm dreaming. I pick up the photo, taken just before I escaped on the adventure of a lifetime. There I am in the middle, bleach blonde crew cut, sad and afraid. I put down that photo and pick up the one we took just yesterday. Rock's on the left, with Dill and their new addition Dill Junior, and yes, the kid is eating a booger he just picked. Scissors hasn't changed at all, with her kissy face and her middle finger. Duggie and Bradline are there, Bradline trying to turn Duggie's face toward the camera.

Nana's there too, sweet Nana, still alive and kicking, still cooking her infamous meals at ninety-eight, eyes as bright as ever. Her arms are around Dad... and Mom.

They're not getting back together, Dad and Mom, in fact she made up some excuse that she needed to take a little trip down the coast, some research into Marsonium for the New WasteWay Corporation.

Ah, yes, New WasteWay: now that lots of Gitanos and their corrupt politician friends are going to jail, the remaining family shareholders, led by Angel, have been extremely eager to merge with an actual, legitimate, law-abiding corporation like Groupie/AceSpace, beginning a thorough scrubbing of their organization from top to bottom. So the name's been changed, and the charter revised to research and distribute Marsonium as a fuel to the government and countries around the globe. New WasteWay will still play a key role in mining on Mars, distilling, purifying, keeping the process safe, and more, employing even more Fillers – who can travel as they wish, wherever they wish – than before. So Mom is gone for now, in another old Honda, no surprise, but Voomvoom is here, sitting in my lap right now as a matter of fact, so I know she'll be back soon.

Voomvoom points to the photo. "Is she a sister too?"

He's pointing to the fourth sister, the one to my left. Aurora. She's gone now, too, off to release the *Rocket Girl* album and prep for the tour. Before she left, she wrote the final lyrics to "Rocket Girl" on the back of the photo:

> *Rocket Girl / I'm goin' far*
> *Gotta leave now / Sail through the stars*

If you look real hard / I'm that dot in the
    black
Will you be waitin' / If I ever get back?
Will you be waitin' / If I ever get back?

Rocket Girl / Time has come
Leave the stars / Learn where you're from
If I look real hard / into the blue
You're running to me / And I'm running
    to you.
You're running to me / And I'm running
    to you.

Voomvoom reaches up and wipes the tear from tip of my nose. He turns the photo back around. "There's me. And Angel. And you."

And there we are, a weird sort of family of our own. Angel's got his hand on Voomvoom's shoulder, he's going to make such a great dad someday, I know it. He's leaning left and kissing me on the cheek and smiling like he just won a trip to a chocolate factory. I can't wait to marry that boy.

And there I am right in the middle, not the sad and afraid girl from what feels like a million years ago, but a more complete Paper, all grown up, surrounded by possibilities, freedom, and most of all, love.

I take a deep breath of the Everpresent Stink and smile.

"Ahh. Smells like home."

ALSO BY ROB DIRCKS

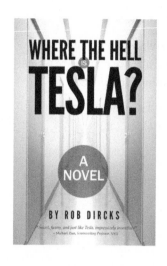

Where the Hell is Tesla?

SCI-FI ODYSSEY. COMEDY. LOVE STORY. AND OF COURSE... NIKOLA TESLA. I'll let Chip, the main character tell you more: "I found the journal at work. Well, I don't know if you'd call it work, but that's where I found it. It's the lost journal of Nikola Tesla, one of the greatest inventors and visionaries ever. Before he died in 1943, he kept a notebook filled with spectacular claims and outrageous plans. One of these plans was for an "Interdimensional Transfer Apparatus" – that allowed someone (in this case me and my friend Pete) to travel to other versions of the infinite possibilities around us. Crazy, right? But that's just where the crazy starts."

"Hilarious time-travel odyssey" -- *Kirkus Reviews Magazine, June 2017*

"★★★★★ Without a doubt the funniest and craziest syfy adventure I've ever read... I made the mistake of reading this book in public and was laughing like a crazied mad man with tears in my eyes. NO BS. I had people glaring at me and hiding their children like I was some kind of lunatic. Great book. I can't wait to read more from Rob Dircks."

"★★★★★ LOVED IT! I loved this book! Hysterical, interesting, cool, just awesome. I flew through it in a few days and laughed the whole way through. I love sci-fi, I love humor and this is the perfect mix of both. Loved!!"

"★★★★★ We need more Bobo! Where The Hell Is Tesla? is one of the funniest books I've read in quite some time."

"★★★★★ Best comedy sci fi in a decade... a fun and hilarious romp through the multiverse with a group of very likable characters, witty and addictive writing."

"★★★★★ Rob Dircks' narrative style and his characters' surprising wit are a breath of fresh air for a genre that I have a great deal of love for but is all too often hit or miss."

"★★★★★ By far the most amusing, funniest and laugh-out-loud audiobook I have ever listened to!"

ALSO BY ROB DIRCKS

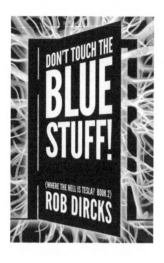

Don't Touch the Blue Stuff! (Where the Hell is Tesla? Book Two)

The sequel to Where the Hell is Tesla? is HERE!

SOMETHING CALLED THE "BLUE JUICE" IS COMING. FOR ALL OF US. Luckily, me (Chip Collins), Pete, Nikola Tesla, Bobo, and FBI Agent Gina Phillips are here to kick its ass, and send it back to last Tuesday. Maybe. Or maybe we'll fail, and everyone in the multiverse is doomed. (Seriously, you might want to get that underground bunker ready.) Either way, I've got to get home to Julie and find out... woah, I'm not about to tell you that right here in the book description! TMI.

WARNING: If you haven't read Where the Hell is Tesla?, I apologize in advance, as you might get completely freaking lost. If you do, just call my apartment, I'm usually around, and I'll fill you in. (If I'm not stuck in the ITA.) – Chip

"★★★★★ **An amusing and unexpectedly crazy ride** - a perfect and hilarious follow-up to *Where the Hell is Tesla?*" - *AudiobookReviewer.com*

"★★★★★ **An incredible, madcap adventure that only Dircks could deliver.** The "Tesla" books are living proof that original stories are still out there waiting to be discovered."

"★★★★★ **I love this series!** It gets better and better. Love wins!

If you haven't read *Where the Hell is a Tesla?*, you must. You'll love both. I promise. Thank you Mr. Dircks!"

"★★★★★ **So damn funny and insanely entertaining!** Loved the first one and this was just as fun."

"★★★★★ **You never know with sequels... Fortunately, you don't have to worry about this one.** Dircks' second in the *Tesla* series delivers every bit as well as the first - in the same balls-to-the-wall writing style that made the first book so entertaining."

"★★★★★ There isn't another writer like Rob Dircks in the entire multiverse."

"★★★★★ **The CHIP MASTER IS BACK.** My second favorite of all audiobooks I've ever listened to... only because *Where the Hell is Tesla?* is number one."

ALSO BY ROB DIRCKS

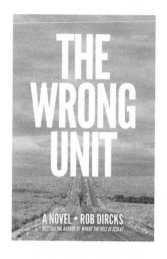

The Wrong Unit

I DON'T KNOW WHAT THE HUMANS ARE SO CRANKY ABOUT. Their enclosures are large, they ingest over a thousand calories per day, and they're allowed to mate. Plus, they have me: an Autonomous Servile Unit, housed in a mobile/bipedal chassis. I do my job well: keep the humans healthy and happy.

"Hey you."

Heyoo. That's my name, I suppose. It's easier for the humans to remember than 413s98-itr8. I guess I've gotten used to it.

Rob Dircks, bestselling author of *Where the Hell is Tesla?*, has a "unit" with a problem: how to deliver his package, out in the middle of nowhere, with nothing to guide him. Oh, and with the fate of humanity hanging in the balance. It's a science fiction tale of technology gone haywire, unlikely heroes, and the nature of humanity. (Woah. That last part sounds deep. Don't worry, it's not.) "Rob Dircks manages to bridge the tricky divide between science-fiction and humor so effortlessly that a comparison to Vonnegut is not a hyperbolic stretch." - *Ruth Sinanian, Literature Reviewer*

"★★★★★ The Wrong Unit is the right story for today... it reacquaints us with our human ingenuity and shortcomings, our deepest longings, and, most notably, our great capacity to love."

"★★★★★ FUNNY. HUMAN. A GREAT RIDE! The Wrong Unit is a fun and twist-turning journey that keeps you on the edge of your seat."

"★★★★★ I'm such a fan of this book that I'm going to recommend it for next month's Book Club pick!"

"★★★★★ OUTSTANDING!! With The Wrong Unit, Rob Dircks has established himself with this potentially prophetic view into humanity's future and the consequences of our growing reliability on and appetite for technology."

"★★★★★ The Wrong Unit is such a great ride!! The pace is fast, the dialogue is smart and sarcastic and witty. The sci-fi world created by Dircks is new, imaginative, and so original. No easy feat! I loved the main characters Heyoo and Wah. Laugh out loud funny and sure, I'll admit, I got a little weepy at some spots. Highly recommended!"

ALSO BY ROB DIRCKS

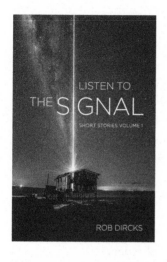

Listen To The Signal: Short Stories Volume 1

Like episodes of The Twilight Zone or The Outer Limits, the sixteen stories contained in Listen To The Signal, Short Stories Volume 1 ask questions like, "What would happen if an iPhone game was addictive - to everyone?" and "Are we all living inside a simulation? And if so, who's running it?" and "When a pilot has to emergency land in a remote town near Area 51 what does he find?"

Hi, Rob Dircks here. I'm the Audible bestselling author of Where the Hell is Tesla?, and I've been writing and narrating these stories since 2016 on my podcast, Listen To The Signal. But now I've made them available ONLY here in this book. They include: Dakō • Today I Invented Time Travel • End Game • November 8, 2016 • Quick Fix • Horatio Breathed His Last • Purgatory • Out of the Blue • Tick Tick Tick • Rose • Red Parka • Bloop • Their DNA Was No Longer the Same • The Last One • Mister Personality • Christmas in Silver Peak.

"★★★★★ There is no one writing scifi as well as Rob Dircks right now, and this short story collection proves it.
I listened to all of these stories when they originally came out on his podcast, and was blown away every time by the quality of his writing and his mastery of the short story form. He knows the tropes and how to subvert them. He can build a world in a few

paragraphs so that you understand it intuitively. He creates characters that are uniquely relatable and gosh darn it, he's funny to boot.

That is when he is not making me tear up. Add to all that the fact that he does a terrific job narrating his own stories and you have a very appealing package.

But now that I have been able to re-listen to all the stories again via this collection, hearing them all together rather than strung out over a series of months, I perceived something I had not noticed before. Something that unites not only these stories but also his novels. Something special that only Rob Dircks can deliver.

It's a sweetness, a love of life and humanity, that shines through all of his characters and all of his imaginary worlds. I feel instantly better when I finish something he has written, I feel uplifted and hopeful. What a wonderful gift Rob has to allow us to see the good in one another, and how lucky we are that he is sharing it with us through his art.

Can't wait for the next collection."

ABOUT THE AUTHOR

Rob Dircks is the Audible bestselling author of *Where the Hell is Tesla?*, *The Wrong Unit*, *Don't Touch the Blue Stuff! (Where the Hell is Tesla? Book Two)*, and a member of SFWA (Science Fiction & Fantasy Writers of America). His prior work includes the anti-self-help book *Unleash the Sloth! 75 Ways to Reach Your Maximum Potential By Doing Less*, and a drawerful of screenplays and short stories. Some of these sci-fi short stories appear on Rob's original audio short story podcast *Listen To The Signal*, also narrated by the author. Rob's a big fan of classic science fiction, and sci-fi conspiracy theories (not to believe in them, just for entertainment.) When not writing, he's helping other authors publish their own work with his own little imprint, Goldfinch Publishing. He lives in New York with his wife and two kids. You can get in touch at www. robdircks.com.

facebook.com/robdircksauthor

twitter.com/RobDircks

instagram.com/Rob.Dircks

goodreads.com/robdircks

amazon.com/author/robdircks

Made in the USA
Las Vegas, NV
29 July 2021